Susan

Emma's Nurse

or

The Garrick Hall Murder

DESIDERATA PRESS

LONDON & CAMBRIDGE

**To Jeff and Pauline
In love and friendship**

Published by Desiderata Press

This novel is a work of fiction. Names and characters are the product of the author's imagination and any resemblance to actual persons, living or dead, is entirely coincidental.

First published in The United Kingdom in 2002 by Desiderata Press
London & Cambridge
PO Box 112
Cambridge PDO CB4 3SU

ISBN 0-954 1678-1-3

Typeset in Times New Roman
Printed and bound by CPI/Bookcraft,
Midsomer Norton

Acknowledgements

Thanks to all those who have helped in the production of this book.

Special thanks to Inspector Martin Gregory for his help with police procedure

To Robert Wood for his editing.

To Hatty and Charlie for their tolerance, and to all my children and grandchildren for their encouragement.

To my friends, especially Margaret Goddard, Liz and Woody Littlefield, Val Goodsell and Linda Moore - for always being there ready to listen and advise.

And to my dear husband Bernard for everything that is good in my life.

Acknowledgements

Enmity's Nurse

Prologue

Autumn 1999

It was almost eleven o'clock in the morning when the knock came at the door. Zoë sighed as the familiar faces greeted her. She thought Inspector Harper looked rather sad, his faced laden with doom and despondency, but then it had always looked that way to her.

The other one, Barnes, looked excited, as though he was particularly pleased with himself; but then he usually looked pretty cocky.

'Come in,' Zoë said with resignation. Bracken gave a muffled growl.

'Quiet, Bracken,' she snapped. She immediately felt guilty; the dog was only doing what dogs were supposed to do

She ran her fingers through her hair, a gesture uncannily like that of her mother.

'What is it now?' She said none too politely. She was tired — she'd been up half the night.

Afterwards, when she ran and reran the scene through her head, she thought she'd seen Barnes snigger. But she couldn't be certain. The older one had just looked extremely troubled, but then she knew that he fancied her. He wasn't going to enjoy the mission was he? Even a hardened copper wouldn't have liked the thought of fancying a murderer.

The two policemen looked at each other; Barnes raised his eyebrows and Harper nodded.

'Zoë Louise Elliot, I'm arresting you on suspicion of murder. You do not have to say anything but —'

She heard no more, the carefully structured sentences merged into a long stream of babble. Two words, just two, repeated and resounded in her head, words not unfamiliar in the day to day ordinary run of things, but odd, disjointed, frightening words when applied to Zoë Elliot: *arresting — murder — murder — arresting — arresting — murder— murder — murder*. The words screamed through her skull, and at the sound of them her world fell apart; caved in on itself and crashed about her ears, surrounding her with a deafening destructive explosion. All she held dear toppled around her and fell into oblivion.

A foul, terrifying sense of decay assaulted her body, seeping into every bone and every joint, sweeping into her brain and robbing her of all logical thought; creeping into her mouth, swelling her tongue and making it tarnished and dry; invading her throat and robbing her of speech; oozing down to her lungs and depriving her of breath; spreading into her heart and making it beat fast and erratically; attacking her hands, making them shake and tingle. Finally, it poured into her legs and robbed her of the strength to support her exhausted, quaking body.

She sat down heavily and put her hand up to her face. All that she valued, all the things that mattered to her, evaporated and drained away. Then came a second attack, a second wave; her normal bodily functions slipped into another gear; she thought she might vomit, or worse, lose control of her bowels or her bladder. Her breathing quickened, her stomach churned, her hands trembled.

She realized that Theo was in the room, and she heard him say something like, 'Wait a minute.' But his words were lost to her, overshadowed by the two words that still screamed around her head; *arresting — murder — murder — arresting*. She needed to go to the lavatory; any minute now she would disgrace herself, and yet she couldn't move; her muscles simply wouldn't obey her brain. *Arresting — arresting — murder — murder*. Her chest was so tight and so painful, that even if she'd had a coherent thought, she could not have voiced it.

Theo was still speaking, or was it the policeman? She couldn't tell; whoever it was, seemed to be a long way away. She squinted, trying to concentrate on what was being said, trying to rejoin the others in the normal world.

Her world still kept moving, folding in on itself, crashing and toppling into a fragmented wilderness. She had no control, there was nothing she could do about it; there was no one to help prop it up, no one to help her rebuild it.

She couldn't communicate, couldn't cry out or express her fear and her pain. She was suffocating, dying, literally falling apart. Couldn't they see that she was disintegrating before their eyes? Didn't they care? Was no one willing to help her?

Her stomach gave another sharp jolt, she was going to be sick. Couldn't they see that she was going to vomit; didn't they have an ounce of pity in them? The words, the two obscene words still played and replayed in her brain — m*urder* — *murder.* Oh God, she'd never see her child or Theo again, it was the end for her, she was dying. *Arresting — arresting — murder*, the words throbbed around her brain, *murder — murder — murder.*

'But . . . ' she managed to say.

Theo was talking again, but she couldn't hear properly, and her vision was distorted. He was saying something about a lawyer, and picking up the telephone.

'But . . . ' she stuttered. 'I didn't, I didn't . . . '

Chapter 1

December 1996

Zoë turned over and squinted at the bedside clock. Oh, God, it was almost ten o'clock; her mother would be there in a little over half an hour. She threw her hands above her head and groaned. Half-past-ten her mother had said, that meant that she would arrive at twenty-five to eleven, Lavinia was always a polite five minutes late, even when visiting her own daughter. Well it was something to get up for, a little excitement in her otherwise extremely dull day. She struggled from the bed and made her way to the bathroom, she peeped at her sleeping daughter as she passed the Lodge's second bedroom.

She quickly washed and cleaned her teeth, wiped the work top and the basin with her damp flannel, cleaned around the lavatory bowl with toilet paper, picked up several items of clothing and stuffed them into the linen bin, and finally tossed two dirty disposable nappies into the waste bin.

She stood back and surveyed the room, sniffed the air and turned up her nose, grabbed the waste bin, and, with bare feet, and wearing only the baggy tee shirt she had slept in, she took it outside and emptied it into the dustbin.

She replaced the bin in the bathroom and made her

way to the tiny sitting room. Her eyes widened as she imagined the scene through her mother's eyes. She was quite appalled by her own mess, what was happening to her? She debated whether to tidy the room or get dressed. She settled on the former, and hurriedly collected glasses, mugs, several dirty plates, Elizabeth's supper dish caked with dried-on baby food, and a deal more unpleasant items, and took them to the kitchen. She had to make several journeys; she dumped all the offending items in the sink, squirted some washing-up liquid over the crockery and turned the hot tap on. Next she grabbed a red clothes basket and, from the sitting room, she hurriedly collected dirty baby clothes, old newspapers, an odd blue slipper, empty crisp packets, a half eaten chocolate bar and other debris. Tucking the basket under one arm, she grabbed a vase containing dead flowers and green slimy water with her free hand, and pushed everything just inside the kitchen door. She shut the door firmly and wiped her hands. From there she rushed back to the sitting room, plumped up the cushions on the sofa, and straightened the fireside rug. Satisfied, she ran her fingers through her unwashed hair as she made her way back to the bedroom. What was happening to her? She was turning into a slob.

She grabbed a pair of jeans. Dear God, she was getting fat, they were far too tight for her. She pulled them up above her thighs and fell back on the bed so that she could zip them up. She pulled the ill-fitting tee shirt up over her head, and then hunted for her bra; she even looked under the bed, but she couldn't find it, so she slipped a grubby pink sweater over her naked torso. She pulled a brush through her long blond hair, made a face as it caught and snagged, and bunched the hair into the nape of her neck fixing it with a tortoiseshell slide.

She looked in on Elizabeth again, and saw that she was still soundly asleep. It was hardly surprising, as neither mother nor daughter had gone to bed before two o'clock that morning. Zoë was making both herself and her daughter nocturnal, sitting up until the early hours, nursing the child on her knee, watching whatever movie came on the television. What else was there to do? She lived like a hermit, just she and the child in the Lodge, with an occasional visit from her mother and father, and return visits to them up at the Castle. It was better when Tiggy, her sister, or her twin brothers were home; none of them could leave Elizabeth alone, so the holidays were great fun, with loads of company, but in dreary term-time Zoë was extremely lonely.

'Hello, darling.' Her mother had arrived. 'All right if I come in?'

Stupid question, Zoë thought, seeing as she was already well and truly in. She cast a nervous eye around the sitting room. 'Of course, come through.'

'Hello, darling.' Her mother kissed her cheek. 'How are you? And where's my little Betsy-boo?'

Zoë felt irritated, if she ever called Elizabeth, Betsy, her father reprimanded her, yet they did it all the time. But instead of voicing her irritation, she smiled and told her mother that Elizabeth was still asleep, and invited her to make herself comfortable in the sitting room whilst she put the kettle on.

Lavinia looked at her watch. 'But, darling, it's almost ten forty-five, it's rather late, isn't it? Are you sure she's all right?'

'Of course she's all right, she had a bad night. She's teething.' Zoë didn't look at her mother as she spoke.

'I'll just go and check,' Lavinia said. And without pausing she made her way down the passage to Elizabeth's room.

'Mother!' Zoë called, but Lavinia was well out of earshot.

A few moments later Lavinia appeared in the kitchen cradling her six-month-old granddaughter.

'Here we are, she was wide awake, and she's got an awfully wet bottom. Where are her nappies, darling? I'll change her.' It was then that Lavinia took in the messy state of the kitchen. 'Good heavens, darling, it looks as if a bomb has dropped in here.'

Zoë had a wealth of answers, but they were all forgotten, her bottom lip quivered and she burst into tears.

Chapter 2

'So you see, Josh, we have to help her.' The Elliot's had just finished lunch and Lavinia Elliot was pacing about in her own kitchen at Hulver Castle, having left her daughter back at the Lodge with the assurance that she would make things right. Her husband, Lord Hulver, was watching her closely, a wisp of hair had escaped from her neat French pleat and she absently tucked it behind her ear. 'She'll be fine when Tiggy gets home. And I'm going to send Doris in to give her a good spring clean on Wednesday, so that will keep her occupied. And I thought we could take her with us when we fetch the boys on Friday.'

'There won't be enough room in the car,' Josh said, still watching her intently.

'Then I'll stay here with Betsy, and Zoë can go and fetch the boys with you.'

He grabbed her hand. 'No, Vinnie, I like our time together. We could leave here early and have a nice lunch on the way. Spend some time together, before all hell breaks loose and the house fills up for Christmas.'

'Oh, Josh.' She kissed the top of his head. Sometimes Josh was impossibly possessive; he'd been that way ever since . . . she swallowed . . . ever since she'd committed adultery, that was the word. Even now, ages after it was over, she didn't like to use, or even think about that

9

shameful word. That's what had changed Josh, her adultery — but that was silly, he didn't know about it, did he? He didn't know she'd been unfaithful to him almost to the point of leaving him, did he? Sometimes she thought he knew; he often seemed so needy and insecure, what else could it be? She pushed her thoughts away from Josh and back to her daughter. 'We're talking about Zoë. I fear for her, Josh. I actually think she could be clinically depressed.'

Josh turned his mouth down. 'What's that mean? I mean, what's the difference between being depressed and clinically depressed?'

'Oh, Josh, I don't know — does it matter? I'm trying to tell you about our daughter. She needs us, Josh.'

Her husband didn't seem to be listening.

'And I thought, since Tiggy and the boys are going on the ski trip at New Year we should take Zoë to Scotland with us — we can't leave her here on her own,' she said.

'It seems funny to think of our daughter having a sex life,' Josh said absently.

'What?'

'Zoë, you know, having a sex life.'

'She doesn't. In her words, she lives like a hermit.'

'You don't have a child, unless you have a sex life.'

'Josh, that was ages ago. She had an affair. She's not, well . . . you know, not now.'

'But she and Steve Jarvis were— ' Josh started to

10

laugh. 'Did I ever tell you? That night, you know, when I caught them together.' Lavinia looked heavenward. 'There was Zoë riding Steve like she was set to win the Derby, and there's me at her bedroom door, asking what she was doing,' he was laughing heartily now. 'And then she says to me, "Daddy, it's not what you think," and I said—'

'Yes, Josh, everybody knows what you said. But I want to talk about Zoë.'

'Talking about sex, Vinnie, how about—' he nodded his head toward the ceiling. 'Everybody will be home by the weekend, there'll be no more afternoon sessions for at least a month.'

'Oh no?' she said looking extremely skeptical.

That was another thing about Josh, he'd always been extremely sexy, delightfully sexy, in fact. But now it was as if he was testing her; he would ask to make love at odd times in the day, especially if she'd been out alone as she had that morning visiting Zoë. It was ridiculous of course. Zoë only lived at the bottom of the drive, admittedly it was a very long, scenic drive, but even so, she'd hardly had time to see her daughter, bed a lover, and cook Josh's lunch.

'Well, maybe, but we'll need to plan a bit.' He placed his hands on her breasts, lifting first one and then the other. He had his eyes closed. 'Mmm,' he said. 'You could make me a happy man right now.'

She laughed. 'Josh, you're sixty- seven years old.

Shouldn't you be—'

'Yes, indeed I should be,' he said running his thumbs around the shape of her hardening nipples.

'I was going to say, shouldn't you be calming down a bit at you're age?'

'You ought to make the most of it. This may be the last time. I may be nearing my sell-by date.'

She touched her hand on his weather-beaten face, ran her fingers down his jaw and placed her index finger on the slight indentation in his square chin. Josh Elliot's looks seemed to improve with the years, the greyer his hair became the more his brown eyes twinkled; and the ruddier his complexion, the whiter his teeth and the broader his smile.

She slipped out of her shoes and eased herself up onto the kitchen table in front of him, pushing both her feet between his thighs. 'We'll go to bed, just as soon as I get your promise.'

He had his head under her jumper and was running his tongue down the line of her bra. Lavinia's breathing was very erratic.

'Promise? What promise?' His voice was muffled.

'That we'll take Zoë to Scotland for New Year, and when we get back, we'll find something to occupy her. She can do a course at the Tech' or something like that.'

Josh pushed Lavinia's skirt higher up her thigh. 'Can't very well take her to the McTodd's, what with Steve and all that. God, Vinnie, you're beautiful.' He slipped one of his thumbs inside her panty leg.

'It's the Jarvis's now, Josh. Phillip McTodd is dead and Steve and Ailsa are married.'

'Exactly, Zoë never really got over finding Philip with his brains blown out. Going to Cameron House might make her very emotional. And with Steve married to a woman twice his age,' he paused and kissed her neck, 'he's bound to have a roving eye. He might decide to rekindle his feelings for Zoë.'

'Oh, Josh, Zoë's well over him now. She lived with Elizabeth's father for the best part of a year after she'd finished with Steve. Besides, Ailsa will be there, she'll not let Steve out of her sight.'

'She may not be able to keep an eye on him, she must be kept pretty busy with — what is it? Three children in as many years.'

'And a fourth on the way,' Lavinia said. 'I hope they have a girl this time — four boys would be hard to cope with.'

'God, what's wrong with the man? He's at it like a buck rabbit.' Josh's voice was muffled again; he was running his tongue around his wife's nipples.

She pushed his head away. 'Josh?'

'All right, I promise, I promise, I promise — now come to bed.'

She slid down off the table and gave a hop skip and

jump toward the door. 'I bet I can be undressed, and in bed, by the time you reach the top of the stairs,' she said with a giggle.

He walked swiftly after her. 'No, Vinnie — wait. I want to be the one that undresses you.'

14

Chapter 3
December 31st 1996

Steve Jarvis rolled over onto his stomach, he squinted at the luminous dial on his watch but couldn't make out the time. It was still pitch black, but in that part of Scotland, and at that time of year, dawn didn't break until almost eight o'clock. He decided it was still very early. The fat girl was lying on her back, her breathing was loud and even and she made little whistling noises as she exhaled. He rolled over on top of her; she made a startled, slightly panicky, noise as she woke.

He was hard for her again; he'd better be quick though, he had a lot to do. It was a really unlucky break, Ailsa being carted off to the infirmary just before the shoot. She was too old to be producing babies. Why she wanted yet another child was a mystery to him — weren't three enough? As for that pompous doctor giving him a lecture about his wife's advancing years and the dangers of late pregnancies! He should try telling Ailsa that, not him. He didn't want to be surrounded by a dozen kids, and at the rate they were going that was sure to be the outcome. He'd obliged her of course, you didn't say no to a woman like Ailsa; and he loved his boys, they were the light of his life those lads were. He wouldn't be without any one of them. But surely three was enough, well four, if this one went according to plan. That would have to be it, the doctor had said as much; but it wouldn't be easy convincing Ailsa, he knew that. Maybe he should just have the cut? Not tell Ailsa, just go ahead and have it done. She was going to be in hospital for a while now, in all likelihood until her confinement. He could have it done, and she'd be none the wiser. She'd just assume that her childbearing days were over and at forty-nine they damned well ought to be.

With both hands he took one of Kirsty's breasts and teased the nipple until it stood proud.

'You've got nipples like marbles,' he said.

She giggled.

He sucked the nipple into his mouth, pulling it right in until it was practically on the back of his throat, his mouth was filled with her flesh. God, these were a pair of tits to die for, shame the rest of the package was of a similar proportion. Ailsa was quite a busty lady but her boobs couldn't hold a candle to the size and feel of Kirsty's.

He tightened his jaw.

'Owch,' Kirsty said, as his teeth caught her.

But Steve hardly heard her; he was sucking greedily, first one twin peak then the other. He idly wondered if it were possible for her to suck her own breasts, decided that it was probably an impossible feat even for someone of Kirsty's charms, and carried on devouring her. He'd ask her sometime though, at a more suitable moment. Meanwhile he had things to do, but not before . . . He

16

unrolled a condom, sheathed himself, spread her ample thighs and proceeded to mount her.

'You may be a big girl,' he said. 'But your muscle tone is pretty good.'

She was working with him now; her energy never ceased to amaze him, whether she displayed it in the care of his boys or as now, in his bed; or to be more precise in her bed. She was a surprisingly athletic girl; she was young, just turned seventeen, but give her a few years and she'd be an extremely sexy woman. She was certainly keen to learn; all she lacked was a little experience, and Steve was quite willing to give her as much of that as she wanted, especially now that Ailsa was out of the picture for a while. He had no problem with her size, unless he thought about it too long and too carefully. Then he found the image of his slim muscular body rutting her voluptuous flesh, rather comical and slightly distasteful. But he didn't think of that now, he was getting carried away, sucking great mouthfuls of her breasts and leaving raised red wealds on her pale skin.

He felt her contract and shudder, and he answered her with his own orgasm.

'Christ, you're a good fuck,' he said.

He felt her squirm and knew that she was blushing.

'Whew, it's bloody hot, isn't it?'

She didn't answer him. That was the trouble with a girl the size of Kirsty, the heat she gave off was beyond belief. He rolled off her and pushed the bedclothes away

17

from his sweaty chest. He edged himself to the side of the bed, lay for one or two moments more and then staggered to his feet. He made his way along the passage to his and Ailsa's empty bedroom, pealing off the used condom as he went. Snapping on the light he saw that it was still only five-thirty – earlier than he thought; good, he had a lot to do before his guests arrived.

He hadn't mentioned Josh Elliot's telephone call to Ailsa, and he was glad now that he hadn't. She'd only get upset to know that Zoë was coming with the party, and it wasn't good for her to get upset, not in her condition. Ailsa would get all sorts of ideas into her head, ideas that wouldn't be much good for her blood pressure.

Steve got into the shower and turned the jets on full, he took a palm-full of shower-gell and soaped under his arms, over his belly and down to his genitals. He caressed himself and thought of Zoë. Despite the fact that he'd made love to Kirsty less than fifteen minutes ago, he became visibly excited at the thought of seeing Zoë again. He pulled his foreskin back and closed his eyes. 'God, Zoë,' he said. 'Me and my mate here have really missed you. We're going to give you a very big welcome, a really, really big welcome.'

Why else was she coming? She obviously wanted to pick up where they'd left off. Well, that would be easy now that Ailsa was out of action. He must make sure Kirsty didn't mention Zoë's presence when she took the boys to

18

visit their mother. Ailsa mustn't be upset; her blood pressure was sky high as it was.

He finished showering, dressed and went downstairs. Apart from Kirsty, the boy's nanny, who lived in, none of the staff had arrived for work. He went into the study; his desk was, as always, neat and tidy. He sorted through a few papers, placed a list of jobs on the top of the pile, and took a handful of shoot-cards out of the top drawer. He was to go out with the keeper after breakfast to place the pegs ready for the morrow's shooting.

He rubbed his hands together. It was his second New Year shoot. Only, last year he hadn't dared ask the likes of the Elliots. But this year Ailsa had persuaded him they should invite all the old crowd; he'd been more surprised than delighted when they'd accepted. But now that he was used to the idea, it felt good to be playing host to the landed and titled gentry. Especially to Josh Elliot, his one-time boss. Not so long ago, he'd been doffing his cap to his elders and betters, now they were beholden to his hospitality. Oh, yes, it felt good, very good indeed.

He went through to the kitchen and out to the stable yard; he flicked on the arc light that lit up the whole area. Several dogs barked as they heard him approach. He opened three sets of kennel doors, and a mixture of canine energy bounded into the yard; a black and a yellow Labrador and several border collies of a variety of sizes and colours.

He took a pressure hose and began to wash out the first kennel, then he saw the tri-coloured Collie, lurking in the back.

'Come on, Bracken,' he said. 'For goodness sake, do you always have to wait to be told?'

Bracken shot from the kennel, and made his way to the back of the other dogs where he lay down as if waiting for further orders.

Steve shook his head. Bracken was a shy dog and a good worker, but much too nervous for Steve's liking. He liked a dog with a bit of an attitude. He liked to pit his wits against an animal and come out the winner. How could you break a dog like Bracken? A dog that hadn't a rebellious bone in its body, a dog that lived to please.

Steve washed out the other kennels and then, throwing the dogs a handful of chews, he ordered them back to their sanctuary. As always, Bracken was the first to obey, his brown eyes looking to Steve for approval.

Steve softened. 'Okay, Bracken, you're a good dog.'

The dog pricked his ears and his tail gave the slightest of wags. Steve shook his head again. There was something about the dog that reminded him of Zoë, always eager to please. Let's hope she's still of the same mind, Steve thought, unconsciously rubbing his crotch.

Chapter 4

It was almost seven-thirty when Steve returned to the house. The kitchen was a bustle of activity. Kirsty, with baby Duncan on her hip, was spreading toast for the elder two Jarvis boys, Roderick, known as Rory and Steve and Ailsa's middle child, Stuart. Mary McDonald, the Jarvis's cook, was stirring porridge in a saucepan on the ancient Aga.

Mary smiled broadly when he entered the room. She was a woman in her late sixty's, with a pleasant face, a jolly smile, and a delightful lilting Scottish accent.

Steve put his arm around her. 'And how are you this fine morning, Mary?'

She playfully pushed him off. 'Oh, get away with you, Mr Jarvis,' she said, 'and tell me what I can be getting for you?'

'You can be getting my name right. It's Steve, not Mr Jarvis.'

'Oh, no, now that would not be right. The man of the house has a right to a Mr. 'twas always Mr and Mrs McTodd, and now 'tis Mr and Mrs Jarvis. And you should know that you can't teach an old dog new tricks.'

Steve laughed, rubbed the back of his hand against Kirsty's ample breast as he passed, winked at her, and seated himself at the kitchen table, where Mary served him a large bowl of porridge. He was wearing an old pair of faded jeans; they felt tight for him around the crotch, were they too small? Or was he already carrying a desire for Zoë in his loins?

'Can I help you to some porridge?' Mary asked Kirsty.

Kirsty shook her head. She was, she said, starting a new diet. She sat down next to Steve with an apple in front of her.

Steve put his hand under the table and squeezed her fat knee. 'That's a shame,' he said. 'I rather like you as you are.'

She blushed to the roots of her mousy brown hair. Then to Steve's surprise, her chubby hand nestled in his crotch, and gave him a squeeze. Steve almost choked on his porridge, what did the girl think she was doing? He stared at her in disbelief and was rewarded by an exaggerated wink. He'd have to have a word with her; she couldn't do that, not to him. He was her boss. What if Mary had seen her?

After breakfast, Steve went out with the keeper to place the pegs that would mark the stands for the following day. Then he ordered two excited collies into the Land Rover and went off to check the sheep. He had a large flock due to start lambing in five days time. If he could fatten the lambs up in time for the Easter trade he'd make a healthy profit. The weather was turning cold, too cold; he ought to bring the flock into the yard.

When he got to the field, he saw that one of the sheep had miscarried, and another was labouring away beside the hedge.

'Damn and blast,' he said. Old Donald, the retired shepherd had told him this would happen if he didn't get them under cover. Well he was damned if he'd let Donald poke fun at him in the village pub. He drove over to the far hedge and he bodily picked up the uncomplaining ewe and put her in the Land Rover. She was so far gone, that she didn't even mind being close to the dogs.

He opened the gate, called the dogs, and together they herded the sheep down to the big covered yard that he and Ailsa had prepared for the lambing. Once there, he unloaded the ewe into a pen, gave her food and water, and made her comfortable. Then he drove back to the field, loaded the food troughs into the Land Rover, picked up the stillborn lamb and returned to the lambing yard. There to his horror he saw that two more ewes were trailing water-bags behind them.

'Shit,' he said. He looked at his watch; it was almost lunchtime. 'Bloody hell, Ailsa, this was supposed to be a joint venture,' he cursed. He penned the two ewes, checked on the first ewe, and then made his way back to Cameron House. Stuart, his two-year-old greeted him, his nose was running and he was wiping it on the sleeve of his sweater. Steve smiled down at his son. 'What's this? Don't you know you can get into trouble for selling candles without wicks?'

Stuart giggled.

'Come here,' Steve said, and taking the boy gently by the arm he wiped his nose with his own handkerchief. He kissed the child's forehead. 'Now where's Kirsty?'

'She's in playroom,' the boy replied slowly. It was still an effort for him to string his words together. Steve's middle son was more like Ailsa than the other two, he had blond, almost red, hair and although his eyes were brown, they, like Ailsa's, were of a paler hue than his fathers' and brothers'. Rory and Duncan were both very like their father; they had dark curly hair and dark brown, almost black, eyes.

Steve kicked off his shoes and went through to find Kirsty. He explained that the flock had decided to lamb early, and that she must take the boys to the infirmary to see their mother that afternoon. Steve sent a message to Ailsa saying that he would telephone her as soon as he had a minute to spare.

Steve grabbed a sandwich for lunch and made his way back to the lambing yard, where he toiled until almost five o'clock. That was the trouble, once you brought the sheep in, they needed far more care than when they were out in the field

At five, Steve went back to the house to change. Donald, the retired shepherd, agreed to keep an eye on the flock until midnight. He lit the stove in the old shepherd's caravan that stood in the corner of the yard and settled himself in for the evening. It was so warm in the caravan that Steve was afraid that the old man might fall asleep on the job, but there was nothing he could do, he had little choice, he had guests arriving.

It had started to snow, and a raw north wind cut through the yard. Steve was bitterly disappointed. If things continued as they were he wouldn't be able to go out with the shoot on the next day, and he'd put in hours and hours of practice with the clays. He did so want to impress the hoi polloi with his newfound skills.

Back at Cameron House, Sir Henry and Lady Osbourne-Pennington had arrived, and he greeted them with their full titles.

'Oh please,' wailed Lady Osbourne-Pennington. 'We're guests in you're house, you must call us Henry and Brooke.'

Wow! Henry and Brooke. Hey, now he *was* coming up in the world. Would his ex-boss, Lord Hulver, ask him to call him, Josh? He doubted it.

Kirsty was back from the hospital. Mrs Jarvis was looking much better, but it was Kirsty's opinion that she was drugged up to the eyeballs, she'd hardly said a word but slept most of the time that they were there; she'd even slept through Duncan crawling all over the bed. She did send a message though; she said she was sorry about the sheep, they must be a bit like her, she said, not very good with dates.

Steve showered and changed. The Elliots were late
— they'd said they expected to be there by six, it was now
well past seven. The night was very dark, and the earlier
sprinkling of snow had turned into a blizzard. Why didn't
they 'phone? Perhaps they'd got lost?

Chapter 5

'We've come too far, Josh, we've just passed a signpost that said Oban four miles, we should have turned off this road miles back.' She turned her head to the rear seat. 'Isn't that right, Zoë?'

Zoë had her eyes closed. She wasn't exactly pretending to be asleep, she just couldn't be bothered to enter into the conversation. Elizabeth, however, who was in the baby seat next to her, really was sleeping; she looked completely relaxed, her little face pink from the heat of the car.

'They're both sound asleep,' Lavinia said. She peered forward into the black snowy night. 'Look there's a turning up ahead; I think you should pull in, and make your way back the way we came, until we see the right road.'

'Maybe if I take this road, it'll bring us round onto the road that leads to the Glen. They're bound to connect eventually.'

'No, Josh, it's safer to—' But Josh had already taken the right turn.

'Josh, this is silly, we'll get hopelessly lost, and we're late already. And look at the weather, we might even get stuck in the snow.' There was an edge of panic to her voice.

Zoë gave a quiet sigh and settled herself further

27

into the corner of the car. Her father hated to turn back on himself; it was as if he saw it as a kind of defeat. Elizabeth stirred, gave a little cry, and went back to sleep.

'Doesn't Zoë remember the way?' Josh asked. The snow was falling hard now and he was bent forward, his head almost touching the windscreen.

'I told you, she's asleep.'

'Will she be all right?'

Zoë was suddenly touched by her father's concern, she felt almost guilty for eavesdropping.

Lavinia lowered her voice, but Zoë could still hear her quite clearly. 'I think so, I think she sees it as a kind of a test — she wants to lay a few ghosts. I'm sure she'll be fine. Ailsa will be sweet to her, but she'll let her know, in no uncertain terms, that Steve is unavailable. I hear she keeps him on a very tight leash.' She glanced back at Zoë, and smiled indulgently. 'Besides, Zoë's no fool, once bitten, twice shy.'

Laying a ghost? Zoë wanted to laugh. Yes indeed, she'd like to lay a ghost, provided the ghost went under the name of Steve Jarvis. Her stomach churned at the thought of him. What fools her parents were, they'd been determined that she shouldn't end up with their hired help and instead she'd ended up with an illegitimate child whose father was long gone; they'd have done better to let her have the man she really loved. Sending him off to Scotland to help the windowed Ailsa may have proved a good move for them,

28

and for Ailsa, but for Zoë, it had been a disaster, it had only made her want him more. Zoë wrapped her arms around herself and smiled into the neck of her jumper. Now her parents, Lord and Lady Hulver, were being entertained by their one-time odd job man. That really *was* funny. And they'd been put in a position where they couldn't say no. If they had, it would look as if they were the most frightful snobs, and saying yes made them look like turncoats. Oh yes, the whole situation was very funny, very funny indeed.

'Zoë?' Lavinia whispered.

Zoë ignored her and continued with her musings.

'It's all right, she's sound asleep, and so is Betsy.'

Josh took another right turn. 'Look, there you see, isn't this the road to the Glen?'

Lavinia pretended to study the map, although it was clearly too dark to see anything. 'It could be,' she said reluctantly.

'It is. I'm sure it is, look, isn't that the wood Philip was so proud of planting?'

'It could be,' she said again.

Zoë's stomach was really churning now, what would she say to him? What would he say to her?

'What will you call him?' Lavinia asked Josh.

'Call him? Steve, of course, it's his name.'

'Well, what will he call you?'

'What do you mean?'

'Well, you can hardly expect him to call you, Sir,

or Lord Hulver, and you call him Steve, can you?'

'I don't see why not?'

'Don't you?'

Zoë squeezed her eyes together a little tighter, what would Steve call her? Darling? Lover? He could call her anything, so long as it was intimate.

'I'd find it difficult to call him Mr Jarvis,' Josh said.

'Perhaps we can get away without him calling us anything? He's certainly not going to call me Lavinia.'

Josh steered the big car through the gates of Cameron House.

'Here we are,' he said. 'Not too late, are we?'

Zoë stretched as if from waking.

They drew up in front of the turreted house. Steve came running down the steps to greet them.

He held his hand out to Josh. 'Welcome, Sir,' he said. 'I'm really very honored that you decided to come and join us.'

Josh gave him a very broad smile. 'Well, thank you, Steve, we're all delighted to be here. Sorry we're late, we got a little lost, I'm afraid — it's a few years since we were in this part of the world.' He glanced toward his wife. 'My excellent navigator soon got us on the right track though, didn't you, darling?'

Steve shook Lavinia's hand. 'Welcome, Lady Hulver,' he said.

Zoë was standing behind her parents with a very disgruntled Elizabeth on her hip. Steve almost pushed between the elder Elliots in order to greet her. 'Miss Zoë,' he said, and made as if to touch his forelock. 'And this must be the lovely Miss Elizabeth — my mum can't stop talking about her. Wait till my boys meet her, they could do with a bit of feminine company,' he laughed, 'to help civilize them.' He grabbed a couple of cases from the car, and shepherding his guests before him, he welcomed them into his home.

Chapter 6

Steve Jarvis had filled out, his shoulders had broadened. He'd always been muscular, but now his body had matured into manhood, and he walked with the swagger of confidence. His broody smiles were now readily given and his merry eyes twinkled. He'd done well, and he acted as if he knew he well deserved the praise given him. The McTodd's estate flourished under his management, but of course, there were no McTodds anymore, that name had died along with Ailsa's late husband. Philip and the old family name had been blown away with a single shotgun cartridge, on a New Years day, in the corner loose box of the Cameron House stable yard. Now Ailsa was Mrs Steve Jarvis, and all Philip's old friends — friends who swore they'd never set foot in the place when Steve took over, were gathered in the large drawing room of Cameron House to see in the New Year.

Everyone agreed that Steve was a good man, a man that had given Ailsa all she could possibly want: a profitable estate, a devoted husband, and three healthy sons: — Rory, Stuart and Duncan. The eldest, a sturdy boy just turned four, the youngest, not yet a year old, and Ailsa seven and a half months into her fourth pregnancy.

Everyone also agreed that it was a great pity that poor Ailsa had been rushed off to the infirmary. Several of the women offered to visit her on the following day. But Steve said that he thought that was probably not a good idea. Kirsty took the children to see her in the afternoons, and the evening visiting hour was reserved for husbands only.

'I was wrong,' Lavinia hissed, as she and Josh hurriedly unpacked and changed before going down to join the other guests for dinner.

'Not like you to be wrong, or—'

'Or admit I'm wrong? Is that what you were going to say?'

Josh, who'd been tying his shoelaces, straightened up; he put his hands on his back and stretched. 'It's funny being here without Philip, isn't it?'

'Josh, Philip's been dead for five years. But you're not listening to me.'

'Has he really? That long? I *am* listening to you, you said you were wrong. About Steve, I suppose? He really does know how to behave, doesn't he? Ailsa must have trained him well. Knows his place, doesn't he?'

Lavinia spread her fingers out by the side of her face; her jaw was tight. 'Josh will you stop rabbiting on, and listen to me?'

'Sorry old—'

'Josh!'

'What?

'You were going to say 'old thing' weren't you?'

33

'Old darling, actually.'

'Josh, listen to me. I was wrong about Zoë.'

'Zoë? How come?'

'Don't pretend you didn't see the way she looked at him? You didn't, did you?'

'I thought he greeted her very politely, and he was charming to Betsy. One always warms to a chap that's nice to children.'

'I'm not talking about the way he greeted her. I'm talking about the way she greeted him. I know that look, Josh, she was . . . '

'What? What was she?'

'Having the hots for him.'

'Vinnie!'

'Well, I don't know any other way to put it. He could have flicked his fingers, and she'd have fallen into bed with him, just like that. And Ailsa's not here. Oh dear, Josh, what are we going to do?'

Josh put his arms around his wife. He shook his head. 'You're wrong,' he said. 'Even if Zoë's still carrying a torch for him, he's not daft enough to put all he has here in jeopardy. Look around you — he's not going to risk losing all this, now is he? If Ailsa divorced him, where would he be?'

Lavinia sat down on the edge of the bed. She was very quiet.

'I make sense, don't I?' Josh said.

Lavinia nodded. She stood up and continued to dress.

'My, God,' Josh said. 'Have you seen the nanny?'

'Couldn't help but see her.'

'Certainly wouldn't like her to mistake me for a chair,' Josh chuckled.

'Josh, that's so unkind. She's probably a lovely girl.'

'Yes, she probably is, underneath all that . . . well you know. What on earth possessed Ailsa to pick such a—'

'Josh!' Lavinia said warningly.

'Well you have to admit, she's rather a battleship, isn't she?'

Lavinia laughed. 'That's just it. Ailsa doesn't want Steve to get tempted.'

Josh raised his eyebrows. 'Well, she does have a point, doesn't she? He's not likely to rove in that direction, is he?'

There was a tap at their bedroom door. It was Steve; he wanted a quiet word with Josh. He explained about the lambing, and he wondered if Lord Hulver might be prepared to take the shoot out tomorrow as he'd be tied up in the lambing yard all day.

Shooting was Josh Elliot's greatest love, and to be in charge of the shoot was his idea of heaven. He felt extremely warmly toward Steve, the boy obviously knew what he was doing, after all. He might have asked Henry

Osbourne-Pennington or Rufus Henchforth to take charge. But no, he'd done the sensible thing and asked Josh.

As Josh and Steve descended the stairs together, Josh put a paternal arm around Steve. 'You know, Steve, we're all equals. Why don't you stop this Lord Hulver lark and call me, Josh — everyone else does.'

Chapter 7

The evening was a huge success. Steve felt warmed by his guests' responsive conversation and their kind and generous words. He spoke little to Zoë, in fact he purposely avoided her, but he was forever aware of her presence and he studied her from the corner of his eye. His wife Ailsa was still a sexy lady, but she was old, she'd soon be past it, and Zoë was young; how nice it would be if Zoë were the hostess for his weekend party. He glanced over at her, and accidentally caught her eye; she was gagging for it, anyone could see that; but he was too wise to let her distract him from his important company.

He drank little, he didn't want the alcohol to voice his thoughts and let him down. Besides, he had the sheep to deal with once everybody was safely tucked up in bed. His abstemious behavior was not, however, reflected in the general company; even Lady Hulver was quite merry.

After a large and lavish dinner, served with the finest wines and in a style befitting the aristocracy, Steve went over to Lady Hulver and, in a low voice, he said, 'Lady Hulver? I'm going to check on the boys, and I wondered if you'd like to come and take a peek? You'll meet them in the morning of course,' he wrinkled his nose, 'but I can't wait to show them off. Besides, they're quite angelic when they're asleep.'

With a broad smile, Lavinia followed him from the room. Zoë's face showed alarm at seeing them disappear, and she went to follow them. But Steve barred her way. 'Miss Zoë, I wonder if you'd top the port glasses up for me?' He winked at her and, still looking disgruntled, she backed away.

Steve guided Lavinia up the impressive staircase and along the wide carpeted passage to his sons' room.

'They're all in together,' Steve said. 'They're each other's best friends, and they don't like to be parted.'

'The twins were exactly like that, when they were small. They still are, come to think of it,' Lavinia mused.

Steve silently opened a door and gestured Lavinia into the room.

'Do you remember this room?' He whispered.

She nodded. 'Indeed, I do,' she spoke in a voice barely above a whisper. 'It was a dreary old room once upon a time. I think Philip used it as a general glory hole, a dump for unwanted boots and cartridge belts and probably every copy of the Shooting Times ever published.' Smiling, she shook her head. 'You've done wonders with it.'

The room was decorated in bright, primary colours. A train set ran at skirting-board height around the walls and the lighting resembled hot air balloons, with baskets of soft toys suspended underneath.

'Wait until Betsy sees this, we'll never drag her away from the place.'

This was his opening; the old girl was playing right into his hands. Old girl? He'd better be careful; she was about the same age as his wife.

'That's what I'm hoping.'

The lighting was low — only a faint glow given off by the boy's nightlight — a ceramic creation in the shape of a toadstool; but even so, he saw Lady Hulver's face drop.

He put his hand out and touched her arm. 'Lady Hulver? Surely you don't think?' he beckoned her to the door and out into the passage. 'No, no, you've got the wrong idea. I admit I was hoping to persuade Miss Zoë to stay on for a week or two, but not the way you're thinking.'

At least her ladyship had the decency not to deny what she was thinking; she even blushed.

Steve swiftly went on, 'You see, I'm going to be really busy with the sheep, and Ailsa's coming home on Tuesday, and I was thinking how nice it would be for her to have some company. You see, although she's coming home, the doctors say that she'll not be able to do too much, and well, you know Ailsa, it'll be difficult to keep her confined to bed-rest unless someone's here to keep an eye on her.' It was a lie of course. Ailsa was really quite ill and he knew very well that she wouldn't be home until after the baby was born. Well, even she wouldn't expect him to live like a hermit; he wouldn't expect her to live like a nun if he were indisposed.

Lavinia was looking thoughtful. 'Tuesday? She'll

definitely be home will she?'

'Oh yes, definitely. I spoke to the doctor this evening, just before you arrived. You see, Kirsty's a nice enough girl, but, well, without being unkind, she's a simple soul. She's none too bright — don't get me wrong, she's lovely with the kids, but she's not well educated, and she's very young, and she and Ailsa don't have much in common.'

'Zoë's young too, Steve.'

Steve scratched his head. 'Yes, I know, but— Oh dear, I'm making a real pigs ear of this, aren't I? And I know I'm not making much sense — 'course I know I'm not of yours or Ailsa's class, nor am I educated. But frankly, that's the difference between Kirsty and Zoë.'

'I understand what you're saying, Steve. But I think there's something you should know.' She had a rather superior look on her face.

Here it comes, he thought. He knew the old dear was going to tell him that Zoë fancied him. He turned a look of wide-eyed innocence on her.

'You see, I don't think Zoë's quite over you,' Lavinia confided.

He looked puzzled, his brow creased into a deep frown. 'Not over me? But surely — I mean, she's had a baby and—'

'I think she turned to Chris on the rebound from you.'

40

'Really? That's incredible, but surely after all this time? Oh well, in that case, you're right, you should take her home with you. I'm very fond of Miss Zoë, I think of her, well,— like she was my sister, I wouldn't want to cause her any heartache . . . ' He stopped short. Careful Steve, don't push it too far, he thought

Lavinia looked confused. Steve moved in for the kill. He guided her over to the boy's bedroom door again, and beckoned her inside. He put a finger to his lips.

'This is where my love lies,' he whispered.

'But—'

'Here, and in the infirmary.' He led her first to Duncan's cot and then onto the bunk beds occupied by his two angelic looking sons.

They both gazed at the sleeping infants for a few moments before Steve led his guest back to the door.

'I made those bunk-beds myself,' he said proudly. He was winning, he could tell he was by the way she looked at him. 'Those little lads are my finest achievements. And you know what? Even if I did still have desires on Miss Zoë, which I don't, I wouldn't risk losing my kids, — not for anyone.'

'That's what Josh said.'

Wow, a direct hit, he thought.

'He's right. Besides, can you imagine Ailsa letting anything go on under her roof?'

Lavinia smiled.

Steve gently closed the door on the sleeping children, and led Lavinia over to a pair of Jacobean chairs that stood against the far wall of the passage. Lavinia sat, but Steve hovered as if awaiting Lavinia's permission to sit.

'I think I ought to tell you straight, Lady Hulver. You see, I know what they,' — he nodded toward the wide staircase, 'all think of me. They think I'm a real upstart. They don't really consider me as an equal, for all they drink my wine and eat my food, and it *is* mine as well — it's food and drink I've worked for. They think I married Ailsa for her money, and that I'm not capable of staying faithful to her. After all, she's a good twenty years older than me. What else, apart from her money, could I see in her? Isn't that right?'

'Actually, Steve, you're wrong. I've heard nothing but praise for you, and for what you've done for her.' She held his eyes steady. 'I'm the doubting Thomas amongst the party,' she said evenly.

Steve raised his eyebrows; this was going to be easier than he thought.

'I don't blame you,' he said. 'To tell you the truth, if I was an outsider, looking in, I wouldn't have much time for me, if you see what I mean. Well, it's a fair cop,' he said. 'You're right. I came here, and I saw the main chance, and I took it. You can't blame me for that. Even I don't blame myself for that. Ailsa is one hell of a sexy lady — she knew where it was at. It was on offer, and I took the offer up. Then when she got pregnant — well to tell you the truth, that were an accident. I was amazed, I didn't think women of her age could— well I suppose the truth is, I didn't think very carefully at all, did I? Then when Rory was born, it changed my life, I know that sounds . . . what's the word?'

'Dramatic?' Lavinia offered.

God, how the upper-crust liked putting the likes of him right about long words.

'Yeah, yeah, that's right, dramatic.'

'So what *are* you trying to say, Steve? That you won't be trying to get into my daughter's panties?'

Knickers, he thought, they're bloody knickers, not panties, even M and S call them knickers. He coughed.

'I'm saying that Miss Zoë and I, well, we were first lovers, you know that, and I'll always have a soft spot for her, but that's the point, I'm not in the business of—' he sighed. 'Look, let me put it another way. When I was a kid, I accepted everything just as it was — you do, don't you? Like, well, like we didn't have a lid on the loo, you know, the bit that fits over the seat, well we didn't have one, and as I didn't know they existed, I never missed it.'

'And now you have several, and you wouldn't want to be without?' Lavinia said.

He thought he detected a note of sarcasm in her voice, maybe he was taking the wrong road. Maybe the woman was cleverer that he thought. On the other hand, maybe she was a lot dimmer than he thought.

He ignored what she said. 'And when I was a kid, I didn't have a dad, but I knew they existed.' He stopped mid flow. 'You know Lord Hulver was a bit of a father figure to me. I really looked up to him, I still do. If the next is a boy, I want to have Jocelyn as his second name.' Good move, Steve, she was really warming to him now, this was going to be really, really easy; she was following the plot right on cue. He'd definitely hit a home run; her eyes were looking all misty.

'Anyway, my boys have got a dad, and they're not going to have to go without, and what's more, they're going to have a dad they can look up to.'

Lavinia was giving him one of her misty eyed, maternal smiles.

'So Zoë's safe?' She smiled.

'Lady Hulver, she 's like my little sister, I'd not see her harmed. In your heart of hearts, you know that. But if she 's, well, not quite over me, then I think you're right, she shouldn't stay on, no matter how much Ailsa would benefit.'

He'd won; he'd beaten the battle-axe at her own game. He was home and dry, he could tell he was, she was looking all dewy and sentimental.

Strangely enough most of what Steve said was perfectly true, except that he certainly didn't look on Zoë in a brotherly fashion. He just wanted Zoë as a distraction, but he wouldn't have risked losing Ailsa for the sake of having her.

'You know Steve, sometimes we all need to learn a lesson, and Zoë's no exception. It's probably time she learned that relationships change, and sometimes love goes altogether and sometimes it just changes and is replaced by friendship. And friendship is often far more precious, and a lot longer lasting.'

Oh, God, what cheesy, sentimental claptrap, he thought.

Lavinia put out her hand and he helped her to her feet.

'Zoë's twenty-four, Steve. I'm sure she's well able to make her own decisions.'

Too right, thought Steve.

'And if Ailsa's back next week — I really can't see any harm in her staying on.' Lavinia moistened her lips. 'I'll tell you this in confidence, Steve. Zoë's been quite down just lately — her father and I have been very worried about her.' Then she said almost to herself, 'She's been more like her old self tonight, though.' Lavinia paused for a moment; they had reached the top of the stairs. 'In fact, I think it's an excellent idea, it's probably just what she needs. A change of scenery will do her good.'

They began to descend the stairs; Lavinia had her arm hooked into his.

'You know, Steve, I think you should try and get over this Lady Hulver business. My first name's Lavinia and I'd very much like you to call me by it.'

Steve smiled. Jack-pot, he thought.

Chapter 8

'So you'll stay then, Zoë?'

Zoë shook her head. Steve was mad. Didn't he know the way in which she thought about him? He'd paid absolutely no attention to her the whole of the weekend. In fact he'd shown more interest in Kirsty, the nanny, than he had in her. And now he was asking her to stay for a week or two. Perhaps he was being deliberately cruel, teasing her, he must know how she felt about him, he must.

Breakfast was being served; all the guests were due to leave later that morning. Kirsty entered the dining room; she had Elizabeth on one hip and Duncan on the other.

'I'm going to feed the bairns in the kitchen,' she said.

Elizabeth had her head snuggled into Kirsty's neck, and Zoë felt a pang of jealousy.

'Miss Zoë will be staying on,' Steve said.

'No I won't, Steve. I told you, I can't.'

'Yes, she will,' Steve said. 'So you'll have one more to look after. Not a problem, is it?' He moistened his lips and smiled at Kirsty as he spoke.

The nanny blushed.

Zoë noted the blush and turned to Steve. He raised his eyebrows in a look of mock innocence. Zoë glanced

47

back at Kirsty, she appeared to be rooted to the spot. Zoë tried to put her thoughts in order; the girl was large, very large, in fact she was very, very fat. She had dull, mousy brown, ill cut hair. Her face was quite pretty in a young teenagerish sort of way. But it was the bulk of the girl that first impressed, and it was difficult to see further than her size.

Duncan wriggled. Steve got up from the table and held his arms out to the child; he deliberately brushed Kirsty's full bosom with his hands as he reached for his son. He made no attempt to hide the action from Zoë, but turned to her, and winked at her in a roguish fashion. He kissed Duncan on the forehead, gently stroked Elizabeth's hair and then suggested that Kirsty take the pair of them off for breakfast.

There can't be any competition there, Zoë thought, as she watched the large hips waddle away.

As if to read her mind, Steve said, 'Ailsa chose her. She thought she wouldn't be a problem.' He laughed and slapped his knee. 'She's a clever woman, is Ailsa. But what she forgot was, that big girls like Kirsty are just plain grateful for any attention, and therefore, very, very accommodating. So you see, you don't need to worry — I'm well taken care of. I shan't be trying to get into your knickers, or should I say panties?'

Zoë swallowed, so he didn't want her the way she wanted him. She gazed around the dining-room, fixing her

48

eyes on one of the huge oil paintings that hung on the walls. Sex was just a function to Steve; he didn't care whom he did it with so long as he could get his end away.

'Girls like Kirsty offer it on a plate,' he said.

Zoë stopped looking at the picture and turned her gaze on Steve.

'Well, you weren't here, were you?' he said defensively.

'But Steve, she's so . . .'

'So what? Fat and ugly?'

'Yes,' Zoë said vigorously nodding her head. 'Fat.'

'Fat can be fun,' he said, besides you don't look on the mantleshelf whilst you're poking the fire, do you? Then he winked at her. 'It's a good job you've come to save me though, isn't it.'

'I haven't,' she said.

'Stay, Zoë. I need help with the lambing.'

She laughed, but she didn't feel very merry. Her heart quite literally ached. 'I don't know the first thing about sheep.'

He reached out and put his hand on her thigh. She caught her breath, his gentle touch was like an erotic bee sting.

'Stay,' he said. 'I'll teach you.' He smiled, and slowly edged his hand up her inner thigh stopping just short of her crotch. 'You always were a quick learner, I don't think it will take you long to get the hang of it.' He took her hand and placed it on his own crotch. 'No, you'll soon get the hang of it,' he said.

Zoë swallowed. 'I don't understand you, Steve, you've ignored me all weekend.'

'Tactics, Zoë, tactics.'

'Anyway, it wouldn't be right, not with Ailsa being in hospital.' She hadn't removed her hand and she could feel his reaction to her touch.

'Ailsa's coming home tomorrow,' Lavinia said as she entered the dining room. Zoë's hand shot from Steve's lap. But Lavinia didn't appear to notice. She went over to the sideboard and lifted some of the lids of the covered dishes. 'Gosh, Steve, this brings back a few memories. Traditional English breakfast.'

'Scottish,' he said.

'I stand corrected. Scottish. Next thing, Steve, you'll be calling yourself McJarvis! Mmm, it looks wonderful, and porridge as well.' She then went on to help herself to two slices of toast and poured herself a cup of coffee.

'You disappoint me, Lady Hulver — is that all you're going to eat?'

'Lavinia,' she reminded him. 'Long journeys and big breakfasts don't sit well with me. Besides, you fed us so well yesterday — I really won't need to eat anything else for a week.' She carried her food to the table, but instead of sitting down, she went over to the window and looked out.

'Thank goodness it's stopped snowing, but the roads still look pretty treacherous. We must get off as soon as we can.' She came back to the table and sat down. She smiled broadly at Zoë and then continued to talk to Steve.

Zoë was almost open mouthed with amazement, her mother and the one time odd-job man were in deep conversation and in complete social harmony. Her mother was saying what a shame it was that he missed most of yesterday's shooting, and Steve was replying that he managed to fit the last drive in; and that it was good of Lord Hulver to organize things for him. Then her mother said that he must call her father Josh, and they were looking forward to him coming to shoot at Hulver.

'It can't be this year, Lavinia. Ailsa will need me here — she won't want to travel with a new baby. Next year perhaps?'

Zoë gulped, the world had gone mad, quite, quite mad.

'So, darling?' Lavinia turned her attentions to Zoë. 'You're going to stay on, are you?'

Zoë glanced at Steve, she heard Kirsty humming a tune from the kitchen. Well, her mother did say she should lay a ghost. She bit into her bottom lip.

'If Steve wants me to,' she said, quietly.

'Of course,' he said. 'But don't think you'll get much of a rest, I'll be working you pretty hard.'

Lavinia put her hand out and squeezed Zoë's arm.

'It'll do you good, darling, and Betsy loves the boys. It'll do her good too, and you'll be such good company for Ailsa when she gets home.'

Zoë had the distinct feeling that her mother saw her as a problem and was unloading her.

Chapter 9

Despite the Elliots' good intentions, it was well past two when they set off for Hulver. Lavinia had practically insisted that Zoë and Betsy stay behind at Cameron House. Not that Zoë was complaining. It was, after all, what she had wanted all along; only having her mother's approval defused the excitement in a way she couldn't quite define.

Zoë waved to her parents as they left. She didn't go back into the house until their car had negotiated the long drive and rattled over the cattle grid at the base of the big gates. Then she turned and walked up the steps to the grand entrance door, glancing up at the cartouche carved above it as she went under it. *Pax intrantibus salus exeuntibus*. Zoë didn't know much Latin, but she knew what the words meant, her father had told her often enough, — Peace to those who enter; safety for those who leave. Zoë smiled, for she had not found either sentiment applicable in her previous visits to Cameron House, and she doubted that this visit would be any different. She was about to enter the kitchen when she almost bumped into Kirsty.

'I've just put Betsy down for a nap, and now I'm off to take the boys to see their mother,' she said. Zoë noticed that the girl didn't ever call her by name, but spoke as if she were looking through her. She glanced beyond Zoë, into the kitchen. 'I'll be off then, Steve,' she said. Kirsty hesitated, for what to Zoë seemed like a long time, as if she half expected Steve to call her back. 'I'll be off now then,' she said again.

Zoë felt impatient for her to be gone. She couldn't pass her in the kitchen doorway; there simply wasn't room.

Steve came to the door. Seeing Zoë, he grinned, then very deliberately he put out both his arms and weighed Kirsty's breasts in his hands. 'Lovely pair you've got there,' he said. The girl looked straight into Zoë's eyes, blushed, gave a defiant smile, and then pushed past her, rounded up her small charges, and left.

Zoë stared after her. Steve was leaning on the door jam, his gaze following that of Zoë's.

'Why'd you do that?' Zoë asked.

'Do what?'

'You know what I'm talking about, touch her like that?'

'She likes it, and it pays to keep the staff happy.' He touched his crotch. 'And this staff is very happy, very happy indeed.' He laughed at his own attempt at humour. Zoë did not join in his mirth. 'And, you have to admit,' Steve went on, 'they're a fine pair, aren't they? Although your tits were always pretty special too — you've got the best pair around here, I should say. Ailsa's are a nice size, but they are drooping a bit now. Kirsty's are bloody spectacular, but a man could suffocate in all that blubber, not that it wouldn't be a nice way to go, mind. But yours,' he closed his eyes, 'mmm, good size, what are you? Thirty-eight C? I seem to remember that's what they were when I had regular access to them. But it's the shape of them. You know some girls nipples are dead in the center, Kirsty's are like that, weenie little pink pimples stuck in the middle of all that womanly flesh. Others, like Ailsa's, have got the nipples sort of pointing down, but I expect that's due to the mid-forties droop. Mind you, Ailsa's nipples are another thing altogether, huge brown things like chestnuts, a real mouthful of tit you gets with Ailsa. But yours, Zoë, — you've got the best pair ever — as I said, lovely size, real good handful. Firm and round, pale creamy coloured, almost transparent skin laced with tiny blue veins.'

Zoë blushed; his description was embarrassingly accurate

But Steve was still in full flow; he had his eyes closed and a look of pleasure on his face. 'And those, deep rose coloured nipples, placed high of center, so that when you look at them from the side, they're almost pointing up to heaven. Long nipples you've got, nipples that come out to greet you, nipples that ask to be sucked and played with. Or at least that was the case before the kid were born. Maybe you've got a bit of droop now?'

She hated him, she hated all his dirty stupid talk; she loathed the way he spoke about women and demeaned them. So why was he exciting her so much? Why would she quite willingly strip off her clothes and go to bed with him right then and there? And why was she so flattered when he said that her breasts were the best?

'How about?'

Zoë gulped. 'What?'

'Tea? It's Mary's day off. Come on, let's have tea.'

Zoë had to clench her fists to stop herself from shaking. 'It's a bit early,' she said. Her voice sounded high and distorted.

'It's never too early for a little bread and honey,' he said.

She followed him into the kitchen, pulling off her coat as she went. He put the kettle on the ancient Aga, got out a breadboard and a loaf of bread, and put pots of jam and honey on the table. Zoë sat down in front of the Aga with her elbow leaning on the table in front of her. Steve sat at the head of the table at right angles to her.

He took the lid off the honey pot.

'A simple fare,' he said, 'but served in an interesting style.'

Zoë was feeling quite nauseous. The last thing she wanted to do was eat tea. She shouldn't have stayed. He was teasing her, playing with her emotions, she knew that he must be able to read her like a book, but she was unable to do a thing about it. He was screwing the fat nanny, and he didn't care that she knew about it, in fact he didn't care whom he screwed or who got hurt. He only cared about himself and his own gratification.

He leaned over toward her; he was acting very calmly.

Zoë sucked in a gulp of air. She neither moved nor objected when he undid first the top and then the lower buttons of her blouse. She sat as if hypnotized by him.

The kettle boiled, he got up and pushed it off the hob. On the way past her he expertly undid her bra and, reaching inside her blouse he slipped the straps off her shoulders.

Leaning over her shoulder he dipped his first two fingers into the honey-pot; scooped up a tablespoon sized quantity of the runny honey and smeared it first on one, and then on the other nipple.

'Whew, Zoë, you haven't changed. What's more these haven't changed — having the kid hasn't altered them. Look at them, they're bloody perfect.' He came around to the side of her and took her nipple deep into his mouth, sucking it and then noisily letting it go, leaving it elongated and pointing upward.

The pattern of her breathing had changed, now she was snatching at the air in short sharp gulps. How dare he? Her brain screamed. But in answer, her heart yearned for him. She was his, she always had been and she always would be. He could do with her as he willed and she was incapable of doing anything about it.

He went around the other side of her and gave her other breast the same treatment. He pushed her chair back so that it tipped backward on the two back legs and rested on the bar of the Aga. Then he undid the popper on her jeans and slid the zip down. He took the honey pot and poured some on her navel, it spilled over and ran down between her legs, and his mouth and his tongue followed after it, licking and sucking, and making her almost mad with desire.

She wanted him so much, so, so much, but she wanted confirmation of his love, not his lust.

'Do you love me, Steve?' There was despair in her voice.

'You know I do.'

'And Ailsa? Do you love Ailsa?' She had a sneaky feeling that Steve loved anyone that was prepared to sleep with him.

'Yup, 'fraid so, it's different though.'

'And Kirsty? Do you love Kirsty.' It was difficult for her to talk. His head was buried between her legs, his tongue was darting back and forth, and she was about to explode with passion.

'What?' He mumbled.

'Kirsty? Where does Kirsty fit in? Do you love her?'

He came up for air and grinned at her. 'Ah, now that's different. She's a good girl, she does what she's told, and she doesn't make trouble.'

'And is that what you'd like me to be, Steve? A good girl that does as she's told?'

'No, Zoë, my love. I want you to be a very naughty girl that does as she's told.'

He stood up and unzipped himself. He dipped his penis in the honey pot.

'And the first naughty thing I want you to do, is clean all this sticky stuff off my John-Thomas here.'

Zoë practically fell upon him to oblige. The sickness she was feeling she realized had another name: that of erotic desire.

Moments later, Steve said, 'Christ, Zoë, who taught you to give head like that?' Then a moment or two after that; 'hold on, I'm going to come if you're not careful.' He pushed her head away from him.

He straightened his back and fumbled inside his jeans pocket.

'Damn and blast, they're in my other jeans,' he said.

She tried to pull him back to her. 'It'll be all right. I can't wait any longer for you.'

He shook his head and laughed. 'You girls are always the same, always gagging for it. Totally irresponsible the lot of you. I want you, Zoë, look at me, you can see how much I want you. Christ after what you've just done to me, I'd be a saint not to want to finish the job. But I'm not an irresponsible bastard, and I never will be.'

He prized himself away from her. 'Back in a minute,' he said. He staggered from the room, holding his jeans at thigh height, and kicking his shoes off as he went; carrying his erection before him like a beacon.

Minutes later, he was back. Seconds after that, Zoë was lying across the kitchen table with Steve grunting on top of her.

He talked to her in the same rhythm as his lovemaking.

'Never,— ugh, — ever, — ugh, — do, — ugh, — it, — ugh, — unless, — ugh, — your, — ugh, — partner, — ugh, — wears, — ugh, — a, — ugh, — rubber, — ugh, — ugh — Oh God, — Oh Jesus-fucking-Christ.' He was suddenly very still. Then he laid his sweating brow on Zoë's breast. 'God, Zoë, you always were magic.'

He gave a huge, contented, sigh. 'Did you come?'

'No,' she lied. 'You owe me one.'

He pulled out of her and looked at his watch. 'I'll have to check the flock, and by that time, the boys will be back. Looks like I'd better come to your room later on, doesn't it?'

He tucked his shirt in, zipped up his jeans, and headed toward the door.

Zoë scrambled to her feet. She too, hurriedly rearranged her dress, the sticky honey was still all over her and her clothes adhered to her skin. 'Wait, Steve. I'll come and help you with the sheep.'

She followed him, pulling her coat on and forcing her feet into a cold pair of Wellington boots. When she got to the door Steve had already reached the far corner of the stable yard and was disappearing round the corner in the direction of the lambing yard.

'Come on,' he shouted. 'Chop-chop, thought you said you'd help me.'

'I'm coming,' she replied cheerfully. But she didn't feel in the least bit cheerful. She had what she wanted, so why didn't she feel particularly happy? Why did she feel let down and ill-used, like an animal caught in a trap.

Chapter 10

'So you see, Zoë, you must leave her just long enough to make sure she's not going to lamb naturally. You know — don't interfere unless you have to. They say it's easier to kill a lamb or a ewe by early or rough lambing, than it is to shoot it.'

Steve shifted his position, his warm breath condensing into a thick cloud around his face.

'That's right — tip her up a bit so as I can get my hand in,' he said.

Zoë pulled the ewe up and pushed a straw bale into its back with her foot. She had tied a rope to each of the animal's back legs and had looped it around her own neck, which meant that she was taking a huge amount of weight on her shoulders. Despite the chill in the air she was sweating.

Steve sprinkled the ewe's rear end with copious amounts of soap flakes, and gently pushed his hand inside her. 'Uh-uh, she's got two lambs coming together, no wonder she's got problems. Here,' he said, 'you have a go at this one, Zoë. You've got a smaller hand than me — she's only a shearling.'

'Shearling?'

'A year old, she's only been sheared once, so she's small, this is her first lambing.'

'Oh.'

Steve took the rope and changed places with her.

Zoë smeared her hand and arm with antiseptic cream. She wished that Steve had offered her a rubber glove, but she didn't like to ask, — she didn't want to appear wimpy.

She slid her hand into the warm body; hot fluid gusted out as she did so. She felt a tangle of lambs; she could feel two heads, one on top of the other, and two feet.

'What shall I do?'

'You tell me, you've seen it done often enough.' He grinned. 'Come on, Zoë, you're better at this than I am, and I'm pretty darned good.'

She gentle pushed both lambs back into the sheep's uterus, and, taking a thin piece of cord, she slipped it over the top of the nearest lamb's head. Holding the cord with her left hand, she carefully ran her hand down the small body and traced its legs and feet. Then, still keeping a hold of the cord, she brought both front feet forward, and secured them with a second piece of thin cord. That done, she pushed the second lamb back, whilst gently tugging on the cords in order to bring the first lamb forward. Then, she patiently and slowly brought the lamb out, letting the ewe do most of the work. The second lamb followed on without any problem.

Steve let go of the rope and allowed the ewe to lick her young. He looked up at Zoë. 'Well done.' He laughed.

'By the size of that smile plastered all over your face, you'd think you'd given birth yourself!'

Zoë wiped her brow on her arm. She knew she was grinning from ear to ear. 'I feel as if I have,' she said. She smiled down at the trio. 'But it's lovely, isn't it, Steve? It really gives you a buzz to think you've probably saved a life, doesn't it?'

Steve put his arm around her shoulders. 'You women are so sentimental. I'll bet you never eat a leg of lamb again.'

She turned up her nose.

'But seriously, you know, Zoë, you're a natural.'

She laughed.

'No, I mean it, you're bloody good. I think you've found your vocation.'

She laughed again. Steve's praise was music to her ears. But what he said was perfectly true, she was good, and she loved working with the animals.

'You ought to train as a vet,' he said.

She grinned again happily. 'I don't have seven years to spare,' she said.

'Got something else planned, have you?'

Yes, she thought; marriage, children; a nice little farm to run. And most importantly, Steve Jarvis by her side, serving as her partner and her helpmate. But of course she couldn't voice her thoughts. So she shrugged her shoulders.

'I'm serious, you've got the knack. I don't just

64

mean the lambing, lots of women are good at the midwifery bit. But look how you handled the flock yesterday, we got the whole lot vaccinated in one morning, it normally takes me a couple of days.'

She knew he was flattering her, but she mopped up his praise all the same. She felt deliriously happy.

'And look at old Bracken there, he never leaves your side. He's a good judge if ever there was one, 'aint that right, Bracken?'

The dog wagged his tail and moved in a little closer to Zoë.

'He'll miss you when you go,' Steve said. And Zoë's happiness was dulled. She didn't want to go, she didn't ever want to leave Cameron House, she didn't want to leave the sheep, or the dog, or Steve's boys, but most of all she didn't want to leave Steve.

The Jarvis household had settled into a predictable routine. Kirsty looked after the boys and Elizabeth in the mornings, whilst Zoë helped Steve with the sheep. After lunch Zoë put Elizabeth down for a nap, and when the child woke she played with her until Kirsty and the Jarvis children got back from their hospital visit. Supper was eaten early, usually in the kitchen with all the children, and in the evenings Zoë took charge of the lambing whilst Steve went off to visit Ailsa. When Steve returned, they spent another couple of hours in the lambing shed together.

'We're one big happy family,' Steve often

announced at supper, a sentiment that prompted the big nanny to glare at Zoë; a look of profound unhappiness written on every surface of her face and misery seeping from every angle of her ungainly body.

Most nights, Steve came to Zoë's bed and rose only when it was time to do the desired two-hour checks on the flock. Occasionally he was up most of the night with a difficult birth, or so he said. Sometimes Zoë woke to find the bed empty and she would wonder if Steve were really with Kirsty; she couldn't believe he would be. She couldn't believe that he'd have that amount of energy for a start, and she flattered herself that Steve must prefer her graceful healthy body, to Kirsty's lumbering mass.

On two occasions, when finding the bed empty, she'd risen herself and made her way over to the lambing yard; only to find Steve with an upended ewe and a difficult birth on his hands.

'Checking up on me, Zoë? Or come to help?'

'To help of course.'

'Good, because I've already got one wife to rule me, and I don't want another.'

For three weeks, lambing had been intense, but in the last week of January it eased up a little.

Steve consulted his calendar and announced that he expected three or four days of calm, and then a second onslaught of lambs.

'How do you know?' Zoë asked, amazed by his

precise knowledge.

He looked heavenward. 'Dates and times that the tups were in,' he replied. 'Really, Zoë, it's no wonder you produced a cuckoo in your nest.'

Zoë became flustered. 'She's not a cuckoo. I intended to have her. Betsy was a wanted child, she wasn't a mistake.'

'Wanted by you, perhaps, but what about her daddy?'

'That's none of you're business, Steve Jarvis.'

'That's where you're wrong. Look, I was born the wrong side of the blanket — I didn't have no dad. So it is my business, see?'

'No, it's not. Betsy is nothing to do with you, neither is her father.'

'No? Well if you'd had your way, I would have been her father, and father to a few more as well. You're just about the most irresponsible woman I've ever come across.'

'You're a fine one to talk, you told me that Rory was a mistake.'

Steve was getting angry. 'Yeah, well, I married Ailsa, didn't I? And yeah, it was my mistake. I told you, I thought Ailsa were past it. But I've always taken care of you haven't I and—'

'And all the other bits you've got on the side? Is that what you were going to say?'

'Yeah, yeah, that's right.' He was white with rage.

Words were spat back and forth. It wasn't until later that evening that Zoë tearfully realized that it was the first serious argument she and Steve had ever had. At supper he'd seemed totally unaffected by it, whereas she could hardly bring herself to speak or to swallow the food that Mary had so carefully prepared for them. The situation obviously pleased the nanny; Kirsty was very buoyant, and very chatty.

Later that evening Zoë didn't offer to go out and check the flock with Steve, but excused herself and went to bed early, where she tossed and turned and slept fitfully.

It was almost one o'clock when Steve joined her in her room.

He gently shook her shoulder. 'Need a bit of cheering up?' He asked.

She turned over in her bed and smiled. She moved over to make room for him. 'I'm sorry about earlier,' she said. Then she suddenly blinked her eyes open; someone else was in the room. She shook herself awake as she realized that Kirsty, fat and naked, was standing at the bottom of her bed.

'Come on girls,' Steve said, flicking on the light. 'I want you both to be friends, kiss and make up.'

Zoë snatched the sheets up around her own naked body.

'No, no, Zoë, that's not the idea at all. Kirsty's showing you her considerable charms, and you should do likewise.' He pulled the sheets away from her.

'Come on, Kirsty, come and show yourself. Now Zoë, what do you think to those tits? Magnificent aren't they?'

Zoë swallowed, what the hell was Steve up to? Surely he didn't think . . . he couldn't possible imagine that she'd be willing to . . .

Before she'd thought it all through, Steve said, 'come on girls, let's have you in the sack, kiss and make-up, remember.'

Zoë wanted to point out that it was she and he that had quarreled, Kirsty hadn't been involved. But before she could say anything, Kirsty moved to the side of the bed.

Zoë saw that the girl was extremely nervous, she was literally wringing her hands and biting into her bottom lip.

Zoë eased herself over to the far side of the bed, and was about to get to her feet, when Steve thwarted her plan by jumping into the bed beside her. At the same time Kirsty eased herself into the other side, so that Zoë was sandwiched between them.

'Now isn't this nice?' Steve said. 'Me and my two favorite girls altogether in the sack.' He rubbed his penis against Zoë's thigh, and she could feel that he was very hard. He tried to kiss her, but she spun her head away from him and was faced first by Kirsty's large breasts, and then by the vision of Kirsty who leaned toward her, her lips puckered, ready to bestow a kiss.

Zoë let out a cry. 'You're perverted, both of you,' she screamed. She wriggled from between them and crawled to the foot of the bed. She grabbed her dressing gown and fled from the room.

She made her way along the passage and down the stairs to the kitchen. She plonked herself down at the table and, with her head in her hands, she tried to put her thoughts in order. But try as she might, she couldn't seem to find any sense in anything.

Ten minutes later Steve joined her. He just walked into the kitchen and put the kettle on the hob.

'Sorry about that,' he said casually. 'She was convinced that I was screwing you. She thought you were some sort of nymphomaniac, so I suggested that she found out for herself. I did it for us — we can't have Ailsa finding out can we? We don't want Ailsa to know that you're here. We don't want Kirsty spilling the beans, do we? It would be easy for Kirsty to let it slip out one afternoon, wouldn't it?'

'I don't believe you, Steve.'

He gave a funny little laugh. 'What? You don't think I was thinking of a threesome, do you?'

'Yes, I do, I think you know how much I love you, and I think you thought I'd do anything for you.'

'You might have enjoyed it,' he said.

'I saw how excited it made you,' she went on.

He slipped his hand under his dressing gown and

70

exposed himself. 'Be a bit difficult for me to hide a thing like this, wouldn't it?' He laughed. 'But how about you, Zoë? Excite you did it?'

He felt between her legs, she was moist, and he smiled.

'I thought so,' he said.

'I wasn't excited by Kirsty,' she said hastily.

'No? It must be this then.'

He drew her up from the chair and, placing her hip against the back rail he bent her forward over it. Standing right behind her he fitted himself with a condom, and he roughly entered her.

'This excite you, does it, Zoë?'

She didn't answer.

'Perhaps not then,' he said, and pulled out of her.

'Oh no, Steve please, please.'

'Ah, I see, so you do want it?'

She could feel him pressing on her buttocks, she tried to stand on tiptoe and maneuver herself onto him. 'Yes, yes, I want it.'

He put the very tip just inside her. 'Is that all right? Or do you want it a bit deeper?'

'Steve,' she was practically screaming. 'Do it, do it now.'

'What was that? Deeper, did you say? Did I hear a please?'

'Yes, yes, yes, deeper, deeper, now please, please.'

'Right,' he said. 'I'm always happy to oblige.'

He grabbed her hips and thrust into her, she in return pushed back onto him.

The coupling was brief and very noisy.

Afterwards, Zoë, still bent over her chair, stood very still; her eyes tightly shut, Steve was cleaning himself up, and then he made a pot of tea.

'You all right, Zoë? Stuck to the chair are you? Or are you hoping for a bit more? If so, you'll be disappointed. I have the staff to service as well, you know. I can't be expected to do an encore.'

Zoë squeezed her eyes even tighter together. She must get away from Cameron House, she knew that, she must leave, the whole situation was unhealthy. She was obsessed with him. She'd even begged him to make love to her; it was degrading, she'd do anything he wanted her to do. She might even be persuaded to form a threesome if things were allowed to continue. And Ailsa would be home soon, then what? Her love would always be one-sided. Steve didn't love her, she doubted if he loved anyone apart from himself. No, no that wasn't true, he loved his boys; there was no doubt about that. But she must go. If she stayed she couldn't be held responsible for her actions.

Chapter 11

Zoë stirred, the telephone sounded a long way off; Steve was deeply asleep.

'Mm, Steve? Steve?'

'Uh?'

'The phone, it's been ringing for ages.'

Steve pulled himself up onto his elbows and let his head flop back on the headboard. 'Shit, it's bloody two o'clock, who'd be ringing at this hour?'

'Don't know, but they're pretty insistent.'

He swung his legs out of the bed, pulled on his jeans and a jumper, and staggered to the door.

He yawned. 'I ought to check the flock anyway,' he said. 'Back soon.'

He made his way to his and Ailsa's room, swung over the bed and snatched up the receiver. 'Yeah?'

He hardly heard what the voice on the other end of the line was saying, he caught only key words and his brain tried desperately to string them together. Emergency — toxaemia — caesarian — very ill. Sheep got toxaemia if they weren't vaccinated especially and thier nutrition wasn't properly managed, surely that wasn't the case with Ailsa?

Ages ago, when he'd first started to share Zoë's bed, he'd perfected his alibi should he not hear the telephone. He'd the wonderful excuse that he was in the

73

lambing yard. And now he recited the rehearsed lines, but the person on the other end wasn't Ailsa, and they didn't care where he'd been. They only advised him to make haste and get to the hospital.

'Where are you going?' Zoë had followed him; she had a bath towel wrapped around her body.

'It's Ailsa, they're taking her to theatre. I have to go. You'll have to manage things here. Keep a special eye on the ewe in pen thirty-three, will you? I'll phone as soon as I know anything.'

He took Zoë in his arms. 'Christ, I'm scared, Zoë. I think they were telling me that she might die.' He gulped back tears. His face was white and his eyes were huge black, fearful, discs.

'Die?' Zoë said.

'Well they didn't exactly say that, it's not what they said, it's the way that they said it. Oh, Zoë, what would I do if she died?'

He gave her a squeeze and bolted along the passage to the big staircase.

'I'll let you know what's happening,' he called over his shoulder, as he bounded down the stairs. 'Don't worry.'

He slipped into his old Barber jacket, thinking as he did so that it was probably not quite the thing to wear in a sterile environment, covered as it was in sheep debris. He grabbed a set of keys from the hook and debated if he should take the car or the Land Rover; the car would be quicker, but the roads were hazardous, and the Land Rover would be more reliable. He had chains he could fit if the weather closed in.

He went out into the yard, for once he had no thought for the flock, he could rely on Zoë. He climbed into the Land Rover and turned the starter. The night was bitterly cold and the engine coughed and spluttered before bursting into life.

The roads were worse than he'd anticipated, and he was driving too fast; even so, it took him almost an hour to reach the infirmary. Twice he skidded, once with near serious consequences.

By the time he reached the hospital swing doors, he was like a man demented. Ailsa, oh Ailsa. What if anything should happen to her? He'd been so casual about their relationship. He'd always found it rather a comfort that theirs was a marriage of convenience. Her money, his youth, and between them they traded each other's high sex drives; as a result they had a fulfilling marriage and a deep sexual harmony that suited them both well. They had, in the beginning, used each other; neither had ever denied it. But Ailsa, oh, Ailsa, she *must* be all right, she had to be. The boys needed her, he needed her — Oh, God, he loved her, he bloody loved her. It wasn't just the money, and it wasn't just the sex thing. Steve had money enough of his own now, and he was dashing and handsome and had the gift of the gab. Women had always gravitated toward him; girls like Kirsty and Zoë were always willing. But money and sex couldn't replace Ailsa, nothing could.

The night staff informed him that Ailsa was still in theatre, and they told him that the doctor would come and see him as soon as he possibly could. A kindly nurse showed him to a waiting room and gave him a cup of tea.

Ailsa. Oh, Ailsa.

What to Steve seemed like an age later, a middle-aged man, smartly dressed in a dark suit, entered the room. He was holding a thick manila file. He had a pair of gold rimmed glasses perched on the end of his nose, a bald pate and, despite his smart appearance, a five o'clock shadow on his rather podgy chin, an observation that prompted Steve to look at his watch; it was four o'clock.

'Mr Jarvis?' The man held out his hand. 'I'm Mr Cowley, consultant obstetrician.'

Steve made no comment, but held his breath. He couldn't bring himself to ask how Ailsa was. If the news was bad, and by the look on the man's face, it was, he didn't want to know.

'Your wife's still in recovery, she seems to have responded well, but I'm afraid she's not out of the wood yet.'

Steve swallowed, there were things he didn't want to contemplate.

The doctors lips twitched into a sympathetic smile.

'She's a strong women and.....'

'Ailsa?' He whispered.

The consultant guided him to a chair.

'It's my experience, that once we deliver the child, the mother's health quite rapidly returns to normal, but I'd be deceiving you if I told you that was always the case.'

'Ailsa?' Steve swallowed. 'Do you mean she might die?' There, he'd said it; he'd asked for the answer that he dreaded most.

Mr Cowley put his hand out and touched Steve's arm. 'It's rare these days for us to lose a mother, but it does occasionally happen. Your wife's a very sick woman.' Then almost as if it were an afterthought, he said, 'You have a lovely baby daughter by the way.' He consulted the manila file. 'Not a huge young lady, two-point-seven kilo's, that's about six pounds, if you want it in English. But she's strong and healthy, she'll soon make it up. As soon as the pediatricians are finished with her I'll get someone to take you to see her.'

A daughter, Ailsa would be pleased, that's if Ailsa ever . . . no he mustn't think like that, positive thought, that was the thing, he would will her back to health, he would put all his strength into it.

The doctor got up to leave. 'We'll keep you informed,' he said. He looked down at Steve's cup of cold tea. 'I'll get the nurse to bring you some fresh tea. It's going to be a long wait.'

He reached the door.

'She shouldn't have more kids, after this, should she? Steve blurted.

'Not the time to think — but no, your absolutely right. If your wife does get over this, I can't emphasize too strongly that she shouldn't have any more pregnancies.'

Steve nodded his head and looked the doctor straight in the eyes. 'Don't worry, there won't be. I'll not put her through this again.'

Mr Cowley nodded. 'Good man,' he said, and left.

A few moments later, the nurse, with what Steve imagined to be a pitying smile, brought him fresh tea.

Steve paced about the room. He found himself praying, 'Dear God, please, please let her be all right. She's had a tough time, she deserves to see her children grow up.'

Steve wasn't a man given to religion, indeed he couldn't remember a time he'd ever prayed before, unless reciting the Lord's prayer in school counted, which, seeing as he'd altered the words, *forgive us our testicles and lead us not into Templeton,* probably didn't. He wondered if kneeling on the floor might enhance the magic. But he didn't believe in God, and he wondered if his disbelief might work against him. He was pretty sure that Zoë believed in God, and Kirsty probably did as well, and he knew Mary came from a staunch Church of Scotland background. Maybe he should ring home and get the experts on to the job.

'Ailsa. Oh Ailsa.'

Well it was worth a try, he had nothing to lose, unless the God he didn't believe in decided to punish him for his lack of faith.

He got down on his knees. Most men, would, at a time like that, consider doing a trade with God. *Dear God, I won't fuck around anymore if you let her live.* But Steve didn't consider infidelity to be much of a sin, and therefore he didn't consider it a fair trade. Ailsa was worth more than that.

He put his hands together, interlacing his fingers, and squeezed until his knuckles were white.

'Dear, God, please, please, please, please let her be all right.' He squeezed his fingers harder, as if the more pressure used, the more potent the prayer.

He was still on his knees when the nurse came in to fetch him; he wasn't in the least bit embarrassed. She, on the other hand, blushed to the roots of her hair, as if, thought Steve, she had caught him masturbating.

'I was praying,' he said.

She coughed. 'Doctor says that you can come and see the wee girl now,' she said with forced cheerfulness.

'Ailsa?'

'Is that what you're going to call her? That's a bonny name.'

'No, no, well, I don't know. I meant how is she? My wife?'

The nurse shook her head. 'No news yet I'm afraid, Mr Jarvis. But come along now and see the wee girl. She's in special care at the moment, but don't worry, it's just a precaution because she's a wee bit premature.'

He was led down a short corridor with doors on either side. He wondered if Ailsa was behind one of them, surrounded by tubes and pipes and worried doctors. He desperately wanted to see her; there were things he wanted to tell her.

The baby was lying in an incubator. Nothing to worry about, they told him. It was just a precaution. All being well she'd be out of there by morning.

Baby of Ailsa Jarvis, the tag on the bottom of the Perspex dome read and his heart lurched. Ailsa. Oh Ailsa.

The child looked exactly the way Duncan had looked, with a shock of very black hair and creamy mottled skin.

'She's a bonny wee lass,' the nurse said. 'And she has your colouring.'

Steve gulped. How could he explain that he wanted her to look like Ailsa, with her pale skin and flaming red hair?

It was almost eleven o'clock in the morning when he was finally allowed to see his wife. He was surprised, almost shocked, to find that there were no tubes or monitors, only a saline drip running into the back of her hand.

He'd spent hours waiting to see her, hours with no real information, and even when they'd finally told him he could go in, they hadn't told him what the state of play was, or perhaps he'd been too scared to listen?

But once he was by the side of her bed and she had sleepily opened her eyes, he heard a nurse say, 'She's had a narrow escape, Mr Jarvis.'

Then another nurse said, 'We've left you to tell her the good news.' Both nurses then tactfully blended into the background.

Ailsa gave a weak smile. 'Gave you all a fright, didn't I?' She whispered, her voice sounded hoarse and her lips were dry and cracked.

'Oh, Ailsa.'

She frowned. 'The baby?' she asked. Steve registered the fear in her eyes; like him, she had been too afraid to ask. 'They said you'd tell me.'

'A girl—'

'She's al—'

'She's fine. She's—' he laughed, he felt euphoric. 'She's a bonny wee lass,' he said, mimicking the nurse's Scottish accent. And he laughed again.

Ailsa smiled, she looked dreamily content.

'They'll be no more,' he said rather sternly.

She nodded, 'I know,' she said.

'I'll take care of it,' he said. Ailsa gave in much easier than he had expected. 'Don't worry, I'll do the deed.'

He laughed, and to his surprise, tears pricked his eyes.

'Ailsa. Oh, Ailsa. I love you, you'll never know how much. Hell, I didn't even know myself until I almost lost you.'

'I've always loved you,' she said, 'right from the very first time, do you remember? At the Osbourne-Pennington's?'

'Oh, Ailsa.'

'Steve? I'll be home soon, you'd better send Zoë back to Hulver.'

'How the hell—'

'Lavinia wrote me, just after New Year.'

'You knew all the time? But why didn't you—'

'I love you, you're a very sexy, needy man, and I wasn't there for you.'

'Ailsa. Oh, Ailsa, you're something else.'

'Only, be kind to Zoë, let her down gently. Don't go crashing in there and break her heart, will you?'

'Ailsa, I love you.'

'Ditto,' she said, contentedly closing her eyes.

Chapter 12

Where was Steve? He'd said he'd telephone and let her know what was happening. It was almost lunchtime and she'd not heard a word from him. Zoë turned the ewe over and, holding the animal between her legs, she bent over. Taking a warped plastic basin in one hand, she gently squeezed and pulled on the ewe's teats and milked out a good quantity of colostrum.

She talked to the sheep as she worked. 'There,' she said, 'if you refuse to feed your lamb yourself, then I'll just have to do it for you. What sort of mother do you call yourself, anyway?' She leaned over and looked at the ewe's ear tag. 'Number fifty-eight. Well let me tell you, number fifty-eight, you're going to get a really black mark in the lambing book, and it's your own fault.' She released the ewe from her hold; and a very small lamb immediately tried to suckle. The ewe swung round and head-butted the pathetic little creature into the corner of the pen.

'For goodness sake,' Zoë said, scooping the lamb up into her arms. 'This is your baby, you stupid skittish creature, what do you think you're playing at?'

With the lamb tucked under her arm, and the basin of first milk in her hand, she climbed over the side of the pen and, holding the lamb by its forelegs, she positioned herself on a straw-bale. She placed the small trembling body between her knees and expertly slipped a red rubber feeding tube down the lamb's throat. She then proceeded to administer half of the colostrum she had milked from the ewe.

'There you are,' she said. She slowly removed the tube and took the lamb over to the orphan pen where, with an aerosol spray, she wrote *fifty-eight* in red numbers on the side of its tiny body. 'Don't worry,' she said to the lamb. 'When Steve gets back we'll put that neglectful mother of yours in a foster harness and you'll get all the nourishment you want, and she can take one of the other orphans as well, she's got gallons of milk.' She put the lamb under a heat lamp and proceeded to the sink to wash the tube.

Where was Steve? She needed him; she couldn't get the ewe into the fostering pen on her own. Maybe she should ring the hospital and find out what was happening. What if Ailsa died? What would happen to her and Steve? Would they become an item, a partnership? Would Steve marry her? And if he did, would she ever trust him?

She submerged the tube in Milton, then she poured the rest of the thick colostrum into an old yogurt pot and placed it to one side ready for freezing; it would be lifesaving to a rejected or orphaned lamb. The first milk was rich in antibodies and without it a lamb had little chance of survival.

She looked at the time again, it was almost one o'clock, time for lunch, but she didn't want to go into the house and face Mary and Kirsty. She knew that Steve hadn't telephoned; they'd have come and told her straight away if he had. She couldn't go over to the kitchen and eat Mary's carefully prepared food; she was fidgety and her thoughts were all over the place, her imagination was running wild.

One moment her sentiments were good and noble, the next they were far from honourable. One minute she fervently wanted Ailsa to live, not for Ailsa's sake, and not for Steve's, but for the little boys. The next moment, her thoughts did a U-turn and she imagined life without Ailsa; she even imagined the funeral and all the sadness associated with it; and she placed herself center stage, comforting the grieving widower, and playing a very maternal role in bringing up his children. Then she thought about Elizabeth and she imagined that it was herself that lay dying, and Ailsa about to take over the care of her child, and she immediately felt guilty and began to pray that Ailsa's life might be spared.

Round and round the thoughts and scenarios went, yet they always ended up with Ailsa being no more, and she and Steve together. Well, if that was to be the case, Steve had better get one or two things straight. There would be no more screwing around. The fat girl would have to go. But who would replace her? Zoë had the sneaky feeling that fat or thin, young or old, Steve would still find his way into her bed.

Zoë went into the lambing hut and pushed another

log into the cast iron stove, then she pulled the kettle off the hob and made herself a mug of instant coffee. Cradling it in her hands, she flopped down on the wooden makeshift shepherd's bunk. The hut, a sort of wooden caravan on wheels, was warm and welcoming compared with the bitter chill of the lambing shed. Zoë hadn't bothered to go back to bed when Steve had left that morning, but had come down to the yard and caught up on the task of docking and castrating the newborn lambs. She stifled a yawn, her eyes felt gritty and her eyelids heavy. She slipped off her Wellington boots and curled her feet under her.

Once more her thoughts wandered back to Steve and what would happen if Ailsa didn't get better. She'd hire a man, not to look after the sheep, but to care for the children, yes, that was the answer. After all they now lived in a world of equal opportunities, there were probably dozens of men willing to become nannies. Of course, they'd probably be gay; but so what? Steve was totally homophobic; he would never allow a gay man to look after his boys. There must be heterosexual men who liked kids; hang on a minute, why would a fully grown macho man want to care for children? He wouldn't — not unless he was some sort of paedophile. Oh shit; was there no answer to this problem?

Zoë took a gulp of her coffee. Problem? What problem? Ailsa was probably fine and Zoë shouldn't be thinking otherwise. Besides, if Ailsa did die, Zoë would feel guilty for having such thoughts and planning her future, as if her thoughts had somehow caused Ailsa's demise. No, it was very wrong of her to make such plans in advance of the event. She should just wait until Steve came home and then—'

'What's this? Unofficial tea break?'

Zoë started so violently that she spilled her coffee. 'God, Steve, you frightened me to death, I didn't hear you creep in.'

'I wasn't creeping, you were miles away, deep in thought, you were.'

'Here,' he said, handing her a champagne glass.

Zoë's heart sank, and the words she ought not to have uttered, slipped out. 'Ailsa's not dead then?' They were said with blatant disappointment, and once out, Zoë would have done anything to bite them back again.

But Steve didn't seem to notice. 'No, thank, God. It was a close call though. I don't mind telling you, Zoë, I was shit scared, I really was. Do you know? At one point I got down on my bloody hands and knees, and I prayed, I prayed with all the strength I had in me. Me! Can you imagine, *me* on my hands and knees, praying?'

Zoë swallowed, but didn't reply.

Steve poured two glasses of champagne.

'Anyway,' he clinked his glass on hers. 'Here's to my wife, and my bonny daughter, that's what they said she was, "a bonny wee lass". How about that then, Zoë? Me and

Ailsa have got ourselves a daughter. Are you happy for us?' He had a broad smile on his face.

'And Ailsa's all right?' Zoë asked weakly, gilt and disappointment were settling on her shoulders in equal proportions.

'Yeah, she's fine. She's tired and all that, but she's fine. She's a tough old bird is Ailsa.'

Zoë fought back tears; she didn't understand what she was feeling, or why she was feeling it. She just knew that the feeling was suffocating and destructive. Ailsa was a nice enough woman, indeed she'd always been very kind to Zoë. How could she have wished her dead? Just so that she and Ailsa's mean, shallow, insensitive, unemotional, husband could be together. I hate him, she thought, I hate him with all my heart.

Steve had settled down next to her on the bunk. Zoë saw that the champagne bottle was almost empty, she wondered if he had consumed the rest by himself or if Kirsty and Mary had been celebrating with him.

He kissed her neck. 'Boy it's warm in here, better take some of these clothes off.'

He stripped down to his waist and then he did the same to Zoë, she neither helped nor hindered him, but sat like a rag doll without a will of her own. They sat together, half-naked on the bunk in the warm hut. Steve was talking and laughing and describing what had happened, and how afraid he'd been, and how beautiful his daughter was. He turned to Zoë, dribbled some champagne on her breasts, then, teasing and sucking on her nipples he licked it off.

'I'm going to miss these,' he said.

Zoë gulped down the rest of her drink and he took the glass away from her. She rolled over and wriggled out of her trousers, consenting to what was required of her, but her face was fixed in stone. He unzipped his jeans and, taking his usual precautions, he was quickly inside her. He seemed unaware of her complacency and her misery. She looked at him as if she was doing a, not altogether unpleasant, duty.

'So, Zoë,' he said spitting out the words in the same rhythm as his thrusts. 'You - don't – need – to – go – yet – not – until – after – the – week – end – in – fact – I could – do with – you – here to – host – the – cock – shoot.'

Zoë had her head turned to the wooden boards of the hut; it smelled of creosote. Her head was being pushed back onto the wall behind her, the rough wooden boards tore at her hair. Tears ran down her cheeks. She wanted to curl up in a ball and die. She wanted to be anywhere but under Steve and yet, at the same time, she never wanted to be parted from him; she wanted to be permanently welded to him, she didn't ever want to pull her body away from his.

'Of course, Steve,' she whispered. 'I'll do anything to help you, you know that, anything at all.' And she spoke as if her heart was breaking.

Chapter 13

Sir Theodore Sheldon-Harris whistled as he stuffed his things into a canvas bag. He felt excited by the thought of three days of freedom. He needn't have left until the following day, but he'd decided to take it slowly, drive as far as the borders, stay there overnight and make the rest of the way to Cameron House on Friday.

'Theo? Theo?' His wife, Isobel, was coming up the stairs.

'Dressing room,' he shouted.

'Are you decent?' She asked from outside the door.

He sighed; he was always decent; if he were less decent he'd have walked out on her years ago. 'Yes,' he said, 'I'm decent.'

She burst into the room. She was a thin faced, deep voiced woman in her mid fifties, a good ten years older than her husband.

'You're going then?'

'Yes,' he said firmly. 'I'm going.'

'I don't think you should,' she said.

He didn't answer.

'I didn't think you liked shooting,' she said.

'I don't,' he said, 'but Ailsa has asked me, and I feel it would be rude not to go.'

She threw her hands into the air. 'Why? Why must

you go? What's Ailsa McTodd to you? Not one of her conquests are you?'

Theo sucked in his bottom lip, he mustn't quarrel with her; that was precisely what she wanted. If they quarreled he'd never get away.

'Ailsa is our friend, at least she was *our* friend, once.'

'She's a wicked, evil, woman.'

'You used to like her.'

'That's before I saw the light.'

When Isobel Sheldon-Harris said these words, she quite literally meant them. Six years previously, she had woken from a dream to find a spirit guide standing in the corner of the bedroom. His message was clear, she had a gift, a gift she must use to help others, and in order to do this she must mend her ways, and live a sober and respectable life. She took the vision very much to heart; in fact, she saw the light.

Seeing the light became her mantra, and she went on and on about it. She also went on and on about Gerry, her first husband and apparently her soul mate. He knew from the telephone bill that she spent hours on the telephone to him. Well, good for her. With any luck her guilt at leaving him and her child all those years ago would drive her back to him and leave Theo in peace. Isobel's contact with her first husband had brought Charlotte, Isobel's daughter, to Garrick Hall. She was neat and vivacious and a real spark of life. She'd been sixteen when Theo had found himself a stepfather; sixteen, beautiful, sexy, and very, very manipulative. At times the frustrated Theo had found it difficult to keep his hands to himself. She'd flirted outrageously with him, an act that confused, embarrassed, and yet thrilled him. Then, four years later, he was to be even more confused when, at the magical age of twenty, Charlotte had introduced him to her lover Helga. After Helga had come Dinah, and then her currant partner, Flora, a big, soft, feminine girl, with a pretty face and an endearing smile. It was Flora's rounded hips and ample bosom that now fed Theo's fantasies.

Isobel minded that her daughter was a lesbian, she minded very much. The once very unmaternal good-time woman now decided that she wanted grandchildren, a continuance of hers and Gerry's genes. And although she loved and welcomed Charlotte she refused to have anything to do with any of her daughter's lovers and had taken a particular dislike to the pretty round-faced Flora. Theo for his part thought the girls affection for each other was a terrible waste. Charlotte and Flora had a lot to offer, but they ought to be offering it to a man, not each other.

Theo placed a folded shirt in his bag. He was getting away; his fingers tingled with excitement and anticipation.

'I was thinking about Gerry,' Isobel said.

Theo sighed, oh no, not now, he had to get on his

92

way.

'You know, we did him a terrible wrong,' she continued.

We? We? Where did the *we* come from? Theo didn't look at it that way at all. Isobel's first marriage had been her concern, not his. Just as he'd never lain the blame of his first marriage break-up on Isobel, he'd never felt he should carry the can for Isobel's divorce. He'd never given a thought to Gerry. For Theo's part, he had walked out of a very boring marriage; leaving a plain unexciting wife in return for the charms of Isobel. The price had been higher than Theo ever cared to admit. His wife Anne had taken their small son with her, and refused Theo any contact. Theo had thought he would bide his time, and make contact when the boy was older and no longer tied to his mother's apron strings. But it wasn't to be. The child had been drowned in a ferry disaster just off the French coast. Even so, for the first nine years of his marriage to Isabel he considered it a very fair trade. But even before she'd seen the light, Isobel had not turned out to be quite the woman Theo had hoped she was. Ten years his senior, she was articulate and bright, and put her clever tongue to good use. She charmed, cajoled and manipulated everyone she met. She entertained in a lavish, outrageous style, was generous but wasteful with his money and was sexually indiscreet. Theo hardly noticed his old friends dropping off, because they were replaced by new, exciting, daring, people; people such as

Ailsa McTodd, who'd been an acquaintance of Isobel's long before she was a friend of his. But then Isobel had seen the light, and friends such as Ailsa became *persona non grata*, and overnight sex became very much a thing of the past.

And things had gone downhill from there. Isobel became a changed woman. Alcohol was banned from the house, as was the eating of meat. For now she declared herself one of a chosen group; she could see and hear Spirit and her body and mind must be kept clean and receptive at all times. She moved out of Theo's bedroom and created a bedroom for herself in the nursery wing. A bedroom comfortably furnished, but littered with religious and magical icons, including a huge crucifix hanging over her bed. Not that she conformed to any conventional religion, she didn't. Indeed she was very much against most forms of conventional worship. But she told Theo that the cross of Jesus acted as spiritual protection for her, guarding her against negative energies and evil spirits. Even though she was no longer committed to Christianity, the cross still represented goodness and purity. She spent hours and hours in her room. Theo had spied her through the crack in the old nursery door, a crack used by he and his sister in their youth to spy on old Nanny Sheldon-Harris. Instead of seeing the elderly retainer he now spied on Isobel, sitting cross-legged or kneeling, talking to the spirit world, praying and begging forgiveness for her past sins and Theo's present sins. When she wasn't communicating with the world beyond the grave, she was nagging Theo and pointing out the error of his ways; or visiting Mrs Hapgood, a medium and spiritualist who guided Isobel and kept her mind focussed on a straight and narrow path that was way beyond his understanding.

Theo zipped up the bag and turned toward the door.

'I don't think you should go, Theo.'

'Oh?'

'Killing is evil, those little birds have harmed no one, they do not deserve to be murdered.'

'Don't worry,' he said lightheartedly, 'you know what a bad shot I am, I think they're pretty safe with me.'

'That's not the point, you're going out with murder in your heart. To think a sin is to commit one.'

Theo could think of no good answer. He shrugged his shoulders. He was no match for his wife. He must not argue; he knew he would end up the loser.

'I may not shoot,' he said weakly.

'Then don't go,' she said, baring his way.

'I have to, I've told Ailsa's husband I'd go. I can't let them down.'

'Ailsa McTodd is a fornicator.'

'Jarvis,' he said. 'Ailsa has remarried.'

He shouldn't have corrected her, her mouth was working back and forth; he could see the anger rising in her face.

'Fornicators,' she spat. 'You're going into a den of

95

fornicators.'

For a brief moment he wanted to laugh and add a verbal, 'I wish,' but he so wanted to go, and he knew that if an argument ensued his chances of getting away would be minimum.

'Ailsa's just had a baby,' he said weakly, as if the fact made fornication impossible.

'The devil's child,' Isobel said. 'That child is the devil's child. Philip killed himself, because of Ailsa's fornication and that child is the fruit of her sin.'

This was too much. Theo took a deep breath. 'Philip killed himself because of Lloyds, you know that. Haven't we been through the same mill?'

She looked unconvinced.

'He had financial worries, for God's sake.' As soon as he'd said the G word he knew he was done for.

'Thou shalt not call the Lord's name in vain,' she screeched.

He tried to push past her. 'I must go, it's a long drive.'

'I forbid you to go,' she growled.

She's mad, Theo thought, as he caught the glint in her eye. She's stark staring mad.

The telephone rang.

Theo took a deep breath. 'That's probably Mrs Hapgood. She rang earlier, she had something urgent to tell you.' It was a lie, a blatant lie, but he had to get away. He'd go crazy if he didn't get out of this madhouse.

Isobel rushed past him to the telephone.

'I'm off then,' Theo called. He was already halfway down the stairs; he hadn't even picked up his toothbrush and wash things. He'd stop and buy new on the way; nothing was going to stop his escape.

He threw his bag into the back of his ancient Volvo and patted the steering wheel. 'Right, old girl, we've got a long journey and I'm relying on you not to let me down.' He pushed it into gear and made his way to the main gates. There was a tractor and trailer parked outside the cottage on the drive; to pass it he would have to run over his tidy grass verge, and there was nothing Theo hated more than ruining his carefully tended lawn. He glanced in his mirror; there was no sign of Isobel. He stopped the engine and got out. Andrew Culper and his girlfriend Cathy were carrying a large sideboard toward the trailer.

They heaved the sideboard onto the trailer.

Andrew touched his cap. 'Morning, Sir,' he said.

Cathy smiled and nodded.

'You're really going then, Andy?' Theo said.

Andrew looked down at the ground. 'I have to, Sir. I can't work with the bloke,' he shook his head, 'I'm sorry, Sir, but the things he says about Cathy can't be repeated. If I stay, I'll end up by flooring him, I swear to God I will.'

Theo frowned. 'Maybe I should get rid of *him*. I don't want to lose you, Andy.'

'He'll not go without a fight and it'll cost you a packet in redundancy, Sir.' Andrew looked embarrassed. 'I hate to let you down, but lambing don't start for another two months, you've time to get a replacement, and, well, if you ever gets stuck, you know me and Cathy will always help you out.'

Cathy nodded vigorously. 'You can get hold of us through my mum,' she said.

'Thanks for lending us the tractor and trailer,' Andrew said. He wiped his hand on his overalls and held out his hand.

Theo took it, and reluctantly shook it. 'I'm sorry about everything,' Theo said. Wondering why he felt the need to apologize for his cantankerous foreman.

'It's not your fault, Sir.'

Theo glanced behind him, the drive was still quiet, but nevertheless he felt uneasy and wanted to be gone. He coughed. 'I wonder if you could just move the tractor Andy? I need to get going.'

Without further ado, Andy jumped into the cab and, instead of maneuvering it into the turning area outside the cottage, he pulled it off the drive and onto Theo's carefully manicured verge.

Theo closed his eyes, and sighed. He gave Andrew a smile and a wave, got into his car, and drove off.

Chapter 14

Isobel replaced the receiver. She was disappointed. It wasn't Marjory Hapgood, it was a call from a local wholesaler asking for Theo. Well, she certainly wasn't prepared to run after him for that.

She hesitated for a moment, her hand hovering over the telephone. She'd like to ring Marjory, but she didn't feel she should disturb her. The mornings were usually the times when the medium got most of her clearest messages. It would be unfair to burden her with questions, but oh dear, she wanted to know what Marjory thought about Theo going to Scotland. She desperately needed to know whether this act of defiance heralded any danger for her.

She repressed the urge to phone. After all, Theo was away, so she knew she'd be safe. She must wash; she should have ignored the telephone and washed as soon as he was out of sight. She went into her bathroom, filled the basin with icy cold water and submerged her hands and face; she counted to three, pulled out the plug, refilled the basin and repeated the ritual.

In the eyes of the world Isobel knew she was not a particularly wicked woman, she'd told white lies occasionally, who didn't? And on occasions she'd drunk a little too much, but all in all, since marrying Theo, she had become quite respectable, her past life forgotten. But it was that past life that troubled her. Theo was her second husband, she had divorced and deserted the first, along with her seven-year-old daughter Charlotte, and although she couldn't bring herself to admit it, she had set her cap at Theo and blatantly wrecked his first marriage, not caring that he was the father of a year-old son.

It had been all too easy. Seventeen years ago she had been an extremely attractive woman. She'd started off her career as the lead singer in an operatic company, that's how she chose to remember it. In fact, she'd been an entertainer, and she'd never minded taking her clothes off to please the audience; indeed, pleasing the audience was, at that time, her stock in trade. Later she'd met and married Gerry Bridges and together they had perfected a double act, an act that had been a mixture of mind reading and clairvoyance. It had all been contrived of course, a series of clever signals from Gerry had convinced even the most skeptical. They'd never made it big; in fact most weeks they'd hardly made enough to feed themselves But the act had brought a bonus with it, they'd been asked to perform at parties and receptions. That's how Issie Bridges had met Theo and his wife Anne. Theo had been a pushover; even Gerry, her first husband, partner and agent, had understood. 'Go for it, Issie,' he'd said, but don't ever forget where you started, nor who you started with.

And she'd gone; life on the road was tiring, and

motherhood even more tiring. She had never thrived on the demands of a young child. So one day she'd dumped Charlotte off at Gerry's sister's house, bid Gerry a fine farewell, and joined Theo and Anne at Garrick Hall, Theo's Norfolk mansion. It wasn't a mansion of course, but to Issie, after living for years in seedy B and B's, it had seemed like one. Gerry had been so sweet, he'd encouraged her; he understood. How could a poverty stricken entrepreneur compete with a Knight of the Realm? Lady Sheldon-Harris had a much better ring to it than Issie Bridges — one time strip artist and mind-reader. Ousting Theo's wife had been even easier than seducing Theo. Isobel shuddered, she wasn't very proud of that now. It had never troubled her before, but now it did. Since she'd seen the light, a lot of things troubled her. Perhaps she should make peace with Anne? She'd made peace with Gerry, although she'd never told Theo; she had a feeling that he would disapprove. And since seeing Marjorie at the weekend she determined to confide in Theo even less than she did already.

Isobel pursed her lips as she remembered her first few years at Garrick-in-the-Willows; she'd been shunned of course. None of the county set had wanted anything to do with her. Those that had so happily employed her to entertain them, now talked about her in hushed voices. She was good enough to perform for them, but not good enough to sit at their table. They'd even got her act wrong. According to local gossip, she hadn't been a mind reader,

101

not even a striptease artist, a porn star; that's what they'd said. Well she didn't need the county set then and she didn't need them now. She had the house, she had the title, and she had the money. Although she'd always had to wheedle every little penny out of Theo, they'd lived well. Theo had had no regrets, she was sure of that. He'd missed the boy of course, but he hadn't missed Anne. She'd given him a good time; she'd shown him how to get the best fun out of spending money. They'd lived life to the full, at least she had. Theo had always been reluctant to leave his precious farm. Now she knew about Theo's past incarnation even his desire to stay home in Norfolk slotted into place, oh yes — everything was now explained. Then the Lloyds insurance market had crashed and Isobel's foreign holidays and visits to health farms had ended overnight, leaving her sour and resentful. Theo was impossible, he never got anything right. He was dashing and handsome — he had the looks of a film star — but he just couldn't get anything right, and the quarrels had begun in earnest.

Then, after a particularly nasty quarrel with Theo, most likely about money — Isobel had forgotten — she saw the light, and everything had fallen into place. And she'd discovered that fate had blessed her with psychic powers. She smiled; she'd been as surprised as anyone to find that she really could communicate with the world beyond. Gerry had been amazed. He hadn't believed her at first. But she'd soon demonstrated her talent, and he'd been terribly impressed. He, like Mrs Hapgood and her spirit guide, thought she should share it with others, but she wasn't ready for that yet. Her main task at the moment was getting Theo to understand what fate had in store for him, and Theo was proving very difficult to convince.

Isobel closed her eyes and wondered what her life might have been like if she'd stayed with Gerry. Gerry understood her, they were soul mates, they always would be, and she would spend all her incarnations with him at her side. He was the only person she could really trust. She should have stayed with him, but how was she to know that Gerry would eventually make his mark in the world of entertainment? He was now a rich man, the owner of a string of strip joints, not only in England but all over the world. The only thing he lacked was a title. Strange how things had worked out, he was now far more wealthy than Theo. The crash in the Lloyds insurance market had used up all of Theo's riches, or so he maintained. The land he once owned and still farmed now belonged to a large insurance company and he was merely a tenant. He still owned the house and the park, but that was all. The estate had been handed over at about the same time as Isobel had had her vision. Theo had kept the title of course, so although he had suffered a loss of wealth, he hadn't lost his status. It wasn't generally known that he'd had to sell out in order to survive, so life went on as it always had.

Isobel bit into her bottom lip. She had been the

instigator, the other woman in Theo's marriage breakdown, and after the vision, that, and deserting her first, and apparently only true husband and child, were the sins that weighed most heavily on her conscience.

From an ornate carved box she removed a little book and read a list of her own personal ten commandments.

'Be non violent,' she said, her voice loud and firm. She knew that she had the power to evoke spirit, and even by threatening another with violence could have a devastating effect on that person. That's why she'd been careful not to wish Ailsa Jarvis dead. She didn't want more crimes on her conscience.

'Be honest. I must tell the truth, even though the truth may hurt those that hear it.' She nodded her head, glad that she hadn't spared Theo when telling him the truth about Ailsa. He needed to know the truth, and she would be failing in her duty if she hadn't told him.

'Don't take anything that doesn't belong to me.' Isobel gulped. Once again she was back to her own sin. She had taken Theodore away from Anne and his child. Theodore hadn't been free when she met him. Isobel had stolen him.

'Avoid Sex. Sex enslaves people, and absorbs all their psychic energy.' She had her eyes tight shut, and the vision of herself and Theo in their early days flooded into her mind. She shook her head. 'No, no, no, get away from me.' She took a deep breath and tried to concentrate her mind on the cross, trying to think of a white light surrounding it, radiating compassion and love and wisdom. But all she saw was herself and Theo in a passionate embrace, their hot sweaty bodies slipping over each other, their breath and desires urgent. She covered her ears with her hands, snapped her eyes open and studied the next commandment.

'Always be clean and fresh.' That meant her house, her mind and body, and even the food she ate. She had excelled at this commandment. She didn't watch television, nor did she read popular fiction, she saved her thoughts for the things that really mattered. She didn't eat meat or drink alcohol, nor did she indulge in any stimulants, no tea or coffee passed her lips. She didn't even eat chocolate.

'Always be aware of what is happening around you.' She smiled. That was a very easy one for her; she complimented herself that she never missed a thing.

'Use your talents.' She did that all right, she had a talent for organizing, a talent for knowing what was right and what was wrong and she used her gift well. And soon she'd do what Gerry and Charlotte asked of her, and use her psychic talents to help others.

'Don't worry about the future.' Isobel sighed. That had been another easy commandment, until last Friday when she'd had a personal session with Marjorie Hapgood and Marjorie had contacted a channeller. It had been

105

extremely frightening for her; in fact the guide had been so powerful and so strong that it had completely overwhelmed her. The guide had been sympathetic but nevertheless insistent. And now she knew the truth about Theo. She already knew that he drew her energy away from her, leaving her weak and helpless. That's why she tried not to have too much physical contact with him. She tried not to share food with him, she didn't use the same hand-towel as he, and she even kept her own cooking utensils separate. If Theo had noticed, he'd never commented. But now she knew why he had such a negative effect on her, now her guide had shown her the light and she wasn't quite sure what she should do about it.

To the outside world Theo looked like a respectable country gentleman, but people were blind. If only they knew his real soul, his real purpose; if only they knew that he had a master plan. Theo with his sweet words, always appearing friendly and helpful, had evil in his heart. His purpose was to create a situation where people became beholden to him. Only she could see it, only she was aware of his emotional blackmail. She must be strong and stand up to him. But in view of what she now knew it was going to become more and more difficult. Oh she did so wish she could consult Marjorie. She needed to know whether she should confront him and let him know that she knew his real purpose in life. At least she now knew she had to be extra vigilant, she must make sure that he never got hold of a lock of her hair and she must be sure never to turn her back on him. Marjorie had told her that she could cut herself off from his influence by folding her arms and crossing her legs when she spoke to him; and she must always, always, wash herself in cold water after leaving him. But would that be enough? Would she be able to prevent him killing her in this life, as he had in her past incarnation?

She shifted her position, she was getting cramp in her legs, — a sure sign that Theo's bad psyche was affecting her. She must act quickly to be rid of it. She stood and took off her shoes, then, dipping her hand in water, she went to each of her four walls and drew two large triangles in the air, one inverted on the other. Then she did the same with the floor, and with the ceiling, finally she drew an imaginary star on both the door and the window; there, she was safe, she was protected by the magic, as long as she remained inside the room, nothing could harm her.

But even so, the thoughts of her past life kept creeping back. She put her hand up to her neck, she closed her eyes, she could feel the rope biting into it. At first she'd thought that she'd helped the farmer kill his wife, and that the pressure on her neck was the hangman's rope. After all she'd been Theo's mistress, hadn't she? But no, Marjorie had explained, that the wife had been strangled and that the rope biting into her was grasped by Theo's hand. But what was scarier still was the fact that Marjorie had said that he'd try it again in this life, he'd find himself a mistress and he would murder her again. Not necessarily in the physical sense of the word, but he would certainly try and murder her spirit. She must be vigilant; she must break the mould and stop history from repeating itself.

Chapter 15

'You see, Steve, he's such a difficult bugger,' Theo said to his host.

'Then why don't you just get rid of him?' Steve replied.

'It sounds simple enough, doesn't it?'

'Well, isn't it?'

'He's been on the farm for thirty years, besides, apart from his lack of social skills, he's a bloody good worker. He knows his job and he knows the farm, and he's only five years to retirement. He'd never get another job.'

'Huh,' Steve said. 'I wouldn't think twice about it. A man has to think of himself, not the serfs that work under him.'

Theo clenched his jaw. It wasn't long ago that Steve was one of the serfs he was now so callously referring to. Steve held no sentiments for the men who worked under him, perhaps that's why he was so successful.

Theo moistened his lips. 'That's all well and good, Steve, but farm workers aren't two-a-penny these days. Quite frankly, the way things are going he won't be easy to replace. Young folk don't want to stay on the farm any more, anyone with any go doesn't want to stay in rural Norfolk — it's the big cities that attract them, and the big money. Farm wages are crap, and we can't pay more. Farm margins are declining rapidly and the work is becoming more and more technical. Gone are the days when any unskilled chap can work the land — and pretty tied cottages and free range eggs don't appeal anymore. Andy, the chap that Trevor has just driven off, is a good worker, but he wouldn't have stayed long at Garrick, he's got his sights set on bigger things. He wants to become his own flock master.'

'Flock master?' Steve said raising his eyebrows.

'Yes, they don't call themselves shepherds anymore.'

Theo's heart gave a sharp jolt as Zoë entered the room. She had dressed carefully, yet simply, tight fitting jeans and a pink checkered shirt with a white sweater draped casually around her shoulders. She'd lost weight, the hard physical work of shepherding suited her; she looked lean and well toned and had a glow of golden health about her.

It had been an eventful week for Zoë. For the first two nights after Steve returned from the hospital she had barred her door against him, and had lain seeped in misery and loathing. On the third night, she'd gone in search of him, but he'd not been in his own bed, nor out in the lambing yard; an ear to Kirsty's door had soon told her all she needed to know. She'd then gone back to her own room and returned to her own private hell, feeling that she might well die of sorrow.

But girls of Zoë's age and constitution rarely die of

a broken heart, and, after a day or two of facing what her mother would describe as reality, she began to make plans to leave Cameron House and return to her parent's estate at Hulver. But as yet that was all she had done, made vague plans. The thought of returning to her old life and the thought of endless empty hours stretching ahead of her, made her shiver, and she did nothing to contact her parents or take any concrete steps toward returning home.

It was now Saturday and the last day of the shooting season. Zoë had not been needed to act as hostess to the shooting party, as Ailsa, looking robust and in rude health, despite her recent ordeal, had returned to Cameron House the previous afternoon.

Theo gave a low whistle under his breath. 'Who's the leggy blond?' He asked.

Steve smiled. 'That's *my* shepherd,' he said. His three words indicating the exact nature of the relationship. He smiled as an idea took root and grew. ' Funnily enough, she's looking for a another job.' He laughed. 'Well, now Ailsa's home, I don't think I'm allowed to keep her.' He winked at Theo. 'In fact with Ailsa home I doubt if I'll have enough energy to keep her. She's pretty hot stuff.'

Theo laughed along with him. The girl was beautiful; he could understand Ailsa not wanting her around. Even before Steve made his next remark the fantasy had begun. The girl established in Garrick cottage, and Theo visiting her. Theo wining and dining her, Theo dancing with her. Theo making love to her. Oh, God, yes, what a dream — what a dream. But if what his host implied was true, how could Steve possibly consider letting her go. If she were his, Theo wouldn't let her out of his sight, let alone out of his bed. He chuckled, this was an amazing household; perhaps Isobel's assessment of the situation wasn't so very far off-key after all.

'She comes from your part of the world,' Steve said. 'Come on, I'll introduce you.'

Theo was happy to be led across the room to Zoë.

'Zoë, this is Sir Theodore Sheldon-Harris. He's a shepherd short, I told him that you're looking for a job.'

'Am I, Steve?' She said and, turning her back to him, she smiled and held out her hand to Theo. 'We've met before,' she said, 'at Hulver. It was years ago. I don't suppose you remember me?'

'I don't think I'd have forgotten someone like you,' Theo said, wishing the words sounded genuine and sincere, but knowing that they sounded false, like an adolescent chat-up line. He swallowed. 'When did we meet?'

'Oh, I don't know, some shoot or other. I remember your wife. She was stunning,— she was wearing the most amazing dress, and all the men, including my father, were drooling over her.'

Theo felt stung, yes he remembered those days. He wasn't happy even then. He'd been jealous and frustrated, but they seemed like good times in retrospect.

Zoë must have noticed Theo's look, because she said, 'I'm sorry, shouldn't I have said that? I meant it as a compliment.'

Theo smiled. 'No, no, it's fine, she'll be flattered that you remembered her. It must have been a long time ago; I was just wondering? You say we met at Hulver, we must have met at the Elliots then?'

'Yes, I'm Zoë Elliot.'

'Good Lord, but you were—'

'A rather chubby shy little thing with braces on my teeth?'

He smiled. 'The change has been remarkable,' he said. 'Tell me, how are Josh and Lavinia? I haven't seen them for a very long time. It must be all of eight years.'

Eight years, it was a landmark in his life, eight years since Isobel's vision, eight years since he'd seen his old friends.

She smiled, and oh, what a smile. He was fascinated by her, his mind drank in the evenness of her small white teeth, the tiny droplet of saliva on her lip as she spoke, the way her eyes sparkled and darted around the room. The fantasy grew and then dissolved before his eyes, he was being ridiculous. Even if he wasn't married, he was years older that she was; he was being stupid.

'My parents are well — very well in fact, thank you.'

'Remember them to me,' he said, and then felt ridiculous for not being able to hide his confusion. 'I mean, remember me to them, of course.'

The girl didn't seem at all put out, she seemed relaxed and perfectly at ease with him. He thought she looked stunning. He'd have liked to have told her that she was wasting her time dealing with sheep,— she ought to be a top London model. But he knew his words would sound crash and pathetic coming from lips twenty or more years older than hers.

'And let me think — yes, you have a sister — don't tell me — pretty name — that's it, Antigone —Tiggy — is that right?'

Zoë seemed pleased by his accurate memory. She nodded. 'She's at Uni' — Edinburgh, she's the brains of the family, she's reading law. Daddy reckons we need a lawyer in the family, says it will save us a fortune when she qualifies.'

He smiled. 'Bravo, I can see his point.' He frowned. 'You've got a brother as well haven't you?'

'Two, the terrible twins! They've just left Edgeford and they're taking a gap year. They start at Bristol next September.'

'Yes, yes, of course, I remember. Full of devilment they were — calmed down now, have they?'

She laughed. 'Oh dear, I hope they didn't give you a bad time? They're all right singly, but the two of them together make quite a formidable duo; and I'm afraid more often than not they *are* together. They even passed their driving tests on the same day.' Then she suddenly said, 'Do you have children?'

That put him firmly back in his place, didn't it?

He sighed. 'No, no, not of my own, I've a step daughter, from my wife's first marriage, but no, we haven't— '

'Is she as beautiful as your wife?'

Theo wasn't sure how to answer that, certainly Isobel had been beautiful, but most of her beauty had come from her personality, she'd been funny and vivacious, and outrageous. And she'd dressed to kill, or if not to kill, certainly to conquer. It would take him a long time to explain whom Isobel had turned into. But that wasn't what Zoë had asked.

'Yes,' he said, 'she's very like my wife — when she was younger.'

The dog Bracken pushed his nose through the door, scanned the room, checked that Zoë was still in residence and stationed himself just outside.

'Well,' said Theo, 'this is nice, very nice.' He wasn't just referring to the scotch he nursed in his hand.

Apart from Zoë and Ailsa, who was sitting at the far end, the room was filled with men. The cock shoot was traditionally a male domain; the wives rarely joined in. There were about twenty guns and these included

115

gamekeepers and a few estate workers as well as single guests. It was a tradition: the party split itself in two, and half were occupied in beating in the morning whilst the other half shot, and in the afternoon they swapped places.

Ailsa had the baby in her arms. She had undone her blouse and, not seeming to care that her employees could clearly gaze on her milk-filled breast, she offered it to the baby. But the baby seemed reluctant to take it.

Steve was sitting on the arm of her chair. He leaned over her and, taking her nipple he squeezed a little of the milk out onto his finger and offered it to the child's lips. The fretful babe sucked hungrily. Steve squeeze a little more out and rubbed it around the nipple, he then guided his daughter onto it; the child grabbed hold and sucked greedily.

'A remarkable household,' Theo mused.

'Ugh,' Zoë said. 'It's gross. You'd think he was with one of the ewes. It's gross to do that in front of all these men. It's disgusting.'

Theo smiled benignly. 'Putting it a little strongly, aren't you?' But then he caught the pain in her face. 'Hurt you badly, has he?'

He saw tears cloud her eyes. 'I'm sorry,' he said, and he meant it. 'It's none of my business,' he added, but wished for all the world it was.

'So it's all settled then, is it?'

Neither of them had noticed Steve approach.

'What?' Theo snapped. Ten minutes ago, when

talking to another male guest he'd described Steve as 'a pretty good show', now he despised him for causing this young girl pain.

'The job. You said you needed a shepherd, — well, you can't get a better one than Zoë here, she's a natural.'

'I'm not,' Zoë protested. 'I've just picked a few things up from Steve, that's all. I really don't know what I'm doing.'

'She's being modest,' Steve said. 'When would you like her to start? I tell you what, you could give her a lift home tomorrow. Yes, that would work out well.'

'What's the matter, Steve?' Theo heard Zoë hiss under her breath, 'Can't wait to be rid of me?'

Steve glanced over at Ailsa, but she was deep in conversation. Theo followed his eyes, then looked back at Zoë; she looked deeply unhappy and extremely uncomfortable. Theo swallowed and instantly made up his mind.

'Yes,' he said firmly. 'That would be great, the shepherd's cottage isn't up to much, but I can get one of the men to give it a coat of paint and—'

'But I can't,' Zoë said, 'I've got a cottage over at Hulver. The lodge, you know, the one near the main gates.'

'Good, so you'll have some furniture. I'm afraid there's not much of anything in Garrick cottage.'

'Yes, I've got furniture, at least, it's Mummy's and Daddy's but, you don't understand, I can't, I don't *really* know what I'm doing — besides, I have a child.'

Theo swung round and gave Steve an accusing look. Then he went back to Zoë. 'Child's no problem, there's a good crèche in the village, or you can take her or him to work with you.'

'She,' Zoë said. Her voice was little more than a whisper.

Steve had a look of triumph in his eyes, and Zoë looked as if she might cry.

'Is that your dog?' Theo said to Zoë, he was hoping he might get her away from an obviously fraught conversation and cheer her up.

'Yes,' said Steve, 'damned good worker he is, as well.' He patted Theo on the shoulder; an action that made Theo shy away. 'You'll get two for the price of one.'

A flush spread over Zoë's face. 'You're giving me Bracken?' She looked pleased and amazed.

Steve shrugged. 'Well, I'll not do anything with him when you go, will I? He's your dog all right, he never did do for me.'

Zoë ran her fingers through her hair. She glanced at Ailsa and the baby, then back at Steve. She drew in a sharp breath and then, with a look of defiance in Steve's direction she said, 'Yes, please, Sir Theodore. I'd like the job, and I'll do my best.'

For about five seconds Theo felt blissfully happy, but then he wondered how he was going to explain things to

118

Isobel. He took a long drink of his scotch. God it tasted good. Maybe it was high time he asserted himself with Isobel. After all, the arrangement was purely business. But in that case, why did he feel as if he were engaging a mistress not a shepherd; a mistress who was to live not six hundred yards from his own home and the home of his crazy wife?

'That's settled then,' he said. 'I'll drink to that, and by the way Zoë, you must call me Theo.'

Chapter 16

It took over nine hours to drive from Cameron House to Garrick-in-the-Willows. Frequent stops had to be made in order to cater for Elizabeth's and Bracken's needs.

Theo rubbed his eyes and yawned. He was reluctant to ask Zoë if she wanted to stay at a Travel Lodge or somewhere overnight. He felt as if it would sound as if his intentions were not quite honorable, which, of course, half the time they weren't; besides, Isobel was expecting him, and were he to stop, no matter how proper the arrangement, it was bound to lead to difficulties. He did suggest that he take Zoë straight to Hulver, it was little more than twenty miles out of his way. But he was relieved when she said she'd rather go straight to Garrick Cottage; he was afraid that Josh and Lavinia would persuade Zoë not to take the job. They'd probably heard how crazy Isobel had become and would advise Zoë to have nothing to do with Garrick or its occupants; and it was suddenly very important to him that this pretty, lively girl came into his life, be it only as an employee. Then he worried that the cottage might disappoint her. Zoë Elliot had been brought up at Hulver Castle, one of the grandest houses in Norfolk; much bigger and more palatial than Garrick Hall. Garrick Cottage was a mean little affair; he'd have to convince her that it could be made homely.

The long journey gave them ample time to talk, and after sometime, Theo decided to take the bull by the horns and ask her about her and Steve's relationship.

'He was my first lover,' she said. 'I never got over him.'

'And do you suppose you ever will?'

'I don't know,' she said honestly.

'Is he Elizabeth's father?'

Zoë glanced behind and smiled on the sleeping baby, Bracken wagged his tail.

'No, but most times I wish he were.'

Theo felt a pang of unreasonable jealousy

'How old are you, Zoë?'

'Nearly twenty-four. Why?'

Theo gulped. He was being ridiculous, he was twenty-two years older than she; he was dreaming up a fairy tale. Far better to take her to Hulver and forget all this nonsense. She obviously knew nothing about sheep, she had said as much; and Steve's compliments were tools he'd used to get rid of her. Theo was letting Steve make a fool of him.

'I was just thinking that you'll get over him, that's all.'

'How old are you?'

'Forty . . . ' he toyed with lying. He looked young for his age, or so he thought; he decided on the truth. 'Forty-five.'

'And have you fallen out of love?' She said. ' I

mean, you fall in love, and it's for life, right? You don't actually get over falling in love, do you? All these glib statements about giving things time and all that. You're forty-five, have you got over your wife?'

'My wife? Do you mean Anne? My first wife?'

Zoë covered her mouth. 'Oops, I didn't know you'd been married before. I'm sorry.' Then she added softly, 'Did she die?'

'No, I changed models, I traded in a rather unsophisticated saloon and in exchange I thought I'd got myself a snappy little sports model, only . . .'

Zoë giggled.'Only?'

'Only, it turned out that the milometer had been fixed — it'd gone round the clock at least twice. The chassis was okay and the bodywork was fine, so long as you kept up the maintenance. Damned expensive to run, but looked good. I was very fond of it, in fact I loved it, I never wanted to be parted from it.' He nodded, 'It was much admired, lots of men used to want to test drive it, and then . . .'

Zoë had her hands over her mouth; she was giggling

'And then?'

'Then like a lot of these old models, it became unreliable and unpredictable and it kept on letting me down.' He took his eyes off the road briefly and looked at her. 'So have I got over her? Oh yes,' he said. 'Years ago. Or rather . . . she got over me.'

Zoë had stopped laughing and pulled a face. 'Oh,' she said. She coughed. 'Did anyone ever tell you that you looked like . . . '

He smiled, lots of people had remarked on the likeness, but he was far too modest to own up to it. 'Who?'

'Oh, what's his name? You know, the film star, Mummy's mad about him.'

'Leonardo DiCaprio?' He smiled.

She laughed heartily. 'No, no. Oh what *is* his name?'

'Sean Connery.'

She laughed more. 'No, no, — you're not *that* ancient. Come on, people must have told you — oh what *is* his name?' She smiled then, 'I know, I know — Ralph Fiennes.'

Theo fained puzzlement. 'Do I know him?'

'You must do. He was in *Schindler's List*, and that other one — *The End of the Affair*, or something like that, didn't you see it?'

Everyone said it; in fact once or twice, he'd had the embarrassment of actually being mistaken for the famous actor. Once he'd even been asked for his autograph.

'I was rather hoping you'd say Joseph Fiennnes, he's the good looking one, isn't he? I believe he's the one that makes the girl's hearts flutter.'

'There, you knew all along who I meant. I bet everyone tells you you're like him.'

123

He smiled, he felt pleased that she'd noticed.

'Actually,' she said. 'I prefer Ralph to his brother. He's sort of steadier, he reminds me a bit of my father.'

'That's put me firmly in my place.'

She giggled; she sounded as if she were having fun. 'I'm sorry, I didn't mean it like that.'

He put his hand out, and almost but not quite touched her arm. 'I know what you meant, I was only teasing.' He was acting like a fool, what the hell was he doing? Bringing Josh Elliot's daughter to his cottage in the middle of the night?

'Are you sure that you wouldn't like to go to Hulver?' He asked.

'Gracious no. Mummy will have a fit if I turn up in the middle of the night with a strange man and a dog. She's got the keys to the lodge, so I can't just creep in. No, it's far better if I come to Garrick. Besides, if I go home I might not have the courage to come back. It's a big step for me.'

They were passing through the village of Garrick-in-the-Willows; it was almost too late. He didn't want to turn back, but part of him knew that he should.

He drew through the ornate gates, drove two or three hundred yards down the drive, and pulled into the turnaround in front of the single storied cottage.

'It's not much of a place,' he warned her. He should have put the men in as soon as Andy left. A coat of magnolia emulsion would have made all the difference

He retrieved the key from under a brick by the door.

'I'll get one of the men to paint the place through,' he said apologetically as he guided her around the cottage. 'You'll be surprised what a difference it'll make.'

He looked at the girl; she had her head on one side as she looked into the sitting room.

'Do you want me to run you to Hulver?' He asked.

Her face burst into a smile. 'Oh, Theo, it's not that bad. I was thinking I could paint it myself. Can I use bright colours? I'll get Mummy and Daddy to send my bits and pieces over, and the place will soon be lovely, you'll see.'

Theo studied the little cottage; he couldn't quite imagine the mean little house as ever looking lovely. The doubt showed on his face.

She pushed his arm. 'Don't worry, Theo, I can do it. Give me a week and you won't recognize the place.' She stretched out her arms, and flicked her hair over her shoulders. 'I'm going to be happy here, Theo, I know I am.'

Their eyes met, hers' full of innocence, his . . . he pulled away, embarrassed by his thoughts. Steve had already hurt her, she was vulnerable; he wasn't tared with the same brush as Steve Jarvis, was he?

He turned away from her. He took a card form his pocket. 'This is the number of my account at Temples. Buy any paint and stuff that you need,' he jotted the number down. 'I'll 'phone them in the morning and authorize it.

They have one of those paint mixing machines. You'll have a lot of fun with colour.'

She took the card and smiled. 'I'll have to wait until Mummy or Daddy come over; I don't have any transport to get to Temples.'

Theo swallowed. 'I forgot to mention, there's a Land Rover comes with the job.' It was a lie. Trevor Skinner, his difficult foreman, had use of all the farm vehicles, and he could easily manage without the old Land Rover. 'It's not much of a thing, but it'll get you from A to B. It'll certainly get you to Temples and back. I'll drop it in to you in the morning.'

'When do you want me to start with the sheep?'

Theo gulped, that was another thing altogether. He'd have to explain his decision to take on an unqualified woman, well, girl really, to both Isobel and the loathsome Skinner. Neither of them would accept the news with any great joy.

'Have this week off,' he said. 'Get your daughter settled in the crèche, organize the cottage, then start next Monday morning.' That should give him time enough to pave the way.

'Fine, only I'd like to see the sheep set-up before then, if I can?'

He smiled. 'Yes, yes of course you would — I'll collect you tomorrow, what? About five?'

Zoë's eyes widened 'AM?' she asked weakly.

126

'No, no, in the afternoon.' He'd calculated that Trevor would have left for home by then.

'But, it'll be dark. I want to see the flock.'

'Of course it will, how silly of me. Better make it lunch time, twelve-fifteen?' Trevor would be at lunch.

She smiled. 'OK.'

'Are you sure you're going to be all right here tonight? There's not even a sofa. God — hope there's a bed.'

They explored the bedrooms, in the third, and smallest, a single mattress was propped up against the wall. On it was a note in Andy's writing saying that Cathy's dad would come by and pick it up on Monday.

Theo was seized with a bizarre panic. 'Look, you can't stay here. I don't know what I was thinking of. I'll take you to a hotel for the night — or I'll run you over to Hulver. There's no bed and no bed linen, there aren't even any curtains up at the windows.' He scratched his head. 'I somehow thought that this place was part furnished.'

'It's got carpets,' Zoë said, 'and the curtains don't matter, the light will wake me in the morning.'

'I can't possibly—'

'Please, Theo, I want to stay here.' She put her hand on the radiator. 'The heating's working, and Daddy will get my stuff over tomorrow. He'll bring my bed and all the essentials — I don't want too much stuff here until I've got it painted. Elizabeth can sleep in her car seat, it won't hurt her just for tonight. Look see, she's very comfortable.'

She pulled the mattress down on the floor. I'll be fine on this — I'm so tired I could sleep anywhere.

Theo shrugged his shoulders; there was no arguing with her. Besides he wanted her there, he was afraid that if she went away, she might not come back. He helped her unpack her things from the car, and then he took off his overcoat and threw it over the bed.

'Unconventional blanket,' he said. 'Tomorrow we'll go shopping.'

'Tomorrow Mummy will bring my own things. And she's got loads of bits and pieces, bed linen and suchlike left over from the B and B's. I think she'll be glad to get rid of them, they bring back unpleasant memories.'

Before he left, he placed a hand on either of her shoulders and kissed her chastely on each cheek.

I shouldn't have done that, he thought as he drove away. Now she must know how much I want her. Then he reasoned with himself. He was being ridiculous; she saw him as an old and trusted friend of her father's. What harm was there in kissing an old friend's daughter? He was only wishing her goodnight.

Chapter 17

'Come on, open it,' Lavinia said.

'Oh, Ma, you're such a child when it comes to parcels.'

A fortnight had passed since Zoë had returned from Scotland, and a package had arrived that morning at Hulver Castle; it had a Scottish postmark and the return address was Cameron House.

'It's Ailsa's writing,' Lavinia said. 'I wonder if it's something for Betsy?'

The Elliots had turned up unexpectedly at Garrick Cottage. Zoë offered them coffee and then, realizing that she was out of milk, Josh had gone off to the village to get further supplies.

Zoë sighed; she'd rather have been on her own when dealing with any correspondence that came from Cameron House.

She sliced into the brown parcel tape that bound the box, pushed up the cardboard flaps and studied the contents. There were two books on sheep husbandry and a third on general farming. Zoë retrieved them from the box and a single page of script fluttered to the floor. Both Zoë and her mother made a grab for it but Zoë got there first. It was little more than a note, and had obviously been written in great haste.

Dear Zoë, it read, *Steve thought you might like these. Good luck with the job, Theo Sheldon-Harris is a fine man, he's a good boss and you should get on well together — a friendly word of advice though. Don't go hopping into bed with him. Isobel isn't as tolerant or as understanding as I am! I hope Bracken is working out all right, he always was a woman's dog. Steve used to say that he reminded him of you!   Yours Ailsa.*

Zoë folded the paper in four and slipped it in her back pocket.

Lavinia looked enquiringly. 'What's she say?'

'Nothing. She just sent some books that she thought might be useful.' Zoë smiled. 'Along with some useless advice.'

'Oh?'

Zoë's smile turned into a frown. 'What sort of woman can just ignore the fact that . . . '

'That?'

'Well, that her husband isn't faithful,' she said softly.

Lavinia raised her eyebrows. 'In Ailsa's case, a very wise woman,' she said. 'I think that—'

'Zoë? Zoë? Look what I've found.' Theo's shout cut into Lavinia's words. He stumbled into Garrick Cottage, a rug tucked under one arm, a large framed picture tucked under the other and a very large brass cauldron balanced precariously between the two. 'Zoë? Oh, Lady Hulver, I didn't know that you, that is to say, I didn't see your car.'

Lavinia looked amused. 'No, well, Josh has just popped to the village for milk. And Theo, why on earth are you calling me Lady Hulver?'

'Dunno, Lavinia,' he said. 'You took me rather by surprise, I didn't expect to see you here.' He went over to her and gave her a peck on either cheek. 'How are you? What do you think of your daughter? She's made this place into a little palace hasn't she?'

Lavinia smiled and nodded her agreement. 'She certainly has, I've never seen a place so transformed in what? How long have you been here darling?'

'Fifteen days tomorrow,' Theo said. 'Isn't she a wonder?'

Lavinia's face held a quizzical look. 'Oh, yes, quite a wonder.' She sounded bemused. Then she said. 'Theo, why don't you put those things down?'

'Ah, yes, I'll put them down here in the corner. I'll pop by later and sort them out with you,' he gave Zoë a nervous half smile.

Lavinia would later describe him as looking like a naughty schoolboy caught in some clandestine act.

He pushed his treasures into the corner of the hall and brushed off his hands. 'Well, I won't interrupt, we can go through them later.' He hesitated for a moment and turned to go, he stood still as if in deep thought and then turned back again. 'I — er, I don't suppose . . . well I did wonder . . . '

'Yes?' Both Lavinia and Zoë said at the same time.

'I wondered if Zoë might be free for lunch? But I suppose, what with your parents here, it's not a good day? Is it?'

'Oh, we're not stopping, Theo,' Lavinia said. 'We only popped over to bring Zoë a parcel that arrived at the Castle.' She glanced at Zoë, 'I think it's a splendid idea. I'll take Betsy over to Hulver with me; I'll bring her back before bedtime. It'll be good practice for next week.'

'Ma's going to look after her during the afternoons, so I can get on with vaccinating the flock,' Zoë explained to Theo.

'Off you go, Zoë, get yourself changed, you can't sit at Isobel's table looking like something the cat dragged in.' Lavinia said.

Theo coughed, opened his mouth as if about offer some sort of explanation, changed his mind and looked down at the floor.

With no objection, Zoë shrugged her shoulders, and went off toward her bedroom to change.

Theo muttered something about the weather, asked after Josh and the rest of the Elliot family, and then went into a long diatribe on the merits of running a second hand Volvo.

When Zoë returned she was wearing a long, tight fitting, black skirt, a red scoop-necked tunic and knee length black boots. She had a black scarf knotted at her neck. Her hair was neatly brushed, and her lips were enhanced with a very pale pink lipstick.

'Darling, you look lovely,' Lavinia said. 'Now off you go and have a nice time.'

Theo led the way, followed by Zoë, with Lavinia and Betsy at the rear. Theo got into his car and Lavinia, seizing her moment, placed her hand on Zoë's shoulder and whispered, 'I know this sounds ridiculous, but there's nothing I should know, is there?'

'What?'

Lavinia nodded toward the car.

'You're right, Ma, that *is* ridiculous.'

'It's just that it's—'

'What? What is it?'

Lavinia shrugged. 'Nothing, darling, have fun.'

Zoë kissed Betsy and her mother and got into the passenger seat. Theo carefully backed the car away from the cottage and turned in the direction of the main gates, not toward the Hall.

'Valentine's Day,' Lavinia whispered thoughtfully. 'Today is St Valentine's Day.'

Theo took the road that led to Kings Lynn, but turned off it just below the Sandringham turn, from there he drove due west to Collop-in-the-Marsh and stopped at a little restaurant that Zoë had never heard of. But then Zoë had not exactly led an exciting social life in the past few years.

The restaurant was decorated in minimalist style, with lots of black and chrome and stark white table-linen.

Theo was given a warm and sincere greeting. A bottle of champagne was already on ice standing next to his table.

'Wow, champagne. What would you have done if I hadn't come?'

He pushed his bottom lip over his top lip. 'That's a difficult one to answer — I could say that I'd have asked someone else, but I don't know anyone else I'd have wanted to bring,' he chucked. 'Nor anyone else mad enough tp come with me. So if you want the truth, I'd have cancelled my table.' He laughed again. 'You bring out the honesty in me.' Then looking a little guilty, he said, 'I'm afraid your mother rather misunderstood, she seemed to think we were lunching with Isobel.'

Zoë joined in his laughter. 'She asked me if there was anything between us, I told her that was ridiculous.'

She saw him smart, as if her words were a physical slap across the cheek.

'Ridiculous? Yes, yes of course it is,' he said and his laughter evaporated, as he made a concentrated study of the menu.

The meal was delicious, exotic, and extremely expensive; the carefully chosen wines a perfect accompaniment and a willing accomplice in the loosening of Zoë's tongue. She was light-headed and giggly.

She took a spoon of coeur-a-la-crème, and smiled as the waiter came over and handed Theo a single red rose, which he presented to her. 'Oh, Theo, that's lovely, that's really lovely.' She smelled it, but it had no perfume.

'So, will you be my Valentine?' He asked, he was laughing, 'Just a joke,' he added, but the laughter was on his lips not in his eyes.

'It's Valentine's Day?' She seemed surprised. 'Yes. Yes of course it is, how stupid of me.' She giggled. 'I can't believe I forgot and I can't believe I'm spending it with you, I mean—' Too late, the words were said, how she wished she could bite them back.

'I'd have thought you'd have had loads of Valentines,' Theo said, clearly embarrassed.

She shook her head. 'No, so I guess you have a clear run.' She giggled again, she was trying to retrieve the situation. Theo was such a kind man, she couldn't bear to hurt him. 'I can't believe I forgot. When I was at school it was just about the most important day in the year. I can't tell you how important Valentine's Day is in a girl's school. You have no idea, just no idea.' She smelled the rose again, and closed her eyes.

'Does it have a perfume?'

'No, but I'm imagining it does.' She opened her eyes and looked boldly into his. 'No wonder my mother threw a wobbly. She asked me if there was something she should know! Ridiculous, isn't it?' There, she'd done it again, why couldn't she keep her mouth shut, besides she'd altready told him what her mother had said.

'Ridiculous,' he agreed again.

'Oh, and she's not the only one. That foreman, — Skinner, is his name? He called me your tart the other day.'

'He did what?'

'Oh, Theo, don't look like that. It's funny, it's so way out'

'All the same.'

'Don't worry, I can handle him. He had a hair-slide in his hair yesterday. And when he bent over to pick a bale up, I swear I saw a pair of women's panties sticking out of the top of his trousers. I swear I did.' There, she'd succesfully steered the conversation away from Valentines.

'I did hear that Skinner has a bit of a problem with gender identity. All the same, he can't talk to you like that.'

'Ma and Skinner aren't the only ones. I had a letter from Ailsa, and she warned me not to hop into bed with you, so you see everyone thinks I'm either already sleeping with you or about to.' The wine was making her talk very loud and very fast. How had she managed to steer the conversation back to bed again?

'I wish,' he said. Then he laughed. 'Idiotic thought, isn't it?' There was a kind of pain written on his face, a look that sobered Zoë up a bit.

'I mean,' he continued, 'what would a beautiful

young girl like you see in a dried up, middle aged man, like me?'

'Kindness, and consideration,' she said quietly and sincerely.

'So, I'm in with a chance then, am I?' His laugh was very hearty. 'Providing I'm kind and considerate, of course,' he said the words as if they were a joke.

He had fear written all over his face. The same look that Zoë's face had held a million times when looking into Steve Jarvis's eyes.

She leaned over the table and took his hand. He'd done so much for her; she had the power to do something for him. He'd rescued her, she was happier than she'd been for years. She needn't actually sleep with him, but it wouldn't do any harm to let him think that she found him attractive, indeed it would be cruel not to. It was, as her mother would say, a kind gesture in a cruel world.

'Of course you're in with a chance. You're a very, very, attractive man.'

He cleared his throat. 'Right,' he said, 'Faint heart never won fair lady, did it?'

She looked confused.

'So, will you sleep with me, Zoë?'

She was becoming more and more sober by the minute. What had she done? What *had* she said? She had to think quickly, she had to get out of it without hurting his feelings, how could she have let things get this far?

'What?' She was truly shocked. How had they got to this so soon, surely he knew she was just idlely flirting with him? What she said next came out all wrong, she was trying to show him how impossible the situation was.

'Not at the cottage, not there, it wouldn't be right would it? Not with your wife being so—'

'No, no, of course not.'

She saw his Adams apple move as he swallowed.

'The weekend? Would your mother look after Betsy? You could say we're going to look at some sheep.'

'Weekends aren't very good,' she said quietly. Oh God, what was she doing? What was she suggesting? that mid-week would be fine but week-ends were out?

'Monday? So much the better. You do mean it? You're not stringing me along are you?'

Oh, God, what was she doing? She'd better make it clear right now before things got out of hand. But it was as if her tongue and her brain were no longer connected. She thought one thing and said another.

'Of course I mean it. Monday it is. I'll ask Mummy to have Betsy, I'll ask her tonight when she brings her home. And I'll tell her I'm going to visit Tiggy, Mummy might get the wrong idea if I say I'm off buying sheep with you.' Oh God, what was she saying?

Theo filled her glass again. 'I'll drink to that?' he said.

Chapter 18

Lavinia couldn't resist washing the few breakfast dishes and giving Zoë's sitting room a quick tidy before leaving Garrick Cottage. Her daughter had certainly improved her housekeeping skills since she'd got back from Scotland. Whatever had happened between the Jarvises and Zoë had to have been a good thing.

Josh came behind her as she stood at the sink and shook his head. 'Vinnie,' he said, 'you're such a mother!'

She laughed. 'Is that such a bad thing?'

He kissed her. 'No, I like it. But I wonder if Zoë might think you're interfering.'

'Interfering?'

'You know, sort of criticizing her, in an indirect way, for not washing up after breakfast?'

'Don't be silly, she'll be delighted. That's if she notices, which I doubt.'

Lavinia dried her hands.

'Come on Betsy-Boo, let's strap you in your car seat.'

Josh took the seat from Lavinia's hand and carried it out to the car, where he spent ages trying to work out how it fixed onto the seatbelts.

'Here, let me have a go, Josh. You're all fingers and thumbs.'

'No, no, I can do it. I do wish they didn't make the dratted things so complicated.' He continued to tug and pull at the seatbelt.

'It just threads through there, look. No, through that eye at the top.' She was getting impatient.

Josh stood back. 'I'll let you do it, I haven't got my engineering degree yet.'

'It's not *that* difficult,' she said, deftly threading the belt through the eye and fixing it home in three seconds flat.

'Of course not, not if you're a woman. I applied logic, and there's no logic whatsoever in child safety-seats. And if you think I'm going to attempt to fold the buggy, you've got another think coming. I've had enough humiliation for one day.'

She stretched up and kissed his cheek. 'Sounds like a cop-out to me,' she laughed.

A car drove up the drive so fast that Lavinia grabbed Elizabeth closer to her, half-afraid that it would plough into them all. She raised her eyebrows to Josh, as Isobel Sheldon-Harris parked at right angles to their car, blocking their exit. She alighted from the vehicle, slammed the door, and strode over to the cottage. Her face was a mask of anger, but the mask lifted as soon as she saw Josh and Lavinia.

'Isobel? I haven't seen you for ages,' Josh said. 'We're just taking Betsy home with us for the day. Zoë has just—'

'Gone out with a girlfriend for lunch,' Lavinia interrupted. 'I do hope that's all right with you and Theo, she's not supposed to work today, is she?'

'But you said—' Josh began.

'That's right, darling, I said I didn't think Theo or Isabel would mind.' She gave Josh a warning look.

'So, is Zoë — your Zoë?'

'What?' Josh said.

'Skinner, our foreman, just cornered me and told me that Theo had taken on some untrained girl and—'

'He has — our Zoë,' Josh said. There was an element of pride in his voice.

'Actually, she's very well trained,' Lavinia said defiantly. She moistened her lips. 'One of our old employees has given her a very good grounding. You may remember him, Steve, Steve Jarvis, married Ailsa McTodd?'

'Oh, yes, I've heard all about the McTodd - Jarvis alliance,' Isobel said shortly. 'But I didn't realize that Theo had taken a girl on, he hasn't mentioned it to me. Is she pretty?'

Lavinia looked uncomfortable, but Josh was already launching in.

'Pretty? She's beautiful, she's clever too, she's—'

'Josh, I think you're sounding rather too much like an overbearingly proud father,' Lavinia said as Josh continued to wax lyrical about his elder daughter's charms. 'Isobel, this is our granddaughter Elizabeth, but everyone calls her Betsy.'

Isobel's face relaxed, she smiled at the child. 'So Zoë's married? That's all right then. Skinner was none too complimentary about her.'

Lavinia gave Josh another warning look, but he was already launching into an explanation.

'No, no, she's not, actually, and it's a darned good thing too. She met this ne'er-do-well and decided to marry him, only he turned out to be not quite the ticket, if you know what I mean? They never actually tied the knot, thank goodness. He was rotten through and through. She had a lucky escape.'

Isobel pursed her lips. 'So the child is illegitimate?'

'Come now, Isobel,' Lavinia said, 'that's hardly unusual. It doesn't matter in this day and age. No one gets married these days.'

Isobel glared at Lavinia. 'That doesn't make it right,' she said. She drew in a deep breath. 'I'd better be getting along, I've an appointment in fifteen minutes.' She turned abruptly and, without glancing in Lavinia's or Josh's direction, she got into her car and drove away.

'What was that all about?' Josh said.

'Oh, Josh, you shouldn't have said that Zoë was pretty — women of her age can sometimes feel insecure.'

'She's about the same age as you, isn't she?'

'She's got a good five years on me,' Lavinia retorted, 'and she looks as if she's got ten.'

'I didn't say that she wasn't a disaster area, did I?'

'No, but you know, even *I* might feel a bit threatened if you took on a twenty-four-year-old novice and forgot to mention it to me. Especially if she was blond, vivacious, and had a figure like a cat-walk model.'

Josh's brow creased. 'Vinnie, I'm confused. I thought you said that Theo was taking Zoë to lunch?'

'He's taken her out.'

'Oh. But I thought you said he was taking her to the Hall.'

'That was my assumption — I must have been mistaken.'

'But why didn't you tell Isobel that Theo had taken her out? She didn't seem to know. Why'd you tell her that Zoë was out with a girlfriend?' He paused. 'You don't think?'

Lavinia gave a funny high-pitched laugh. 'Goodness no. In fact I mentioned it to Zoë and she thought it was highly amusing. I expect Theo just forgot to mention it to Isobel. You heard her say that she'd got an appointment. I expect Theo was at a loose end. Theo's years older than Zoë, I can't believe that there's . . . ' her voice died away as she caught her husband's eye.

'A sensible chap doesn't shit on his own doorstep,'

Josh said. 'Besides, Theo's a good man. I wouldn't, well, you know — not Theo.'

'He's a very good man,' Lavinia agreed. 'Only, only—'

'Only?'

'Only, I hope he realizes how vulnerable Zoë is.'

'His wife's a bit dotty though, isn't she? Did you see what she was wearing? Bare feet and open toed sandals. It's February, for God's sake, and that funny black tunic thing? She looked like a, well, like a . . . '

'Hippy nun?' Lavinia said helpfully. 'Apparently, she's got a bad case of some new religion.'

'I heard it was spiritualism.'

'I heard that, but apparently she quotes the Bible as well.'

Lavinia put Betsy in her car seat and strapped her in. 'Oh, dear,' she said. 'I've just stopped worrying about Zoë and now this.'

'Zoë's got her head screwed on, she's not going to fall for a man of Theo's age. She came here for the job. She's very keen on that, not Theo Sheldon-Harris.'

Lavinia sighed. 'You weren't here, Josh. You didn't see the way he looked at her, he was like an adoring puppy.'

'Vinnie, you're reading things into this that aren't there. Anyway, I'm not concerned with Theo. Zoë's all right, look what she's done to this place. I nearly had a fit when I first saw it, look at it now. She's transformed it — she's made it into a really comfortable home. Perhaps she should do something like that for a career, you know, interior design, she's got a real flare.'

'Fine, except for the fact that she wants to work with animals. I think she thinks they're more reliable than people.'

'Maybe we could get her her own flock, and set her up at Hulver?'

'That wouldn't do. Zoë needs to make her own way in life.'

'Ga-ga,' Elizabeth said.

'Oh, Lord, sorry, Betsy. Here, give me the key, Josh. I'll put it under the brick. Come on — let's make tracks. It's no use worrying about it. Things will sort themselves out. But I will have a word with her when I bring Betsy back.'

Chapter 19

Tiggy Elliot scraped her notes together. It had been an interesting lecture, but had gone on far longer than she had anticipated. She looked at her watch; Bruce would be furious with her. He couldn't understand why she'd wanted to go anyway, Bruce did the minimum of work; there was no way he'd come to an evening lecture no matter how interesting it promised to be; he was quite disparaging about her ambitions. He didn't understand how difficult it was for a woman to make her way in a man's world. She stuffed the papers into her rucksack. Funny, she could have sworn that she knew the visiting lecturer, but that was impossible; he was a barrister from London who specialized in criminal law. She shrugged; maybe he'd been to visit the university before. He was certainly very knowledgeable, and very attractive, she thought wryly, and then she qualified that by adding, for a man of his age.

She flung the rucksack onto her shoulder and, on glancing toward the stage, she saw that the lecturer was making straight for her. She definitely did know him, but she couldn't remember when or where they'd met. He had a smile on his lips; he was almost up to her now, she looked around, maybe he was making a beeline for someone else? No. No, he was definitely making his way toward her. She looked at her watch, damn, she'd promised Bruce that she'd be in the Spotted Cow before ten; she was late already and she had to get a bus halfway across Edinburgh. Why Bruce insisted on drinking in a pub so far away was a mystery to her. It was true that the beer was a few pence cheaper but what they saved on drink, they spent on bus fares. But then Bruce was never very logical.

'It's Tiggy Elliot, isn't it?' he held his hand out in front of him.

'Yes but—'

'Alex Kirby,' he said.

'I know,' she replied pointing to the poster advertising his lecture. 'But I don't remember—'

'I used to B and B at Hulver.'

'Oh. Oh, I thought I recognized you — I just couldn't place you. How are you?'

He nodded. 'I'm good, and, and how is Hulver? Your parents? Well, are they?'

'Yes, yes, very well. They don't do B and B anymore.'

'Yes, yes, I know — unfortunately for me.'

'Yes, right, well.' She looked at her watch. 'I'd better be going. Brilliant lecture, by the way.'

'Thanks, um, how's . . . how's your mother? — Well? — You say.' Tiggy thought he sounded bitter.

'Yes, yes she is. She's very well. She's a granny now and enjoying every minute of it.'

'Yes, yes, I knew that. Zoë's little girl?'

'Yes, she's adorable.'

Tiggy looked at her watch yet again. 'Look I'm sorry Mr Kirby. I promised to meet someone, and I have to get right across the city.'

'Pity. I was hoping I could persuade you to have a drink with me.'

She shrugged. 'Sorry. Another time, perhaps?'

'Yes, another time.'

'Well, goodbye, nice to have met you,' she said.

She had reached the doors of the lecture hall when he came after her. 'Look, why don't I give you a lift, my car's over in the car park.'

Tiggy looked at her watch for the umpteenth time. She hadn't a hope of getting to the pub before closing time unless she accepted his offer. 'It's a bit out of the way.'

'I've nothing better to do.'

She smiled. 'All right, thanks.'

The Spotted Cow was a dark, not very salubrious little pub, but the landlord was very liberal and the students liked the relaxed atmosphere. Tiggy didn't remember asking Alex Kirby to join her, but he did anyway.

They fought their way across the bar to where Bruce, and a party of about ten other students, were gathered. Sacha Wright was sitting on Bruce's knee, and Tiggy could see quite clearly that Bruce had both his hands under Sacha's pink jumper and was kneading her breasts as if they were made of Plasticine. He didn't bother to remove them when Tiggy appeared but started to kiss Sacha's neck and eventually her mouth.

'Hi,' Tiggy said with forced cheerfulness. 'This is Alex Kirby, he's just given a brilliant lecture on the criminal mind.'

'From a barrister's point of view. I'm not a psychologist,' Alex said.

'Good for you,' Bruce said. 'Time for a round of drinks, I think.'

'I'll get them,' Alex said.

'Get me a couple of pints, Alex, will you, it'll save the last minute rush to the bar. Little-goody-two-shoes will give you a hand.'

Tiggy blushed and went with Alex to the bar. 'I'm sorry,' she said. 'He's obviously had too much to drink. He acts in a very immature way sometimes.'

'We were all young and immature once.' He winked at her.

Alex ordered the beer, getting an extra one for Bruce.

'You're not going to pander to him?'

Alex smiled. 'Of course, there's nothing I like more than seeing a big mouth like him falling flat on his face. Sorry, is he your boyfriend?'

'Sort of.'

'Ditch him, you're worth more.' He smiled in a disarming manner. 'Why'd you choose him anyway? A girl like you can just click her fingers and they'd all come running.'

She laughed and strugged her shoulders, then seized with sudden devilment she said, 'Maybe it's sex, maybe he's the best.'

'Not as good as me.'

Tiggy put her hand over her mouth. The pub was very noisy and she was having to shout over the din. 'I was only joking. I was trying to shock you.'

'Oh dear, the first thing you should learn is that a chap in my profession is pretty unshockable. Besides there's many a true word spoken in jest.'

Alex handed the barman a fifty-pound note. He turned it over and held it up to the light, appeared satisfied, and took it over to the till.

They loaded the beer onto a tray and began to make their way back to Bruce and his friends.

'I'm afraid your boyfriend will be too drunk to put in a good performance tonight though.' He grinned mischievously.

'Good, let's hope Sacha dies of disappointment.'

'The criminal mind I can understand, but a woman's mind is beyond me.'

When they got back to the table Bruce and Sacha were missing.

'He's just taken Sacha outside for a breath of fresh air,' Tom said, nudging Carl with his elbow. 'Said to say he'd be back in a minute.'

'Yeah, never takes Bruce above a minute, does it, Tiggy?' Carl said, bursting into fits of giggles.

Tiggy appeared perfectly calm. 'Give him a message will you?' she said. 'Tell him I'm sorry I couldn't wait, Alex is taking me out for a curry.'

'Am I? Good,' said Alex. 'I'm starving.'

'Oh, and can you tell him something else?' She said.

Carl, still laughing, nodded.

'Tell him to fuck off.'

'Well done,' said Alex as he wriggled into his overcoat. 'That was the best legal argument I've heard for years. Clear, precise, no use of unnecessary words, no overt use of legal jargon, no doubt as to what you're trying to say. Yes, Miss Elliot, you should go far.'

'Everyone does it,' she said wistfully. She was very close to him, she could smell his aftershave.

'What? Are you talking about Bruce and what's-her-name?'

'Sacha. Sex — everyone does it. I mean it doesn't mean anything. It's a bit like having a meal, it's variety and change that we go for now, and it doesn't mean anything anymore. It's not like when my parents were young. If you slept with a bloke then, you expected them to marry you.' She laughed. 'I'm even having to cover for my sister Zoë, she's going to spend a night with her boss! I'm having to tell

151

Mummy that she's coming up to visit me so that Mummy will have Betsy for the night. And how about this? She's sleeping with her boss because she feels sorry for him! Can you believe it? He's done a lot for her, and he's got this really frightful wife, a real loony she is, and so Zoë is going to do something nice for him. He's as old as the hills as well.'

'Right, I see — times really have changed.' He laughed. 'So tell me, how many men have you slept with Tiggy? If it's not rude of me to ask.'

'Four,' she said without so much as a blush, she was begining to enjoy herself, the wine was going to her head and it was nice to see the others glancing in her direction, she was the centre of attention 'But really only with Bruce, properly — you know?'

He looked bemused, she wondered if he were laughing at her. He nodded goodnight to the students and escorted her to the door of the Spotted Cow.

'And were they good meals?'

'Meals?'

'Yes, you said—'

'Oh, I see, well one of them couldn't get it up when it came to — you know, — the actual business. That was just plain embarrassing. Then another was quite the reverse he, well, you know, all over my leg. He couldn't even get the thingy, you know — the condom, on in time.'

'And number three?

'Ah, number three was Professor Giles, only please don't tell anyone. God, I really fancied him, and he must be about forty.' Tiggy smiled as if it was a fond memory. 'He did loads of foreplay and really got me going, only he never actually did it, you know, put it in.' Tiggy slapped her hand over her mouth. 'God! Why am I telling you all this?'

'You have to finish now.'

'He just wanted, a — Oh, God, what do you call it. A blow job? Is that it?'

'And did you?'

'Well, I did my best, but he sort of took over with his hand, and then he, well, — you know, and then he just got up, got dressed, and went home! Then the next time I saw him he couldn't even look me in the eye let alone speak to me.'

'So it was back to poor, pathetic, Bruce?'

She laughed. 'You've just about summed him up.'

'Tiggy?' he put his hand out and rested it on the back of her neck. 'Let's forget the curry. Come back to my hotel and we'll get room service.'

'All right,' she said, and turning her head, she sucked his thumb into her mouth.

'I ought not to eat anyway, I'm getting really fat.'

Alex laughed heartily at that. 'You're as slim as . .' He broke off his sentence. But Tiggy didn't seem to notice, she was pulling her stomach in and pressing her hand down as if trying to flatten a bulge that didn't exist.

Chapter 20

Zoë placed herself as far away from the reception desk as possible. Theo had loaded her up with a coat hanger holding his shirt, trousers, blazer and tie. Then he'd cheerily said, 'Hang onto these as well, will you?' And handed her a pair of slip-on shoes which were desperately in need of polishing. It was all too sordid and embarrassing. Tiggy would die of laughter when she told her.

She glanced over at the reception desk. The girl caught her eye and smiled, Zoë gave an awkward half-smile in return. Oh God, what was she doing here? She didn't want to be associated with Theo; he was at least twenty years older than she; not quite as old as her father, but getting on that way. What was the receptionist thinking? They were clearly not married. She comforted herself by thinking that she probably looked like his daughter; until she heard Theo say, 'Double, please, and non-smoking.'

He signed the register and came over to her; he was all smiles. 'Let me take those,' he said. 'Sorry, I'm not the most organized of people, I'm afraid. I left in a bit of a hurry.'

She handed the shoes and the heavily laden coat hanger back to him and picked up her own neat overnight bag. Whatever was she doing here? Whatever had possessed her? She liked Sir Theodore Sheldon-Harris, liked him very much, but not enough to want to spend the night with him. He was married — very unhappily — her own eyes had witnessed that. But even so — *Those whom God hath joined together* — and all that, only He hadn't; it had been Theo's second marriage and conducted in a registry office, not a church. But even so, it didn't make what she was doing any better.

'Penny for them,' Theo said as they walked down the long hotel corridor.

'I was thinking about, those whom God hath joined together — let no man put asunder.'

'What a very intense young lady you are. Highly moral, all of a sudden, aren't we?'

She hadn't worried about Steve being married to Ailsa had she? But that was different, Steve had been her love first, long before he'd been Ailsa's, or so she believed.'

'Here we are, room one hundred and four.' Theo swiped the plastic card in the slot.

The room was beautifully furnished, but very small, and Zoë felt a moment of real panic as if she were in a trap that she couldn't escape from. What *was* she doing here?

Theo put a hand on her shoulder. 'You all right, Zoë?'

She smiled weakly. 'Yes, yes I'm fine.'

Why was she doing this? Getting at Steve? Is that what it was? Damn Steve, she'd only taken the job with

Theo to get at him, but how was that getting at him? Some perverse form of punishment? He'd used her, used her yet again. He'd shared her bed and worked her nearly to death, only to leave her high and dry once Ailsa and the baby came home. It was Steve's fault that she was here, not directly of course, but he'd had a part to play, hadn't he? She felt hurt and defiant.

She glanced over at Theo; he was whistling and hanging up his blazer. She didn't want to make love with him, but that was the deal she'd made, wasn't it? She couldn't pull out of it now, could she? She'd look such a fool and besides she would hurt him and he had been so kind to her.

Theo checked the time. 'It's almost six-thirty, shall we have a bath and a drink before dinner?'

She smiled and nodded her head. Theo was such a nice man, surely she could explain it to him. Tell him that she'd only agreed to come out of a sense of gratitude. She gulped. No, she couldn't do that; it would be too cruel.

'What would you like?' he asked opening the mini bar.

Something that will get me drunk very quickly, she wanted to say. 'Oh, I don't know, what are you having?'

He looking inside the little fridge and brought out several miniatures. 'Bloody Mary, I think.'

'Great,' she said. 'I'd love one, too.'

She scurried into the bathroom and ran the bath,

she was in and out of the water in a moment, half-afraid that Theo would bring her drink into her and find her naked. She wrapped a thick white bath towel around her, and went back into the bedroom.

'Gosh, you were quick.' He handed her the drink and then let his hand rest on her shoulder 'I'll try and be as speedy.' He rubbed the muscles at the back of her neck. 'You're very tense, I brought some oil. I could give you a massage, would you like that?'

She took the drink and smiled but didn't answer him. Once he was out of the room she took a large gulp of the thick red liquid, and then topped the glass up with another miniature of vodka. There was nothing else for it, she would have to get drunk. She pulled the bedclothes back and, keeping the towel wrapped tightly around her, she got into bed.

There was only one way of dealing with it so as not to hurt his feelings. She'd get it over with as soon as possible, then, when they had dinner, she'd persuade him to drink a lot, so that he'd sleep, then tomorrow they'd go back to Garrick and that would be that. She switched on the television and tried to concentrate on the news. She could hear Theo whistling in his bath.

Then, in what seemed like no time at all, he was in the bed with her. He tried to pull the towel away from her, but she hung onto it.

'Sorry,' he said. 'I just wanted to see you.' He was

158

apologetic and seemed embarrassed.

She swallowed and laughed. 'Maybe I'm shy, or,' she bit into her bottom lip, 'maybe I'm a control freak.' Her voice was high pitched and edged with panic, the vodka had had no effect on her at all, her panic hadn't dulled, in fact she was as acutely fearful as she'd ever been.

He ran his fingers against her thigh and up between her legs. She was feeling far from sexy, his fingers caught and dragged her skin.

She gave an involuntary gasp. 'Sorry,' she said, 'that hurt, maybe we could do with some of your massage oil.'

He leaned out of the bed and grabbed the oil from his bedside table.

'Sorry,' he said as he fumbled with the cap. 'It's sealed, I can't seem to get it open.'

Zoë stared at the ceiling; this was terrible, why didn't he just hurry up and get it over with? She took the bottle out of his hand, deftly opened it, poured some in the palm of her hand and rubbed it between her legs. Then she took another palmfull and rubbed it on him. The sooner she got it over with the better. His excitement was obvious and urgent. She muted the television and rolled over onto her side facing away from him, still keeping the towel wrapped tightly around her. It would help if she didn't have to look at him, he could do it from behind, then she could even imagine it was Steve.

And then he was in her, and it wasn't Steve. He was much more than Steve had ever been, and from wanting it never to start, she now wanted it never to end. Round and round, together and forever, arms and legs entwined in the mating dance, the wonderful, life saving, exhilarating mating dance. She was lost, lost in the dance, drowning in the sensation of it. Joining in, leading him, taking him onward in the complicated steps, the pulsating rhythm.

All her inhibitions were forgotten. The towel was abandoned.

'Oh, God, Zoë. I'm lost, I'm done for. I'm finished,' he groaned.

They were both saturated in sweat. Zoë's hair was sticking to her back. She flopped down on his chest and buried her head into his neck; she couldn't quite bring herself to look at him.

He sighed and blew his hair away from his forehead. 'God, you didn't give me time to— You *are* on the pill Zoë?' He murmured.

Pill? Pill? Of course she wasn't on the pill, she never had been, what use did she have for pills? Before she'd gone to Scotland there'd been no man in her life. And Steve had always been so careful, he'd always used protection, never once failing to do so, he was almost paranoid about it. He'd even used a condom when she was having her period. Pill, why would she need to take the pill?

'Mmm,' she murmured, neither affirming his

assumption, nor denying it. She sat up and dangled her rosy-red nipple into his mouth. And the orchestra struck up a chord and the mating dance resumed, but this time the melody was slower, gentler and just a little old fashioned.

Chapter 21

Theo was light hearted as he swept the hotel freebies into his toilet case. Zoë plucked a shampoo miniature back again. 'God, I can't believe you're taking this. It's awful stuff, it'll make your hair fall out.' She was standing very close to him, and she was naked. There was no hint of yesterday's shyness. He put his arms around her and kissed her.

'We're supposed to be out of the room by eleven,' he said.

She had her arms around his neck, and her body was pressing close to his. 'Maybe we could extend the deadline?'

He needed no more urging, he reached over to the telephone and arranged to relinquish the room at four that afternoon.

'We could get room service for lunch,' she said.

'We had room service for dinner and breakfast, don't you think it's beginning to look rather tacky? As if I'm ashamed to be seen out with you?' They were lying on the bed and he was kissing her stomach.

'I don't care how it looks,' she said. 'It feels great.' She was rubbing her breasts against him and exciting him.

Later, much later, as they attempted to pack for the second time, he touched her cheek and said, 'Zoë, dear,

dear, Zoë, I don't believe what's happened to me.'

'Nor to me,' she said. She thought for a moment, then she added. 'Theo, I have a confession to make.'

He frowned. 'Will I like it?'

'No, and yes, I hope so.'

'Intriguing.'

She placed a hand either side of his jaw and looked into his eyes. 'I didn't want to sleep with you, I wasn't really attracted to you, not in that sort of way—'

He shook his head. 'It didn't seem—'

'Shush, let me finish, it's important for me to say this. I liked you, so, so much, and I was sort of grateful to you, for getting me away from Steve and all that, and giving me a job. I didn't want to go back to Hulver. Mummy and Daddy are lovely to me, but I . . . '

'Wanted to make your own way?'

'Yes, and I agreed to sleep with you, sort of to say, thank you.'

'And?'

'And now I never want to stop sleeping with you.' She smiled coyly. 'I hope that's not going to be a bore for you?'

His heart sung out, his eyes danced and he smiled. 'I think I'll cope,' he said. He kissed her tenderly. 'I'll give it my very best shot.' He closed his eyes. 'My, God, Zoë, you just don't know what you've done for me. I was living in an emotional desert, and now I've stumbled across a wonderful oasis, where all my needs are fulfilled.' He sighed. 'It'll be hard going back to Garrick.'

'No it won't, I'll be there.'

He hadn't expected to feel what he felt for her, he'd wanted to bed her, but if the truth were known he'd felt that for a long time, about any attractive female that came his way. Now she was saying that she'd be there for him. 'Will you?' he whispered. 'Always?'

'For as long as you want me, I will.'

'Prepare to hole up then, because I'll always want you.' He was mad making that sort of commitment. He gave an involuntary shiver. He'd said similar words to Isobel once; it seemed like a lifetime ago. But he'd been just as sincere then as he was now.

After he'd dropped Zoë off at the cottage, he drove the rest of the way down the drive, parked neatly in front of the Hall and with a spring in his step, he entered his home and called out to his wife. She was upstairs on the second floor, right at the top of the house. She had been standing facing east, looking over the rooftops toward Garrick Cottage. From there she'd seen Theo's car enter via the ornate gates and disappear into the turnaround in front of the cottage. The low winter sun had been mirrored in the windscreen, so she hadn't been able to tell who was in the car. It was some moments before the Volvo reappeared and continued down the drive.

Isobel had been putting things away in the attic

rooms. Things she'd decided were worn, tacky or decadent, things she no longer wanted in the house. Whilst there, she'd noticed that there were several things missing, a Jack Vettriano print of couples, in full evening dress, dancing on a beach — a ridiculous picture that Theo had brought home after a visit to the flea market in Fakenham. She'd only placed it there a couple of weeks ago, and a brass cauldron was missing, a hideous thing with Roman men frolicking about on it. Theo had liked it and had for years used it for firewood, but Isobel had finally put her foot down and demoted it to the attic. And then there was the little Persian rug that used to be in front of the library hearth; it had a lot of red in it, and Isobel had taken a dislike to red — it was the colour of adversity — and replaced it with another. But where was it now? Perhaps Theo had moved it?

She went down the stairs; her footsteps landing heavily on each tread, and met Theo at the top of the first landing.

'Hello, Theodore,' she said. 'Good trip?'

Theo became immediately anxious; how could this woman make him feel this way, at times he felt he was actually frightened of her. He hated it when Isobel called him by his full name, as it usually meant trouble.

'Fine, fine — looked at some sheep, but didn't buy — they were too pricey.'

'I don't understand you, Theo, you don't know one end of a sheep from the other. I can't see how you could consider yourself qualified enough to actually buy them.'

'I'm not — that's what I decided — that's why I didn't.'

'Were the people disappointed?'

'What people?'

'The people you stayed with, the people who wanted to sell you the sheep.'

'Oh, those people? Yes, they were, of course they were, but they were very decent about it.'

'Did you have a comfortable night with them? I'm told that these remote farms can be a bit rough.'

Theo was feeling rather hot and nauseous, Isobel didn't generally question him in this way, she never appeared to care where he'd been or what he'd been up to. 'Yes. Yes, I was fine, yes, it was a bit rough, but . . . no it was fine, really, just fine.'

'What did the girl say?'

'What girl?' Theo thought he might actually faint, he was clenching his fists so tight that his hands were shaking.

'You know perfectly well who I mean.'

He gulped. 'Zoë, do you mean Zoë?' The game was up.

'You just called in to see her, I was in the attic and I saw your car.'

'Right,' his heart was pounding in his chest and fine beads of perspiration clung to his top lip. 'I called to tell

166

her about the sheep. She was disappointed of course. It would have been nice to expand the flock, but there you go.'

'You know who she is, don't you?'

'Zoë?'

'She's Josh Elliot's daughter.'

He needed to sit down, he couldn't keep this up, he briefly wondered if it had been worth it. Oh yes, it had been worth it, very, very much so. He coughed. 'Really? From Hulver? I hadn't realized, well you can't find fault with a pedigree like that, can you?'

'Huh, unmarried and has a child!'

'Oh. Oh yes, the child. But surely Isobel, everyone's allowed one mistake, everyone deserves forgiveness. I mean — if she made a mistake,' he licked his lips, 'she may have been taken advantage of, you just don't know.'

Isobel suddenly changed the subject, but her new line of inquiry was almost as painful as the last.

'Theo? Did you take some things from the attic?'

'Things?'

'Yes, a rug, and that brass thing you used to put logs in, and that hideous Jack Vettriano print.'

Theo's brow creased as if he were trying to recall the items.

'Well?' She said.

'No. No, I can't remember the last time I went up to the attic.' Beads of sweat were forming on his forehead, he simply wasn't very good at deception.

Isobel shrugged. 'Perhaps I put them somewhere else, only Charlotte's coming at the weekend, and I thought she might like them. Did I tell you that she and Flora are moving into a new flat?'

'Yes, but look Issie—'

'Isobel, my name's Isobel.'

He sighed. 'Isobel. Those things are mine, I don't particularly want to give them away.'

'Well, I can't now, can I? They've disappeared.'

'No, well, please don't give my things away.'

She didn't answer, but pushed past him and descended the stairs to the hall.

'You'll have to get yourself some supper. I've a meeting with Mrs Hapgood,' she called.

Minutes later he heard the front door slam and her car drive away.

Theo went into his bedroom, from the back of his wardrobe he retrieved a bottle of scotch and, using his tooth mug he poured himself a good measure. He'd go to the supermarket in Lynn tomorrow and stock Zoë up with booze. All of his cravings would soon be satiated at Garrick Cottage.

He unpacked his bag. He picked up his dirty shirt and inhaled, it smelt very faintly of Zoë's perfume and he wondered what it was called, he thought it the most wonderful scent in the world, and he wanted to buy her gallons of it.

He tipped all the dirty washing into the laundry basket, tossed his toilet case into his bathroom, and stretched out on the bed. He put his hands behind his head and closed his eyes; and there she was, as clear as anything in his mind's eye. Slim and beautiful, big breasted, slim waisted, with that delicious smile. He adjusted his trousers; he was wanting her again. He tried to get comfortable, but his need of her was becoming urgent; and she was only at the bottom of the drive. He unzipped his trousers feeling he might masturbate; but this was stupid, she was less than six hundred yards away. 'Old habits die hard,' he said aloud. He picked up the telephone.

'Zoë?'

'Theo,' she purred.

'I was wondering?'

'Yes?'

'Well, when . . . I mean, I wondered if I could—'

'Yes,' she said. She sounded as short of breath as he was. 'Shall I ask Ma to keep Betsy another night?'

'See you in two minutes.'

He packed himself away, threw a sweater over his shoulder, grabbed a front door key and left the house via the side door. From there he cut across the north lawn, through the orchard and the walled garden and arrived at the back door of Garrick Cottage.

She looked flushed and fresh from the shower, and

was dressed in a red Chinese robe.

'I'm going to fetch Betsy in the morning — if I can get the time off work,' she quipped. Her words were casual but spoken with a breathless urgency.

'Isobel's out for the evening.'

Zoë stepped back to let him pass. He pushed the door to with his foot and undid the tie on her robe. Falling to his knees he ran his tongue down her body from navel to pubic hair and back again. He pushed his mouth between her legs and could taste that she was already moist. He lifted his hands and cupped her breasts.

'Zoë. Oh Zoë, I can't get enough of you.'

His sweater joined the robe on the hall floor, his shoes and his trousers were discarded just in front of the bedroom door and the rest of his garments were littered around the bedroom.

'I didn't think that middle-aged men had this much energy,' she whispered half-an-hour later.

'You bring out the best in me.'

He was kissing her neck just below her chin, and Zoë was idly thinking that she must get to a GP tomorrow and get herself put on the pill, when a loud rap came on the back door.

Theo rolled off her. 'Shit! Who's that? I didn't think your mother was bringing Betsy back tonight?'

'She's not.'

Zoë sprang from the bed and peeked through the

bedroom door. Andy was standing just inside the hall looking straight at her. There was no use her pretending she was out, he was already inside the house and he had already seen her. They hadn't even bothered to shut the back door, let alone lock it. Zoë's dressing gown was in a heap on the floor; Bracken sniffed at it. She grabbed Theo's shirt, put it on and went into the hallway.

At the sight of her, Bracken rushed forward, picked one of Theo's shoes up in his mouth and ran manically around the tiny room.

'Calm down Bracken,' she smiled. 'Thanks, Andy, I hope he's behaved himself.'

'Yeah, he's been fine. I checked the flock for you yesterday and today. Skinner didn't think much to it.' He laughed. 'I took the dog — in fact I had him working,' he nodded toward Bracken. 'You know, Zoë, he's the best.'

Andy waved his hand around the room. 'Well, I'd best be off.' He gave an awkward smile. 'Sorry, Zoë, I should have rung first. I didn't realize you had company.'

'I haven't', she said defensively.

'Right,' he said. 'I see.' He took Theo's shoe out of Bracken's mouth and placed it gently on the floor.

Bracken, deprived of his entertainment sniffed around the floor, then, realizing that Zoë's bedroom was occupied, he pushed his nose through the door, and, on recognizing his old friend Theo, he bounded through it and landed slap-bang in the middle of the bed. The bedroom door was wide open, and Theo, the ruffled bedclothes barely covering his modesty, was in full view of Andy. Their eyes met for the briefest of seconds.

'Well,' said Andy, as if he hadn't even noticed the man in Zoë's bed. 'I'd best be off, Cathy's expecting me for me tea.'

'There's no one here,' Zoë said. She was looking at him with extremely wide eyes.

'No. No of course not, Zoë, I can see that.' He winked at her. 'Good luck to yer,' he said. Then under his breath, he added. 'And good luck to him, if his Missis ever finds out.'

'He's a good man,' Theo said, after Andy had left. 'He'll not mention it to anyone. He won't even tell Cathy. I know Andy, he'll keep his mouth shut.'

He returned to the Hall well before Isobel got back from Mrs Hapgood's. She was in a good mood and chatted away about some new people, a clairvoyant and her husband, whom she had met that evening.

Theo smiled and made the odd encouraging remark. He was so happy, he was invincible, he had love for the whole human race, even Marjorie Hapgood. His mind kept wandering back to Zoë, he wondered what she was doing, sleeping probably, she'd had very little sleep the night before. He closed his eyes. He too was short of sleep, but he didn't want to succumb to unconsciousness, he wanted to be with Zoë, be it in mind or body. He wanted to relive every moment in his imagination, every action, every touch, every kiss.

At ten he went to bed. At one, he woke with longing. At two, he got up, dressed, and made his way through the moon-lit garden to Garrick Cottage, where his lover welcomed him with open arms and a warm bed. At six, he retraced his steps back through the garden to the Hall where he showered and changed. And for all his lack of sleep, he felt better than he had done for years.

Chapter 22

Theo slammed the door of the silver Volvo and whistled as he made his way over to the tractor and trailer that stood idling in the farmyard. Trevor Skinner hadn't seen him approach; he had his back toward him and he was shouting to make himself heard above the din of the engine.

'He's probably got the hots for her. Dirty old bugger. She thinks she's something special, she does, thinks 'cause she's got a fancy, la-de-da title she's better than any of us. Title? Huh, she's only a bloody 'Onorable for God's sake, and for all her airs and graces she's been caught with her nickers down once, aint she?'

Bob saw Theo coming toward them. 'Ay-up,' he said nodding his head in Theo's direction. 'Boss's here.'

But Trevor was in full swing and was taking no notice of his panicking work-mate.

'And as for that damned stupid mut of hers — it don't know nothing, it don't. My mongrel could control sheep better than that can. Bet I know what she's got it trained to do! I've seen it sniff round her fanny, I have. Bet she takes it to bed with her these cold nights.' He cackled with laughter.

Theo coughed. 'Morning, Bob. Morning, Trevor. Got a problem?' he nodded toward the standing tractor.

Bob immediately dusted his hands. 'Best get on,'

he said climbing up to the cab and leaving the tractor door open for Trevor to join him. It was the custom to leave the sugar beet harvester on the field and come down to the farmyard for breakfast in the tractor.

But Trevor wasn't going anywhere until he'd spoken his mind, and if he could speak it in front of Bob, so much the better.

'That lass, the Elliot girl, she's not turned into work this morning. It's not that I mind checking the flock, but it does take time, and I ought to be getting on with beet harvest, don't want to lose out on our permits do we? That girl, she's a lazy beggar, Sir Theodore, and no mistake. Half the time she doesn't turn in for work and when she does, nine time out of ten, she's late. I had to check the flock myself again this morning, I did. I came in early and it were hardly light. I knew she'd not turn in, she had yesterday off see, pretending she were sick, no doubt — wrong time of the month I expect. I tell thee, Sir, women and farming make poor bedfellows. Women on the land spell trouble, you mark my words. She got Andy to do the job for her yesterday, she must have known you were away for the day — and I thought Andy were out of here.'

Theo looked both troubled and confused. But the look on his face masked a deep tremulous fury; an angry volcano that threatened to explode. As arranged with Zoë, he'd checked the flock himself that morning; she was leaving early to drive to Hulver to collect Elizabeth. He'd been out on the meadow by seven o'clock, and, what's more, there had been no sign of Trevor, either there or in the farmyard.

'So, it'll be an hour's overtime on me timesheet, I'm afraid, Sir — still I don't expect you begrudge me—'

Theo rubbed his eye. 'What time did you say you checked the flock, Skinner?' His voice totally belied his anger; he spoke with a perfectly calm voice. Trevor should have been warned by Theo's use of his surname. Bob certainly saw what was going down, he tried to signal to Trev, but Trevor was not to be stopped.

'Seven o'clock, Sir — well I started a bit before that, but I won't quibble over the odd quarter of an hour. It's a good job I went when I did though, there was one of them there old ladies on her back, it took hell and all to turn her.'

'Really? That's interesting.'

Trevor beamed. 'Like I say, Sir. The Elliot girl,' he turned up his nose and shook his head. 'Best be rid of her, Sir, she's not a good deal.'

Au contraire, thought Theo.

'You'll never get your money's worth there. In fact — well, you know me, Sir, I gets on with anyone—'

Even Bob shook his head at this.

'And I don't like to call folk behind their backs, but she can't stay here, she's—'

Theo frowned. 'How do you get on with her, Bob?'

Bob took his cap off and scratched his head. 'She's

176

all right,' he said, and then added with some conviction, 'I've no complaints.'

Trevor looked to be digesting Bob's opinion. He drew in a deep breath. 'Well, I have, Sir Theodore. In fact, it's her or me.' He nodded his head convincingly. 'That's about the size of it Sir — her or me.'

'Really?' Theo's brows were raised. 'You're serious? They're your terms, are they? You or her? I have to make a choice?'

Skinner continued to nod vigorously, his thin lips were screwed up in his rather rounded face. He had the look of a confident man, a man that knew his own worth.

'Well, Skinner, we'll be sorry to see you go. You've been on this farm a good while — worked for my father, didn't you? But so be it. I'll need your cottage of course for the new man — or woman, that replaces you, but the council will no doubt house you. Right — end of the week? I'll pay you a month's wages in lieu of notice, it's demoralizing for the other workers to have someone working out their notice.'

Theo turned on his heels and walked back to his car, leaving both Bob and Trevor open mouthed. He felt good, very good. At last he was taking charge of his life again. He suddenly felt a surge of enthusiasm for the estate; it was the first time he'd felt that way since the Lloyds crash had forced him into the sale and leaseback. He'd been dead for a few years; now he was alive, very much alive.

He switched the radio on and whistled to a tune as he drove toward Cathy Porter's house.

Cathy's mother opened the door to him. 'Oh! Mr—er—Sir Sheldon-Harris,' she was extremely flustered. Theo thought she was about to curtsy.

'I came to see Andy, is he in?'

'Oh yes, Sir, 'cept they're still in bed. But if you're worried about, — well — you know, the young lady — Andy knows when to keep his mouth shut, he'll not breath a word to a soul.'

Theo was stunned, it hadn't occurred to him that Andy would even tell Cathy let alone Cathy's family. His feelings were a strange mixture of fear and pride. Proud that the world knew that Zoë was his, yet at the same time afraid of the consequences of such an alliance. But of the two, pride got the upper hand, what was it he'd said to Zoë at lunch last week? That he'd rather be in jail than in love? Well that wasn't true anymore.

He looked at his watch; it was well past nine-thirty. He ignored Mrs Porter's remarks and asked when she thought Andy might be up.

'Come you in, Sir, I'll go and give them a shout now.'

Theo followed Mrs Porter inside the semi-detached council house and the woman scurried away toward the stairs. He looked around him, the house was neat and tidy and spotlessly clean. Two places were set for breakfast, by the look of the place settings, Mrs Porter was about to cook Cathy and Andy a full English breakfast. He suspected that she probably did so every morning.

'He'll be down in two shakes, Sir.' The woman bustled into the room. 'He's late this morning, he's usually up long before now — well, you know that yourself, of course.'

'He's not working then?'

'No, Sir. He's applied for one or two jobs, but no luck yet. He's got the experience but not them bits of paper, from the colleges like. Bosses want qualifications these days, don't they? And there's no work for farm labourers this time of year, is there? Come summer, harvest and all that, he'll be turning offers of work away.'

Theo tried not to look too relieved as Andy appeared in the doorway. His hair was sticking up on end and his ruffled appearance made him look younger than his twenty-eight years. He gave Theo a sheepish grim.

'Sorry, Sir Theo, I slept late, couldn't seem to get up this morning,' he grinned. 'Cathy was laying on me shirt.'

Mrs Porter tutted. 'I'll make some tea,' she said, 'and let you two talk in private.' She scurried into the kitchen, but didn't shut the door.

'Sit down, Sir Theo,' Andy said pulling a straight-backed chair away from the table and settling himself in another. 'If it's about last night at Miss Zoë's place, I'll not

179

say anything, it came as a bit of a shock like, but I won't say—' he followed Theo's eyes over to the open kitchen doorway where Mrs Porter could be seen placing cups and saucers on a tray. 'She'll not say anything either, you knows that, Sir Theo.'

Theo rubbed his chin. 'I didn't know you knew Zoë,' he said. 'I didn't realize that you were looking after her dog.'

Andy laughed. 'Bless you, Sir. I've know her years. I grew up at Hulver. My dad worked on the Hulver Esate for years, and even after he retired he did odd jobs and helped out in the castle gardens — until the staff cuts, of course, then he got the chop, like. But as I said, he were way past retirement anyway. He were always a good man, Miss Zoë's dad were. Always treated my family fair and square. I were surprised at Miss Zoë shepherding though — me sister Val met her at the crèche, she's got a little-un, — Storm, she named him, a right little devil he is, and all. Anyway, Val recognized Miss Zoë and they got to talking, and Val said that I'd look after the dog anytime like, and that's how we met again, so don't you worry that I'll say ought, I won't. I'd not see Miss Zoë harmed, that I wouldn't. Always a lady Miss Zoë were, just like her mum.'

'Thank you,' Theo said. He'd have liked to have added that he didn't care whom Andy told, but he was rather afraid that he did care. For the time being, fear had overtaken pride. 'But I didn't come here to talk about—' he

180

couldn't quite bring himself to mention Zoë's name again.

'I was wondering if you've got a job yet?'

Andy rubbed his hand around the back of his neck. 'No, Sir, I haven't, and to tell you the truth I regret the day I gave you my notice. I let Skinner win, didn't I? I played right into his hands, and now it's me that's unemployed, it's me that's out of work.'

'That's why I came, Andy, I wondered if you might like the foreman's job?'

Andy blinked. 'But what about Skinner?'

Theo laughed. 'Well, Mr Skinner just gave me an ultimatum, — him or Zoë.' It felt so good to tell somebody, so very good.

Andy slapped his hand on his knee. 'No contest,' Andy screeched 'No bloody contest. Whoops! 'Scuse my language, Sir.'

'No contest,' Theo agreed. 'So of course I regretfully had to tell Mr Skinner that his P45 would be ready for collection on Friday.'

Andy's jolly face suddenly became serious. 'Watch old Skinner, Sir Theo. He's trouble, he always has been. There's something not quite right about him.'

Theo shook his head. 'I'm not worried, Andy.' He genuinely felt that nothing and no one could touch him. 'But what I need to know is, when can you start? Monday be too soon would it?'

The smile came back onto Andy's face. 'Monday's

great. Tell you the truth, I was really getting worried. I was really regretting leaving you, Sir. I thought I could just walk into another job, just like that.' He flicked his fingers.

'I'm glad you didn't.'

'So am I, now.'

'I'm afraid it might be a while before Skinner gets out of his house though.'

'We get Skinner's house as well?

'Of course, goes with the job.'

'Just a minute,' Andy said. 'I've got to ask Cathy something.'

He rushed to the bottom of the stairs. 'Hey, Cathy, Cathy.'

She came to the top landing and looked down over the banister rail. Theo was amused to see that her night attire was almost the same as Zoë's; a long baggy tee shirt.

'What?' She said.

'Would you consider marrying the foreman of Garrick Farm?'

'What, old Skinner?'

'No, you daft bugger, me. Me, Andy Culper. Will you marry me?'

'Andy!' She rushed down the stairs and into his arms; her tee shirt rode up and exposed the lower portion of a rounded pink buttock. Theo smiled, last week the sight of feminine flesh would have filled him with envy and longing, but not now, not anymore.

Mrs Porter came through with the tray of tea and plonked it on the table. She handed both Theo and Andy a cup; it was very weak and very milky.

'Cheers,' Andy said clinking his cup on Theo's. 'And you and Zoë shall come to the wedding.'

Theo gave a weak smile. Not only were he and Zoë a couple in his own mind, but in Andrew Culper's mind as well.

Chapter 23

'Zoë? It's Tiggy.'

'Hi! Just a minute, let me get Betsy out of her high-chair.' Zoë released her daughter, and the child crawled off in the direction of her toy box.

Zoë flopped down on the sofa, picked up the telephone and, curling her legs under her, said, 'right, I'm all yours now.'

'So how was lover-boy? Bad as you thought or worse?' Tiggy asked.

Zoë had a sweet smile on her face, but before she could answer, her sister cut in, 'If I don't tell someone I shall burst. Oh, Zoë, I'm in love.'

'Not Bruce?'

'No, no, his name's Alex and he's, he's, he's, he's wonderful, he's gentle and kind and he's been around a bit, he's experienced and, and he's handsome, he's got these wide apart blue eyes that just make you want to melt, and he's, well,— he's just everything. I can't stop thinking about him, it's all I can do to stop myself 'phoning him every five minutes—'

'I'm in love too,' Zoë chopped in, a hint of urgency in her voice. 'Only I haven't told him yet.'

'What?' Tiggy snapped. 'Not with old what's his name? Theo? But he's so old.'

'He's forty-five, and he's everything you've just told me about Alex, apart from the blue eyes, that is. And what's more he's a wonderful lover.'

'He can't be as wonderful a lover as Alex.'

'You've slept with him!'

'You sound like Ma. Besides, you've slept with what's-his-name, Theo.'

'That was only because—'

'I know, you felt sorry for him.'

'Yes, well, I certainly don't feel sorry for him anymore, — at least I do, but not the way I did before.'

'Zoë, I've never felt what I feel with Alex. I've never had an orgasm with a man before — it was, well, spectacular.' She paused for a moment, 'You know, Zoë, I've just thought, I think he's probably about the same age as your Theo.' She giggled. 'So I'd better take back what I said about him being old, maybe what they say about older men is right? God, I can't believe I'm saying all this.' She giggled again. 'Did Theo make you . . . you know . . .did you get there?'

Zoë swallowed, she felt terribly shy suddenly, and yet Tiggy had always been her confidante.

'Well? Did he?'

'About the same number of times he got there,' she replied, 'maybe a few times more.' She too burst into a fit of giggles.

'I wish I could place your Theo. I know you say

185

that he used to come over to Hulver to shoot, but for the life of me, I can't remember him.'

'You must remember him, he looks like Ralph Fiennes, only he's much taller, about six-three or six-four, and he's a really gentle, loving person, and he's so sweet to Betsy and he's so kind and so—'

'And so married.'

'In name only. She doesn't give a damn about him, they have separate rooms and—'

'A likely story, that's what all married men say when they want to get their leg over.'

'He comes and visits me in the night once she's in bed, he couldn't do that if they were sharing a room, now could he? Anyway, what about Alex? If he's so wonderful he must be attached, if not married.'

'He was married, but he's divorced. And he was going out with someone, but she was married, and when it came to the crutch, she couldn't leave her husband and her way of life. He was very cut up about it at the time — but you know what they say, — her loss is my gain. When are you seeing Theo again?'

'Tonight, I hope, — that's if she goes to one of her spiritualist meetings. Oh I must tell you, she believes in reincarnation, and she uses all this mumbo-jumbo, and somehow gets in touch with her previous lives, and it appears that in a previous life, she and Theo were married, and Theo murdered her! Anyway, she's determined that he won't get her again. That's why she sleeps in another room, — she's afraid that Theo might do away with her in the middle of the night!'

'She sounds crazy to me.'

'I think she is. It's a bit worrying though. You see, before — in her previous life, that is, Theo was a farmer, and he took himself a mistress, and the farmer and the mistress plotted together and murdered his wife. They were found out, and both hung from the gallows on top of Gibbet Hill. You know, the hill that overlooks Applegate Farm?'

'Of course, we used to fly kites from there when we were children. It's true that about two hundred years ago, a farmer and his mistress killed the farmer's wife and were hung for it. The bodies were left up there to rot, to act as a warning to anyone who might be tempted to do the same. Don't you remember that nanny we had who was always on about it? She didn't like going there because she said it was haunted.'

'I seem to remember that it was a pretty eerie place, — don't you remember all those noises we heard up there?'

'Oh, Zoë! That was the wind.'

Zoë laughed. 'I know, I know, but it was just a bit scary, wasn't it? The way the wind whistled through the trees in Applegate wood and over the top of the hill.'

'Yes, it certainly was. I remember the nanny getting us going once or twice. It was her way of getting complete control over us. I was scared out of my wits, but you were very daring, you used to laugh at her, and I remember you used to creep up behind her and make her jump.'

'That wasn't me, that was you. I was always the scare baby, you always put me to shame. I hated my baby sister being braver than me.'

'Was it me? I don't think so. Anyway, that nanny had complete control over us. She used to tell us that if we didn't do as we were told, the ghosts would follow us home.'

Both Tiggy and Zoë were giggling. 'And it worked beautifully didn't it? I think that's Lady Sheldon-Harris's plan as well. She tries to frighten Theo into doing what she tells him. Anyway, I asked Mummy about it, and do you know? That's how the Hulver Estate got Applegate Farm. Randall, that was the farmer's name, didn't have any children and after he was hung there was no one to take over, so our great, great, great grandfather took it on. Everyone said that he'd be cursed for it. But our lot seem to be pretty lucky, don't they?'

'I'm surprised Mummy told you, she always used to clamp up when we asked.'

'We were children then. We won't be influenced by all that superstitious nonsense now.'

'Did you know that the mistress's name was, Zoë?' Tiggy asked.

'It wasn't! Was it?'

All Zoë could hear was Tiggy's helpless laughter. 'Oh, Tiggy, I believed you for a minute there, you really had me going. Anyway, if Theo and I decide to do away with her ladyship, I'll expect both you, and your barrister friend with the big cock, to bail us out.'

'I didn't say he had a big cock, did I?'

'No, but I expect he does.'

'I've nothing to go on really, except—'

'Except?'

'Except, well you know, that professor, the one I nearly went to bed with, but didn't, because he only wanted me to suck him off?'

'Yes?'

'Well it was a good mouthful, I almost choked.'

There were squeals and giggles coming from both ends of the line.

'What about Bruce?'

'Oh, he's about four, five on a good night, nothing to write home about. What about Sir Theodore? Is he well blessed?'

'I told you, he's larger than life in every way, he's tall and very handsome, everything about him is slightly exaggerated.'

Tiggy giggled. 'God, Zoë, I'll not be able to keep my eyes off his crotch when I meet him.'

'So long as you keep your hands off his crotch!'

'Don't worry, my hands will be fully occupied. So Sis, you over that bastard Steve, are you?'

'Steve? Steve who?'

'Good, I've been waiting to hear you say that for the past four years or more.'

'Steve was special, Tiggy, and that's just it, he *was* special. He isn't anymore.'

'Bravo.'

'But tell me about Alex, when are you seeing him again?'

'I'm going to stay with him this weekend, in his house in London. Only don't mention it to Ma and Pa, will you?'

'Of course not, you won't mention about me and Theo either, will you?'

'Don't be daft, of course I won't.'

Zoë saw Theo's shadow walk across the lawn and enter via the back door. 'Sorry, Tiggy, I have to go, I'll ring you later.'

'Ah, enter Sir Theo?'

'That's absolutely right. I'll call you tonight.'

'Do that, and if the police come for you, don't say anything until you've spoken to a lawyer.'

Zoë laughed. 'I won't.'

She replaced the hand-piece into the cradle and rushed into Theo's arms.

Chapter 24

Trevor Skinner entered Home Farm Cottage. He didn't know how he was going to tell her; she was a very understanding woman, but she could be difficult, — very difficult. Maybe he needn't tell her; maybe he could just carry on as if he were working? He hung his coat on the hook inside the porch door, went through to the kitchen and slid his tuck box onto the worktop. From the back of the kitchen door he took a flowered wrap-around apron, slipped his arms into it and tied the tapes firmly around his waist. Then he fished into the pocket and retrieved a thick pink hairnet. He removed his glasses and placed the hairnet on his head, tucked his wispy grey hair into it and replaced his glasses.

'That you, Trev?' Jane called.

He went through to the sitting room; she was watching television.

'Oh, Trev, you do look nice,' she said. 'But you've forgotten your lipstick, and what's this? No mascara? You bad boy, you should make an effort when you come home.'

'Sorry, dear,' he said. 'I'll pop upstairs and do it now.'

'Do that,' she said, 'and there's a little pressie for you on the bed.'

Trevor climbed the stairs wearily; he just didn't

know how he was going to tell her, he didn't think he'd get away with pretending he was going to work everyday. Sooner or later she'd hear about it. Garrick-in–the–Willows was a hotbed of gossip.

There was a neatly wrapped parcel on the double bed. He reached over for it; the thoughts of his problems already fading, he ripped into the brown paper and removed a pink lacy nylon nightgown. He smiled and held the garment up in front of him. He gazed at himself in the mirror. The nightdress had a thick ruche at the hem and shoestring straps. He licked his lips; he couldn't wait to try it on. He sat down at the dressing table and rubbed some cream on his face. Next he dabbed foundation into his skin applying it with a small natural sponge; it made a loud rasping sound as it came into contact with his twelve-hour stubble; he should have shaved first, but he was eager to get on with his makeup. He carefully applied eyeliner, mascara and blusher; last of all, he outlined his thin mean lips with a plum coloured lip-liner and, taking a small flat brush he filled in the rest of his lips in with a peachy-toned lipstick. He pouted at himself in the mirror, and blew himself several kisses. He felt good, he felt very good.

He got up to leave the room, but then his eyes rested on the new pink nightgown. He couldn't resist it; in no time at all he stripped out of his flowered apron and the rest of his clothes. Then he went over to what Jane called his special drawer, where he found a bra and two soft pliable breast enhancers. He put the bra on and filled the cups with the rubber substitutes. He pushed his penis between his legs and admired himself in the mirror. God, he looked good, but his penis was getting hard and refused to remain between his legs.

He removed the hairnet and, taking Jane's brush, he parted his hair down the center and pinned it back with two diamante hairslides. He was pleased with the effect.

Jane came into the room. 'Oh, Trev,' she said. 'Your hair looks lovely.'

'Trev? What are you calling me that for?'

She smiled indulgently. 'Sorry, Theresa.'

He smiled at her as he slipped a pair of mauve frilly panties on, they felt good next to his skin, he adjusted his penis and poked his hips forward.

'Oh, Theresa, look what you've got there, I shall have to smack you if you start playing with that.'

A thrill went through him; he put his hands between his legs and held himself. She was a good woman was Jane, a very understanding woman. She wouldn't understand how he'd lost his job though, that was for sure.

He slipped the new nighdress over his head, and then he turned this way and that grinning at his reflection in the mirror.

'Oh, you look grand,' Jane said, 'really grand.' She took a belt from the wardrobe and secured it around his waist. 'Right, now I'll lend you this just for the evening, but you must let me have it back if you do something naughty and I need to punish you.'

'Yes, Jane,' he said. God he hoped he'd do something worthy of punishment. He was getting all peculiar just thinking about it. That was the thing that always brought him off, that and only that, and Jane enjoyed it too, he knew she did. She loved giving him what for. It had always been that way, even when he was very young and his mother had caught him dressing in her clothes, it was the punishment, the beatings, that had given him the thrill. Jane was such an understanding woman. When she'd wanted the kids she'd had to beat him nearly black and blue to get him to do it. Over her knee he'd been and he'd had to tell her when he was on the brink so that she could whip it in quick, just before he shot his load. The technique had worked well, although it had taken a good many attempts. Two girls they'd produced, two lovely girls, both grown up and left home, but neither of them married.

Jane pushed her hand down between his legs.

'Theresa, I think I'd better use that belt now,' she said.

He was swaying from side to side. 'You won't make me go to work in my frilly panties, will you?'

'I think you must.'

He rubbed his thighs together, my God, this was exciting.

'And the hair slides, you must wear them for work

tomorrow.'

Oh, God, the hair slides as well, he'd have to keep his cap on all day. This was exciting, so exciting, nobody would know they were there except he and Jane.

Jane was smiling; she still had one hand on his penis. 'Theresa, this isn't good enough.' She picked her hairbrush off her dressing table and sat down on the side of the bed. Trevor, knowing his lines, bent himself over her knee, she slipped his panties down around his thighs, and brought the hairbrush down hard on his bare buttocks. The pain was bliss; it seared through and through him. Whack, whack, whack, she pushed one hand down on the back of his neck and brought the brush down harder still. His skin was red and inflamed, whack, whack, whack. His orgasm seemed to be coming from a long way off rolling on and forward, building from his stomach and his groins. Whack, whack, his penis was trapped between the mauve panties and his wife's ample thighs and he could feel his load shooting into the soft nylon.

He cried out, she released him and he fell to his knees. She picked up the front of the nightgown; he was very wet. She brought the flat of her hand down across his face. 'You're a bad, bad, boy,' she said. 'Now go in the bathroom and clean yourself up — your tea's nearly ready. And wash your nickers out, you fifthly cunt.'

She got up from the bed and she smiled as she produced a pair of feminine thongs from the drawer. 'Put these on love, you'll look nice in these.'

Trevor scurried into the bathroom; he had such a good life, such a very good life. If he didn't have to go to work he could dress up all he wanted; and he and Jane could play games all day. He wished he dare ask her to go a bit further. Maybe next week, when he was at home more, he'd pluck up the courage. He put water in the basin, washed the mauve panties with hand soap and hung them on the line above the bath. He'd had a good orgasm, but he still felt slightly unfulfilled. He locked the bathroom door and fumbled into the back of the bathroom cabinet bringing forth some cotton wool and some lighter fuel; he moistened the wool with fuel, and stuffed one end up his anus. He was trembling with excitement. He took a match and set fire to the protruding piece of material. It ignited immediately and sent a searing pain through his body, his ejaculation was so strong and fierce that it splattered the bathroom wall opposite.

His heart beat wildly as he removed the strip of burned cotton wool. His anus was singed and painful and he knew that it would hurt every time he sat down, and he knew that he would probably ejaculate every time he used the lavatory, he was like that, it was his way, his nature.

'Your tea's ready, Theresa love,' Jane called up the stairs. 'Come and eat it whilst it's hot.'

Trevor went back to the bedroom and stuffed his feet into a pair of high-heeled shoes and joined her in the room below. Jane served up two big plates of Irish stew, which they ate in silence, watching the six o'clock news.

It was after the weather forecast that Trevor dropped the bombshell.

'I've got some bad news, Jane.'

'Really, Theresa, what's that then?'

He drew in a big gulp of air and said it straight out. 'I got the sack today.'

Jane's mouth fell open. 'What'd mean, you got the sack?'

'Well, I told old Sheldon-Harris it were either me or her, you know, the Elliot tart, and he said he'd choose her, and I could pick me cards up on Friday.'

'He can't do that, not to you. You're only four years from retirement.'

'He's done it already.'

'But he can't, he can't. Did he tell you why?'

'No, except I were reporting that the bit of stuff hadn't come to work. It's my job to keep an eye on her.'

'Course it is. So he sacked you with no good reason.'

Trevor fingered the top layer of the pink nylon. Jane was raising her voice. He liked that; it excited him. He shifted uneasily in his chair, his arse hurt and his new thongs were cutting into it, and it felt good, he was beginning to get an erection again. He wasn't quite sure that he could manage a hat trick, but he was willing to try.

'Well I know why it is,' Jane said firmly. 'It's because you're a cross-dresser, and he can't sack you for that.'

'He doesn't know,' Trevor said.

Jane smiled. 'He will tomorrow, won't he?'

'Will he?'

'Yes, because you'll be going to work all dressed up tomorrow, won't you?'

'Will I?' The prospect excited him more than he'd have thought possible, he was very erect now and his penis was straining against the women's panties.

'Yes, you will, and if anyone asks why he's given you the push, that's the reason you'll tell them. You'll get thousands in compensation, thousands and thousands. I read about a similar case in *The Sun* only last week. We'll be millionaires, we will, bloody millionaires. Now, as soon as I've tidied up the kitchen, we'll decide what you're going to wear in the morning.'

Trevor smiled. 'It'll be sort of like coming out,' he said happily. 'But—'

'But what?'

'I thought you'd be cross with me.'

'Do you want me to be cross with you?'

He moistened his lips and nodded his head.

'Good,' she said loudly. 'Because I'm fucking furious with you, you're a naughty little tart, and I'm going to beat you till you're sorry.'

She pulled the leather belt from his waist. 'Come on, over my knee.'

Trevor did as he was told. For the second time that evening she pulled the nightdress up and pushed his underwear down as far as his thighs. With strong violent strokes she rained the belt down on his buttocks until ugly red welts appeared. Trevor closed his eyes. This was bliss, complete and utter bliss.

'I'm shooting,' he breathed as he ejaculated into the feminine underwear. 'I'm shooting my load.'

'Then you really are a very bad boy,' Jane said bringing the belt down even harder. 'What are you?'

'A bad boy, a very bad boy.'

She stopped hitting him and he was slightly disappointed.

'Now get off my knee, you're too heavy.'

Trevor stood upright.

'Look at you.' Jane said. 'Look, you've made a real mess of your new clothes. You can just stay in them and do the washing up to make up for it. Do you think I've been put on this earth just to wash your dirty knickers?'

Trevor started to clear the table, he was a happy man; he was to be allowed to wear something fancy to work tomorrow, something showy. He smiled over at his wife. He wondered what she would choose.

Chapter 25

Isobel Sheldon-Harris rushed into her bathroom and filled the basin up with cold water. She pulled off her jumper and, taking a flannel, she washed all of her exposed skin. Theo had come so close to her that she'd panicked and pushed past him and she'd actually touched him. She could feel her energy being sapped away. She felt frantic, would she never be free of his evil influence? She emptied the basin, washed it, then refilled it and submerged her face in the icy cold water. She held her breath for as long as she could before repeating the ritual a second, third and fourth time. Then she set about making her room safe by drawing the star signs on her walls, floor and ceiling. But still she felt discontent. What if Theo had managed to get something of hers, a personal item or, and this thought was unbearable, a lock of her hair? She checked her hairbrush. It looked remarkably clean and free from hair. Perhaps Theo had managed to take some of her hair from it, perhaps that was the reason she felt so depleted.

She dressed in fresh clean clothes and bravely made her way to Theo's bedroom. She hadn't been in there for months. She thought it seemed dark and sinister, and she sensed that evil vibrations were all around her. She checked his bedroom, his dressing room and finally his bathroom. Nothing; no sign of any mischief. He was clever, she musn't forget that, he was both clever and cunning. She opened his toilet case and tipped the contents out onto the vanity unit, shampoo, soap and bath gel fell out; all bore the logo of a Cumbrian hotel. At that moment she lifted her eyes and looked out of the window. Zoë Elliot was walking along the edge of the north lawn on her way to the farmyard. She had the child strapped to her back and a dog at her heels. Isobel glanced again at the hotel freebies. Zoë Elliot — now it all fell into place. Taking one of the shampoos, she went into Theo's bedroom and dialed the hotel number printed on the lable. She told the receptionist that her name was Sheldon-Harris and that she and her husband had stayed at the hotel and she wished to book another excursion, she particularly liked the room they had last time, and would like the same room if possible. As if on cue the receptionist pressed a few buttons on her keyboard and announced that Mr and Mrs Sheldon-Harris had stayed in room one-hundred-and-four.

Isobel replaced the receiver. She felt sick. Not that she cared that Theo was having an affair, far from it. The thought of his life force flowing away from her, pleased her. But when two evil beings got together in sexual antics, then the Devil was given power. The Devil rode on the back of fornication. She went back to the window and looked in the direction that the girl had taken. She was a small dot in the distance now. The child on her back made her look hunchbacked and the dog at her heels like a black shadow stalking her. Isobel nodded her head; it was exactly what her guide had warned her about. Theo had taken a mistress, and they were out to kill her in this life, just as they had in the last life. Zoë Elliot was beautiful; that probably meant that she was a fallen angel, and thus a very dangerous woman. Isobel must be on her guard at all times, she must make plans to protect herself.

She replaced all of Theo's things carefully. On no account must he suspect that she had discovered the truth. She went back to her own room and once more she ritually washed herself. Then she went down to the kitchen to wait Zoë Elliot's return. Unconsciously, she had noted the girl's habits and so she was ready when Zoë appeared at a little after twelve o'clock. This time Zoë was walking on the south side of Garrick Hall, just as Isobel knew she would. Isobel, with perfect timing, walked out and met her close to the cattle grid that separated the Hall gardens form the open parkland.

Isobel pasted a smile on her lined face. 'You must be the new shepherd,' she said.

The girl looked frightened, as well she might. She was holding out her hand to Isobel, but of course she couldn't take it; she had to keep her arms tightly folded across her chest to protect herself from the girl's evil psyche.

'I'm Zoë Elliot,' the girl said, still holding out her hand.

'I know exactly who you are, and I know that you

have a bastard on your back.' Isobel watched with contempt as the girl's hand slowly dropped back to her side.

'This is my daughter Elizabeth,' Zoë said.

The dog gave a low growl and, going down on his belly he edged his way between his mistress and Isobel.

'It's the Devil's child,' Isobel hissed. She could see that she was making the girl feel uncomfortable, she was red in the face and trembling.

'She's beautiful, Lady Sheldon-Harris, how could you say that?' The girl took a step backwards and the dog started to patrol up and down between the two women.

Despite the fact that she had resolved to keep her knowledge secret the words slipped out 'You're Theo's mistress, and you should know that you won't get me this time. This time, I'm prepared for you.'

Zoë swallowed. She looked from left to right as if she might make a run for it, but, for the moment, she stood her ground.

Isobel began to laugh. She was enjoying this, the girl looked frightened half out of her wits. Isobel was protected, and she had taken the Devil by surprise.

Without a word, the girl quite suddenly turned, and walked away from her.

Isobel watched her receding back. How she would have liked to have stabbed a knife in between the shoulder blades, but no, she mustn't even think that. She already had the Devil on the run, this time she would overpower him and all his evil works.

Chapter 26

Zoë's heart was pounding, she had tried very hard not to run away from Lady Sheldon-Harris, but it had been almost impossible not to break into a trot. Once she reached the cottage she slipped inside and locked the door behind her. Elizabeth was crying, and Bracken was equally disturbed; he was so close to her legs that she very nearly fell over him. What a fool she was, how could she have imagined that she and Theo could get away with it? Especially as she lived not four hundred yards away from Theo's home. What would her parents say? She'd let them down once again. More to the point, what would Theo say when he knew that his wife had found out? Would he ditch her? Probably; he had a lot to lose, didn't he? And what would she do without Theo? She loved him more than she cared to admit, she worshipped him; she'd do anything for him. She wondered if he knew that his wife knew, or if he had gone out that morning totally unaware of the earthquake that was about to happen. Oh God, she wished she could get in touch with him, but he was in Norwich having lunch with his bank manager.

She hadn't seen Isobel Sheldon-Harris up close and she was surprised by the woman's plain appearance. She had imagined that Isobel would be very glamorous. She had gleaned from her parents that Isobel was the original *femme fatale.* She'd been unprepared for the mean mouth, the dark darting eyes and the wild hair pulled severely back from her face. The woman's appearance had frightened her. She looked somehow sinister, and she stood in such a strange way, with her arms folded and her legs crossed. Zoë had thought that she might well topple over at any minute. One thing was sure, she'd stop walking past the Hall to get to the farm. She'd start going the long way round by the road. She wouldn't risk another confrontation like that one in a hurry.

Zoë made herself coffee and sat down to wait. Theo was bound to call at the cottage before he went home, he always did. She rang Andy to tell him she wouldn't be in to work that afternoon, and asked if he could check the flock for her and if Theo called down at the farm he was to tell him to call on Zoë first before he went home.

'There's trouble brewing, Miss Zoë,' Andy said. She'd told him a dozen times to call her Zoë, but he still lapsed into his old style of address. 'Bob came up to see me. Apparently Skinner's going to the tribunal for unfair dismissal. He went into work this morning all dolled up in his missus's clothes. Bob says he looked a right ponce, and he told him as much. Skinner even had a ribbon in his hair.' Andy started to giggle. 'He reckons that Sir Theo's sacked him because he's different. Reckons he's a cross-dresser or something. Anyway, poor old Bob's in a state about it, because he told Skinner what he thought of him, and he also told him what Sir Theo thought of him, and Skinner got it all on tape, say's he's been discriminated against and that he's been harassed. Just say the word, Miss Zoë, and me and me mates will bloody harass him.'

'Don't do anything silly, Andy. I'll tell Sir Theo if I see him first, but if you see him, for goodness sake ask him to call at the cottage, *before* he goes home, it's really important, Andy, really, really important.'

Zoë paced up and down, she couldn't eat and she couldn't be still, and both Elizabeth and the dog seemed disturbed; both were begging for her attention. At one point Zoë went into her bedroom and put some of her clothes in a bag. It was best that she left this place. She couldn't stay, not now that Isobel knew about her and Theo. A moment later she replaced her things, it was best to wait and see what Theo had to say. She didn't want to leave, she didn't want to leave her job or her home and she especially didn't want to leave her lover.

At three the telephone rang. Theo was in the farmyard and was ringing from his mobile. She'd earlier thought she might ring him, but somehow telling Theo that his wife knew of their affair in front of the bank manager seemed rather bizarre.

'Where are you?' He asked. 'Shirking your duties? Perhaps the lovely Skinner was right about you after all.' He was in a jovial mood.

'Theo? She knows, she stopped me this morning,

she knows. And she said that Betsy was the Devil's child, and she said that we weren't going to get her this time — it's all to do with Gibbet Hill, you know, what you told me, and I was really scared, she's one weird lady and—'

'Calm down, darling, speak slower, I can't understand—'

'She knows, Theo, she knows about us.'

'She's guessing, she can't possibly know.'

'What if she followed you one night?'

'She wouldn't go out in the dark in case the evil spirits got her.'

'Are you sure about that?'

'No.'

'What are we going to do?'

'We're going to keep calm and work through this, like sensible people. You didn't admit anything, did you?'

'Of course not. I just walked away.'

'Well done, the idea is to seem insulted. You should have told her you already had a boyfriend or something, or that I was far too old for you.' He laughed without much conviction. 'Which, incidentally, I am.'

'Of course you are,' she said. Tears were pricking her eyes and beginning to spill over. She sniffed.

'Zoë? Are you crying?'

'No,' she sobbed.

'Look, I'm coming up.'

'You can't, she'll see you.'

'Not unless she's on the drive or in the attic.' He was quiet for a moment. 'I'm coming up.'

'But what if she is watching?'

He was quiet again. 'I'm coming up anyway.'

'Theo?'

'Yes?'

'She frightens me.'

'She frightens me too,' he replied.

Chapter 27

It had been an exhausting day. First his lunch with the bank manager. He hadn't been worried, but it was still taxing to have to have your wits about you all the time. Then all the bother with Zoë; Isobel hadn't said a thing when he got home. He rather thought that Zoë must have imagined what Isobel had said. Read more into it than was there, as it were. Isobel could act in a jolly funny way at times. Then there was all this business with Skinner. That was a turn-up for the book. He'd have to get his lawyers onto it tomorrow. Of course Skinner didn't have a leg to stand on, he'd not sacked the chap for cross-dressing, in fact he hadn't sacked the man at all. He'd been offered a choice between Skinner and the woman he loved, and he'd chosen the latter, who wouldn't? No, he wasn't too worried about that. But all the same he was worn out. He closed his eyes, but his brain wouldn't empty. He'd told Zoë he wouldn't go down to the cottage that night. It was maybe best that he stayed away for a few nights, just until he saw how the land lay.

He turned over and thumped his pillow. He couldn't get comfortable, he was used to having Zoë in bed beside him, and his body was beginning to ache for her. He rolled over onto his stomach; he pulled a pillow under him and burrowed into it. Then he turned onto his back and pulled the pillow onto his stomach. Christ, how he wanted her, he couldn't put up with too many nights without her, she wasn't a want anymore, she was a need. Maybe he should just confess everything to Isobel and ask her to let him go? She didn't want him; it would solve her problems as well as his. He glanced at the bedside clock. It was one-fifteen, he was usually tucked up beside Zoë by now. He could telephone her? But it was hardly fair to wake her; she'd probably be fast asleep, not lying awake like he was.

Once more he tried to empty his mind, but Zoë filled it to the brim; he tried counting sheep, but the shepherdess took over the flock. It was useless, totally useless. He looked at the clock again; it was half-past-two. He put his hand down between his legs, this was madness; he could be in Zoë's bed, in Zoë's arms. Isobel was fast asleep; she had no knowledge and even less interest in his nighttime activities. He would go to his lover and what the hell.

He swept the covers back and, just as he was about to get out of bed, he heard a floorboard creak. He gently replaced the covers and half-closed his eyes. His bedroom door gave the slightest of squeaks, and he saw the outline of his wife in the thick half-light. She was coming toward the bed. He smiled; he'd been wise to stay after all. He turned his head toward her as if stirring in his sleep. He could just make out her face, the features set in a determined pose, she had her arm raised and, too late, he saw the glint of metal. He rolled away from her as she plunged the knife downward; it caught him on his left ear, missing his neck by millimeters. He jumped from the bed falling to his knees. He held the pillow above him as protection from the blows that rained mercilessly down on him. His forehead was wounded, and blood was spurting from his cut ear and soaking into the white linen of the sheets and pillowcase.

'You won't get me this time,' Isobel was saying over and over again. 'Not this time.'

Theo staggered to his feet and backed toward the door, still holding the blood soaked pillow in front of him, he reached back for the light switch and flicked it on. The light seemed to slow her down, her hand froze in mid-air and she allowed the knife to drop to the floor. She seemed horrified by what she had done.

'Theo, I, I . . . Oh, oh, what have I done?'

Theo was trying to staunch the flow of blood, the wound on his forehead was little more than a scratch but his ear was bleeding profusely.

Isobel took a step toward him.

'No,' he said. 'Don't come any closer.'

He reached for his dressing gown and wriggled into it, never for a moment taking his eyes off his wife. 'I'll be back tomorrow for my things,' he said. 'And we'll talk — make fair arrangements. You can continue to live here.'

She nodded. She looked perplexed as if she had just woken from a nightmare.

Theo backed out of the room, made his way down

the stairs and out of the front door. He crossed the garden just as the cold grey dawn was breaking and banged on Zoë's door.

A month previously Theo Sheldon-Harris would have told anyone that he considered that he hadn't an enemy in the world. Now it seemed there was more than one person that hated him.

Zoë answered the door. 'What's happened? Why are you here? I thought — Oh God, Theo, you're hurt, you're bleeding.'

'Don't worry,' he said. 'It looks worse than it is.' He looked at her. He may have enemies but he also had love, and if one had to go with the other, then he'd take them both as they came, and gladly.

'I came for medical assistance, and besides, I've decided that I do want to take you to Andy's wedding after all.'

'What?'

'Never mind, just get your first aid kit. We've got the rest of our lives together — they'll be time enough to explain later.'

Chapter 28

'Mummy would like this house,' Tiggy said pushing her hands under her head and stretching her naked body back into the mattress.

'Would she?'

'Yes, she'd love the pictures especially, and the dinner service. It's Haddon Hall isn't it? It's her favorite, and she loves white linen sheets, and flowers, flowers everywhere.'

'Don't you like those things?'

'Yes, but only because she's taught me to like them.'

'Your sister? Would she like them?'

Tiggy gave it some thought. 'Yes, but not as much as me, she's more like my father, sort of an outdoorsy sort of person. I'm more like my mother.'

'Yes, you're very like her.'

He was lying beside her, also with his hands tucked behind his head and also naked.

'How would you know?'

'I told you, I B and B'd at Hulver many times.'

'I don't think you stayed there that much. I'd have remembered you, I'd have lusted after you even then.'

'You were much too young and innocent.'

'Anyway, you must come to Hulver and meet the

folks. They'll say you're much too old for me, of course, but they'll soon get over it, they can't make too big a fuss.'

'Oh?'

'Mummy's nineteen years younger than Daddy, so they can hardly mind, can they? We'll go next weekend, shall we? I'll 'phone them and organize it.'

Alex rubbed his chin. What the hell was he doing in bed with Lavinia's daughter? There was something slightly incestuous about bedding your ex-mistress's child. If Lavinia had kept to her promise and married him, Tiggy would be his stepdaughter, but Lavinia hadn't seen it through, and Tiggy wasn't his stepdaughter. She was so like her mother, apart from the fact that Tiggy was honey blond and Lavinia was dark. She was just a younger version of the woman that he'd loved; she even made love in the same way, — a way that Alex never wanted to end.

'I don't think that's such a good idea, Tiggy. I don't think your mother will approve of me being with you.'

'Don't be silly, darling, she'll adore you. She'll soon get over the age thing.' She leaned over and kissed him fully on the lips. 'She can't help but like you.'

Alex returned her kiss. 'I don't think so,' he murmured. He reached up and cupped her small firm breasts in his hands. She had the most perfect body, a younger more perfect version of the woman he still hankered after.

' I so want to tell them about you.' She rolled over on top of him and, starting at his nipples, she began to kiss and caress his body, working her way down to his groin.

'Mmm,' he said lifting his hips. 'She won't like it if she thinks her daughter is doing that to me.'

'She wouldn't understand *what* it is, I'm doing,' Tiggy said.

'Oh, I think she would.'

'Hah, a-hah, you don't know my mother very well. She can be quite a prude.'

'Uh, uh,' he said lifting his hips a little higher. 'God, that's good, but watch it, or you'll take me beyond the point of no return.'

'That's okay. High protein, low fat, low calorie, perfect for my new diet.'

He pushed her head down onto him. 'That's good, because you have taken things too far.'

Tiggy coughed and spluttered. 'Christ, Tiggy, you always get it right.'

She swallowed and flopped down beside him. 'You owe me one now,' she said.

'Twenty minutes recovery time, isn't it? Bet I can get it up in ten?'

'You know you can, Alex Kirby, you're bloody oversexed you are. God, and I thought that men over forty were past it.'

'Foolish girl,' he said. He was already becoming hard. He rolled her over, hooked her ankles over his shoulder and entered her. Vinnie, Vinnie, he thought, see

216

what you've driven me to? I don't know if it's her I want, or you. Am I just seeing you in her, or did I see her in you. Is she the one I've been waiting for?

'I do know your mother,' he said as he drove into her.

'What?'

'You said I didn't know her, and I'm telling you I do.'

'You mean from B and B?'

'I was her lover.'

Tiggy started to giggle. 'Alex, don't make me laugh.'

'She was the best fuck I ever had.' It pleased him to use crude terms when speaking of Lavinia. His eyes were tightly shut; a glazed look had overtaken his features. 'Next to you that is.' He was pummeling into her. Sweat was running down his forehead and dripping off his eyebrows onto her chest.

Tiggy pulled her arms up to his shoulders and forced him deeper into her.

'You're fantasizing about her,' she said. She sounded amused as if she were enjoying the game.

'I don't need to now, not now I have you, you're so very like her.'

He suddenly pulled out of her. 'Turn over,' he said. She did as she was bid and knelt on all fours. He entered her from behind. Her back was amazingly like Lavinia's. She even had that funny little collection of moles on her right shoulder blade, or were Lavinia's moles on her left side? Had he forgotten? No, no he mustn't forget, Vinnie was his lifeline, her memory was the only thing that made his life worth living. There'd been girls, lots of them since his affair with Lady Hulver. Dinner dates and one night stands, but no one that he'd wanted to see more than once; until he met Tiggy.

'I love your back,' he said. 'Oh, Vinnie, I love your back.'

He felt Tiggy stiffen. 'You're not serious, are you?' she whispered. 'Alex, I don't really like this game.'

Afterwards, as they lay in bed together, Tiggy mentioned her mother again. 'Alex, you were joking, right? About—'

'About your mother and I being lovers?'

'Yes.'

'How would you feel about me if it were true?'

'It isn't, is it?'

'Answer me first, how would you feel about me?'

Tiggy was quiet for a moment. 'But it isn't true, right? You were joking, weren't you?'

Alex sucked in his breath, there seemed no point in lying, besides, it still hurt, and using it as a weapon to hurt Tiggy would, he thought, lesson his pain. 'Actually, no, I was her lover for four years, then she ditched me.'

'That's not very funny, Alex.'

'No.' He sighed and stared up at the ceiling. 'It's not very funny, not very funny at all, Tiggy. I'm not joking, she really did break my heart.'

'Yes, you are.' She poked him in the ribs. 'You are, aren't you?' She giggled, but there was an edge of panic in her voice. 'My mother and you! Yeah, right, good one Alex.'

He felt slighty annoyed that she didn't believe him. And, even if he could have retracted what he'd already said, he didn't want to. Besides she was bound to find out sooner or later. He had always believed that honesty was the best policy, his job had taught him that. But her face told him that she wouldn't just be hurt, she'd be mortally wounded. For a split second he considered laughing it off, but he couldn't hold back. Memories of Lavinia Elliot haunted his every waking hour, and sleeping with Tiggy was the nearest he'd come to laying that particular ghost. Maybe this was his chance, maybe now he could exorcise it for good, maybe a confession could rid him of his obsession.

Tiggy was leaning up on one elbow, staring down at him. Her face looked very white, and he could see that her bottom lip was trembling.

'Alex, this isn't funny anymore, it's a joke in very poor taste. You're talking about my mother, remember? Now, tell me that you're joking.' It was more of a plea than a request

'No,' he said sadly. 'I'm not joking, Tiggy. I wish

for all the world I was. In fact she came this close to leaving Josh and coming here to me. I filled this place with all her favourite things.' He was watching her intently trying to gauge her reaction. He'd already lost Lavinia, what if he lost Tiggy, her doppelganger, as well.

Tiggy's face relaxed and she fell back into the pillow. 'Oh, yes,' she giggled. 'Now I *know* you're teasing me.'

'I can prove it,' he said.

'Sure you can, mind if you explain how?'

'Well, when she walked out on Josh—'

'My mother never walked out on my father,' she interrupted. 'Alex, you're such a fool.'

Alex ignored her.

'She packed a small case, she was to send for the rest of her things later. She'd arranged to meet me in Starky's restaurant. She came, but only to tell me that she'd changed her mind.' Alex closed his eyes; he could see it as if it were yesterday. 'She went haring off to Hulver and left the case in Starky's cloakroom. They gave it to me. I still have it.'

She laughed again. 'No wonder you win all your cases, you had me going there for a minute. Trouble is,' she pointed her index finger at him, 'I know my mother.'

He was cross that she didn't believe him. Was it so preposterous that a beautiful woman like Lavinia should prefer him to the stuffy man she was married to?

220

'I can show you the case?'

'Go on then.' She was still laughing.

He went to his wardrobe and retrieved Lavinia's small overnight bag. He brought it back to the bed and unclipped it. He watched as the smile disappeared from Tiggy's face and a frown replaced it. She picked up one or two of the garments.

'Where did you get this?'

'I told you.'

'No, no, be sensible, Alex. You stole it, didn't you? You stole it from Hulver.' She had a frantic look about her; her eyes darted around the room as if searching for a logical explanation.

'I'm sorry,' he said. 'Bit of a dramatic way to tell you — sort of thing I'd do in court to shoot the prosecution down in flames — haven't handled things very well, have I?'

Her face told him that she believed what he'd said. She wriggled out of bed, and started to hunt for her clothes.

'Don'tbe stupid, Tiggy, you're overreacting. Where do you think you're going? You can't go back to Edinburgh at this time of night.'

'I'm going to see my mother, I'm going to ask her the truth.'

'I've told you the truth.'

'She wouldn't, I know she wouldn't. She loves my father.

'And your father loves Hulver. That's why she came to me.'

'That is so not true. Daddy loves Mummy more than anything in the world — why, they even had a second honeymoon last year. They went to Venice. Does that sound like a marriage that's breaking up?'

Without knowing it, Tiggy had dealt him a blow — and it hurt. How could Lavinia have holidayed with Josh in such a way? Was he nothing to her that she could forget him so quickly?

'I love you, Tiggy,' he suddenly said. The words sounded right, but he wasn't sure that they were true.

'What?'

'I said, I love you, and if we can work through this, I want to marry you.'

'What? But you've only known me for five minutes.'

'Give me a chance, Tiggy? Let me prove myself to you.'

'And my mother?'

'Was the catalyst that brought us together.'

'But—'

He took her in his arms. 'Just one chance, Tiggy, just one.'

She leaned into his chest. 'But what about Ma?'

'She'll have to learn to live with it.' But then he silently added, and she'll have to learn to live with her mistake, I've had to.

Chapter 29

Isobel Sheldon-Harris paced up and down the kitchen waiting for Theo. Several times she sat down and did the deep breathing exercises that Margery had advised. She wished Theo would come and get it over with. Last night she'd been sorry that she'd acted the way she had. It was against her personal commandments. But this morning, after speaking to Margery, she'd realized that she had acted in the best possible way. She had a duty to try and break the cycle; it wasn't so much Theo she was trying to kill but the evil spirit that inhabited him. It was a case of kill or be killed; it was strange that Randall had come as her husband; according to Margery he could just as well have come back as her father or her son or even her sister. Reincarnates often changed both their sex and their relationships. But Randall had come back as Theo, and Isobel had fallen into the same trap as she had hundreds of years before.

She put the kettle on; some herb tea would calm her. She held her hand up to her head; she was so tired, so very tired. She'd stayed awake all night trying to contact her spirit guide. When that had failed, she'd tried to telephone Margery, but it was still the early hours of the morning, and her friend hadn't picked up. She hadn't got hold of her until almost lunchtime. She hadn't been able to wait that long, so finally, in desperation, she'd called her daughter Charlotte.

She regretted doing that now. Charlotte was quite scathing about Spirit; she thought it nonsense; she was always telling Isobel that she was crazy. Maybe she was right? She hadn't really known what she was doing last night. She'd been quite horrified when Theo had flicked the light on and she'd been faced with all that blood. She didn't remember getting the knife and she hardly remembered stabbing Theo with it. Thank goodness she had Margery to help and advise her, she'd soon made Isobel see the error of her ways; she'd soon made her shrug off all feelings of remorse.

The back door opened and then closed. He had a cheek just walking in like that. She'd expected him to knock. He'd left last night and gone to her. Isabel couldn't bear to speak her name; she'd forever be *her*, an unnamed adversary, whose tools of seduction were sex and wickedness.

'Hi!' Charlotte Bridges swept into the kitchen.

'Charlotte! What are you doing here? I thought you were Theo.'

'What do you mean, what am I doing here? You called me at three o'clock this morning and told me that you thought you'd killed Theo! Three a.m. mother! Flora was furious, absolutely furious. I nearly drove down there and then, in the middle of the night, but Flora wouldn't let me.'

Isobel's lips tightened at the mention of Charlotte's girlfriend's name. She heartily disapproved of her laid-back attitude, the relationship she and Charlotte shared. It was unnatural, the thought of her beautiful daughter and the fleshy Flora in bed together made her skin crawl. Flora, like Charlotte, was an actress and seemed to be more out of work than in. Sometimes Isobel blamed herself for Charlotte's sexuality, maybe if she hadn't deserted the child . . . it was yet another cross she had to bear.

'I can stay the night, but I have to be back in London by two o'clock tomorrow. I've an audition. It's a television play, and they could make it into a series. It's too good an opportunity to miss. I desperately want the part.' She straightened herself up to her full five feet five, 'and I'm going to get it, even if I have to sleep with the producer.' Isobel bit back her question, she was wondering if the producer was male or female.

Isobel swallowed, her daughter sounded exactly as she had when she was her age. Isobel had a lot to answer for. She should have taken the child with her when she left Gerry; the only reason she hadn't was because she'd known Theo would disapprove. At least, that's what she'd convinced herself after she'd seen the light. Of course, it had all been Theo's fault; he didn't like children, that's why she'd had to leave Charlotte behind.

Isobel poured water onto the herbal teabags. 'Theo will be here in a minute. He 'phoned to say that he was on his way.'

'I thought you said you'd killed him?'

'I behaved very irrationally last night.'

'When you stabbed him? I should think you did.'

'No, I mean when I called you.'

Charlotte shook her head. 'Mother, you are the end. What's this all about? You say he's shacked up with a hot little number? Well, who can blame him? He's not getting any juice here, is he?'

'Charlotte!'

'Well, it's true. Theo's a very, very, sexy man. If you don't give him what he needs, it stands to reason that he'll go elsewhere, doesn't it?'

'You find Theo sexy?' Isobel was confused.

'God yes, I had a crush on him from the first time I met him. I've spent every holiday here for the past five years poncing around in my undies hoping he'd make a pass at me, but no such luck.'

'But I thought . . . '

'I'm bi-sexual, mother, you know, AC–DC, that way you get the best of both worlds.'

'Oh God, Theo's evil spirit has bewitched even my child,' Isobel cried out and jammed her fist into her mouth to stifle her grief.

Charlotte Bridges at twenty-four was almost the same age as Zoë Elliot, but she lacked Zoë's fair locks. She wore her ash-brown hair in a bob that swept back from her forehead and finished just below her ears. She had a straight nose, a broad smile and wide-apart, very light brown eyes.

Her complexion contrasted with her hair; her skin was the colour and texture of porcelain and her lips were full and exquisitely shaped. She had a slim, slight, figure, was nimble and light of foot, and she gesticulated wildly when she spoke. She was excitable and given to sudden outbursts of passion, and she liked to be center stage in every situation.

'I don't understand you,' Charlotte said, bending over her mother's chair. 'You used to be quite a girl in your time. I've seen a video of you on stage, yet you come all this prim and proper stuff with me, as if butter wouldn't melt in your mouth. And don't tell me all that crap about seeing the light. It's all in your head, mother. Why don't you go and take those ridiculous clothes off and get into something more, well, more normal. You look like an out of work nun dressed all in black.' She sighed. 'You're still a good looking woman, or at least you could be, if you tried a bit.'

Isobel sighed too. She knew that she must put up with Charlotte's ranting and her skepticism. Margery had explained it to her. It was Isobel's punishment for all the wickedness she'd done in her youth.

'If you want Theo back, then you must make a bit of an effort. I know Theo. Just lay the guilt trip on him a bit, and he'll be back here in no time.'

'But I don't want him back. You see, if he comes back then he and—'

Charlotte jammed her hands over her ears. 'Oh

please! Not all this past life nonsense, not the Gibbet Hill scenario again. There *is* no past life. Theo is not out to kill you.' She shook her head, 'You're one crazy lady, you really are.'

'Charlotte, you just don't understand. Theo has made a pact with the devil—'

'Absolutely right,' said Theo. 'Hello, Lottie, I'm really glad to see you here.' He bent and kissed Charlotte first on one cheek and then the other. He took a step toward his wife but she shied away from him.

He pulled a chair out from the kitchen table and sat himself down. Isobel sat opposite him. He had a plaster over the cut on his forehead, and his ear was covered with a large piece of lint. But his face looked jolly as if he hadn't a care in the world.

'Coffee, Theo?' Charlotte asked.

'Love one,' he replied.

'Not poisoned, is it mother?'

Isobel didn't answer. Charlotte was acting in a ridiculous manner; she couldn't imagine why she'd telephoned her in the night. Theo had sapped her of her strength — that was it. He had rendered her weak and vulnerable.

The three of them sat at the kitchen table.

'So?' said Charlotte, 'What's to be done?'

'Theo must leave.' Isobel said.

'Aren't we forgetting something? This happens to

be my house.'

'You said last night I could stay.'

'When someone's threatening you with a knife, you'll say anything.'

'This is her house as much as it is yours,' Charlotte butted in.

'I don't think so.' Theo said.

'If you want her to leave you'll have to pay her off.'

'I'm broke, Charlotte. Lloyds took every penny I had.'

'Huh, you still have plenty left. This house, alone, must be worth a fortune.'

'Yes but—'

'You'll have to sell it and give Mother half.'

'I can't do that.'

'Why not? She's entitled to it.'

Isobel sat, her arms folded in front of her, looking from one to the other. Then she said, 'I won't leave here.' She spoke very calmly and quietly. 'Spirit tells me I should stay. I must not wander the world.'

'I wasn't suggesting you wandered.' Charlotte said. 'But you must have money to live on.'

'I'll give her half my income,' Theo said.

'It's not enough, ' Charlotte replied. 'She needs a chunk of capital.'

Theo shook his head. 'Lottie, this has nothing to do

229

with you.'

'Yes it does, it's my inheritance you're both talking about.'

'What? But you're not my child.'

'I'm the nearest thing you have. I'm your stepchild.'

'I'll soon have another stepchild, and I may have children of my own.'

'More of the devil's children.' Isobel hissed.

Charlotte scraped her chair away from the table. 'Mother won't divorce you, ever.'

'Your mother tried to kill me last night. Wouldn't it make sense to have a clean break? I could probably borrow enough money to get her a nice little house somewhere and, as I said, she's welcome to half my income.'

Isobel rose, she still had her arms folded in front of her. 'I'm going to my room,' she said. 'Theo, you can take anything you want so long as it's not mine. Then leave, and don't come back. I'm having new locks fitted to the doors this afternoon, so there's no point in you trying to get in.' Never once taking her eyes off Theo she backed out of the room.

Theo rubbed his chin. His jovial mood had left him and he looked sullen and depressed. 'God, Lottie, what am I going to do?'

'You'll have to pay up, Theo, baby.'

'You know that's not the answer. You know she's

quite, quite mad, don't you?'

'I know you're trying to do her down. She needs a chunk of capital, Theo.'

'She does, or you do? What are you doing here anyway?'

Charlotte shrugged. 'She said she needed me.'

'Did she, indeed? You don't usually come at her command.' He shook his head. 'Stay out of this, Lottie.'

'You said you were glad to see me when you came.'

He smiled. 'I was, I thought you were going to talk some sense into her.'

'I'll get her a lawyer.'

'Good idea, as long as he knows I'm not Rothschild.'

'She, Theo. Don't you know that the female is more deadly than the male?'

Theo rubbed his forehead and got up to go. 'Tell your mother I'll let her have a list of what I want, she can send it down to me. It looks like she and I will be close neighbors for sometime to come.'

'You're a fool, Theo. Sell up, split the profit, and go your separate ways.'

'My life's here Lottie, you should realize that. I was born in this house and I intend to die in it.'

'You bloody nearly did,' Charlotte said and laughed.

Theo ignored her. 'And I'm still hoping that my children will be born here.'

'You won't get rid of mother that easily, Theo. You're a fool, Theo, you can't hope to win. Ask my father if you've any doubts about that.'

Chapter 30

Theo's arm flopped over and onto the sleeping Zoë. He snuggled up to her.

'I can't ever remember being this happy,' he said.

She was sleepy, her eyes were heavy and her body totally relaxed. 'Nor I,' she breathed.

'It's Sunday. Let's go to church.'

'Church!' She was fully awake now. She screwed up her nose. 'Church?'

'Yes, you know, that funny Carstone building with a big tower and a lot of seats.'

She poked him in the ribs. 'Ha—ha, very funny, but why d'you want to go to church?'

'To thank God for you, of course.'

'I don't think *God* would quite approve of our relationship.'

'And I think you're wrong, I think it's you that doesn't quite approve. We've been together for over a month, and it's high time we told the world exactly where the land lies.'

'And where *exactly* does it lie?'

He put his hand on her right breast. 'Here, right here my love. My heart is in this land, and my heart is lodged with you.'

'You're such a sentimental fool, Theo.'

'You'll come then.'

'What about Betsy?'

'She'll come too, she's all part and parcel of the deal, isn't she?'

'Yes.'

'You'll come then?'

'Theo, I—'

He kissed her. 'Good, I'll go and make some tea. Betsy's awake, I can hear her singing to herself.'

It was Zoë's weekend off; it was Andy's turn to check the flock.

At breakfast Zoë said, 'Theo? Can we go to Hulver?'

'Hulver! You mean to church? But won't your parents be there?'

She steadily held his gaze. 'Yes, I expect so.'

'But if we're together, what will your father think?'

'He'll think whatever Mummy tells him to think.'

Theo raised his eyebrows.

'Well, it's hardly fair to let them hear though the gossip vine, is it?'

Theo let out a sigh, shook his head, and then smiled broadly. 'We'd better get a move on then.' He left the room whistling.

They were late. Perhaps Zoë took longer than usual to dress and organize Elizabeth in a subconscious effort to arrive at church after her parents. Or perhaps the journey from Garrick-in-the-Willows to Hulver was further than Theo remembered. Either way, the bell was ringing and the gravel path between the dark yew trees was deserted as Zoë, with Theo beside her carrying Elizabeth, breathlessly hurried into the south porch.

Miss Randall, a descendant, no doubt, of the infamous wife killer, smiled warmly at Zoë as she handed out service and hymn books.

Zoë knew that her parents would be sitting in the very front pew on the left. The Elliots had occupied the same place in Hulver Church for generations.

'Let's sit here, at the back,' Theo hissed.

But Zoë either didn't hear, or she chose not to hear him. She walked boldly down the center isle and planted herself in the front right-hand pew opposite her parents. Theo, still holding Elizabeth, followed shyly behind.

The child, who had recently found her feet, immediately spotted her grandmother and tried to wriggle out of Theo's arms.

'Ga-ga, Ga-ga,' she cried.

There was no help for it. Theo released her and she toddled over to her startled but delighted Grandmother, who, with a look of pride, scooped the child up into her arms. Lavinia smiled happily at Zoë and mouthed 'Hello' to Theo. The vicar had by now finished reading the notices, and the organ struck the first cords of the first hymn.

As soon as the service was over and the small congregation had made its way to the back of the church, Lavinia, holding her grandchild by the hand, made her way across the isle to her daughter.

'Darling, how lovely to see you, and, Theo,' she held out her hand, 'how nice of you to bring her over.'

Theo looked guiltily at his feet. Maybe this hadn't been such a good idea.

Elisabeth wriggled free of Lavinia's grasp, and now begged Theo for attention. Theo picked her up and absently kissed the top of the child's blonde head; Lavinia raised an eyebrow.

Zoë, catching her mother's gesture, raised her own eyebrows and looked defiant.

Josh, who'd been talking to the church warden, joined them.

'Theo, how very nice to see you. Hello, darling.' He kissed his daughter and shook Theo by the hand. 'You'll come back for a drink?'

Theo looked at his watch. 'Better be getting back,' he said

'Yes, Pa, we'd love to,' Zoë said at the same time.

'Good, that's settled then.' He took Theo by the arm. 'No good arguing with the women, Theo. I used to try it myself when I was younger, but constant defeat wears a fellow down. Much less trouble to accept the inevitable and give in gracefully.'

Theo smiled and allowed himself to be led away.

'Tell you what,' Josh continued, 'I'll come back to the castle with you in your car, and Vinnie can bring the girls. They'll be full of women's talk, no doubt.'

'Nice of Theo to bring you over,' Lavinia said again, once they were settled in the car. 'I mean, it's quite a drive isn't it? I'm quite surprised that Isobel—'

'Oh, Ma, are you blind? Isn't it obvious that Theo and I are an item.'

'An item? Whatever does that mean? That you're sleeping with him? Is that what it means?' She shook her head and didn't give Zoë time to voice a reply. 'Oh, Zoë, Zoë, think about what you're doing. I knew it, when I saw you a couple of months ago, I knew. It was Valentine's Day, he was taking you out to lunch and I knew then, of course I did. I said as much to your father. I'm not a fool, I could tell he was trying to seduce you.'

Zoë smiled, if anything she was the guilty one, it was as much she as he. She couldn't get enough of him; she was both in lust and in love with him.

'Why are you smiling? He's married, Zoë, he can never—'

'Never what? Make an honest woman of me?'

Lavinia was extremely agitated. 'He'll never leave Isobel. You know that, don't you? She's an unstable woman at the best of times, and she has him wrapped around her little finger. If Isobel says 'jump', then Theodore Sheldon-

237

Harris, jumps.'

Zoë looked rather smug. 'He's already left her — we're living together, Ma. That's what I mean when I say that we're an item.'

Lavinia drew the car to the side of the road. Theo, who was following on, stopped behind them, jumped out and came to Lavinia's window.

'Everything all right? Got a problem?'

Lavinia's face was set. Zoë shook her head and gesticulated that Theo should go away.

'No, everything is not all right,' Lavinia said, winding down her window. 'Far from it. I'm just having a few words with *my* daughter, who is still only twenty-three years old, you know?'

'Ah,' Theo said 'I'll see you back at the castle then.'

Lavinia rewound her window and Theo returned to his car.

'Everything all right?' Josh said.

Theo started the engine and drove away. 'Not really, Sir. Zoë's just explaining to her mother that . . . well . . . . that er . . . that we're moving in together.'

'Who? Not you and Zoë?'

When Theo didn't answer, Josh said, 'Well of course you're talking about you and Zoë, who else?' Then he said, 'she's a lovely girl, my Zoë. She's had a rough ride, what with all that business to do with Steve, and then with

238

Betsy's father. She's over all that now, thank goodness. Let's hope that it's third time lucky.'

'I'll do my best for her, and we'll marry just as soon as we're able.'

'I've no worries there my boy, you're a gentleman and the word of a gentleman still counts, even these days.'

'I'm a lot older than her,' Theo said, as if he needed to get all the facts on the table.

'Good thing too. I know you wouldn't think it, but I'm nineteen years older than Vinnie, and half the year I'm twenty years older than her, so she always says I'm twenty years older, and I always say I'm nineteen.' He chuckled. 'Works well, the woman being younger.' He smiled and looked rather dreamy. 'She needs someone like you, Theo, a bit of stability in her life. But what about little Betsy? Take the child on as well, will you?'

'As if she were my own.'

'Good man. Well, we'll pop a bottle of bubbly when we get home. I think a celebration's in order. Decent of you to come and tell us, better than hearing the gossip. When are you going to, I mean, you'll have arrangements to make and—'

'I already have, we've been living together for about a month.'

'At the Hall? That's more like it, I must confess I didn't much like a daughter of mine cooped up in that little cottage, and shepherding for a living—'

'But—'

'Not that she's not good at it. I take my hat off to her for what she's done, but it'll be nice for her to have a more ladylike existence.'

'Hang on, Josh, I should come clean. I've moved into the cottage with Zoë. Isobel's at the Hall, I could hardly throw her out, could I?'

'I don't see why not, she's as mad as a hatter, isn't she? Someone told me she hears voices from the dead.'

'I can't throw her out, Josh.'

'Well, with any luck she'll get out herself, given time. As soon as she sees there's no welcome there for her—'

'Josh, I don't expect her to leave. Zoë and I are happy in the cottage. Very happy in fact—'

Josh's mind seemed to have gone into overdrive.'The tenancy to Applegate Farm is up in September. Arthur's retiring and his son doesn't want to take it on, he's something in the city. Why don't you move there and rent out your own farm. That way—'

'Thanks, Josh, but I'm already a tenant, remember? I lost the estate to Lloyds? I can't sublet, besides, I wouldn't want to leave Garrick.'

'No, no I can understand that. I know I'd feel the same way about Hulver. Not that I could envisage life without Vinnie, whether it was at Hulver or anywhere else. There was a time when . . . but I won't bore you with all that.'

'Thank you, Josh.'

'What on earth for?'

'Understanding,' he took his eye off the road and glanced toward him. 'Giving us your blessing, I suppose.'

They drew up in front of the castle and Josh went straight to the cellar and retrieved a bottle of champagne. 'Come on, it's a lovely day, we'll take this out to the garden, have it all ready for when the ladies get here. I can't think what's keeping them. Probably discussing wedding dresses and the like.'

'I think that would be a little premature,' Theo murmured under his breath.

Meanwhile Lavinia and Zoë were having a much more heated discussion.

'He's old enough to be your father, Zoë.'

'There's about the same difference between us as there is between you and Pa.'

'That is hardly the point.'

'It's exactly the point.'

'You're father was not a married man, Theo is. And if you think he'll leave his wife for you, you're more naive than I thought. You're just a diversion to him. He'll stay with you just so long as it suits him, and then he'll be back to his wife. Married people like Theo don't walk out on everything for the sake of a bit on the side.'

'Is that why you didn't go to Alex?'

Lavinia's features froze. 'What?'

'Alex Kirby. He was your bit on the side, wasn't he?' Lavinia's eyes widened, her mouth worked but she didn't utter a sound. Her face had become a deathly white.

'I didn't believe Tiggy when she told me,' Zoë gave a funny little laugh. 'I thought you'd deny it.'

Lavinia went to speak.

'There's no point, Ma, I can see it in your face.' She bit her lips together, then said, 'How dare you lecture me? How can you condemn Theo?'

'Because I did the right thing. I stayed with your father, we were going through a very, very, difficult time, what with Lloyds, and all the financial pressure that put on us.'

'Theo went through Lloyds, and he didn't—'

'Didn't what? Didn't go astray, well he's certainly making up for it now, isn't he? He'll go under. Isabel will make sure of that. And he's chosen to drag our family name down with him. You don't know what you're letting yourself in for.'

'As soon as he's divorced we'll get married.'

'Divorced? He'll never divorce, and do you know why? He can't afford to. He'll lose Garrick and he'll not risk that'

'Is that why you stayed with Pa? Because you couldn't bear to give Hulver up? That's what Alex says.'

'How do you know Alex? What did he tell you?

242

'I don't know him, as a matter of fact I've never met him.'

'Then . . .'

'Tiggy's in love with him.'

'What? Don't be ridiculous, he's — well — how, how does she know him?'

'He went to lecture in Edinburgh and met Tiggy and they're . . .'

'What? What are they?'Her eyes flashed.

'Inseparable.'

Lavinia slumped down in her seat.

Zoë put a hand on her mother's arm. 'Ma, I don't want to hurt you, but—'

'Is that why Tiggy doesn't visit anymore? She hasn't been home for ages.'

'I think she intends to come home next weekend, she's planning to surprise you.'

'With him? Is she bringing him with her?'

Zoë nodded.

'But she can't do that — why is she doing that?' There were tears in Lavinia's eyes. 'What does he see in Tiggy anyway? He's doing it to get to me, you know. He's using Tiggy—'

'Ma! Stop it. What are you saying?'

'He loved me, he'll always love me. Don't you understand, it's the one comfort I have.'

'Think of that, when you're in Pa's bed, do you?'

Zoë said scathingly.

'No. You don't understand, you'll never understand. Alex and I had something special, but it has nothing to do with your father or with Tiggy.' Tears were falling fast now; she wiped her cheeks on the back of her hand. 'He's taken Tiggy to punish me. He doesn't love her.'

Zoë was looking very angry. 'How can you possibly say that? How can you *know* what's going on in his head.'

'I know, believe me, I know.'

'I think they're happy together.'

Lavinia sniffed. 'I thought you'd never met him.'

'I haven't, but talking to Tiggy—'

Lavinia grabbed her arm. 'You must try and break it up. He's no good for her, he'll break her heart.'

Zoë snatched her hand away. 'You know what I think? I think you're jealous, jealous of me, and of Tiggy. You're past love and excitement, and you can't bear it that your daughters have found it.'

Lavinia pushed the car into gear and drove off, they continued the rest of the journey in silence and neither spoke until they reached the long drive leading up to the honey coloured castle.

'Zoë? Don't mention this to your father will you?'

'I love Pa, I'm not about to hurt him.'

'Thank you, I only hope in time you'll—'

'Understand?'

'Forgive me.'

'Oh, Mummy.'

'It's been a long time since you called me that.'

'Look, there's Pa and Theo waiting for us, what's he holding? It's champagne, oh how lovely.'

'You'll stay to lunch won't you, Zoë?'

'Well I . . .'

'Please, I'd like you to, we'd both like you to.'

Chapter 31

Josh had looked concerned when she said she was going to London for the day and, not for the first time, she suspected that he knew more about her affair with Alex than he was letting on.

'I'll run you to the station, shall I?'

She'd rather he didn't. She wanted every possible moment to prepare both herself and what she was going to say. But the look on Josh's face robbed her of the ability to decline, and so she dutifully accepted.

'Meeting Brooke are you?' he asked moments before he dropped her off. Long ago she'd vowed she'd never actively lie to him again, the nearest thing she'd come to a lie would be by omission.

'No. No I'm not, not today. Gosh is that the time? I must fly or I'll miss my train, there's bound to be a long queue at the ticket booth.'

Josh checked his watch and compared it to the car clock.

'You've plenty of time Vinnie, it's only—' but she had already gone.

She reached Alex's chambers a good fifteen minutes before her appointment, but she was shown straight up to his room.

He came forward with his arms outstretched.

'Vinnie, how lovely to see you.'

She backed away from him; he grinned at her and dropped his arms. 'You're looking very lovely, and very, very serious.'

He flicked back his cuff and looked at his watch. 'It's almost twelve, lets go and have a pre-lunch drink shall we?'

'I'd rather not. I'd rather say what I've got to say, here.' She sunk her teeth into her bottom lip.

He picked up a black, tightly rolled, umbrella. 'Looks like rain, we'd better take a brolly.' He walked past her to the door. He paused in the entrance and said, 'I only do business here, and you're not here on business, are you, Vinnie?'

'Alex, I—' but he was striding ahead and had already reached the top of the stairs.

She had no choice but to follow after him.

She remembered the wine bar from her days spent with him. Everything looked exactly as it had looked before, the tables held the same high polished sheen and the mirrors around the walls were still blotched and stained in the same old fashioned manner. Nothing had changed, nothing at all, except her relationship to the good-looking man that now sat opposite her.

He placed a glass before her. 'Still Chardonnay, is it?'

She picked the glass up and instead of the intended

sip, found herself taking a large gulp.

She cleared her throat. She felt extremely hot and her voice seemed to have disappeared. He, on the other hand, looked very cool and very relaxed.

'You know why I'm here,' she said, and coughed again. Her throat seemed constricted; she felt she was unable to get the words out.

'Do I?'

'Alex, stop it, stop pretending. You know how I feel about it.'

'About what?'

'You and Tiggy.'

He raised his eyebrows. 'Ah, a little bird's been talking, has it?'

'Zoë told me — Alex, you can't do this.'

'Really?' he smiled and she could have slapped his face.

'I don't understand why you're doing this, Alex? Why Tiggy?'

'She reminds me of you, why else?'

'Tiggy's not a bit like me.'

'Oh, she is, believe me, she is.' He leaned forward across the table. 'She even whimpers like you when she comes.'

'Alex!'

'And the things she does to me, well, I almost believe that you've been giving her lessons.'

Lavinia was shaking, not with anger, but with something deeper than anger, something that verged on hatred. This then, was her day of reckoning. Tears welled up in her eyes, she put her hand close to his and he grasped it. 'Alex please, please don't—'

'Tiggy makes me feel close to you. It's as simple as that. She's the next best thing, I suppose.' He suddenly looked extremely sad. 'But Tiggy isn't you.'

'That's right, Alex, Tiggy isn't me. So why don't you leave her alone?'

'It's in your own hands, Vinnie.'

'Please don't call me that.'

'Vinnie? Why? Is it a name reserved for present bedmates only?'

'That's cheap, Alex.'

'Desperate people get pretty cheap, they'll do anything in order to get what they want.'

'Even break a young girl's heart?'

'Tiggy's heart's not broken. She loves me.'

'But you don't love her.'

'Could you bear it if I did?'

Lavinia swallowed, her throat was thickening up again.

'No, I thought not,' he said. He took a sip of his wine and refilled both of their glasses.

Lavinia took a hefty mouthful.

'I could bear anything for my children, what I can't

bear is you deliberately hurting her.'

He grabbed her arm. 'Vinnie, have you any idea what you did to me that day? Have you any idea how much I loved you?'

She closed her eyes tight. He was saying things that she didn't want to hear.

'I still love you, Vinnie. I will always love you. I'll drop Tiggy tomorrow, if only you'll—'

'What? Leave Josh?'

He held both his hands in front of him. 'No. No, I'm not asking you to do that anymore. I understand, believe me, I do. Josh is getting on and can't have—'

'Long to live, Alex? Is that what this is all about? Well I pray that Josh will live for a very long time. Long enough for me to make up for the wrongs I did to him—'

'No. No Vinnie, hold on. I'm not asking for a full commitment from you. I realize that's where I went wrong before. Just see me, once a week even,' he paused as if he was studying her reactions. 'Okay, once a month — yes? Just once a month?' He thrust a balled fist into the palm of his other hand. 'Don't you see? I'm addicted to you. You drive me mad. I need to see you, touch you, and love you.' he closed his eyes and shook his head. 'Oh, yes — and love you, love you.' He opened his eyes again. 'You're my drug Vinnie, and like any addict, I need an occasional fix.'

Lavinia's throat suddenly cleared. She shook her head. 'No! No! You know, Alex, I don't drive you mad —

you *are* mad. What we had is over and done with.'

He was clinging to her hands again now. 'You don't understand, I love you and I'll always love you. I'm not asking for so very much, am I? I just want a little of you.' His eyes looked wild and his cool demeanor had vanished.

Lavinia was feeling stronger and more in control by the minute. 'But Tiggy — how could you do this to Tiggy?'

He raised his eyebrows. 'Ah, Tiggy, dear, sweet, loyal Tiggy. If you turn me down, then I shall ask her to marry me. She'll accept, you know.'

Lavinia's control was seeping away from her. 'You can't do that.' She spoke too loud, too earnest. Several people standing at the bar turned and looked in their direction. 'You can't, you can't marry her unless you love her.'

'You married Josh, and you didn't love him.'

Her voice dropped. 'I grew to love him,' she whispered.

'And I shall probably grow to love Tiggy. She's a sweet girl, and so like you — it would be hard not to love her.'

'Alex, please don't do this — please, please don't do this. Think of Tiggy.' Then as if inspired, she added, 'Think of me, if you love me — as you say you do, think of me.'

He flopped back in his chair. 'I don't go along with your argument, darling. I'll be good to Tiggy, I'm well established — she'll get an entrée into the courts, she's a very bright girl by the way — she'll make an excellent lawyer. That's another thing she's inherited from you, her quick wit and her sense of reason. And just think our children will be your grandchildren.' He laughed. 'Takes a bit of getting used to, doesn't it?'

Her head was spinning. How could he, how could he? 'I thought you were a better person, Alex, I truly did.'

'Did you? Well now you know I'm not. I'm an imperfect being, just like you, just like Josh, just like the rest of mankind.'

She scraped her chair back and got up to leave. 'I shall tell Tiggy I've spoken to you. And I shall tell her about your offer.'

'Offer?'

'That you'll throw her over if I have an affair with you.'

He smiled, he was such a very good-looking man, she noticed that his temples were grizzled, and she thought that it enhanced his features. It wasn't hard to see what Tiggy saw in him.

He tapped his fingers on his lips. 'Risky. For one thing she won't believe you, and for another she might just spill the beans to Josh.'

'Josh knows,' she lied.

'Really? Knows you're here now, in this wine bar with me, does he?'

She sat down again. 'You hurt my family, and I'll kill you,' she said, She clenched her teeth together.

'Oh please, Lavinia, please.' He picked up her hand and idly kissed her fingers. She did not pull away from him. 'Remember, Vinnie? Remember what we had — what we could have again?'

Yes she remembered; she remembered his touch, his kiss. Her body was waking once again and reacting to that memory, her fingertips tingled and there was a heat in her loins. It would be so very easy, she could solve the problem; she only had to give in to her passion. Her mouth was terribly dry; she took the wine and drained the remainder into her glass and didn't give any to Alex. She took a large gulp and noisily swallowed it. His hand was under the table, rubbing on her thigh. Her days with him had been so filled with passion, she suddenly wanted to drift back into them; it wouldn't hurt would it? As long as she established some ground rules, as long as he didn't expect her to hurt Josh. Her legs fell a little apart, and his hand crept under her skirt.

'You want me as much as I want you,' he said sucking her fingers into his mouth. 'Come back to my place. Now, Vinnie — come round to the house, we've been apart for much too long.'

She got back on her feet. He threw a twenty-pound

note on the table and, putting his arm around her shoulders, he ushered her to the door.

The fresh air hit her hard, and she stumbled.

'Whoops, the sooner we get you into bed the better,' Alex said and laughed merrily.

Lavinia looked briefly into his eyes, then she looked up and down the road. A taxi was just dropping off its fare. She shrugged off Alex's arm and weaved her way over to the curb and got in. Alex followed her and settled himself beside her.

'Liverpool Street Station please,' she said.

'What? But aren't we going home?' Alex asked.

'I am,' she said, 'home to Hulver. I don't know about you. You must make your own decisions.'

Chapter 32

Zoë hung up her Barber jacket. Her back ached, but she didn't care. She'd just delivered a ewe with three fine lambs and she felt justly proud of herself. She went through to the kitchen, and put the kettle on. The kitchen clock told her that it was almost two a.m. She had to be up again in four hours. She switched the kettle off. It was silly to make tea; it would only keep her awake. She swung her head around, decided that her hair smelt of sheep and went into the bathroom. After she'd washed her hair and showered, she crept into the bedroom.

Theo was lying on his back, his arm thrown out across her side of the bed. She slipped in beside him. He stirred and muzzled up to her. 'Where've been?'

'Andy called me — there was a ewe in trouble.' She smiled into the darkness. She considered it quite a feather in her cap to have Andy ask her for help, — after all he was supposed to be the expert.

'You're a clever girl,' he said and rolled over on top of her.

'I'm a tired girl,' she replied, and wriggled out from under him.

'Oh, sorry. You should wear a nightdress.' He rocked his hips against her thigh.

'Why?'

'Maybe I wouldn't want you quite so much. I'm only flesh and blood. However I'll be a gentleman and let you get to sleep.' He turned over, his back toward her.

But Zoë couldn't sleep, he had excited her, she snuggled up to his back and slipped her hand around his waist.

'I can't sleep.'

He turned back to her. 'I have something that might help.'

She felt for him. 'Well we could try it I suppose,' she said playfully. 'How exactly does it work?'

'It's a drug. I have to inject it, then it sort of works by osmosis.'

'Show me.'

'Hang on, I have to prepare the site first.' He slipped his head under the covers.

'Mmm, that's nice, that's very nice.'

They made love, but an hour later Zoë was still not asleep. Turning over in bed she saw a movement outside the window. The moon casting a shadow, she told herself. Theo was gently snoring. She slipped out of bed, went into the kitchen and made tea. She'd promised Andy that she'd relieve him at six-thirty, it was now almost five. She might as well forget about sleep.

She took the tea back to bed and, sitting with her knees up under her chin, she slowly sipped it in the half-light.

Theo stirred and squinted at the clock.

'Sorry,' she said. 'I didn't mean to wake you. Do you want some tea?'

'Is it in the pot, or a bag in a mug?'

'A pot, of course.'

'Then I'd love one.'

She brought his tea back to bed.

'What's the matter, Zoë? Why can't you sleep? You must be exhausted.'

She shrugged. 'I don't know, perhaps I'm overtired.'

'Not worried about this Skinner thing are you? It's his word against mine and who do you think they'll believe?'

Zoë didn't like to tell him that she rather thought they'd believe Skinner.

'He's always around you know. Tonight, when I went down to the farm, it was about twelve, he was lurking about.'

'In the farmyard?'

'No, he was in Parson's Lane, just outside the yard.'

'He was probably taking his dog for a walk.'

'He doesn't have a dog.'

'How do you know that?'

'Andy told me.'

'I think Andy's wrong, I'm sure he has a little

brown mongrel. Anyway, even if he hasn't, I expect he was just out for a stroll. He'll calm down soon, once the tribunals over with and he finds out that he hasn't got a leg to stand on.'

They put their cups down simultaneously and Theo snuggled down into the bed pulling Zoë down after him.

'I know the problem,' he said. 'I didn't give you quite enough sleeping potion. I'm afraid you'll have to have another injection.'

'All right, you're the doctor,' she murmured. 'I'll try and be brave, it won't hurt will it?'

'I'll be as gentle as I can.'

'Oh, Theo, if it has to be done then get just get it over with,' she giggled.

When the alarm went off an hour later it woke them both from a deep, deep sleep.

Zoë collected the mugs from beside the bed and, naked, she took them through to the kitchen. She snapped open the kitchen curtains and gazed over the parkland, it looked wonderful in the early morning light. The movement across the meadow at the edge of the wood was so slight it was barely discernable; and yet it was unmistakable. Skinner was lurking there; it had to be him. She turned away from the window, and, in an effort to hide herself, she scampered into the bathroom and retrieved her clothes. Then she went back into the bedroom and alerted Theo.

Theo hastily dressed and went into the kitchen, but

all looked calm and peaceful. 'You're mistaken, darling, there's no one there.'

But Zoë knew differently, she also knew that the shadow at the window had not been her imagination. Skinner was watching her every move, and she was afraid.

Chapter 33

'Have you seen this?' Theo exclaimed, throwing a bright yellow poster onto the table. 'How dare she? How dare she humiliate me in this way?'

Zoë picked up the poster and read it. In bold type along the top it announced that Issie Sheldon-Harris could prove beyond doubt that there was life after death. The corners of the poster had been torn and it was obvious to Zoë that Theo had ripped it away from a notice board of some sort.

'Where did you get this?'

He didn't answer but continued to pace up and down. 'How could she do this? Has she no shame?'

'Isobel would say that you're humiliating her by moving in with me,' Zoë said gently.

'Isobel, yes, that's another thing. She was Issie when I met her, but it was more than my life was worth to call her by that name. Now it's suddenly trendy to be called Issie, — suits the image, no doubt.' His voice was raised and angry.

Zoë put her hand on his shoulder. 'Theo, it's all right you know — as long as she's caught up with this, she'll leave *us* alone.' It wasn't strictly true of course, and Zoë knew it. Isobel would never leave them alone, but at least the pressure might be reduced a bit. 'Where'd you get the poster from anyway?'

'The village Post Office! Can you imagine? Everyone must be laughing at her behind her back.'

'Then they'll probably understand why you left her.'

Theo stopped his pacing and paused as if in thought. 'Do you really think so?'

'Yes. Yes, I do.'

'No-one will go of course,' Theo said. 'She's a charlatan, and everyone knows it. Look at this, ten pounds a ticket. Who'll go at that price?'

Zoë shrugged and smiled as if she agreed. She'd known about the meeting for weeks and she felt now that she should have mentioned it to Theo. But the moment was never quite right; the last thing she wanted to talk about was Theo's wife. She knew how he'd react. Andy had been full of it, all the farm workers had, and Andy had already told her that several people he knew were going, and, as the meeting was to be held in Norwich, she suspected that the event might well be a sellout. Someone claiming to actually prove the existence of the afterlife was irresistible. Even Zoë was curious as to how definite proof was to be achieved.

'We'll go of course,' Theo said.

'Will we? But surely—'

'We'll be there.'

'But she might see us.'

'That's the intention, seeing us will unnerve her. She won't go through all that Randall nonsense if we're there.'

'But what if she does?'

'Then I'll stand up and tell a few home truths of my own. Only I shall concentrate on this world, not the next. I'll let them know all about Issie Sheldon-Harris, I'll tell them all about the time she was a stage act. She used to do a bit of mind-reading then you know, between taking her clothes off, that is.'

Zoë was shaking her head. 'I don't understand how you got involved with her. I mean, she was hardly your class, was she.'

Theo looked down at his shoes. 'No, but she was a class act, she really was. She was dynamic, and very, very, sexy. I'd never met anyone like her.'

Zoë swallowed, it wasn't the first time Theo had explained his early relationship with Isobel in that way, and she couldn't understand why it hurt so much. But it did hurt; it cut deep into her confidence and made her fear and loath Isobel even more.

Zoë studied the poster again. 'It's next Friday, you'll not get tickets now.'

Theo put his hand in his pocket and produced two tickets the same bright egg-yoke yellow as the poster.

'You will come with me, won't you?'

She nodded. 'Of course, but do you really think it's

such a good idea? I mean surely—'

'Please, I don't want to go on my own, I need you to be there, Zoë.'

She smiled. 'Of course.'

In truth, she was frightened. She and Theo had lived together for over a year, this was her second lambing. She loved Theo more than she'd ever thought possible, but even so, over the months, Isobel and Skinner between them had worn her down, making her afraid of her own shadow.

A house cow had been added to the livestock and Zoë had taken on the early milking; a task she loved. She thrived on the morning ritual, she felt at peace when the world still slept and she was alone with the lusty rhythm of nature. But often when Zoë returned from her early stint at the farm, Isobel would be waiting for her. Her remarks and condemnation hurt, and Zoë was weary of her rival's cutting tongue and obscure accusations. And that wasn't all. Skinner was always watching, always lurking, and he made sure she knew he was there. She was becoming obsessive about him. Theo thought she exaggerated, but he didn't stalk Theo, he stalked Zoë, and sometimes she felt that the whole world was against her. But then there was Theo, good honorable Theo, she loved him so, so, much. What's more, her daughter adored him and her parents had welcomed him with open arms. Compared with her beloved sister, Tiggy, she was in a very enviable position. She loved her man, she loved her work, and she loved the place in which she lived.

If only Skinner and Isobel weren't always on her case, then she'd be the happiest woman alive.

Chapter 34

'Lady Hulver, how nice to see you again.' Alex Kirby grinned and held out his hand.

Lavinia returned his gesture and greeted her daughter's lover.

'You remember, my husband, Josh, of course?'

'Lord Hulver, how nice. Is Tiggy here yet? Or am I too early?'

'Her train's an hour late,' Josh said. 'She says to start dinner without her, she'll get a taxi from the station. We won't of course, and either Vinnie or I will meet her.' Josh patted Alex on the shoulder. 'Come on in, my dear fellow, and what's all this nonsense about Lord and Lady Hulver? You used to call us Josh and Lavinia.'

No, thought Lavinia, *he used to call me Vinnie, or darling or other, more intimate names.*

'I'm glad Tiggy has persuaded you to join us for the weekend. You've rather monopolized her, we haven't seen her for ages. I doubt she'd be coming home tonight, if you weren't here.'

Josh guided him into what was fondly called the small drawing room, but which was in fact a room of quite grand proportions, and proceeded to offer him a drink. Alex declined, he wanted to be sober, he said, so that he could save either Josh or Lavinia turning out to meet Tiggy.

'I applaud that,' Josh said 'Can't be too careful.'

Lavinia helped herself to a hefty scotch; she felt that she needed it.

The trio settled themselves down to await Tiggy's telephone call.

'So,' said Josh. 'What's new? Defended any axe murderers since we last saw you?'

Alex smiled; it was a warm familiar smile, a smile that used to melt Lavinia's heart.

'I did have a very interesting—'

'We went to Venice the autumn before last,' Lavinia interrupted. 'Look I've sorted out the photos. It was a second honeymoon, wasn't it, Josh?' Why was she doing this, what was she trying to prove? And who was she trying to prove it to, Alex? Josh? Or was it herself?

'I don't think Alex will want to see—'

'Oh, but I do,' Alex said, almost snatching the photographs out of her hand.

'Oh dear! Floods were there? What a pity.'

'No. No, it wasn't a pity at all. Actually it made it all rather romantic,' Lavinia said, whilst at the same time Josh said:

'Yes, it was a bloody nuisance, almost ruined the trip.'

'No, darling, it was wonderful.'

'Not really, was it? I mean, when you pay that sort of money and get soaked every day it's not exactly what—'

'Josh, it was wonderful, the rain was an excellent excuse to stay in bed' She gave Alex a look of triumph.

Josh raised his eyebrow at her.

'That was another thing.' Josh said. 'We stayed at the Danielli, first rate hotel — least it used to be. I ordered a double bed, and they gave us singles, what do you think of that? I complained of course, but they didn't seem able to understand. They just pushed the beds together. Poor show, I think, when you pay those sort of prices.'

Lavinia bit into her bottom lip. Why couldn't Josh keep his mouth shut? Here was she, trying to paint a picture of married bliss, and he was destroying it. And she did so wish he wouldn't keep on about money all the time. He was playing right into Alex's hands.

'Ah,' Alex said, as if he'd just remembered something. 'I know what I was going to ask, well, two things really.' He turned and faced Josh. 'I know you're a man of the world, Sir, and I know that you realize that Tiggy and I have become very close.'

My God, Lavinia thought, *he's going to ask for her hand in marriage.*

'The thing is, we're very close and—'

'You're sharing a bed?' Josh said.

Alex nodded. 'I didn't want to be indelicate — but, yes, we live together, when Tiggy's in London, of course, not in Edinburgh, well, if I'm up there then she stays in my hotel . . . Oh, dear, I'm not making a very good job of this.'

He turned back to Lavinia. 'I know you both have very high morals—'

That was cheap Alex, she thought. *Very cheap indeed.*

'What I'm trying to say is, that if you and Josh object—'

'Not at all,' Josh boomed, 'That's between you and Tiggy, she's past the age of consent. I must say though, that we appreciate your asking. Not like in our day, hey, Vinnie? All that creeping about in draughty corridors at dead of night? Things have changed, haven't they?'

'Oh, I don't know,' Alex said. He held Lavinia's eyes with his own. 'There's still a good deal of creeping around corridors in the night, only these days they're not draughty, and it's the women just as likely to do the creeping as the men. Isn't that right, Lavinia?'

'I wouldn't know,' she snapped.

Josh raised his brows, but didn't comment on her sharpness. 'What was the other thing you were going to ask? You said there were two things.'

'Oh yes, this sounds a little silly, but I wondered if you might humor me. When I used to stay here for bed and breakfast—'

Lavinia thought he laid emphasis on the bed, but Josh didn't seem to notice.

'I slept in that lovely room at the top of the stairs, the one with the red drapes? I wondered if I could have that room again. I have such wonderful happy memories of it.' He turned and looked straight into her eyes as he said it.

She wanted to hit him, fall upon him in a mad hysterical rage. She hated him; she hated him so much; she could kill him.

'That's no problem,' Josh said, obviously flattered.

'It's not ready,' Lavinia protested. *Oh, Josh, if only you knew, I was unfaithful to you in that room. This man who sits before you and pretends he's your friend, was my lover. I crept into his bed in the middle of the night — whilst you innocently slept. I loved him and I nearly left you for him.*

'Oh yes it is,' Josh said. 'I know because I went in search of Doris today, my shirt button was loose, hanging by a thread it was. Anyway, I went in search of her and she was in there. She seemed to think that's where they'd be sleeping.'

'I've put them in the blue room,' Lavinia almost sobbed.

'But that's such a long way away from the main part of the house,' Josh said.

I know. I can't bear for him to be making love to my daughter in the room where he did it to me. Can't you understand that? She wanted to say.

'I don't mind, of course,' she tried to recover. 'It's just that I especially got the blue room ready . . . ' her voice trailed away into a whisper.

'There you are then, Alex, take your pick, Vinnie doesn't mind?'

She didn't answer, but took another gulp of her drink.

'Here comes a cab,' Josh said as headlights illuminated the far wall. 'I told her to ring from the station and we'd go and get her.'

A few moments later Tiggy bustled into the room.

'Hi, Pa, would you be a darling and settle the taxi. I've only got a twenty, and he says he hasn't change.'

Josh trundled out of the room and Tiggy looked from her mother to Alex.

'Hello, Ma,' she pecked her on the cheek. 'You do remember Alex, of course?'

'Yes,' Lavinia said. 'Just, — it's been a long time, I barely recognized him.'

Alex turned the corners of his mouth down and grimaced at Lavinia, then he took Tiggy in his arms and gave her a long lingering kiss.

Lavinia stared once then twice around the room.

'Give me air!' Tiggy gasped, and pulled away from him. But he brought her to his chest and, looking over the top of her head he winked at Lavinia.

She wanted to cry, to die even. It wasn't fair; it simply wasn't fair that her sins had come back to haunt her in this way.

Chapter 35

'Dad? Where the hell have you been? It's almost eight o'clock.'

Trevor Skinner, ignoring her question, said: 'Where's your mum?'

'She's gone to Bingo, you know she goes on Fridays.'

'What you doing here, then?'

She sighed. 'Believe it or not, I came to see you.'

'What for?'

Gail sat down on the sofa. 'Come and sit down Dad. I want to talk to you.'

Trevor removed his navy anorak, revealing a frilly pink blouse and what to Gail looked suspiciously like a pair of false bosoms.

'Dad! You've never been out like that, have you? Christ, what will people think?'

Trevor scowled. 'They can think what they like.'

'But, Dad, don't you see.' She stood abruptly. 'Christ, *this* family! It's no wonder you got the bloody sack.'

'Hah, hah-hah, there you see, even *you* admit that I was sacked on account of me cross-dressing.'

'Well you couldn't blame them, a tractor driver dressed up like a bloody fairy, you're the laughing stock of

271

the village.'

'That's just it, aint it? That's why he sacked me. Tribunal wasn't fair, they didn't even consider my point of view, they just took one look at Miss Smarty-pants and that was that.'

'She wasn't even there.'

'I know she wasn't, but they're all in on it. They knew she was one of them, and they came down on her side. Happens all the time. I'm going to take out a private prosecution, that's what I'll do, then they'll have to sit up and take notice.'

Gail sat down again. 'Dad,' she said softly. 'It won't work, the tribunals findings are against you. All you'll do is spend money you can't afford, and make Mum unhappy. It's been over a year, Dad, it's time to let it go. Leave it, Dad, please.'

'Is that what you came to say? If it is, you can get home now, 'cause I'm not listening.'

'I'm not going 'til I've said my piece, Dad. And it's about all this business with Sir Theo.'

'Oh yeah?'

'Yes, Dad, there's rumors going about that you're watching his girl. Is that right, Dad? Is that where you've been tonight?'

'I've been minding my own business, and you, our Gail, would do well to do the same.'

'Dad? What you been up to?'

'If I can't win in court, then there are other ways to win.'

'What? Watching them? What use is that?'

'Not them, *her*. Puts the wind up her good and proper it does, scared the shit out of her six o'clock the other morning, I did.' He chuckled. 'She were in the kitchen, stark naked she were, and she gives me a full frontal.'

'Dad!'

'Huh, she knew I were there, brazen hussy — she is. She wanted to show me what she'd got.'

'Thought you said, you scared the shit out of her.'

'Yeah, well, she runs away as if I had, but now I think about it, why would the tart pull the curtains back when she's in the altogether? No, I bet she knew I were there and she wanted to show me what she'd got.' He clasped his own imitation bosom. 'Big tits she's got, great big firm tits. Bet old Sheldon-Harris nigh on suffocates in them.'

'Dad! Shut up, it's not nice to talk like that. Look at you,' she drew in a deep breath. 'Dad, you could get help you know.'

'Help, help for what?'

She moistened her lips.

'What if she goes to the police, Dad? What then? You could get yourself in a lot of trouble.'

'She asks for it, I told you. Why would she open the curtain when she's—'

273

'They live in the middle of nowhere, Dad. She wouldn't expect anyone to be out there at that time in the morning.'

He chucked. 'She's wrong then, aint she? 'Cause I'm always there, always.'

'Dad, you have to know — what you do,' she shook her head, 'it isn't normal.' She stood again and placed a hand on each hip. 'You know what, Dad, when me and Elaine were growing up, we often didn't know who was our mum and who was our dad. Right confused we were, then later, when we were old enough to understand, — we were ashamed, Dad. We'd never dare bring friends home you know. Christ, I did once, remember? Val Henshaw, it was, Mum said to bring her home for tea. It were fine 'til you showed up and started showing off.'

'Showing off?'

'Yes, you put fancy ribbons in your hair for a start. Val thought you were playing a game with us. Then you went and put a load of Mum's clothes on, skirt and tights and high heels. You even covered your face in panstick.'

'Panstick?' He looked confused.

'That makeup Mum used to use.'

'That's not true, Gail. That weren't your Mum's makeup, or your Mum's clothes. They were mine. I wouldn't dress in your mother's clothes. Not unless she said I could.'

'Give me strength,' Gail moaned, flopping back

down in the chair.

'Dad, are you deliberately misunderstanding me? It doesn't matter whose things they were. It only matters that Val never came round again, and that her parents forbade her to play with me after that.'

'Weren't much of a friend then, were she?'

'Dad, I'm thirty-two, don't you wonder why I never bring a boyfriend home to meet you and Mum?'

'I don't expect you've got one.'

'If I had, Dad, and I've had one or two, I wouldn't dare bring him over. Can you imagine it? This is my Mum, and this is my Dad. My Dad's the one with bigger tits, only don't let that worry you, they're not real, just a pair of falsies.'

Trevor clasped his bosom again. Then he stuck his chest out and smoothed the material of his pink frilly blouse over the humps. 'Are they really?'

'What? False?'

'Bigger than your Mum's?'

'Jesus wept!' She put her head in her hands. A few seconds later she straightened up. 'I'm not getting anywhere, am I, Dad?'

He leaned forward and touched her hand, but she shield away from him.

'I see what you're saying, Gail. But as far as I can see, if the way I am doesn't bother your Mum, than I can't see why it should bother you.'

275

Gail felt exhausted. She shook her head. 'She's as bad as you, Dad, that's the truth of it. You'd never have gone as far as you have if she hadn't egged you on. Don't you see, Dad? It's Mum's way of controlling you.'

'What do you mean?'

'It's Mum's way of making you do as you're told. It's manipulation, Dad. You're putty in her hands.'

'I have to be punished when I do wrong, don't I?'

Gail put her head back into her hands and, bringing it up again, with a defeated sigh she said, 'What's the use, what's the bloody use? Look, Dad — Oh, never mind. Why don't I make us both a nice cup of tea.'

Trevor looked at the clock on the mantelpiece.

'Yeah, all right, Gail. Only look lively, they've gone out for the evening and I want to be there when they get back.'

'Are you talking about Sir Theo?'

'Yeh, and *her*, Miss Smarty-pants. I waits 'til they're in bed, having a little bit of Dr Pepper no doubt, then I throws a little bit of gravel at the porch door. That there damned dog of hers sleeps in the porch. Goes bonkers, he does, and then she has to get up and calm him down. Then once the lights go out, I does it again. Old Sheldon-Harris must be in and out of her like a buck rabbit.'

'Dad, that's terrible, that's a dreadful thing to do.'

'Don't hurt nobody.' Skinner replied.

Gail put her coat on.

'Thought you were going to make us a cup of tea.'

'Changed my mind, Dad. I think I'll be off.' She walked toward the door.

'And, Dad? I hope it rains.'

'What? When?'

'When you're out there, playing silly buggers, and I hopes you get soaked to the skin and catch double bloody pneumonia.' She opened the door and let herself out.

Chapter 36

'Come on, we have to hurry, we'll be late,' Theo said.

'Does it matter?'

'We don't want to draw too much attention to ourselves.'

'But, Theo, I thought you wanted her to know that we were here.'

'That was before I knew it was to be so well attended.'

The meeting was due to commence at seven-thirty and it was almost that when Zoë and Theo finally reached the hall. Cathy had been late turning up to baby-sit Elizabeth, so they'd been late arriving in Norwich. Then they'd had difficulty parking the car. The car park attached to the hall was full, as were the many little side streets running away from it. They'd had to drive some distance before they found a parking space.

Now they were both out of breath as they took two of the few remaining seats at the back of the crowded hall.

Theo glanced around him. 'It's packed. Who on earth would want to come to this sort of thing?'

'The desperate and the curious,' Zoë replied. 'Look behind you, it's standing room only. I've never seen so many—'

'I've just counted the seats, there's fifty rows with

forty seats in each row, that's . . . ' he frowned.

'Two hundred?'

Theo shook his head. 'Thousand, — two thousand.'

'At ten pounds a ticket?'

Theo nodded. 'Twenty thousand pounds.'

'Surely not,' Theo must be mistaken; she did her sums again, breaking the seating down into smaller numbers. 'Let's see, forty in a row, so that's . . . four hundred pounds a row . . . fifty times four hundred—'

'Is twenty thousand.'Theo repeated.

'And that's not counting the ones standing at the back.' She turned to look at them. 'She'll have had to pay for the hall of course, and printing isn't cheap.'

'All the same, not bad for a couple of hours bullshit, is it?'

Zoë laughed. 'Shush, someone will hear you.'

But in fact, the buzz of conversation was very loud, and no one was giving the couple any attention. Every other person seemed to be pulling on a cigarette and the air was blue and hazy. Several times Theo coughed.

'God, I should think this atmosphere would dispatch a few of the audience into the next life,' he said.

It was almost eight o'clock before the doors at the back of the hall were finally closed. Several minutes later the lights were dimmed and the audience were finally hushed.

It was a good five minutes after that, before Charlotte appeared on stage and introduced her mother.

'Lottie?' Theo whispered, 'I didn't know she was involved.'

'Rich pickings,' Zoë whispered back.

Isobel was wearing a long blue robe and open toed sandals, her long, wild, grey hair had been left loose and was flowing around her shoulders.

'Merlin?' Zoë whispered. And was rewarded by an amused smile from Theo, and a black look from a young woman in the row in front of them.

'Zeus,' Theo replied rather loudly giving the same woman a defiant glance.

Isobel smiled. Zoë thought she looked rather handsome, the audience certainly seemed in awe of her. She tested the microphone and asked how many people had been to one of her evenings before.

Zoë and Theo looked at each other. So this wasn't a new venture.

About a quarter of the people put their hands up.

'Now,' she said. 'The most important thing about the evening is for you to participate. If you think that the message is for you, then stand up. It's no good thinking afterwards that it may have been for you, you must speak straight away. Don't be frightened. If the message isn't for you, then it doesn't matter. It's sometimes difficult for me to decipher Spirit. I shall get a lot of Spirit through, but sometimes the messages get confused with such a great number of people.'

There was a slight stirring in the audience.

'But before I begin,' she took a deep breath and smiled. 'So many of you have asked me about Spirit, and about what happens when you pass on and die. And I'd like to tell you exactly what happens.'

'Great,' said Theo under his breath.

'It's only we who are left behind, that have a problem understanding Spirit. Those that have gone on before, come back as Spirit with fun and with love. The other world is full of love and fun and laughter. When you actually pass over, or so we understand from Spirit, you leave your body and you pass through a white light, which is actually your higher self. Once you're through that white light, you are then in Spirit. You don't then instantly go floating around on a cloud.' There was a titter from the audience. 'You are then on what we call the plain of illusion. In fact at this point, you still think you're a person, and it may take many, many years, for that to actually drop away. You could actually eat, and drink, and sleep, although it's not necessary to do so.'

Theo chuckled. The audience seemed transfixed; hanging onto Isobel's every word.

'When you realize it's not necessary, then, of course, you start to move on. At that point, on this plain of illusion, you can see your family who have passed on, they will come back and be the people you expect them to be. And you will see them where you think it is correct to see them. Whether it's relaxing on a picnic or on a beach, or in your own home.'

'I'm confused,' Zoë whispered. 'Can we see them, or they see us?'

Theo shrugged his shoulders, he looked as if he were about to burst into laughter and Zoë found it hard not to giggle.

'When you go to spirit to start with, you learn many, many, things that we don't know here.' Isobel continued. 'Then you will move on, and you won't move on alone, but will be in a group of fifty to a hundred. These are your soul mates and your soul mates will always wait for you, then you will be reincarnated together into another life. But relationships may have altered, a person in one life may be your brother, but in the next life, they may be your son.'

'Or your murderous husband,' Theo said.

Zoë dug her elbow into his ribs.

'The most important thing to know about Spirit, is, that it's fun. You know — I used to go to church and people would say, 'Shush, you're in the house of God'. And I used to think that poor God must have a hearing problem. Because to me a place that is the home of God should be a place of joy and should be full of enjoyment and laughter and joy.'

Theo wriggled in his seat; Zoë put out her hand to

him. He was shaking his head as if in disapproval

'And that's what we try to do here, we try to have a house of joy and laughter, so those that come from Spirit, come because we want them to. Come because they want to say, that no matter how unhappy or sad a passing, however much we may miss them, they want us to know that they are all right. That they've gone through a barrier and they've survived, and they're all right. They want us to know that one day we shall join them, and that it's all right.'

'That's all right then,' Theo said, still struggling to keep a straight face.

'A great comfort,' Zoë giggled.

'Now I don't know what will happen this evening, because I don't know anyone here, well as far as I know, I don't know anyone.'

Theo and Zoë sank a little lower in their chairs.

'Obviously, I can't get around to everybody tonight, but I know that what you will hear tonight, will prove that there is life after death.'

Isobel closed her eyes and said, 'I'm making my link now, and I'm seeing a wedding dress, a lovely wedding dress. Now I feel that someone here tonight has either recently, very recently, either got married, or someone very close to them has got married, within the last couple of weeks. Does this make sense to anyone?'

She looked around the room.

'Because I have a lady here that's very excited

about it. And I'll tell you why. Because she would have either made a wedding dress, or she would have made bridesmaids dresses. But she was very, very, fond of making clothes, and it was the dress the bride wore that interests her, because it was so beautiful. And I feel someone here would know about this. Does this make sense to anybody? Has anyone recently got married?'

The hall remained silent.

'I have this lovely wedding dress, and I'm sure somebody knows.'

Isobel closed her eyes. 'Marilyn? Who's Marilyn?'

A woman two rows from the front stood.

'Ah, Marilyn, good evening.'

Isobel looked around the packed room. 'Before I go on, is there anybody else named Marilyn?'

A woman toward the back stood.

'Ah, we have another Marilyn. Well now, if I go on a bit, we'll soon know which Marilyn's being contacted. I'm still stuck with the wedding dress. I can't get rid of that. I feel that one of these ladies would have known a lady who would have made such a dress. Does that make sense to either of you?'

One woman shook her head, the other, the one at the front, nodded.

'Ah good, now who was the lady?'

In a shaky voice the woman said, 'My grandson got married last August.'

'I suppose a year could be classed as recent.' Theo whispered.

'I thought she said the wedding was in the last couple of weeks.' Zoë whispered back.'

'Shush,' someone on the row behind said.

'Ah yes, and I think it was a lovely day.' Isobel was saying. 'Now let me see, your mother is in spirit?'

'If she's not, she must be about a hundred and forty,' Theo said.

'You mother was there at the wedding,' Isobel said. 'In spirit, and she thought the dress was lovely. It was very silky, quite a heavy dress, but it was lovely. Who used to make wedding dresses?' Isobel asked.

'Dilys once made one,' Marilyn said.

'Ah yes, and she's in Spirit isn't she?'

Marilyn nodded.

'And everything is fine, and there's going to be a baby. Did you know that?'

Marilyn shook her head. 'No.'

'Oh dear, I've let the cat out of the bag. Act surprised when they tell you.'

The hall erupted into laughter.

Zoë glanced at Theo. He had his hand on his chin and he was staring at his wife, he was wearing a half smile. 'She's good,' he whispered. 'She's bloody good.' And Zoë felt a stab of jealousy.

'It'll be a boy,' Isobel said.

'Fifty-fifty chance of her being right,' Theo said.

'Who's Jason?' Isobel suddenly asked.

'My granddaughter's boyfriend,' Marilyn said.

'Right, well, they won't get married, well not just yet anyway, because I think they need time.'

She closed her eyes for a brief moment. 'You're very like your mother,' she said. 'You look very like her and you're like her in personality. Who's John?' she asked.

'My son and my uncle.'

Theo leaned forward in his chair.

'It's a common enough name,' Zoë hissed.

'It's rather nice,' Isobel said, 'knowing that they are all there together in Spirit.'

'My son's not,' Marilyn protested.

'No. No, of course not. But they all want you to know that they are all right. Now your mother, she's been gone several years, but she's not been gone that long, has she?'

'Twenty-five years,' Marilyn said.

'Whoopse,' said Theo. 'I was almost impressed then. Use your head Issie, the old girl must be sixty plus, her mother must have died yonks ago.'

Zoë swallowed, she was beginning to feel extremely miserable. Theo was sitting forward with interest, and he had a strange look on his face which Zoë interpreted as admiration.

'Yes, well, that's not long to her. She'd know all

the children, and she'd know all that was going on. She takes a keen interest in you all.'

'Well recovered,' Theo whispered.

Isobel gestured to Marilyn that she should sit down, and then she closed her eyes again. 'Happy birthday,' she said. 'Whose birthday is it?'

No one got up.

'A wide shot,' Theo said under his breath.

'Sometime this month, someone has a birthday?'

'Well recovered, but not very convincing,' Theo rejoined. The woman in front of him turned around and glared.

And so it went on. Zoë reckoned that Isobel got about fifty percent of it right, but the other fifty percent was way out. She wanted to go home. She didn't like Theo's reactions, he was sitting on the edge of his seat, he seemed to hang on Isoble's every word, and every little while he would comment on how skilful she was.

Isobel had her hand to her forehead. 'Robert I'm getting the name Robert through and . . . and now, I'm looking at a grave, and I feel that there is a child in this grave, because there is a little teddy sitting on it, and there's a beautiful bouquet of flowers. Now, the question is whether the grave and Robert go together? I feel they should do. It's a little boy in the grave. Now somebody knows about that little boy. Does it mean anything to anybody?'

'This is a bit near the mark,' sighed Theo.

'Can anybody accept that?'

The hall was very quiet.

'I have this little boy and, well, first of all, I'm sure Robert is a grandfather.'

The woman who had spent the evening glaring at Theo stood up. And Zoë saw that she was about the same age as her. She had her dull brown hair scraped back into a ponytail and her face was a pasty white.

'Here,' she said, 'over here.'

Then another woman stood up on the other side of the room. But after a few questions, Isobel decided that the message was for the woman in front of Theo.

'Can you tell me what makes sense to you.'

'Robert makes sense, he's the grandfather,' the woman said.

'He's your grandfather?'

'No, the little boy's grandfather.'

'Ah, you know about the little boy? Is he a relation of yours?'

'Yes,' the woman said weakly.

'Pardon?'

'Yes,' she said, choking back tears, which were too far away for Isobel to see.

'He's not your child is he.' It was a statement, not a question.

'Yes,' the woman said. Tears were now flooding down her cheeks.

'He's your little boy?'

The woman, overcome with emotion, nodded.

'I just know that there were some beautiful flowers, you've laid a bouquet of flowers on him?'

'Y-yes.'

'And he . . . wasn't he beautiful? He was only little wasn't he?'

'He was a baby.'

'Yes, he was a baby, only little, and he was beautiful, and he has some little roses for you, and, and his granddad Robert is in Spirit with him isn't he?'

'No, no.' Sobbing, the woman shook her head.

'Well I guess that name has been given—'

'His great-granddad was Bert,' the woman said helpfully.

'Yes, yes, well that would be the same name, so it's his great-grandfather and he's in Spirit?'

'Yes.' The woman was scrubbing at her face with a tissue trying the stem the tears.'

'Well he was the one that has brought this little boy, and he wanted you to know that he was here, and whose Marie? Or May? M?'

'My Mum's named Maureen.'

'So the little boy's grandmother is named Maureen?'

'Yes.'

'And she's here, not in Spirit.'

'Yes.' The woman was weeping inconsolably.

Theo fidgeted. 'This is awful,' he whispered. 'It's cruel.'

'I just want you to know, that he's got these little roses for you. I wonder? Did you put some little flowers in his hand?'

'Yes,' she wept.

'That's right, that's what he's holding. Were they roses?'

'Yes,' the woman sobbed. 'Yes. Oh, yes.'

'And he brings them to you with his love, and, and there will be another little boy.'

'There is,' the woman said. But by now her tears were obliterating her words.

Theo looked extremely uncomfortable. 'This is cruel,' he kept saying. 'Why doesn't she leave it?'

As if she'd taken her cue from Theo, Isobel said 'We'll leave it there,' and the woman in front of Zoë and Theo literally crumpled into her chair.

Next Isobel saw an accident victim — a young man cut off in his prime — who was desperately trying to contact his sister. After that, she linked with someone's elderly mother. And so the meeting progressed. After almost three hours, Charlotte finally came on stage and thanked everyone for coming. She apologized for her mother not being able to carry on. She was, she said, exhausted. However, Isobel was available for private consultations and

Charlotte gave her own telephone number for those wishing to make an appointment.'

'I dare you to go,' Theo whispered into Zoë's ear.

'I will if you will,' she quipped back.

Charlotte thanked everyone once again and the crowd filed noisily out of the hall into the balmy May evening, and dispersed in varying directions. Zoë and Theo, being at the back of the hall made a quick getaway and saw no one they knew.

Afterwards, they discussed the meeting far into the night.

'Perhaps she has something,' Theo said. 'She got pretty close to the bone a couple of times.'

'And she was pretty far out at other times.' Zoë said. Then with a mischievous grin on her face as she said, 'Maybe she has got it. Maybe we should sharpen our knives and get ready to do her in. We can, after all, plead that it was our destiny.'

'Good idea,' Theo agreed. 'Except Randall's wife was strangled.'

Chapter 37

Tiggy had offered to help with the clearing up, but the offer had been half-hearted, and it was Josh that now stood with a dishcloth in his hand wiping the kitchen surfaces, whilst Lavinia replaced the crockery in the cupboards.

Once everything was packed away, Josh said:

'Vinnie, I need to talk to you.'

Fear rushed into her body, drying her mouth and flooding her extremities with adrenaline. He knew; he knew about her and Alex. He'd always known, and now he was to confront her with it. She'd deny it, it was Alex's word against hers, but, what if? What if Josh had followed her to London that time after Zoë had told her about Tiggy and Alex being together? What if he'd seen her entering Alex's chambers? What would be her excuse for visiting him?

'Vinnie, do you ever look at the young in their tight fitting sweaters and their skinny skirts, and wonder what it all has to do with you?'

'You're talking of the girls, of course? You're worried about Tiggy, aren't you? She's getting so thin.' Lavinia was flooded with relief, so that was it.

'The boys too,' he said.

She frowned; the boys weren't on a constant diet. He'd lost her, he didn't ever talk like this; something was wrong, very wrong. 'I'm sorry, Josh, I don't know what you're talking about.'

'Life, Vinnie. Life that doesn't concern us anymore. We're past it Vinnie, we're over the hill.'

Fear was bearing down on her. Something was wrong, very, very wrong, This wasn't Josh talking. Although he was nearing his seventieth birthday, he still regarded himself, if not young, then certainly vital. Josh never spoke in such a downbeat manner. He was the eternal optimist.

Josh was sitting at the kitchen table, and she sat down beside him. She covered his hand with her own and took a deep breath; the least she could do was make it easy for him. It was about Alex and her; the day of reckoning had finally come. The most courageous thing she could do was to make it easy for him.

'Is it because Tiggy brought a man home? Alex is—' She was going to say that Alex was experienced, and she hoped he wasn't busy breaking Tiggy's heart. That ought to open the discussion up. But he interrupted her.

'It's got nothing to do with Alex,' he said.

Thank God,— she was wrong. She felt ashamed by her own selfishness, the world did not completely revolve around her and she ought to recognize that.

'Is it because the children are leaving home? It's me that ought to be suffering from the empty nest syndrome, not you.' She laughed a very artificial laugh.

'Vinnie, I've some bad news, old thing.'

Oh, God, Josh was slipping into that stupid old fashion way of speaking, he always did that if something was really troubling him. This was serious, very serious. Josh must be a very worried man.

'It's not easy to have to tell you this,' he said.

'What Josh? What is it?' Panic was stealing her breath away, she snatched at the air and gulped it in. Why didn't he just come out with it, why keep her in suspense. What was wrong?

'You were busy this morning when I went out, you were flapping about Tiggy coming home, and so I didn't get around to telling you where I was going.'

Josh heaved himself up from the table and got himself a glass of water. Lavinia would have liked a drink as well, her voice seemed to have dried up; it was as if she only had enough strength to ask the really important questions, and asking for water wasn't that important.

She closed her eyes and pinched the bridge of her nose. Of course she remembered him going out that morning, and no she hadn't asked where he was going, she'd watched him put Fen in the car and drive off, only it hadn't been Tiggy she was flapping about, it had been Alex Kirby.

Josh drank almost half the glass of water in one gulp.

'I've know for a long time, of course, I just didn't want to recognize it. Loss of appetite, drinking more and

294

more . . .'

'Oh, God, Josh was ill, that's where he'd gone that morning, to see the doctor, and she, bitch that she was, was all tied up in knots about her ex-lover coming to stay. Josh had needed her and she'd let him down, oh God, oh God, oh God.'

'There's no easy way to say this, Vinnie. You see, it's terminal.'

'Oh, Josh' She gulped, picked up Josh's water and took a long drink. He went back to the sink and filled the glass. She studied her dear husband's back; she loved him so much, how could she face life without him?

'I should have taken her sooner,' he said as he sat down and handed Lavinia the replenished water glass. 'But I just hoped she'd pick up. She's nearly fourteen. That's a good age for a Labrador, isn't it?'

Lavinia slowly nodded her head. 'Yes,' she whispered. She felt as if someone had dealt her a blow in the stomach and she couldn't quite breath in nor out. He was talking about the dog, not himself. She watched as a tear formed in the inner corner of his eye, he blinked and the liquid sped along to the outer corner, where it pooled and spilled over onto his careworn cheek.

'Josh, I'm so terribly sorry,' she said, as if Fen had nothing to do with her. 'How . . . how long?'

'Matter of days, she's got this lump . . . here.' He indicated the right side of his ribs. 'Vet, wanted to, well, he wanted to . . . '

'Put her down?' Lavinia asked gently.

'Yes. I can hardly bear to say it. Vet said that she might go naturally, but that she'd soon be in a lot of pain, and it might be kindest to — well, you know.'

'I'm so sorry, Josh.'

Josh wiped his eyes on a large checkered handkerchief. 'Daft old thing aren't I? She's only a dog.'

Lavinia held onto his hands, she knew very well that Fen was far more than a dog, she'd been part of their family, she'd been the children's playmate, part and parcel of their upbringing.

'No, Josh, Fen's not just a dog. She's been your friend, and your companion, for many, many years, she's not *just* a dog.'

'Vet says that I'll know — you know — when to take her in, if she's in too much pain. He says I'll know. But, Vinnie, what if I don't know? What if I take her before it's time? I don't know if I'll have the strength to have it done.'

'It won't be easy, darling.' Relief had flooded her veins and brought with it more guilt. Guilt, that she should be relieved that it was only Fen that was dying, it wasn't her dear, dear, husband, and her husband hadn't found out about her lover. It was only a dog. She sniffed; Josh's tears were infectious.

'I'll be with you, Josh. I'll come with you. We'll do it together — if it needs to be done.'

He nodded his head. 'I thought tomorrow, — if Tiggy and Alex want to go off for the day, we could drive Fen up to Applegate Wood. I do believe it's her favorite place. We've had some good times up there together. She could have a bit of a run, that's if she's up to it. She'd like that, I know she would.'

He was talking of a world from which Lavinia had been excluded, whilst Josh and Fen were chasing rabbits in Applegate Wood she'd been . . . only that was a long time ago and it didn't matter anymore. All that mattered was her and Josh's life together. And from now on she was going to spend as much of her life as possible with him.

'We'll go whether Tiggy and Alex have plans or not, Josh. They're well able to fend for themselves.'

'They might like to come?'

'No, Josh, this is something just for us. You, me, and Fen. It'll be emotional, and I don't think I want to share that with Alex Kirby.'

He patted her hand. 'Thank you, Vinnie, thank you for always being there for me, always putting me first.'

She closed her eyes. Josh's words were like a knife in her heart.

Chapter 38

Flora Gouch was kneeling on all fours, her legs slightly apart, her head bent forward onto a pillow and her big breasts dangling down under her. Charlotte Bridges was positioned below her, she took first one, then the other breast into her mouth, sucking and teasing the nipples until Flora moaned with pleasure. Charlotte's hands were working expertly, one rubbing herself, the other delighting Flora with the same treatment.

'We could go to one of those centers,' Flora panted, 'you know, A I D they call it.'

Charlotte let her mouth wonder from Flora's breasts. 'That spells aids,— are you sure that's right?'

'Artificial insemination by donor, A I D.' She shifted her position and pushed her breast back into Charlotte's mouth. 'Don't stop, not now.'

'No,' said Charlotte. 'You know the deal, it's my turn now.' Slipped out from under her friend and settled herself beside her. She opened her legs and pushed a pillow under her hips.

Flora turned around, slipped one leg over the prostate Charlotte, bent her head and buried herself in the soft musky smell. Charlotte brought her head up and, in turn, teased and manipulated between the willing Flora's legs.

'Careful, Flora, I don't want to . . . '

Flora sucked even harder, as Charlotte knew she would, and very soon Charlotte's hips were pushed high in the air, and her legs were curled around Flora's neck as the spasm washed over her.

'I love you, Flora,' she said once her breathing had calmed. 'I love you very much. And now I'm going to prove it.'

She saw Flora shudder, a girlish excited gesture that made Charlotte want to repeat her orgasm all over again, but first she must satisfy her lover. She rolled Flora onto her back, and straddled her waist with her neat light body. Flora put her hand up and caressed the small round breasts, and Charlotte made love to Flora until she gave a satisfying cry.

'Up on you knees,' Charlotte commanded, removing the dildo, which was very large and very pink . She fitted a harness to her extremely slim hips, fastened the dildo into place and mounted her lover, at the same time; she leaned forward and caressed Flora's magnificent breasts.

'Imagine it's him,' Charlotte said.

'Ugh,' Flora interjected.

Charlotte's hips continued to work. 'You don't mean that, what I'm trying to tell you is,' she put her bottom lip over her top lip and blew her fringe away from her perspiring forehead. 'That you can get him to do it from this position, and you can pretend that it's me doing it, You don't need to think of it as going with a man, you won't know the difference.'

'I will when he shoots all that stuff into me, Ugh.'

'You won't even know about it.'

'I will, it's all hot and slimy you know, and it burns.'

'It does not. I've had blokes. It just throbs a bit, you know, the prick just jumps and then it's all over. That's why blokes call it jerking off.' She ran her hand around Flora's belly and pushed her fingers up alongside the dildo. Flora was a girl with rounded hips and a full bosom but she had a tiny neat waist, 'you're pretty slimy yourself.' She removed her fingers and balanced her hands on Flora's hips.

'Look, it'll be okay. Close your eyes and think of England. You won't mind once he gets it in, you might even enjoy it. Before I discovered the real thing, I often used to do it with a bloke. It's okay, not like this, but it's okay, and it's soon over with. You might get one encore but you'll not get two, let alone three. Blokes are all right, they have their limitations, but they're all right.'

'Then why don't *you* do it with him? Why don't *you* have the baby? It would really piss your mother off — you'd like that wouldn't you? Why should I have to have it? If you don't mind blokes crawling all over you—'

'But you're better built for producing children, look at these.' She was still thrusting her hips, pushing the dildo in and out rhythmically, and at the same time pulling on Flora's breasts. She gave an extra deep thrust, and smiled when she heard Flora draw in a sharp breath.

'It won't hurt, he'll not be as big as big-John here.' She gave another deep thrust and Flora moaned.

'Why Theo?' Flora panted. 'Why can't I just go to a clinic?'

'Why Theo? 'Cause he's really handsome, and he's from good stock. If I were straight I'd go for him, wouldn't you? You might get any little weed's sperm if you take pot luck.'

'He'll never agree,' Flora said biting into the pillow.

'He's always had the hots for you.'

'Yes, but he's got a girl now.'

'Men like variety, he'll comply, you really don't understand how a man's prick works. Cocks and brains are directly wired, like they're programed to dip in as many honey pots as they can.' As she said this, she softened her pace and slipped in and out very slowly. 'Is that nice my little cherub? Do you like what Lottie's doing to you?'

'Yes, yes, yes,' Flora breathed.

'In and out,' Charlotte said, gently pressing forward. 'Slowly in, uh, right in to the hilt, hold it there for a second, then slowly out. Nice sweetheart?'

'Very nice, very, very nice.'

'You will do it, won't you? Do it for me? Do it for

us?' She tweaked Flora's nipples and bent over and kissed her back. 'He'll come quickly, I promise you he will, God, you're so delicious, I wouldn't be surprised if Big-John here didn't shoot off one of these days.' She cupped Flora's breasts. 'Theo'll not last five minutes with these to play with, I can promise you that.'

'I thought you said his girlfriend had got a big bust.'

'Not as big as these.' She paused for a moment, and then she started to rotate her hips. 'Is that nice sweetheart? Does that feel good?'

Flora answered with a moan, she was rocking her head from side to side. Her speech was slow, and she was breathless.

'Shall I stop now? Have you had enough?' Charlotte smiled, she knew that she had won the battle.

'No, no Lottie, please . . . please don't stop . . . please, please don't stop.'

'Will you do it then, Flora? I love you, Flora. Will you do it for me?'

'Yes . . . yes, Lottie, I'll do it,' she moaned, 'I'll do it . . . I'll do it . . . but why, why does it have to be Theo?'

'We want our baby to have the best possible start, don't we? Theo is tall and broad and he's handsome and clever, and, oh yes, I remember — the best reason of all — he's rich, he's very, very rich.' She suddenly thrust hard into the girl, and caused her to arch her back and cry out in satisfaction. She smiled, 'He pretends to be poor, but he still has his house and his farm, and he's rich enough to keep a bit on the side. So, I think he'll make a very fine father.'

Charlotte pulled out of her friend, unbuckled the dildo and strapped it around Flora's hips. Flora remained on all fours, her pendulous breasts almost touching the mattress and the huge pink rubber penis sticking out from her mound of Venus.

'Come on, roll over it's my turn.'

Flora crashed down onto the bed. 'I'm not sure about this,' she said.

'What? This?' Charlotte said, straddling the pole of rubber, and lowering herself onto it? Or giving us a child?'

'The child bit.'

'You promised,' Charlotte said, digging her nails into Flora's shoulder. 'You promised.'

'Ouch, that hurts, Lottie.'

Charlotte didn't apologize, she didn't even answer, but rapidly lifted herself up and down; she was emotionally satisfied, now she wanted physical satisfaction and she knew that Flora wouldn't let her down on either count.

Chapter 39

It had been Lavinia's idea to gather all her brood under her wing at Hulver that Saturday. 'Please come,' she'd said. 'It's your father. He needs you to be around him.' But it was she, not Josh, that wanted them there, an antidote to Alex Kirby — a living reminder of who she was and what she stood for.

They'd all come without hesitation — the twins from Bristol and Zoë and Betsy from Garrick. 'It's a family thing,' Theo had said, 'best if you go without me.' But in fact it suited his purpose to have Zoë out of the way. Charlotte had asked to see him, she wanted to meet him for lunch to discuss a deeply personal matter. The divorce, thought Theo, and he knew that Zoë would be upset that Charlotte was pushing her nose in. No, it was far better that Zoë went her way and he his, just for the day. He'd listen to what Charlotte had to say; she might be the bearer of good news.

First thing in the morning, Josh and Lavinia took Fen up to Applegate wood. From there they walked the short distance to Gibbet Hill where they sat, leaning their backs on the foot of the ancient gallows, and enjoyed the sunshine, whilst Fen sniffed slowly, yet excitedly, at the many rabbit trails.

'I think she's looking better,' Josh commented, 'maybe . . .'

Lavinia forced a smile. 'Maybe.'

But their faces belied their words.

Zoë and Betsy arrived just before, and the boys just after, their parents returned with the dog. So at lunch Alex was met with the full force of the Elliot family. Oh what a relief it was to Lavinia to have Sebastian and Quentin home again. What balm it was to be surrounded by her family. The childrens' smart quips and gregarious personalities rebounded from every wall, and Lavinia was comforted and confident in the bosom of her family.

The news that Josh's gun dog was losing her battle with illness was met with deep sorrow, yet above the sadness came tales of the times the children and Fen had shared together.

'And there was Pa trying to convince this new keeper that Fen would never dream of touching a pheasant, and the dog rushes past with a hen bird stuffed in her mouth,' laughed Quentin.

'So Pa says that it must have been a dead one she'd found in the woods, and then he starts moaning about the pickers up—' Sebastian continued the story.

'And Fen lets go of the pheasant, and it flies away!' Quentin finished.

Everyone roared with laughter. And Lavinia gave Alex a look as if to say: *This is my family, Alex, so don't toy with it, and don't threaten it. We're bigger than you, there's only one of you, there's six of us.* She glanced over at Tiggy, who was not joining in the conversation and looked quite miserable. *All right, five of us then, but if push came to shove, Tiggy would unite with her family, not you.*

Tiggy stared around the dining room. Everyone was so animated. They'd all been shattered by the news of Fen's demise, but now they were suddenly full of laughter and talking of the past.

There was Zoë, looking like the original mother earth, shoveling food down Betsy's throat, looking fulfilled and wholesome; and Sebbie and Quentin larking about just like they used to. Josh, her father, was the only one looking like he was in mourning. Her mother was all defensive, pretending she wasn't noticing the way Alex was looking at her. It was sick, that's what is was – sick – how could he prefer a forty-something-year-old woman to her, just turned twenty-one? How could he? Admittedly he was forty something himself and her mother was in pretty good shape, slender and sylph-like, still attractive and still energetic with dark refined looks. Both Tiggy and Zoë were fair, like Josh. Quen was fair too, only Sebastian had inherited Lavinia's dark hair and fine features.

She glanced down at her own body. She couldn't afford to put on any weight. At the moment she was slim and fluid, but she'd have to keep a careful eye on herself. She'd intended to stick to her diet, but it was hard at home with all that good food around. In her heart she knew exactly what Alex saw when he looked at her; her body and manner were very like her mother's, even her voice. People still mistook the two on the telephone. But she wasn't her mother, for God's sake; she was a younger, better version. She shovelled a spoon of bread and butter pudding into her mouth, then watched as her mother pushed her pudding plate away; her mother rarely ate puddings, that was probably why her weight stayed so constant. Tiggy loaded another spoon and devoured it; then she scraped up all the remaining custard and ate that too. Her mother glanced in her direction and gave her an odd sort of look. God, how she wished Alex would stop making cow's eyes at Lavinia, she should never have brought him. Tiggy reached over and took her mother's plate.

'Not eating this, Ma?'

Her mother shook her head.

'Mind if I eat it?'

Several pairs of eyes fixed on her.

'What? It's delicious.'Tiggy said defensively.

She took a large spoonful.

'You've met your Aunt, Miss Tiggy Piggy?' Quentin said to Betsy.

Tiggy put her tongue out at him.

'Do you think you should, dear?' Her mother said.

'Why not?' Tiggy sighed and dug her spoon in.

'You seem so obsessed with your weight, that's all. You'll make yourself miserable and start all that dieting nonsense again.'

'Take no notice of your mother,' Josh said. 'You're as thin as a rake. She ought to be encouraging you to eat as much as you can, to build yourself up a bit.'

'Josh, you've misunderstood me. I'm just trying to get Tiggy to eat normal portions, it's either famine or feast with her and . . . '

'Don't come winging to me when your trousers won't do up,' Zoë said and laughed.

Tiggy finished the plate of pudding and leaned back, the waistband on her jeans was uncomfortably tight. She surreptitiously undid the button and let out a deep breath.

'Cheese anyone?' Josh asked.

'Please,' Tiggy replied.

'Clear the desert plates first,' Lavinia said. 'Anyone else want cheese?'

Everyone shook their heads.

'Well at least Tiggy's going to keep me company,' Josh said. 'I much prefer a woman with a bit of meat on her, how about you Alex? Wouldn't you agree?'

'Most certainly,' Alex said, his eyes trained on Lavinia.

'Tiggy-piggy,' Sebastian said, making an hour-glass shape in the air.

Tiggy pushed her pudding plate to one side and helped herself to a large piece of Stilton, butter and water biscuits. She didn't want it, but she was damned if she was going to let anyone tell her what she should or shouldn't eat. Her weight was her own affair and not for public discussion. She forced the food down.

'Seriously, Tiggy,' Zoë said. 'I do envy you. You eat like a horse and yet you never seem to put an once on, just like Ma.'

Tiggy gave a tight little smile. She was slimmer than her mother, surely she was. She'd tried so hard, some days she didn't eat anything at all.

Lavinia got up from the table and stacked the plates, then she took them out to the kitchen. Three pairs of eyes watched her go. Josh, Alex and Tiggy. She was certainly still slim; she moved so beautifully, so lightly, she was soft and flexible.

Tiggy drew in a deep breath, the zip of her jeans peeled open. She felt fat and bloated; the jeans seemed to be straining, not just at her waist but at her thighs and calves as well. The twins were right, Tiggy-piggy, that was the best name for her.

Alex was still staring at the door where Lavinia had exited. Josh had returned to his biscuits and cheese.

Tiggy scraped back her chair, 'I'll just go and give Ma a hand with the coffee,' she said, leaving the room. Once in the hall she walked calmly over to the cloakroom where she locked the door, tore a strip of paper from the roll and placed it double thickness on the lavatory seat. She knelt down by the side of the bowl, pushed two of her fingers down her throat and wiggled them about. Nothing happened, she pushed three fingers down her throat and wretched, her stomach heaved, but nothing came up. She tried again and was rewarded with a bitter bile burning the back of her throat. She forced her fingers down again, her recently eaten lunch shot into the back of her throat and projected down the lavatory pan. She shuddered. She hated the way she was, why couldn't she just eat less, why had she got onto this merry-go-round of eating and vomiting, why couldn't she just be sensible? She continued her forced vomiting until her diaphragm ached and she was absolutely sure that her stomach was completely empty. She flushed the toilet and rinsed her mouth. Then she scrabbled in the cloakroom cabinet until she found a brush and one of her mother's lipsticks. She pulled the brush through her hair, applied colour and blotted her lips. Then she zipped and buttoned her jeans and drank half a glass of cold water. But the taste of the acidic vomit remained in her mouth. She ought to have gone upstairs to her own bathroom to be sick so that she could have cleaned her teeth.

Quentin was waiting outside the cloakroom.

'You all right, Sis? Thought I heard you being sick.'

'I'm fine — you're imagining things,' she replied cheerfully.

'Wouldn't be surprised the amount you packed away in there.' He nodded toward the dining room.

'Don't be so rude,' she said poking him in the ribs as she passed.

She crossed the hall and made her way down the library corridor to the kitchen. She smiled to herself. As long as she was in control of her life, everything would be all right, and she was in control, wasn't she? Very much so. Even when she overate she was able to rectify things; it wasn't a problem. Tiggy Elliot was in control, and nothing and no one could make her lose it; she was in charge of her own destiny. She would make things be all right, she had to, she'd show her mother who was in charge. Alex was hers and no one could alter that, not even Alex.

She carried the coffee tray into to the dining room. Zoë was still trying to persuade Betsy to eat her lunch. Quentin had returned and he eyed Tiggy suspiciously.

'I say, Sis, what are you feeding Betsy on?' Sebastian said poking the mashed up mess on Betsy's nursery dish.

'Fish fingers,' Zoë answered.

'Yuck,' said Quentin. 'I didn't know fish had fingers.'

'Oh, Quen,' Zoë admonished as she shoveled another spoonful into the child's mouth.

'Don't worry about Uncle Quen,' Sebastian said, tickling Elizabeth under her chin. 'He doesn't know anything, he doesn't even know that Cod have balls.'

'Sebbie, you're a fool.' Quentin said, taking the

spoon out of Zoë's hand, pushing some of Elizabeth's food onto it, and offering it to the child.

'Where's a chicken keep its nuggets?' Tiggy suddenly chipped in, and everyone laughed.

Lavinia smiled in her direction. *Give in, Alex,* she thought. *Give in, before you lose face.*

'And where's a beef keep its burger?' Josh said and looked around the table as if hoping for applause.

'No, Pa, you've got it wrong,' Tiggy said, 'you have to have the actual name of the animal not the meat it produces.

'Yes,' Quentin agreed. 'Like you couldn't say, 'where's a pork keep its pies,' but you could say, 'where's a chicken keep its pies.' Get it? And it also works better if you're talking about an actual body part, like fingers or balls. Do you see?'

'Balls aren't an actual body part,' Sebastian explained, 'But we all know what it means.'

Lavinia tutted.

'Right,' said Josh, 'of course.' But it was obvious from his facial expression that he didn't see at all.

Josh looked deep in thought for a moment, then he said: 'So where's a pig keep its trotters?'

'No Pa, because a pig really does have trotters.' Quentin said, but then his face creased into a smile and from there into a hearty laugh and the rest of the family joined him, even little Elizabeth screwed up her nose and chortled, and Josh looked well pleased.

Tiggy flung her hands around her father's neck.

'You really are the sweetest man,' she said. Her face was bright and animated as if she suddenly held the secret of the universe.

Chapter 40

Charlotte took a small sip of the perfectly chilled Chardonnay. She pushed a strand of hair back from her face and anchored it behind her ear.

'I'm beginning to feel quite squiffy,' Theo said. 'I'm not used to drinking at lunchtime.' He smiled at his companion; she was being perfectly charming. He couldn't help but think that she was the bearer of good news, he only wished she'd get on with it. It was difficult for him not to let his imagination run wild. He topped up her glass.

'Theo,' she giggled, 'if I didn't know you better I'd think that you were trying to get me drunk in order to take advantage of me.'

'And if I didn't know *you* better, I just might be trying to do that,' he quipped back.

She raised her brow. 'Really, Theo, how risqué — whatever would little Miss What's-her-name think to that.'

Theo tightened his jaw. 'Zoë, you mean. Her name's Zoë.'

'Don't look like that — I didn't mean anything by it. She's sweet.'

It was Theo's turn to raise his brows.

'Well, I'm sure she *is* sweet, otherwise you wouldn't be with her, would you?'

'Wouldn't I?'

'You know you wouldn't.'

Theo nodded and smiled. Charlotte had never made any secret of her feelings for Zoë; she hated her. He supposed it was reasonable, but all the same he didn't much like the way Charlotte reduced her to a nameless person.

Theo took a sip of his own wine and smiled. 'So, Lottie, what was it you wanted to discuss with me?' The hand under the table had its fingers firmly crossed.

Charlotte scraped her chair away from the table. 'In a minute, I must go to the loo first.'

She scurried away in the direction of the ladies room, where, once inside the cubical, she took out her mobile phone and rang Flora.

'Wish me luck, darling, I'm just about to ask him.'

'Oh no, don't, Lottie. You see, I've changed my mind. I don't think I can go through with it.'

'But—'

'Please, I can't — I just can't — I mean all that—'

'All that what?'

'You know . . . '

'But this morning you were so keen.'

'No, you were the one that was keen, Lottie, not me.'

'Look, I've got to go, we'll talk about it tonight, when I get home.'

Meanwhile in the restaurant Theo allowed himself to dream. If Charlotte gave the word, if Issie was softening, if it were just a matter of money — a final negotiation — a final settlement, then he'd go home and formally ask Zoë to marry him, hell, he'd even get down on one knee and play the subservient suitor. Zoë knew he wanted to marry her, of course she did. They'd talked about it often enough, but the words, the actual proposal, had never been spoken.

The door to the ladies room creaked as Charlotte re-entered the restaurant. She was smiling, he'd never known her so amiable and so noncontroversial. She seemed to agree and endorse everything he said. It must be an omen for good news, it must be.

He topped up both their glasses; hesitated, but decided against buying another bottle. He stood as she slipped into the chair opposite him. She was a remarkable looking woman. Her hair was cut in a severe but sharp and fashionable style, her makeup was perfectly applied to her flawless complexion. She was, thought Theo, the calmest, most businesslike woman he had ever met. Certainly, she was extremely attractive, not that Theo was attracted to her. He had what he would describe as a sincere admiration for the way she ran her life; a life that, because of her sexuality, couldn't have been particularly easy.

Charlotte sipped at the wine and slipped her hand across the table and covered Theo's hand.

'Theo, I need to ask you something.'

Theo's brow broke into a sweat, this was wrong, something was about to happen, something that he hadn't anticipated. He felt puzzled and confused, yet convinced that whatever it was, he wasn't going to like it.

'Don't look so worried, Theo, I'm sure you're going to find my request quite a pleasure.'

He relaxed a little, but somehow, Charlotte's broad smile didn't give him any confidence. He tried to smile back, but his face portrayed more of a grimace.

'Oh, Theo,' she said and nudged his arm. 'Don't look like that! You'll be flattered.' She squeezed his hand. 'You see, Flora and I want you to be the father of our child.'

At first, just as she was speaking, he'd been afraid that she might ask him to go back to Issie. Or that Issie had found some way of making him leave Zoë. He couldn't think how, but then the thought had been too swift to allow time for any rational component. So he'd met Charlotte's request with a certain amount of relief, but then he couldn't believe that he'd understood what she was saying and he needed it clarified.

He frowned. 'Whose child?'

'Flora's . . . and mine, of course.'

His frown deepened. 'You want me to make you pregnant?' He said the word slowly and disjointedly as if he couldn't quite believe what he was saying.

'Not me, Flora.'

'Flora?' he repeated stupidly.

'Oh, Theo, stop acting so horrified.'

'But, but, why do you and Flora want a child?' It

317

was a stupid question, why did anyone want a child? Why did he long for Zoë to have his child? Why should Charlotte and Flora's feelings be different to his?

Charlotte peered over the rim of her glass and smiled. 'Slow down, Theo, you're asking questions the answers to which you don't need to know.'

Theo sucked in a noisy breath. She was right, and, in truth, he was flattered, but the feeling was tinged with amusement. Then a dozen or so other thoughts crammed into his head.

'I'm flattered, Lottie, of course I am. But I couldn't, — I mean I wouldn't want— Flora's a nice girl, I hardly know her of course, but—'

'You don't need to know her, for God's sake!' Charlotte's eyes were darkening and the smile she had worn throughout lunch was fading and was being replaced with a frown. I'm asking you to impregnate her, not marry her.'

A million implications ran through his head, Zoë and Betsy, Issie and this new child. Given that he was still married to Issie, he'd be both father and grandfather to the same child. It was bizarre; the thought brought an involuntary smile to his lips.

Charlotte must have interpreted his smile as a positive sign and she tightened her grip on his hand.

Theo's thoughts were still racing ahead and were now turning to horror, and the thought of Charlotte having a claim on his emotions and his finances did nothing to lighten his fears.

'What's the matter? Don't you fancy her? She's a pretty good lay — I can assure you of that. And she's never been with a man before, it'll be like screwing a virgin.' Charlottes eyes flashed as she spat the words.

Theo snatched his hand from under Charlotte's, his stepdaughter was as mad as her mother.

'Charlotte, I'm very flattered but—'

'But little Miss What's-her-name won't like you bedding another woman? Well it's not you we need, it's the stuff you carry around in your balls.'

Theo watched in amazement as she searched in her bag and eventually brought out a small plastic pot.

'You just need to do the business in this, and leave the rest to me.'

Theo picked up the pot, and turned it around in his hand. He laughed, for a split second his fears lightened. It had to be a joke. If it wasn't, the whole world had gone mad. But then he felt ashamed of himself. What could he have done or said to make Charlotte think he'd be willing to do such a thing. It was true, at first he had been flattered, then amused, but if she was serious, — he was repulsed.

'You're crazy,' he said. 'You're as crazy as your mother.'

'Thanks a million.'

'I'm sorry, but you have to admit it's a pretty hare-brained scheme. If you and Flora want a child, either get yourselves a boyfriend or go to one of these clinics. I'm your—'

'What, Theo, what are you?'

'Your stepfather.'

'I thought you'd left my mother? Anyway, I'm not the one that's going to get pregnant, Flora is.'

'It wouldn't be right, Lottie.' His nostrils flared a little. 'If I father a child then I want to be around to bring it up.'

'We might arrange paternity visits,' she quipped

He moped his brow on his napkin. 'I don't think so.' He pushed his chair away from the table. 'I must go. Zoë will be home from Hulver.' For a reason Theo could not quite define he felt suddenly afraid of her.

Charlotte sighed and smiled. 'Look, Theo, this is no big deal. Do this for me and I'll do what I can concerning mother.' She'd taken a notebook from her bag. 'Some time around the eighth. I think that's when Flora will ovulate, but I'll ring you and tell you exactly. I've bought one of those handy little kits from Boots that indicate the right time . . . ' She hesitated, Theo was shaking his head.

He pushed the little plastic pot back toward her and indicated that the waiter should bring him the bill.

Charlotte picked the pot up and plunged it back into her bag.

'It's her, isn't it? Your fancy bit, that's why you won't?'

320

Theo smiled softly, yes it was Zoë. Before meeting her he'd probably have jumped at the chance of bedding Flora or anyone else for that matter. But not now, he would not allow anything, or anyone, to come between himself and Zoë. Now he had far too much to lose.

Not bothering to check the bill, he handed the waiter his credit card. Then turning back to Charlotte he said, 'Try to understand, Lottie, it's not personal. I wouldn't do it for anyone.'

Charlotte was red in the face. 'But I'm not asking you for very much, am I? A teaspoonful of—'

He laughed aloud then. 'A teaspoonful, Lottie? A teaspoonful of my life?'

'It's not much, is it?'

'On the contrary, Lottie, it's everything.'

He signed the credit card chit, got up and went around the table to Lottie and planted a kiss on her cheek. He was already wondering whether he'd tell Zoë what had happened, decided it was best not to, but knew he would anyway, he would have no secrets from her.

'I'm sorry, Lottie,' he said

She didn't answer him, but her eyes followed him to the door. She watched him cross the road and get in his car.

'You will be sorry, Theo. You and little Miss What's-her name will be very sorry,' she said aloud. 'Very, very sorry indeed.'

321

Chapter 41

Autumn 1999

Theo stirred, lay on his back for a few moments, then turned over. He wriggled down in the bed and sighed. Minutes later he stirred again as a child's urgent cry rang through the cottage.

'Mummy, Mummy.'

He rotated his head, arched his back and pushed out his arm in Zoë's direction.

'Zoë,' his hand was met with an empty space. His eyes snapped open. 'Zoë?' The child's cries were now very urgent; she was becoming extremely distressed.

'Zoë?' he knitted his brow together, and then he relaxed as his fuddled brain reached an explanation. Betsy was suddenly quiet, Zoë must already be up and seeing to her. He turned over and closed his eyes.

'Mummy, Mummy,' it was more of a scream than a cry. 'Mummy, Mummy.'

He swung his legs out of the bed and sat on the very edge for a second or two trying to put his thoughts in order.

'Mummy, Mummy.'

The 'phone call; that was the first thing to come into his mind. It had troubled him at the time and it had kept him awake when they'd first come to bed, but not for long, Theo was an instant sleeper. All the same, he'd run the scene through his head several times before sleep overtook him.

'Mummy, Mummy.'

He dragged his dressing gown from the hook and, pulling it on, he stumbled through the cottage to Betsy's room. She was sitting up in bed; tears were cascading down her cheeks. She must have been crying for a long time; her hair was damp with perspiration and the front of her pajamas was soaking wet.

She sniffed when she saw Theo, and her bottom lip trembled. ' I...I had' . . . sniff . . . 'a dream . . . a bad dream,' she sobbed. 'Where's my . . . m . . . ummy?'

'Shush,' Theo put his finger to his lips. Where indeed *was* her mummy? 'Shush, she's sleeping, we don't want to wake her.' He took the child into his arms, and sat with her on his knee. Betsy continued to shake and sob.

'Tell me about the dream, darling,' he spoke quietly and soothingly as he hugged her frail frame. 'It's all right now, I'm here.'

The 'phone call, he couldn't get it out of his head. It had come about ten o'clock, just as they were thinking about going to bed. Zoë got up early to milk the cow, so they tried to be in bed by eleven, on weeknights at least.

Zoë had answered the call. She seemed to be having some trouble with the person on the other end of the line. At first he thought it might be Isobel. They'd been together almost three years and although things had settled down, Isabel still never missed an opportunity to torment them. Then he wondered if it might be Steve Jarvis. He hadn't heard the call very clearly, he'd only caught little urgent phases like — 'I can't' and, 'I don't want to,' and he'd gathered from Zoë's voice that the person calling was giving her a bad time. He knew Steve was at Hulver, Josh had told him. He knew he didn't have anything to worry about; Zoë was long over him, but even so . . .

He still had the child in his arms and was rocking her back and forth, gently stroking her forehead and whispering comforting words to her.

'There was a monster,' Betsy stuttered, although she was much calmer now, 'and it nearly caught mummy, and then I woke up.'

'That's all right then, isn't it? Nearly's okay, as long as it didn't get her.'

'But, but, it *nearly* got her.'

He stroked the child's fine hair. 'Well it didn't get her, Mummy's fine.' He kissed her forehead. 'Mummy's just fine.'

When Zoë had replaced the receiver, he'd asked her who had called, and from being really heated on the 'phone, she'd became ultra casual. 'It was only Tiggy,' she'd said.

Theo may have be a bit slow on the uptake, but he knew darned well that it wasn't Tiggy on the telephone.

Then he'd said to her, 'Steve's shooting at Hulver tomorrow, did you know?'

And Zoë had answered casually — much too casually, 'Really? That's nice.'

But Theo hadn't been able to leave it there. 'Yes, your father told me. I never thought I'd see the day, did you?'

Zoë had lost it then. She'd snapped, 'Who cares? I'm sick and tired of hearing about Steve Jarvis.'

Then he'd known for certain that it had been Steve on the telephone. Yet still he hadn't been able to leave it alone.

'I wouldn't mind,' he said, 'If you felt you needed to . . .'

'Needed to what? Sleep with him?' Her voice was strained and angry.

That wasn't what he'd meant, he'd meant that maybe she needed to see him. She hadn't seen him for years, — perhaps seeing him would lay a ghost?

'If that's what you needed to do, Zoë,' he'd said.

Zoë had cried then. 'I need to marry you, Theo, I need you to be free. I need that cow of a wife of yours to be gone from here. I need to put our lives in order.' She'd sobbed and sobbed then, much as Betsy had done several hours later.

The child stirred in his lap, her eyelids were looking heavy, and her head was pressing on his arm. He settled her into her bed, pulled the covers up around her shoulders and then sat by her side gently stroking her forehead.

When he got back to his own room he looked at the clock, it was half past twelve. Where was Zoë?

Theo spent the next two hours in a twilight world of waking and dozing. At two-thirty the lights of Zoë's Land Rover played across the bedroom ceiling and he became wide awake.

He saw the lights dim and heard the door of the Land Rover close. He heard Zoë come into the cottage and go straight into the bathroom, and then he heard the shower running for what seemed like ages. Eventually he felt her slip into bed beside him, bringing a damp moist glow with her. He put out his hand; even her hair was damp. She had her back toward him and was lying on the very edge of the bed curled up in a foatal position, he couldn't be sure, but he thought that she was quietly sobbing. He didn't comfort her, to do so would expose him, he'd have to admit that he knew she'd been out and if he did that, then he'd have to ask where she'd been. It was a question that he didn't want answered.

In the morning, she went off to the farm really early, long before he was up. She was never very talkative at that early hour, so her behavior wasn't that unusual. Was she unusually reserved? He didn't know. But from the bed, even in the half light, he saw that her lower lip was cut and very swollen, and she had some angry scratches on her cheek, and when she pushed back the sleeve of her sweater, he saw that her arm was black and bruised. She looked tired and seemed depressed, but that wasn't surprising seeing as she'd had so very little sleep. He didn't mention her nocturnal exploits. He decided that he wouldn't ask, or if he did, he'd ask her that evening, once Elizabeth was in bed.

When Theo went into the bathroom to wash and dress, he spied a black plastic bin liner wedged between the basin and the bath, on examination, he found that it contained a set of Zoë clothes, the ones she had worn the day before. He was puzzled; maybe she was taking them to be dry cleaned? But she always washed sweat shirts and jeans, and besides, everything was there, right down to her underwear, he didn't know what it meant and he wasn't sure that he wanted to know. He bundled the clothes back into the bag and replaced them. He'd ask Zoë about them later, when they got a moment of quiet. There was probably a perfectly logical explanation, of course there was. But the sick feeling that had settled in the pit of his stomach weighed heavily, and it wouldn't go away. This was stupid. He only had to ask her, — and he would ask, — as soon as they had some time to together.

Chapter 42

Angela slapped the plate down in front of him; it hit the table with a dull thud.

Pie, chips and baked beans; pub food, he thought. He might just as well have gone to the Rose and Crown or eaten in the police canteen. In fact he'd have faired better in either. Both establishments would have flooded his plate with gravy, making it easier to swallow the mulch.

'All right for you?' She asked.

'What? Oh, oh yes, yes it's fine.'

He momentarily fixed his eyes on his wife of fifteen years. Any minute now, he thought, she'll peel off her clothes, unpin her hair, and then dance naked on the table. He smiled.

'What? What's funny?'

'What? Nothing, I was just thinking.' He glanced at her again. She seemed to have shrunk over the years; he didn't remember her as being such a little person.

'What were you thinking?'

Then she'll unzip my pants and she shraddle me, and she'll tell me she's riding the tiger and—

'I said, what were you thinking?'

He smiled broadly. 'You don't want to know.'

'I do. I do, Michael. What were you thinking?'

He sighed and dug his knife into the crust of the

pie, scoped out some meat, speared three, rather damp, greasy, chips and pushed the whole lot into his mouth.

'Tell me,' she insisted.

His eyes were drawn to her again. What had happened to the girl he married? Gravity, he thought, studying her double chin, bulbous nose and drooping bosom — gravity.

'Tell me,' she said again. That was typical of Angie, she even demanded to control his thoughts. All of him, that's what she wanted, all of him. When he'd promised to love and honour her, he'd overlooked the hidden agenda, he hadn't agreed to obey her, quite the contrary, but nevertheless, that's what she expected.

He'd been a good and faithful husband, he'd looked, but he'd never touched. But now that Debbie Smith had joined the team it was getting harder and harder not to stray. What was she? Twenty-eight? Thirty maybe? He could check up on that. He smiled. She was his for the asking, that was plain. A slip of a girl, pretty and sexy; he smiled again, she'd be willing to ride the tiger; she'd all but offered, and one day, one day soon, he just might take her up on it.

'Well,' Angie said. 'What are you looking so smug about?'

'I was just remembering that time when we went to the British Legion fund raiser.'

'I don't remember that,' she snapped.

'No? Well you got rather pickled, and you took all your clothes off in the car going home.'

'Don't be ridiculous, I—'

'Ridiculous or not, you definitely—'

'How's your tea? I went to Safeway for the pies.'

'Very nice. Surely you can't have forgotten, Angie?' He placed his hand on his crotch. 'Remember the way you used to ride the tiger?'

'That's enough of that filth, eat your tea before it gets cold.' She scraped her chair away from the table and disappeared into the kitchen.

That's enough. Yes, it was always enough for her, she wouldn't even talk about it, let alone do it. He was only forty-five and Angie wasn't yet forty; why should it all end? He still fancied her, well, that is to say, he still wanted sex. Debbie featured more prominently in his fantasies than Angie these days, but even so . . .

If they'd had children things might have been different. After Angie had been told that she'd probably never conceive, she stopped seeing the point of it, and his sexy laughing wife had turned into a frumpish prude of a woman, seemingly overnight. He pushed some more food into his mouth as Angela returned with a prefabricated syrup sponge.

'I've been asked if I'd like to go over to Fenshaw for a week or two?' He said.

'What for?'

'There's a DI going into hospital, — they're short staffed and so I said—'

'But why you?' She interrupted.

'I'm experienced and—'

'But it's a long way to go every day.'

'I'll probably stay over, get some digs, save on the journey—'

'But that's not fair, what am I supposed to do? Here, in the house all day, on my own?'

'I've said I'd do it now, it's only for a week or two. They've—'

'Well, you can tell them you've changed your mind, tell them that I can't do without you.'

'I want to go,' he said bravely.

'But why?'

To get away, I need air, I need space, I need a rest from you, and I might possibly bed Debbie Smith while I'm at it. He didn't say that, of course. He said 'I'm getting stale, I need a bit of stimulation.'

'But if you're away all day and all night, I'll be on my own. I hate being here on my own.'

'You cope when I'm on nights.'

'But then I know you'll be back in the morning. Don't go, please don't go.'

'I have to,' he said. Then he added brutally, 'I want to. I'm sorry, but I want to.'

She leaned over and snatched his plate away, even

331

though he hadn't quite finished, a soggy chip rolled onto the table.

'What'll you do for food? They'll be no home cooking.'

Home cooking, that was a laugh! Angie's idea of cooking was a pie from Safeway and a packet of oven chips.

'I'll manage, we'll get a good allowance.'

'We? Who's we?'

'Figure of speech, that's all.'

'Who else is going?'

'Me, just me. Look, Angie, don't take on. We're talking about a week or so, that's all, and I won't be away every night. I'll have time off. Tell you what, why don't you get your mum to come over, or better still, go and see her.'

'Why's that better still?'

'It'll give you a break, that's all.'

'A break! What, with my mother? She drives me crazy, you know that. She won't want to come anyway. She hates me, you know she does. Our Alan was always the favorite, I never got a look in.'

Michael closed his eyes, he'd known she'd take on like this; that's why he'd put off telling her. He was due to leave the day after tomorrow; he couldn't have left it much longer.

He dug his spoon into the treacle pudding. It had been left too long in the microwave and one side was hard and chewy, it made his teeth stick together.

'All right is it?' She asked.

'Yes, yes it's fine,' he mumbled, trying to force his tongue between his teeth.

'I'll make some coffee,' she said, and once more left the room.

Michael pushed his plate to one side. Oh Angie; she used to be such fun, — ten years ago she'd have gone to Fenshaw with him. Now look at her, she couldn't even raise a smile.

Angela returned carrying a tray. Michael studied her, noting the straggly hair strieked with grey, the dark, bushy, unplucked eyebrows hovering above darting black eyes, laced with wrinkles. He took in the sagging jaw and fine dark hair bordering her upper lip. She had been so pretty, she just didn't try anymore. But that wasn't really the problem; he was no oil painting. The problem lay in their differing appetites, she no longer wanted him, and he, if truth were know, had an indefinable want, a need; anyone would do, so long as they wanted him. So that, instead of seeing his wife's attributes, he saw only her faults. Not that he would ever dream of leaving her, how could he? She had become so dependent on him. She didn't even drive a car. She couldn't manage anything without him. She went as far as the local Safeway on her own, but that was only a short walk away. The weekly shop involved a trip to the outskirts of town, to Tesco or Sainsburys, and so he had to take her. And that was about the most exciting thing they ever did together.

She poured him some coffee.

'Thanks,' he said. 'You not having one?'

'I've lost my appetite,' she said, pursing her lips.

'Oh?' Like it or not, he was going; he refused to be blackmailed. He couldn't back out now anyway, not unless he went on sick leave and he'd never taken a day's sick in his entire career. Besides, Fenshaw was Debbie Smith's hometown. She'd go home on her days off and he could let her know he'd be there.

'When do you go?'

'Day after tomorrow.'

'It's short notice.'

'It's an emergency,' he lied.

'Oh.' She snatched the coffee cup away from him; once again he hadn't finished.

'I'll just have to manage then, won't I?'

''Fraid so,' he said, standing up and switching the television on.

Angela cleared all the dishes through to the kitchen, scraped them, piled them in the sink and squirted washing-up liquid all over them. Then she ran the tap. This done she came back into the living-room, plonked herself down in an easy chair, turned the volume up on the television and picked up her knitting.

Michael went through to the sink and began to wash and dry the dishes, just as he always did. He had a good view of Angela through the open door, she was chewing on a toffee, and her hands were flying over the knitting needles. It had been a long time since her nimble fingers were put to a more rewarding use.

She sensed him looking at her.

'What are you thinking?' She asked.

'That time we got locked in your bedroom at The Priory,' he said boldly, 'and your—'

'I don't remember that,' she snapped.

'But you *must* remember. Your dad came to the door, and you pulled my zip up so fast, you caught the bottom of your blouse in it, and you—'

'I said, I don't remember. Now leave it.'

'Okay, I'll leave it, but you did ask.' He smiled to himself. He'd always been such a good husband; he'd always stuck to the straight and narrow. Maybe now was the time to break out. He wondered what it would be like with another woman. He didn't want to die in ignorance, maybe, just maybe . . .

'What are you thinking?' Angela asked yet again.

'What a boring time I'm going to have at Fenshaw,' he lied.

She smiled. 'More fool you for going.'

'Yes,' he said. 'More fool me.'

Chapter 43

Grey mist lay before her in the valley, but here on the top of the hill, the sun was breaking through, lighting the treetops and exaggerating the red and gold autumn colours. She looked about her; she was acutely aware of the beauty and tranquility that surrounded her. Her heart felt heavy, she would have liked to succumb to the tears that hovered dangerously close to the surface. In her hand she carried an aluminum milk can full of fresh, warm milk. Bracken, the tri-coloured Border Collie, kept close to her heels. She reached the first gate and climbed it shakily, holding the milk can in one hand and steadying herself with the other; the dog sailed over the top bar with effortless ease. From the gate she followed the sheep track toward the big beech that grew on the side of the hill. She looked mostly to the right, her keen eyes checking the fence, and noting a fallen branch that she must get moved later that day. Apart from the fallen tree, everything appeared normal, but appearances were so often deceptive. Today nothing was right, and she felt that nothing would ever be right again. She had behaved in a stupid, idiotic way; she had committed an unforgivable sin. 'It wasn't my fault,' she said aloud. But deep down, she knew that it had been her fault, she should never have gone. She should never have deceived Theo. She was guilty and she was bound to be found out.

Halfway down the hill, and away from the big beech, she bore south until she came to the water trough. From there she had a clear view of the Hall roof, the orange pantiles, damp from the heavy dew, reflected the gold and yellow of the trees behind it. Leaves crunched underfoot as she walked, but there was no other sound. She rested for the briefest of moments, absently placing her free hand on her abdomen. Then she cut back on herself toward the school house that nestled in the valley, still used for its original purpose, but deserted at this early hour, its young charges still in their beds. The schoolhouse windows exhibited bright paintings, colourful images that seemed out of place in such a rural setting.

She deftly climbed a black iron sheep hurdle, and skirted the school on the southern side of the valley. She drew herself up by a young walnut tree. There she paused: she was a little out of breath. Her hands shook. After last night she just couldn't seem to get it together. The dog lay down on the ground, his ears pricked. She put the milk can at her feet; this time she placed both hands on her flat belly. She looked before her; her face set, and her shoulders slumped. Placing her cheek against the rough walnut bark, she stared ahead. The Hall roof was in full view now. The sun had not penetrated the lower part of the valley and the early mist still overhung the house, making the building look dark and lifeless. The tall chimneys looked black and slightly menacing against the brightly-lit trees in the background.

Zoë stood quite still, her face betraying none of the emotions she felt. She stared at the house as if hoping to penetrate the walls and observe the occupant. Garrick Hall was very still, nothing and no one stirred; there was no movement, no sign of life, but as Zoë reflected, there was rarely any sign of life at that time of the day.

She pushed her sleeve back. Her coat rubbed against her bruised arm, a physical and mental reminder of the night before. She gave an involuntary sob. She looked at her watch, seven fifteen; too early even for the spirit world to stir. Zoë snorted, she had no patience for Isobel's predictions and premonitions.

She picked up the can and, leaving the safety of the walnut tree, began walking over the meadow with the dog following close behind. Everystep of the way brought pain. If she breathed in it hurt, but no more than if she exhaled. She'd got to the point in her journey where she normally felt her most vulnerable, but today her vulnerability seemed to have doubled. She could hardly walk, and she felt exposed, — the watcher now in a position to be watched. She changed the milk can over to her other hand and tried to quicken her pace, but it was no use, her steps still remained slow and heavy. Any other morning should Lady Isobel Sheldon-Harris choose that particular moment to look out of her kitchen window, then she would see Zoë in full view, and if she had a mind to, she would come out and confront her. And there in that beautiful valley, guilt and pain would be taken out and aired in the magic of the morning. For as far as Isobel was concerned, Zoë must pay the price, and pay dearly. Isobel truly believed that Zoë was the reincarnation of Sally Smith, Charles Randall's mistress. But Zoë didn't really know what the price was, Sally Smith had hung alongside her lover in 1769, and Zoë wondered if Isabel would have her hang again, she wondered if, once the price was paid, it would make Theo hers? They had lived together for so long now and marriage seemed as far away as it ever had. Isobel was leaning more and more heavily on Theo, and Theo, from habit or a sense of duty, Zoë didn't know which, danced to the tune she played. Then there was Charlotte, Isobel's spiteful daughter, to contend with. Charlotte, who seemed to have everything going for her; looks, intelligence and money, she wanted for nothing. Everyone knew she was making a fortune from her mother's clairvoyance shows. And she'd had the nerve to ask Theo to sire her lover's child. Zoë felt that her hatred of Charlotte was possibly a bit irrational, but explainable or not, she still hated her. It was an obscure kind of jealousy. It was ridiculous; it wasn't as if Theo had complied, was it?

Why did Zoë stay living in the valley so close to those she despised? The answer was simple. She loved Theo Sheldon-Harris, she loved him more than anything in the world and Theo wouldn't, or couldn't, move, and Zoë wouldn't and couldn't leave him. And so she stayed. She would stay with him as long as he wanted her, and she would do what ever she had to do to make him keep on wanting her. And now she'd blown it, in one stupid act she'd thrown it all away.

'I've been wishing you dead for years,' Zoë said, looking toward the Queen Anne windows. Why was it that it was she, not Theo, who carried the blame of Theo's broken marriage? How she tired of hearing how in a past life she had persuaded Theo to commit murder. She was the scarlet woman, the femme fatal. Theo was all right; he could come and go as he pleased. Isobel was always using him. Yesterday she'd demanded that he go and change a light bulb. He'd gone of course, there'd been not a moment's hesitation. She'd 'phoned, and off he'd trotted. But Zoë had to creep past the Hall like a thief in the night. It wasn't fair; it just wasn't fair. Isobel lived like a queen; and she expected Theo to finance her extravagant life style, even though everyone knew she made a fortune from her seances or whatever she called them. Yet Theo paid up time and time again. 'I want to dance on your grave,' Zoë spat.

She swallowed, such sentiments were not normally in her nature, but Theo was acting in such an irresponsible way. What if she did get pregnant? What if she was pregnant already? They'd always agreed to wait until they were married. Why had Theo acted so irresponsibly? And why had she? Her parent's had been stoic when she had produced Elizabeth out of wedlock, but to do it again? There'd be no point in her telling them that she was twenty-six and well able to make her own decisions. They already knew that; and it wasn't any use her explaining that Theo would marry her tomorrow if he were free to do so; they knew that too. Nor could she use the modern argument, that no one gets married anymore, because in their social circle that simply wasn't true.

'Oh, Theo,' she sighed. Three weeks ago; that's all it had been, three weeks, but things had changed so much since then. She'd been due to start another course of her contraceptive pills. She'd woken in the morning and fumbled for the packet, and then she'd heard Theo chuckle. 'Looking for these?' He'd said. He'd crinkled the foil pack in his hands. 'I think we ought to make a definite commitment to each other, don't you?' She hadn't answered, just smiled, and felt full of warmth and love for him. 'And I think Betsy deserves a playmate,' he'd gone on to say; and then, with perfect aim, he'd thrown the packet of pills across the room and into the wastepaper bin. And Zoë had settled down under the covers, and Theo had snuggled up to her and held her, and made love to her, in that special way of his. And he'd whispered that, 'she should always take the morning price', as he bore into her, and made her want him so fiercely, that she thought she might one-day die of the thrill of him. Even now, despite the pain and the trauma of the night before, as she thought about him loving her in his straight uncomplicated way, she became breathless and needy, and longed for his arms around her. Why had she been so stupid? She'd had everything. Isobel was only a minor irritation, now that it was all changed . She wanted Theo's child; she wanted everything to be as it was before, before last night. Last night? Oh God, last night. What if? Oh God, what if? Why did she now have this added complication? If she had Theo's child before they were married her parents would cope. She straightened her back, the struggle of the night before had torn muscles and sprained ligaments, and whatever was wrong with her breathing? She should confide in someone, if not Theo, then maybe her mother? But her mother was all caught up with Tiggy and that barrister Alex, and her father was always out, tramping around the estate training Fable, his new dog. It had taken him ages to get over losing Fen and it had taken a long time before her mother had persuaded him to buy a new puppy. Now he was besotted with it. Anyway, they wouldn't understand, no one would understand. Perhaps she should go to the police, tell them the truth, and let them sort it out. But then she'd have to tell Theo and her parents. They would be shocked. She loved them, she couldn't put them through all that. She may be twenty-six, but she still didn't want them to be disappointed in her.

Two days ago, Steve Jarvis had come down to Hulver, and for the briefest of moments she hadn't known what she wanted anymore. Steve had spoken and acted as if he had prior claim on her. It was like she and he were

342

married and she was having an affair with Theo, — and she'd been so stupid, so, so stupid. She put her hand up to her cheek; it was scratched and bruised. Why, oh why had she done it? And why hadn't she told Theo what had happened last night? Truth was, she dare not, she was afraid of losing him. She felt Isabel and Charlotte's grip of him was getting tighter. Last night she'd lost her mind, that was the only explanation. Why else would she have acted so foolishly and risked everything.

She shuddered. She was so tired, so weary. Every bone in her body ached; she felt as if all the strength had been sucked out of her. It was all Isobel Sheldon-Harris's fault. If she'd have given Theo his freedom in the first place, then last night would never have happened. By now she'd have been a happily married woman, and she'd probably have several of Theo's children around her knee.

She looked over to the Hall again. 'I want to dance on your grave,' she said again, this time with real venom. 'If you'd have let Theo go, we could have married and everything would be all right. Last night would never have happened.'

She stared down at the cluster of buildings before her. Today the house remained quite quiet and undisturbed, peaceful almost, although Zoë knew from Theo's grief that the house had not known much peace since Isobel dwelt there. Two first floor windows, a guestroom and its en-suite bathroom, overlooked the meadow where Zoë now walked.

Today the windows were closed and the curtains were drawn back. No guest last night, thought Zoë; no ears to hear Isobel's tale of woe, reincarnation and intrigue. There were two ground floor windows below those of the guestroom. One belonged to the kitchen, and the other to a small study, a room where Lady Isobel Sheldon-Harris toiled, endlessly assessing her future finances, adding a list of wants to a list of needs and then adding noughts to the already inflated figures. Or were they Charlotte's wants and needs? It was difficult to tell. Since Isobel started hosting her meetings and taking private clients, Charlotte acted as a kind of manager, and Zoë had no doubt that she influenced her mother and persuaded her to make inflated demands. But no matter who was the instigator, the letters came anyway. Letters that invariably began with, 'Dear would-be murderer,' and ended with, 'I will never forgive you, and I will never give you your freedom in this life, or in the next'.

Zoë crossed the cattle grid and hurried along the south drive. She kept her eyes on the house, all the time looking for signs of movement. The dining room curtains were open; the drawing room curtains were closed. One of the first floor windows on the south side was open just a crack. The lights inside the house, although switched on, were barely visible in the gathering light, but in most rooms a faint, pale glow could be seen. The glass doors of the porch were closed; the inner wooden doors were open. Lady Isobel's car, the big maroon Mercedes, was parked on the gravel in front of the house.

'Lazy cow,' Zoë said aloud. 'Nice car like that and she can't even be bothered to put it in the garage at night.' Her voice echoed the bitterness she felt. For in truth she resented the fact that Theo had been bullied into buying it. Isobel could well afford to buy her own car; in fact she could afford a fleet of cars.

Zoë left the drive and cut across the top of the south lawn, which she noted needed cutting. The last cut of the year, she thought. A few seconds later, she arrived at Garrick Cottage, the home she shared with Theo; her body wracked with pain and her heart thumping with anxiety.

Chapter 44

Zoë gently shut the door of the cottage and leaned against it. She closed her eyes for a few seconds waiting for her heartbeat to calm.

Theo came into the little hallway. 'What are you doing there?' he asked.

She shook her head. 'Nothing, nothing.' Her heart was still jumping in her chest; it had been that way since last night. She must forget about last night. She must wipe it from her memory. No one must know; she would destroy the evidence and carry on as if nothing had happened. But what if? Oh God, what if?

'How is Daisy today?' he asked, as he kissed her cheek. She winced, her face was very sore, she half expected Theo to ask how she'd hurt it; she had her answer all ready, but he didn't ask. He smiled at her, but he looked tired and troubled.

'Acting very awkwardly, and I think we'll have to put her in calf again soon.' Zoë unconsciously stroked her stomach as she spoke. 'Her milk's drying up, and besides, we could do with a hunk of beef to boost our supplies.'

Theo laughed. 'You won't say that when she presents you with a soft, brown-eyed calf — in fact you will seriously consider becoming a vegetarian. I know you.' His eyes looked troubled but his mouth had a merry, teasing look; the look she loved so much. Immediately her heart felt lighter. Theo murmured something else, but it was drowned by the noise of the pajama clad Betsy dragging a book bag though the hall and into the kitchen.

'Mummy, Theo says I must finish the Cornflakes before I open the Rice Krispies.'

Zoë looked at Theo, who shrugged his shoulders. 'Well, it's a waste,' he said defensively.

'I agree with Theo,' Zoë said. 'Waste not, want not.'

'It won't be a waste if you and Theo eat them,' four year old Elizabeth replied. She flounced around the kitchen; her straight, almost red, hair bounced and shimmered as she moved.

Zoë ignored her daughter and turned back to Theo. 'Theo, she's not even dressed yet, let alone started to eat breakfast. She'll be late for school.'

Theo made a feeble effort to help Elizabeth remove her top. But Zoë slammed the milk can down and, holding her ribs, she almost dragged her into the bathroom. Elizabeth looked heavenward and Theo laughed and winked at her. Moments later, Zoë returned with the child neatly dressed, in grey and navy, ready for school.

She sat Betsy down at the table and poured her a bowl of cornflakes, adding fresh milk from the can, and sprinkling the top with sugar. The child turned her nose up but dug her spoon in and started to eat.

'Mummy, how did you hurt your face?' Elizabeth asked.

Zoë shook her head, as if to tell the child to be quiet. 'I tripped over Bracken,' she said barely above a whisper.

She glanced over at Theo who was seated at the same table; he didn't seem to be taking any notice of the exchange but was ticking off cheque stubs against his bank statement.

'Who's A. F. Bennett, twenty-seven pounds?' He asked.

'Shoes,' Zoë replied absently pouring some corflakes into her own bowl, her hand shook a little, she couldn't get the events of the previous night out of her head.

'What shoes?'

'Betsy's school shoes,' she sighed. *What's it matter what shoes?* She thought, *don't you know what I've done? I've let you down. Once you know what I've done you won't give a damn about shoes, you'll just stop loving me.*

'But she only had a new pair a few weeks ago. Why does she need more?'

Zoë pushed her straight blond hair away from her eyes in an exaggerated manner. 'It's been months since she had new shoes, not weeks. Children's feet grow, you know, they don't stay the same. If you didn't want to buy them you should have said so.'

'I didn't mean . . . I mean, of course I don't mind

348

buying her shoes, but it *has* only been a few weeks since . . . '
he started to flick through the cheque stubbs.

'Why can't we have proper milk in proper bottles?'
Elizabeth asked, her freckled nose smelling the milk newly
poured on her cornflakes. 'Proper milk like other people?'
She added, still wrinkling her nose and sniffing.

Zoë snatched the cheque book out of Theo's hand,
her ribs delivered a searing pain. She tried to catch her
breath, then, as she caught Theo looking at her, she flipped
back the stubs to October 1st.

'Look,' she said, 'Isobel Sheldon-Harris, one
thousand, five hundred.' She went back further. 'September
first, Isobel Sheldon-Harris, one thousand, five hundred.
August first—'

Theo drew a deep breath. 'All right, all right, I take
your point. You don't think I want to make these payments,
do you? But she is my—' he hesitated.

'Your wife, why don't you just say it straight?
She's you wife, and I'm only, your — what am I? Your bit
on the side?' Zoë sniffed back her rage. 'Do you know what
I found myself wishing today?'

'That she were dead?' Theo asked simply.

'Something like that,' Zoë said quietly and sniffed.
'I imagined myself dancing on her grave, and that's a
terrible thing.' She stood up and folded her arms, she felt
cold, although the cottage was very warm and cosy. 'Maybe
she's right. Maybe we are reincarnated. I certainly have

more hate for her than one lifetime could build.'

'Mmm,' Theo shook his head. 'Nevertheless, she is my—'

'Wife,' Zoë snapped.

'My . . . my responsibility. I have to — well — provide for her, don't I? I wish to God I didn't. It cripples me, you know that.'

But Zoë wasn't finished. 'And Betsy,' she nodded toward Elizabeth, 'is nothing whatsoever to do with you, is she? She's not your wife or your daughter, so why should you buy her a piddling pair of shoes? Except, of course, that I not only feed you, and clean, and care for you, I also work on your two-bit farm for forty or more hours a week for nothing. Whilst her bloody ladyship swans about the place, conning the public and making a fortune to boot, dining out and maligning me. What's it matter if my child goes barefoot?'

Theo had his hands up in the air, as if to physically ward off his lover's verbal blows.

'Why can't we have proper milk in bottles like other people?' Elizabeth repeated, seemingly unaware of her elders' discord. 'Granny has proper milk.'

'Because, Theo would rather have me playing milkmaid than deprive her high and mighty ladyship of two pounds a week,' screeched Zoë fleeing from the room. 'And eat your breakfast, and don't go giving it to Bracken,' she shouted as she headed in the direction of her and Theo's bedroom. She slammed the door shut and lowered herself into the warmth and safety of their double bed, where, doubled up in pain, she sobbed with guilt and frustration. Oh God, what had she done? She should tell Theo, tell him straight, tell him what happened last night. He would understand, he loved her, he would forgive her; he would forgive her anything. But then a little voice of doubt crept into her head *anything, but that,* it said, *anything but that.*

Theo was left in the kitchen to cope with Elizabeth. He murmured that Mummy was tired, she'd had a bad night; sometimes she gets cross, but she doesn't mean it.

'It's my fault because I had a bad dream, isn't it?' the child said in a matter of fact voice. 'Where was Mummy, Theo? Where did she go?'

'Nowhere sweetheart,' Theo said, his voice troubled. 'She was right here, asleep, in our bed.'

'But . . . ' the child frowned.

'But what?'

'Nothing,' the frown remained. 'How did Mummy get hurt?'

'She told you, darling, she tripped over Bracken.'

'Theo? You do still love Mummy, don't you?'

'Oh yes,' he replied. 'Oh, God, yes, more than anything.'

'More than me?'

Theo, smiled as he looked down on Zoë's child. He smoothed her hair with his big hand. 'I love your mother more than anyone,' he said, 'but you come a pretty close second.'

She pursed her lips, as if to give his words due consideration. 'But, Theo, why can't we have proper milk like other people?'

352

Chapter 45

Zoë sat stiffly in Dr Armstrong's waiting room, her fists and jaw clenched. She'd lived in Garrick-in-the-Willows for over three years and she knew almost everybody. Old Mrs Yates sat opposite her, her toothless rubbery gums working back and forth as if she were chewing gum. She stared ahead of her and straight in Zoë's direction but she made no sign of recognition.

A young mother, whom Zoë didn't know, sat to her left cradling a small fractious infant, and next to her, Ted Lea, one of Theo's farm workers, was nursing a bandaged hand. He nodded to Zoë and held his hand up.

'Caught it in the kettle steam, I did, Mrs Sheldon-Harris, it's hell and all painful as well.'

Zoë blushed. People had started to refer to her as Mrs Sheldon-Harris. It had just happened, and she'd never bothered to correct anyone, it seemed easier to let it go; besides, she liked it. Only she wasn't Mrs Sheldon-Harris. She was Zoë Elliot, and she was here to ask Dr Armstrong to help her.

She was a nervous wreck by the time she was called into the surgery. Twice she'd almost decided to take potluck, and had got up to leave, but the thought of being pregnant, with all its implications, had sobered her up. She couldn't have a child, not now, not after what had happened.

'Zoë,' Dr Armstrong beamed at her. 'What can I do for you?' He was an old friend of Theo's. She wouldn't be able tell him the truth.

She bit into her swollen bottom lip. 'I need . . . I'm afraid I've been rather stupid, I've um, I've . . . er, had unprotected sex . . . and . . . er.' There it was, she had said it.

'When?'

She swallowed. 'Last night, I wondered if . . . if I could have the morning-after pill? . . . or . . . or something.' Now it was all out, but she didn't feel one jot better.

Jeremy Armstrong looked at Zoë's records. He frowned as he studied them. He was a small neat man with a bit of a potbelly. He wore his glasses attached to a string around his neck, and now he fumbled for them and studied her notes even more carefully.

'You're on the pill. Forget to take it, did you?'

'No, I mean, yes. No, I mean . . . I didn't start them at all this month, you see Theo and I thought . . . well, we thought . . . well, we're never going to be able to get married, we thought she'd never divorce him, so we might just as well get on and . . . '

'Have a baby?'

'Yes.'

Dr Armstrong looked at her, it was, she thought, as if he was looking into her heart and could see her guilty secret.

'And now you've changed you mind?'

'No, no, not that, not really, it's just that other things have changed, it's just the wrong time for me to be pregnant, you see . . . '

Dr Armstrong nodded his head. 'I see.' Although it was blatantly obvious that he didn't see at all.

He pulled a prescription pad toward him and wrote on it.

'Take one of these as soon as you can — preferably with food, then you must take the other pill exactly twelve hours later. The instructions are on the box, read them carefully.'

He signed the prescription.

Zoë was biting into her lip, an action that opened up the scar that she'd got the night before.

'You're sure about this, Zoë?'

'Very sure.'

He plucked a tissue from a box on his desk and handed it to her.

'Your lip's bleeding.'

She tried to blot it, but missed, and he took the tissue from her and gently patted the cut.

'This could do with a stitch,' he said. 'But it'll leave a scar if I put one in.'

He went over to the wash-hand basin, moistened another tissue, and, placing the cool damp wodge on her lip he said, 'Suppose you tell me, what this is *really* all about?'

She shook her head, and ran her fingers through her hair, she felt very close to tears. Dr Armstrong pushed her hair away from her forehead and revealed the bruises and scratches.

'Good heavens, how'd you come by those?' he turned her face toward the window, which threw light on her scratched cheek. He opened a drawer and took out an antiseptic wipe and dabbed it on the red angry welds.

It stung, and she put her hand up, Jeremy caught hold of it and pushed her sleeve back revealing more bruises and scratches.

'What happened Zoë? Theo hasn't . . . '

She shook her head vigorously. 'No, no please, it's nothing . . . it's all sorted now. Please don't say anything, not to anybody . . . you won't, will you?' She grabbed the prescription and got up.

Jeremy Armstrong stood between her and the door. 'Someone should talk to Theo, he can't just—'

'Please, please don't mention this to anyone, you must promise me, you won't say anything will you?' She was almost pleading.

'No, but—'

'Thank you, Dr Armstrong,' she said, she was already halfway out of the door.

'Zoë?' she heard him call as she made her way back to the waiting room. But she didn't stop, she carried on through the waiting area and out to the Land Rover, clutching the precious piece of paper that she knew would solve all her problems.

Chapter 46

Charlotte Bridges swung the white Porsche through the gates of Garrick Hall with the ease of a confident driver. She slowed down as she neared Garrick Cottage.

'Don't want to mow the Betsy-brat down,' she said to Flora, laughter in her voice. 'That would never do!'

Once past the cottage she picked up speed, so much so, that she had to brake quite sharply and arrived at the Hall in a cloud of dust.

Tom Farrow, the gardener, shook his untidy grey head. 'Like mother, like daughter,' he said aloud.

Farrow had worked at Garrick Hall for the past twenty years. He took a pleasure in witnessing the comings and goings of the family. He could not, under any circumstances be described as a loyal retainer, loyalty didn't feature in his vocabulary. But he did have a high regard for Sir Theo, perhaps because he, as a general rule, had quite a low opinion of women; so as a result of his gender, Sir Theo scored points.

Farrow decided to make himself scarce. He had no desire to pass the time of day with Charlotte Bridges. He quickly slipped inside the potting shed on the pretext of attending to some young seedlings. He hung his tattered check jacket on a nail hammered into the back of the door and rolled back the grubby sleeves of his coarse, checkered shirt. He leaned against the potting bench in such a way that his extremely ill fitting trousers looked more baggy than they truly were. Thus he positioned himself so that he could watch the new arrivals.

Farrow was a man of almost seventy. His wiry grey hair contrasted sharply with his neat black eyebrows. He was square chinned and his mouth had long since taken on a downward turn, making him look dour, an impression confirmed by his speech and attitude.

'Wait here, darling. I'll just worn mother that we've arrived,' Charlotte shouted as she hopped out of the car. She'd had her dark hair cut and styled to look thick and bouncy. Her wide smile exposed perfect white teeth confirming that her orthodontic treatment was money well spent. She was well groomed and her face was evenly tanned, but today, her quick movements lacked rhythm. She was in a happy, almost manic, mood. She was always that way after taking the car on a long journey. She got a kick out of driving, akin, she said, to any drug-induced buzz.

Charlotte was wearing very tight black trousers, a white sweater and black ankle boots. A black embroidered Pashmina was slung carelessly over her shoulder. In fact she was a perfect match for the car with its white body and black seats. Even the numberplate had a sense of order about it, GER 1234. The car and Charlotte went well together. Sleek, expensive, coordinated and powerful.

She went to the front door and pressed the brass

bell. At the same time she turned the knob on the glass porch. Seemingly certain that it would open, she put her full weight against it, but the door was unyielding and she banged her nose and forehead against the glass.

Flora opened her window. 'Idiot!' She laughed.

Charlotte stopped rubbing her nose just long enough to put out her tongue in Flora's direction. Farrow eased his position, a smile played on the down-turned lips; he was enjoying the display.

Charlotte glanced over to the potting shed. She was well aware that Farrow was watching.

'Funny,' she said. 'Mother never locks the glass doors during the day.' She rang the bell again and again. She could hear it ringing deep inside the house, but her mother did not come.

'I'll go round to the back. Don't look so worried, Flora. Mother will be pleased to see you.'

'Oh yes? I bet she will,' Flora grimaced, narrowing her eyes as if to add weight to her conviction.

Charlotte returned a few moments later. 'There's no sign of her. She must have popped out to the shops or something, or maybe she's had to go and see a client. She's expecting us, so she can't have gone far.'

'Correction, my love,' said Flora. 'She's expecting you, or at least she *was* expecting you, yesterday. She'll be really cross that you've brought me, you know. I really think you should have stuck to the original plan and seen her alone. If you want to talk business, she won't want me around.'

Charlotte put her hands on her hips. 'I told you Flora, I don't want to talk *business,* as you put it. I just want to thank her for the holiday, in fact we should both thank her.'

'Perhaps she got wind of me coming, and decided to batten down the hatches and hoist up the drawbridge.'

'Oh, don't be silly, darling, she really likes you. You imagine these things.' Charlotte folded her arms and rubbed the sleeves of her sweater. She glanced over to the potting shed and forced a smile in its direction. She knew Farrow was there and she wasn't sure how much he could hear.

'Your mother looks at me as if I'm a bad smell, and don't tell me that I imagine it, because I know I don't.'

Charlotte sighed; she had to bring the conversation to an end. She leaned over the car window, turned her body a little so that Farrow got a clear uninterrupted view, and gave Flora a deep and passionate kiss, fondling her breasts as she did so.

There's a nice little show for you Farrow, she thought.

Flora enjoyed the kiss for a few moments, then, seemingly alarmed, she pulled away.

'What if your mother's watching?'

'She knows the score.'

'And she doesn't like it.'

'She's disappointed at not having grandchildren, that's all. If only you'd . . .'

'I can't, Lottie, I told you. I've thought and thought about it, and I just can't go through with it.'

'You once said you'd go to a clinic and—'

'I changed my mind, I'll never have a child.'

Charlotte smiled. She bent back over the car and kissed her again.

'Dirty unnatural buggers,' Farrow said, a glint in his eyes.

'Don't take any notice of Mother,' Charlotte whispered to Flora 'It's just her way. I'll go and ask Farrow where she is.'

Her small, neat rear disappeared towards the potting shed.

'Well, Miss,' said Farrow in his slow Norfolk drawl, 'I ain't seen her all day. Not at all today, and it's payday tomorrow as well. I hope she hasn't gone out or anything. Sir Theo brings the money down to Lady B on a Tuesday and I picks it up from her on the Wednesday.' He took out a large silver pocket watch and squinted at it. It told him that it was almost eleven o'clock. Still squinting, he looked up at Charlotte. 'I ain't set eyes on her all morning, and I've been here since seven. I'm meant to finish at eleven. I'm only part-time, you know. I suppose she *will* pay me tomorrow?'

The last statement was issued in the form of a question, and when Charlotte didn't respond, he repeated it in rather too loud a voice.

'I said, Miss, that I suppose she'll pay me tomorrow?'

'What? Oh yes, I expect she will.'

Charlotte rubbed her forehead. She felt as if she were on stage, putting on a performance especially for Tom Farrow. Well, she was supposed to be a rising star, wasn't she? She'd give an Oscar performance. She'd act as if her life depended on it.

Chapter 47

After leaving Dr Armstrong, Zoë went first to the chemist and then to the village shop where she bought a packet of digestive biscuits and a pint of milk. That done, she drove to the farmyard. In one of the loose boxes she ate two of the biscuits and drank half of the milk, then she swallowed one of the two tablets, ate two more biscuits and finished off the milk. She decided that she was feeling a little better, her chest didn't seem quite so raw. Maybe it was the relief at having swallowed the tablet.

It was eleven-thirty. She'd have to wait up that night in order to take the other tablet. Theo liked to be in bed by ten. She'd have to make an excuse, she'd tell him that she wanted to see the eleven o'clock news.

She went out to the yard and put a handful of straw into the drum of the incinerator. Then she went into the tractor shed and came back with some old oily rags; she placed the rags on top of the straw and set light to it. Next she took the black plastic bag of clothing out of the Land Rover, and carefully added her sweatshirt to the pyre, next came her underwear and finally her—

'Zoë? What are you doing?' Theo startled her. The jeans fell from her hand onto the earth.

'I . . . I didn't hear your car,' she said defensively.

'I walked. I thought maybe I'd take you out to

lunch.' He frowned and put his hand up to his cheek. 'But never mind that — why are you burning your clothes?'

Tears flooded her eyes. 'They're dirty. I don't want them, they're filthy.' She was sobbing now. 'I don't want them . . . Oh Theo, I don't feel very well.' That was true, she was suddenly feeling extremely ill. It wasn't so much her chest now, it was her stomach, she felt as if she might vomit at any moment. 'I think I'm going to be sick.'

'There's only one old girl not tupped,' Andy said coming into the farmyard with Bracken at his heels.

'What?' Theo said, putting his arm around Zoë and guiding her to the Land Rover.

'Those old ewe's that missed the ram. Zoë said to put them in again. They'll be late lambing but . . . Is Zoë all right? She looks awful, and where'd she get all them bruises?'

Theo sounded irritated when he answered. 'No, she's not all right. Now open the door for me and help her in.'

'I'm fine,' Zoë said, 'I'll be all right in a minute, just let me catch my breath.'

'You look as white as a sheet,' Andy said.

'Thank you, Andy,' Theo said, 'that'll be all. Now find yourself something to do, there's a good chap. Zoë will be fine.'

Andy nodded and made his way over to the incinerator. Zoë opened her mouth to tell him to leave it; she would see to it, but instead of speaking, she retched. She leaned back on the Land Rover seat, the door was open and her legs dangled out.

'Have you eaten something funny?' Theo asked. Then his face brightened. 'Maybe you're pregnant?'

She shook her head, but again she retched, she mustn't be sick, she must keep the pill down. But it was hopeless; she pitched forward out of the Land Rover door and was very, very sick. She vomited until her stomach hurt, and her bruised ribs ached, her forehead was beaded with sweat and her hair stuck to the back of her neck.

Theo held onto her until the convulsions subsided. Then he helped her back into the vehicle. He went over to Andy and told him to make sure that the fire was safe, then he climbed in the driver's side and started the engine.

'I think I'd better take you home to bed,' he said.

Zoë didn't argue; she just nodded her head. She was frightened, really frightened. She wondered if the vomiting had made the pills ineffective. Dr Armstrong hadn't mentioned it. She had glanced at the leaflet inside the box, but the print was so small and her vision was cloudy, she ought to read it now, but she could hardly do that in front of Theo. she did know that whatever else she did, she must make sure she took the other pill that evening. She patted the pocket of her Barbour jacket, for in it lay her salvation.

Andy watched them drive away. He frowned as he

poked the fire, the clothes were slow burning. Ted Lea joined him; he seemed to have appeared from nowhere.

'What you doing?'

'What's it look like? Here take over will you? I need to get old Bracken a drink of water.'

'Carn't do that,' Ted said, holding up his bandaged hand up. 'Got to keep this clean.'

'Okay, you give the dog some bloody water, and I'll do this.'

Ted looked as if he was going to argue, thought better of it, and went over to the tap.

'Them looks like good clothes,' Ted said when he returned. He picked up the jeans. 'Look at these.'

Andy took them from him and held them up. He turned his mouth down and raised his eyebrows. 'Bloody Levi's,' he said suprised. 'Why she want to get rid of these?'

'Fit your Cathy, wouldn't they?'

'Not at the moment, she's six months gone.'

'Oh right, forgot that. Ere, do you think that's what's wrong with her? She were in the doctor's this morning.' he nodded toward the road.

'Could be, I suppose. Be nice if it was, wouldn't it?'

'Would explain why she's getting rid of stuff,' Ted said.

'And it would explain why she's just been as sick as a dog.'

Andy held the jeans up again. 'Yer, but burning a pair of Levi's!'

'They'd fit your Cathy after the baby comes.' Ted said.

'Probably would,' Andy nodded. He took the jeans over to his car and put them in the boot. 'Best keep it to yourself, Ted. I'm sure Zoë wouldn't mind, but you never know.'

'Shan't tell a soul, Andy. Now what would you like me to do?'

Andy scratched his head. 'Well, she's forgotten to take old Bracken home, take a walk over the park and deliver him to the cottage, will you? Only, mind the she-devil at the Hall don't see you.'

Ted threaded a piece of orange string through Bracken's collar and, whistling happily, he made his way out of the farmyard and toward the cottage.

Chapter 48

Charlotte's eyes were fixed on her mother's bedroom window. She could see that the lights were on even though it was a clear sunny day.

'You go off, Farrow,' she said, and she turned abruptly.

Farrow's mouth turned even lower and he snorted. His opinion of women was not to be altered.

Charlotte hurried towards Flora who was leaning against the car. She had the collar of both her blouse and her blazer turned up, and her sleeves were pushed back. She was leaning against the car door, her legs crossed at the ankles and her hands plunged into the pockets of the blazer. She was a handsome girl, but in an old fashioned sort of way, fleshy and curvaceous, and, despite, or maybe because of her sexual preferences, she was extremely feminine. Her dark features were even and clearly defined, and dimples appeared in her cheeks when she smiled. Of the two girls, she was by far the prettier.

'Flora, Mother can't possibly have gone shopping. Her car's still here, and she would never walk to the village, she's not into that. Look, all the lights have been left on.' She pointed to the drawing room windows. 'Perhaps she's been taken ill or something.' A frown clouded the perfectly made-up face.

'Come on, Lottie,' Flora said, 'aren't you over-reacting? Since old Theo foots the electricity bill your mother has never been known to stint on the illuminations. In fact I suspect she burns as much as she can, just for the hell of it.'

'That's not fair, Flora. Mother feels safer when the house is lit. It's hardly her fault that Theo ran off with a farm girl, now is it? Poor mother has problems enough living in a huge house like this, without you making that sort of comment.'

Flora raised an eyebrow, a rehearsed expression that emphasized her pretty features.

'Come off it, Lottie,' she laughed. 'What's got into you? Why are you talking like this? You hate the sight of her most of the time.'

Charlotte flushed. 'You don't understand. I may complain about her, but she *is* my mother.'

'Before you reduce me to tears, aren't you forgetting something?'

'What?'

'Well, she has no need to stay here, for God's sake. It's Theo's family home, poor sod, it must be costing him a fortune to run. I don't know why he doesn't just throw her out. Besides, your old lady is raking it in, she's holding at least one meeting a month, and then she has all her private consultations.'

'She doesn't make *that* much, Flora.' She turned

on her heels and began walking away from the car. 'Why should she get out and let Theo and his floozy live here? She has every right to stay as long as she pleases. Now come on, we're not going to have another row about it. The bathroom window is open and Farrow has a ladder. We'll let ourselves in, and make sure mother's all right.'

Flora caught up with her and, putting her hand on her shoulder, she turned her around.

'Just a minute Lottie. We need to have this out, you've changed your tune. Only a month or so ago you said that your mother ought to settle and give Theo his freedom. As you pointed out, if she doesn't get a slice of Theo's money before she dies, then we won't inherit a brass farthing from her.'

'We, Flora? We? Don't you mean me?' Charlotte said through clenched teeth.

'You know what I mean, Lottie.'

'And please don't talk like that about my mother. It's her life, and it's her money.'

'It's about the baby, isn't it? That's what this is all about. Even if I was prepared to go through with it, which I'm not. I don't want to saddle myself with a child, things are really taking off for me at the moment.' She slipped her arm around Charlotte's waist, and kissed her cheek. 'I thought you'd accepted it.'

Charlotte pulled away from her.

'Look, Lottie, if it really means that much to you,

371

why don't you have one? I'd help all I could. You could approach Theo again, or go to a center. Only I just don't want to go through nine months of disgusting pregnancy, give birth and then find out that I can't get a part.'

Charlotte suddenly brightened. 'I'm sorry, darling,' she said. 'I shouldn't go on about it, only I fancy you something rotten, and I'd fancy you a whole lot more if you were pregnant. I keep imaging your breasts filled with milk and—'

'Bad reason to bring a child into the world,' Flora said.

'You'd change your mind,' Charlotte said. 'I know you would, once you found yourself pregnant, you'd want it as much as me.'

'Well, unless we're into the Immaculate Conception, I'm never going to find out, am I.'

'Things happen,' Charlotte replied.

'What? Big-John the dildo going to shoot me a load, is he?'

Charlotte shrugged. 'You never know.' She laughed. 'Come on, let's go and get this ladder. And Flora?'

'Yes?'

'I love you.'

'I love you, too.'

Once the ladder had been put in place, there was a slight disagreement as to who should enter the house. Charlotte hated heights, whereas Flora didn't mind them at all. Even so, Flora didn't relish the thought of coming face to face with Lady Sheldon-Harris whilst breaking and entering.

'She might be having a bath,' Flora said.

Charlotte looked thoughtful. 'That's a point, and she would probably lock the door beforehand.'

She thought for a moment more.

'No, Flora. She's expecting me. She wouldn't have a bath now, nor would she go out. Something is wrong, I know it is. She should be here.'

'Okay, okay, but who's going up the ladder?'

'It looks awfully high, Flora. You know I'm not good with ladders and heights and things.'

She stood looking gloomily up at the window. Farrow stood watching from the shrubbery. He made no effort to help, but he didn't seem prepared to leave either. He was still enjoying the entertainment.

'All right, I'll go up the ladder,' Flora said. 'You hold the bottom and keep it steady.'

Charlotte did as she was bid, and Flora, who was surprisingly nimble, scooted up the ladder. The sash window opened smoothly and Flora slipped into the bathroom with ease.

Once inside the eerily silent house, Flora felt an inexplicable sense of foreboding. She crossed the bathroom and entered Lady Isobel's bedroom. The bed had been made, but it was untidy, as though she had lain on it and ruffled the bedspread.

'Well, at least she's up and about,' she said aloud.

She left the bedroom and went along the book-lined landing. Nothing seemed amiss; she descended the sweeping staircase. At the bottom step, she hesitated and listened; the very air in the house seemed oppressive, it was just too quiet. She admonished herself for being silly. Old Issie was out and no mistake. What's more she'd go mad if she thought that the girls had entered without her permission. She decided that Isobel had probably forgotten that Charlotte was coming, or had gone out to teach her a lesson.

Flora's footsteps echoed as she walked across the hall with its marble floor. Reaching the solid front door, which stood open, she passed through, admiring the big oak doors as she did so, and slid back the bolt on the glass outer door. With a deep bow, she swung the door back and let Charlotte in.

'Good afternoon, Madam, do come in. So sorry about the class of butler Madam is having to employ now-a-days, but you know, what with Sir Theo living it up with his floozy, times is very hard and one has to take what one can get.'

Charlotte giggled. 'Oh, Flora, you're such a fool.' She put her hand over her mouth; she couldn't seem to control her giggles.

'It wasn't that funny,' Flora said.

374

'Shush,' Charlotte rejoined, starting to control herself. 'She might hear you.'

'Oh no she won't, she's not here. The place is as dead as the Dodo.'

They went into the drawing room. The ashes lay cold and still in the hearth. Charlotte drew back the curtains and switched the lights off.

'That's funny. Ruth hasn't cleaned up in here today.'

'I expect Issie's having to cut down on cleaners now, it's hard for her to make ends meet on her measly allowance.'

Charlotte pretended to take a swipe at her.

'Don't take the micky out of my mother,' she said, she was still close to giggling. 'She can't help it, Flora, she was so hurt when Theo left. She has a problem with forgiving him, especially when he was responsible for, well you know, all that business in her past life.'

'Oh spare me!' Flora exclaimed. 'You're not going to pretend that you believe in all that? Oh come on, you've told me what you think of her spirits and all that lark.'

'Well you never know. Besides, she believes it and you never know what—'

'You mean you're changing your mind! I don't believe it!'

'I didn't say that, I just said that she believed in it. She moans and groans about money and things because she's hurt, that's all.'

'I hear you, but I don't buy it. She was soon on to your dad, wasn't she?'

'They were friends, that's all. It's not what you think. Look Flora, let's not argue, let's check upstairs and make sure mother's not ill, and then we'll make some tea.'

They toured the house, beginning with Lady Isobel's bedroom and then working their way through the maze of bedrooms, bathrooms, and sitting rooms that comprised Garrick Hall. Finally, they checked the dining room and Theo's old study.

'There you are, darling,' Flora said. 'I told you there was nothing to worry about. She probably spied me in the car and made a bolt for it.'

Charlotte still couldn't seem to control her giggles.

'What's the matter with you?' Flora asked.

'You're funny, that's all,' Charlotte spluttered. 'Go and put the kettle on, and I'll tell Farrow that it's all right.'

'I climbed the ladder, you make the tea. I'll tell Farrow.'

Charlotte seemed suddenly serious, 'No, no, you make the tea. I'll tell Farrow.'

Flora shook her head. 'Too late,' she said and she ran toward the door.

When Flora returned to the house she found Charlotte standing with her hand on the kitchen door-jamb.

Her eyes wide and her mouth open as if to scream, but the only sound to be heard was that of a distant clock striking the hour.

Lady Isobel Sheldon-Harris lay on her back with her legs bent under her. She was wearing a red woollen wrap-around skirt and a white blouse. The blouse was torn at the shoulder, and the skirt was bunched up around her waist. Her underwear was torn and her lower body was exposed. A pair of flat red shoes was close by. Her face was swollen and distorted. A piece of orange bailer twine cut deep into her neck.

Flora had an urge to laugh, she really couldn't reason why. A thought flitted through her head: it was, she thought, the only time he had ever known Isobel Sheldon-Harris silent.

Chapter 49

Michael Harper had had a bad start to the day. Angela had been quiet and sullen at breakfast, then they'd argued, and then she had cried when he left for work. She'd 'phoned twice during the morning, asking him to run errands, and emphasizing her need of him. Now it was almost lunchtime and the day was definitely getting worse.

'You can't be serious,' he said to Soames. 'You can't be. Fenshaw is fifty miles away. There must be someone nearer — there must be.' A look of panic had seized his features. Angie had reacted in such an extreme way, he'd half decided to try and wriggle out of going, it simply wasn't worth the hassle, better to give in and live a quiet life. Debbie was probably just leading him on, anyway. Women could do that these days, and chaps like him couldn't do a thing about it. Before they knew where they were they were up for sexual harassment.

Chief Inspector Gordon Soames laughed; the ginger freckles that splattered his pale face getting lost in the ample creases of flesh. 'Aren't you getting a bit carried away here, Mike? You were due over there tomorrow, anyway. Seemed to me that you jumped at the chance to get away from home for a week or two.'

Had Michael not been in such a bad mood, and had he not felt so guilty about leaving Angela to cope alone, he'd have laughed, and made some comment about marriage and balls and chains. He knew Soames had had a previous disastrous marriage followed by a traumatic divorce, he also knew that his superior had ended up in a near as perfect second marriage. He wondered if his boss had forgotten all the mean and misery that two married human beings could inflict on one another; he wondered if Soames ever counted his blessings.

Gordon Soames looked more intently into Michael's face. 'Will it cause problems, Mike?'

They had known each other for years and enjoyed promotion at the same time, although Gordon had in the last few years pushed more and more ahead of Michael. But that didn't mean he had forgotten their early years together.

Michael shrugged his shoulders, his face still bearing a look of utter misery. He'd jumped at the chance to get away, that was true, but Angie had taken on so, and she'd looked so miserable when he'd left that morning . . .

Gordon was still talking, 'You see, you're not actually working on any case of great importance at the moment, and everyone else capable of dealing with this is very tied up just now. Charles Hastings, the DI at Fenshaw, who'd normally take the case is due on sick leave tomorrow. There's no point in him starting on the case; he'll be in hospital for at least a week, and then he'll be off for at least another two weeks after that.'

'There's a good chap at Fenshaw that can work

along side you, a trainee DI by the name of Barnes. He can do a lot of the leg work.' Soames said brightly, as if offering a bribe to a truculent child.

'Then why can't he take the case?'

Soames shook his head and bit into his bottom lip. 'They need a bit of muscle behind this one. Barnes is new, and this woman — the victim, is a Lady somebody or other.'

Michael didn't reply.

Soames sighed. 'Look, Mike, is there a real problem?'

Michael looked up. 'We had a row that's all.'

'What, you and Barnes? I didn't know you knew him.'

'No — Angie. Me and Angie.'

'Oh, I see,' and with a strong hint of sarcasm in his voice, he added, 'So we have to stop a murder inquiry because the man who ought to be in charge has a tiff with his missus?'

Michael swallowed. 'Well,' he said, suddenly realizing how unreasonable he was being. 'I know it sounds silly, but I hate to go on a sour note. Angie ought to get herself a job,' he said, as if that explained everything.

'How long have you and Angela been married, Mike?'

'Nearly sixteen years,' Michael said with misery in his voice.

'No kids, that's your mistake. It's surely not too

late though? Look at me. You should think about it. I can thoroughly recommend it,' he said, proudly glancing at the framed photograph of his wife and son.

Gordon continued to elaborate on the joys of fatherhood, seeming not to notice Michael's expression. Suddenly he stopped short. 'What's up, Mike? Did I say something wrong? You're looking a bit twitchy.'

Michael blew through his teeth. Yes, the day was definitely getting worse.

'Gordon, we wanted a family, we tried for years, and we had every test you can think of. We had blood tests and x-rays and God knows what, and still nothing happened. If you think it's left me twitchy, you should see Angie. We gave up years ago.'

'Hmm,' Soames cleared his throat, embarrassed now. 'We never had a great deal of trouble,' he said.

The remark was made in an open flat manner, and as such, could have been interpreted in a number of ways. But whichever way it had been meant, Michael read it to mean that he, or Angie, or maybe both of them, were either incompetent or incomplete.

The subject was dropped and Soames produced a piece of foolscap on which were written a few sketchy details: the address where the murder had taken place and the hotel where Michael had been booked to stay the night

Michael leaned over and took the paper from him. 'I suppose it's too much to hope that it's a cut and dried domestic, isn't it?'

Gordon, with obvious relief that Michael was no longer objecting, smiled broadly.

'Well, I don't know the details, except that she was a Lady with a capital L. But you never know, — perhaps the butler did it.'

Michael got up to leave.

'Why don't you 'phone Angela before you go?' Soames said, gesturing toward the telephone on his desk.

'I'll do that,' Michael replied. He also looked at the telephone. 'From my own office, I've taken up enough of your time already.' He went out and closed the door with a gentle click.

'Suit yourself,' said Soames, picking up the photograph from his desk and studying it. 'We didn't have any trouble,' he mused to himself, as he gazed at the fair-haired boy grinning out at him 'No trouble at all and I'm two years older than Mike.'

Chapter 50

At home, Zoë vomited twice more and then felt perfectly all right. If it were possible to feel all right with what seemed like all the cares of the world resting on her shoulders. She'd have liked to have telephoned the surgery and asked Dr Armstrong if the sickness affected the effectiveness of the pills, but Theo was hovering around and fussing over her and she didn't dare risk him overhearing.

'I've 'phoned your mother and asked her to pick Betsy up from school,' Theo explained.

'But why?' She felt insecure and wanted her child close by. 'There's no need, I'm perfectly all right now.'

'You're tired,' he said, touching her cheek. 'You need some time off. Besides you don't want Betsy to catch your bug, do you?'

'It's not a bug,' she objected.

'What is it then?'

She blushed. 'Something I've eaten.' Well, that was true enough.

'Oh? Even so.' He sat down beside her and put his arm around her. 'What really happened, Zoë?' He said softly.

'What do you mean?'

'Well, just look at you, you look as if you've just done six rounds with Cassius Clay.'

'Who?'

'He was a boxer.'

'Oh.'

'So?'

'I told you. I fell. I was in the yard, early this morning, when I went to milk Daisy, Bracken got under my feet and I tripped.' She could see by his face that he knew she was lying. He looked immeasurably sad.

'Sure?'

'Of course I'm sure, I should know what happened.'

He tightened his grip on her and a sharp pain shot through her ribcage.

'Ouch.'

'What? What is it?'

She put her hand on her ribs. 'Nothing. I must have strained myself when I was sick.'

Theo got up and paced the room. 'Zoë, this isn't . . .' he looked up sharply as a car sped down the drive. 'Dr Armstrong? What's he doing here?' The car passed the cottage and drove on toward the Hall.

'Isobel must be ill,' he said, 'or Lottie. I saw her and that other girl arrive some time ago.'

Zoë tried to draw a deep breath but couldn't. Her ribs really did hurt, she hadn't really noticed the damage last night, but now the pain was getting worse. She gave a strained cough.

'You all right?'

She nodded.

'Can I get you anything?' he asked.

'Cup of tea would be nice.'

'Is that wise? Seeing as you've been so sick'

'I'm fine now, it's something I've eaten. I've got rid of it all now.' She shuddered. She was rather afraid that she had ejected the precious pill.

Theo went through to the kitchen and put the kettle on. Both the kitchen and the sitting room faced south and overlooked the drive. Theo frowned as a second car sped down the drive, this time it was a white police car.

From the next room Zoë also saw the car, the sight of it brought the nausea back.

Theo came through to her. 'Did you see a police car going down to the Hall?'

She nodded.

'I ought to go and see what's going on.'

'Theo, please don't, please stay here with me.' She was extremely alarmed, whatever the police wanted it couldn't have anything to do with them, could it? But perhaps they were looking for her; perhaps they'd meant to go to the cottage but had gone to the Hall by mistake. But how could they know? They couldn't, no one could know about last night, apart from the two people concerned and she knew the other one wouldn't be talking. And no one must know either. Theo would never forgive her, never. She

385

closed her eyes and leaned back on the sofa. Oh God, she felt awful, she was light headed from lack of sleep and her brain wasn't working properly. She couldn't think straight, she was incapable of putting things into context. Her whole body ached, she felt abused and violated.

A third vehicle raced past the cottage, this time a white van followed soon after by another police car.

'What the hell?' Theo said strutting toward the door.

'Don't go, Theo,' she pleaded.

'Why not?'

'I don't know, why not, Theo. I just don't want to be on my own.'

'She's probably been burgled. Don't forget that most of the stuff that's in that house is mine.'

'Stay, Theo. If they need you, they'll come and tell you.'

A loud click told them that the kettle had boiled. Theo went through to the kitchen and made the tea. Yet another car went by. This time it was a metalic blue golf Escort and was driving at a far more sober pace. Theo put the tea on a tray and brought it through to the sitting room.

The telephone rang and Zoë snatched the receiver up to her ear. It was her mother asking her how she was, and telling her that they would pick Elizabeth up from school and take her over to Hulver for tea.

'It's all right, Ma. I'm perfectly all right. I've just

been a bit sick, that's all.'

'Morning sickness? Could you be pregnant?'

Zoë was silent for just a little too long.

'Darling, that's wonderful. And don't worry about your father — you know, — you and Theo not being married and all that. He understands,' she gave a little laugh. 'I'll make him understand.' She gave another funny little laugh and said without conviction: 'No one gets married these days, do they? It's quite the norm, I mean, even if Theo wasn't married already, you probably—'

'Ma, I'm not pregnant,' she almost shouted, causing Theo to look at her searchingly. 'You don't understand. It's not that, it's not that at all.' She started to cry. It was as if she was no longer in control of anything, least of all her emotions.

'Darling, whatever is wrong?'

But Zoë couldn't answer. Her misery had robbed her of the ability to speak. She shook her head as if trying to shake the words loose, but all she managed was a small, strangled, cry.

Theo took the telephone from her. 'Lavinia?'

Zoë could only hear the Garrick side of the conversation, but she could guess what her mother was saying. Theo was promising that he'd take Zoë to the doctors and that he'd telephone Lavinia later to let her know how she was. When he finally put the receiver down he said:

387

'Come on, Zoë, your mother says I'm to put you to bed, or did she say I was to take you to bed? I can't quite remember which.'

But Zoë couldn't even raise a smile at Theo's feeble joke. Breathing was becoming difficult; laughter would have proved impossible.

'Zoë, darling, what's wrong?'

'Nothing,' she sobbed. 'Nothing's wrong, I'm tired, that's all. Ma's right. I need an hour in bed and I'll be fine.'

He nodded. 'Come on then.' He went to help her to her feet, and at that moment yet another police car zoomed down the drive.

'What the hell?' he said. 'Look, darling, I won't be long, but I must go see what this is all about.'

Before Zoë could draw breath, he'd rushed out of the cottage and was running down the drive.

He was back in less than five minutes.

'She's dead, Zoë. Issie's dead.'

Zoë had never heard him call his wife Issie before and, for some inexplicable reason, the familiarity hurt.

'Dead? Are you sure? Perhaps you—'

'There's a policeman at the door, he wouldn't let me in—'

'He told you she was dead?' Zoë breathed.

'No, no, he wouldn't tell me anything. Jeremy Armstrong was there, he told me.'

'What did he say? I mean, how—'

'Murdered, Issie's been murdered. Who would do that?'

His eyes roamed over Zoë's bruised and battered face. 'Oh God, Zoë — not — Oh God . . .'

Zoë put her hand up to her forehead.

'Theo, you can't think — Theo, I — Theo, you must trust me — I couldn't help — Oh God . . .' Her sobs returned with a greater force

If she told him the truth she was damned and if she didn't, she was doubly damned.

Chapter 51

Angela Harper walked boldly into the police station. She knew the police sergeant by sight, but not by name. He, however knew very well who she was.

'I think he's out Mrs Harper, but I'll ring through and make sure.' He smiled politely. 'I'll do my best to track him down, although I think he's gone off to Fenshaw. Take a seat, and I'll see what I can do.'

Angela slid herself into one of the red plastic chairs in the waiting area. Surely he couldn't have left so soon; he'd rung her less than an hour ago. She'd been furious with him, and her anger had not diminished, she was still furious. All his protestations about 'something important' coming up, that was a likely story. He just couldn't wait to get away from her, that was the truth of the matter. He was just plain bored with his plain little wife, he was having, — what did they call it in the women's magazines — a mid-life crisis? Yes that's what it was, a mid-life crisis. 'What about your clothes?' she'd asked. 'You haven't got anything clean with you.' He'd been pretty casual about it. Someone would call and collect them and take them over to Fenshaw for him. He didn't even have time to pop home and say goodbye. Well, he'd no need of that now, because she'd come here to see him. If Mohammed wouldn't come to the mountain, then the mountain would have to come to Mohammed, wasn't that what they said?

A boy of about thirteen with a little dog on a lead entered the station, he fidgeted at the desk whilst the sergeant made his calls. Angela imagined a telephone ringing somewhere deep inside the building, an impenetrable defense protecting her husband from the likes of her.

After a few moments of the boy not receiving any attention, he spoke up.

'Me mam says, I'm to bring 'im here. She says she's 'ad enough of 'im.'

The desk Sergeant put his hand over the receiver. 'Wait your turn, sonny, the lady's before you.' He nodded toward Angela, his voice was gruff; a totally different tone to that with which he'd greeted the Inspector's wife.

The boy glanced in her direction, eyed her up and down and then, as if he'd summed her up, he turned back to the man at the desk. 'I'll just leave 'im here then, shall I?'

The policeman put his hand over the mouthpiece again. 'No you won't, we're not a stray dogs home. RSPCA is who you want, or maybe the dog warden will take it off your hands. But you definitely can't leave it here.'

Angela stood up. 'I'll take him,' she said.

The boy and the policeman stared at her.

'Right, okay, I'll tell her,' the sergeant said into the telephone.

'He's left for Fenshaw, Mrs Harper' he said to Angela. He looked at the boy. 'Now, son, what's all this about?'

Angela was petting the dog. It was small, very small; perhaps it was still a puppy? Oh dear, she hoped it wouldn't grow too big. She'd spoken hastily, she knew she had. Michael would probably have a fit, but then Michael wasn't here, was he?

'Don't matter,' the boy said. 'The lady says she'll 'ave him.'

'Now hang on,' the desk sergeant said.

'What's his name?' Angela asked.

'Mam calls 'im, fucking nuisance,' the boy said laughing at his joke, but he soon pulled a straight face when he saw Angela's look of disapproval. 'I call him Butch, you know, like Butch Cassidy and the Sundance kid? Me mam's boyfriend's got that on video — he's got a really cool collection.'

Angela looked puzzled.

'It's a really, really, old film,' the boy added helpfully. 'It's about a couple of cowboys and—'

'All right, all right,' the policeman said.

'It must have been going when you were young,' the boy added.

Angela didn't respond. She had returned to petting the dog, which was nearly all white with a few areas of ginger.

'Right then,' the boy said handing over the lead. 'See yer.' He got almost to the door when he turned back and said, 'E's a proper breed, miss. E's a Jack Russell. E ain't no mongrel, only his mum were a rough and his dad were a smooth. An' 'is birthday is May eleventh, and e aint ad is jabs, 'cause mam couldn't afford them, right?'

Angela smiled, holding onto the lead — she resembled a child herself.

'Hang on a minute,' the policeman said.

The boy didn't take any notice of him, but continued to walk toward the swing door. Just before he pushed through it, he looked back at Angela. 'Look after 'im Missis, won't yer?'

It seemed to Angela that at that moment, a tough little would-be thug dissolved into a vulnerable child.

'Try and explain to 'im why I couldn't keep 'im, won't yer?' he pushed a little way through the door and hesitated. 'You'll be kind to 'im, won't yer, Missis?' he wiped his nose with the back of his hand and pushed through the door and into the street.

Angela watched as he walked away, his head bent and his walk slow and deliberate. The little dog pulled on the lead and whimpered after him, cocked his head on one side, looked up at Angela, and whimpered again.

The sergeant shook his head. 'Cheeky little . . . '

Angela knew that her presence was the only thing that kept him from swearing.

He picked the telephone up and started to dial a number. 'I'll 'phone the dog warden and get it picked up.'

'No, no, I meant it,' Angela said. 'I'll take him.'

'But you can't. He'll have fleas and worms and hell and all knows what.'

'Then I'll take him to the vet's and get him sorted, sergeant. It's really not a problem.'

He shrugged. 'I'd like to see his highness' face when he knows,' he said under his breath.

Angela pretended she hadn't heard. Michael wouldn't mind, would he? It would give her something to do; something to help pass the time.

She'd gone to the station on the bus, but now she would walk home. She stepped into the bright autumn sunshine with the dog trotting at her heels

'Come on, Butch,' she said. 'We'll have a nice walk home, and then I'll make you an appointment with the vet. Then I'll have to go to Safeway and get you some food, only you won't be able to come in there with me, because it's a food shop, you see, and dogs aren't allowed.'

The dog pricked up its ears and gave a little jump.

Angela puffed and panted all the way home, she realized that she was extremely unfit. Michael was always on about her getting a bit more exercise; well, Butch would make sure she did, wouldn't he?

At five, pretty Debbie Smith called to collect Michael's bag. Angela couldn't believe how fast the day had flown. She had to ask Debbie to wait whilst she finished packing the bag. The dog greeted the girl as if she was his long lost friend and the girl was all over the dog.

'You're a friendly little chap,' Debbie said. 'My mum's got one of these at home.' And then the questions came, how old was he? Did he like this? And did he do that?

Angela couldn't quite grasp how dramatically her life had changed. Poor, sad, introverted Angela had at last come out of her shell. In the park that afternoon she'd spoken to at least a dozen people, more people than she'd spoken to in the last three weeks.

After Debbie had left with Michael's bag, Angela put the dog on his lead and made ready to take him to the vet. She was fumbling for her house keys when she caught a reflection of herself in mirror on the hallstand. Debbie Smith was an awfully pretty girl, she wondered if Michael had ever been tempted.

'I'm getting dowdy, Butch,' she said. 'You know, if you'll be all right on your own for an hour or two, I think I'll go and get myself off to the hairdressers. I might even have a bit of a tint put in my hair, or a few highlights, just to liven it up a bit.'

She looked down at her clothes. 'I think I'll have to invest in some smart walking clothes as well, because you and I will be going on a lot of walks won't we? And you know what, I could get myself one of those bicycles with a big basket on the front, and I could bike up to the common with you in the basket. You'll like it up there. You can run about without your lead.'

The dog jumped vertically, almost as high as Angela's waist.

'There's a clever boy,' she crooned.

She went out of the front door and shut it behind her. She smiled at her neighbour of five years. Until today, they'd never so much as given each other more than a curt nod. But today the dog Butch was admired and petted, and before they parted, they were on first name terms.

It took her a long time to get to the vet, so many people stopped and spoke to her, well more to Butch than to her, but even so . . .

Angela Harper smiled, the whole world was suddenly her friend, and, for the first time in almost ten years, she felt blissfully, blissfully happy.

Chapter 52

Detective Inspector Michael Harper was a big man, well over six feet four, with broad, powerful shoulders. Had he followed an acting career he would certainly have been type-cast into the role of his chosen career, probably the rank of sergeant in the uniform branch, not the exalted rank of DI.

His first view of Garrick Hall caused him to take a sharp breath. It was perhaps the most beautiful eighteen-century house that he'd ever set eyes upon, perfectly proportioned, a dolls-house, a picture postcard, perfectly symmetrical from the full-length windows on the ground flood to the carved dormer windows in the roof. Virginia creeper, still with a few rust-red leaves, clung to the impressive facade. A perfectly shaped round porch protected the weathered oak door. It was hard to imagine anything as undignified as murder could take place in such a beautiful place.

'Not a bad little shack,' Ian Barnes quipped as they stood back and surveyed the surroundings.

'Not bad at all,' Michael agreed, thinking of twenty-two Saxon Way, the modern box of a house that he and Angela shared.

'At least this case will be more comfortable than the last one you were on,' mused Barnes.

Michael gave a rye smile and thought back to the case he'd been telling Barnes about as they'd driven to the scene.

'On the other hand, this one might not be quite so easy to solve. Also we might get a bit more pressure from the powers that be.'

His last case had been the murder of an itinerant. He never had found out his name, but he had, by a fairly simple process, discovered whom the murderer was; another tramp, who probably found the prison cell he now occupied a good deal more comfortable than his life on the road.

The usual scene greeted their arrival at the Hall. Michael noted that there were at least four police cars, a small white van, and a cluster of private cars. They had asked directions to the Hall in the village of Garrick-in-the-Willows from a plain, round faced woman, who wore a dirty mackintosh, although the crisp autumn afternoon looked far from bringing rain.

'Would it be Sir Theo or Lady Sheldon-Harris, you would be wanting, Sir?' She said speaking in a broad Norfolk drawl.

'Just the directions to Garrick Hall.' Bad news obviously didn't spread quite as fast as it was rumored.

'Well, you see, if it be Lady Sheldon-Harris, you want the first turning on the right after the farm track, but if it be Sir Theo you'll be wanting, you take the second turning that will bring you around by the main drive and past the lodge. You can go that way if you want Lady Sheldon-Harris, but it's quicker to take the first turning and go to the Hall by the back entrance. 'Tradesman' it 'as on the gate.'

'Thank you,' Michael said wrinkling his brow. He wondered if he was classified as trade.

He smiled at Barnes, thankful that his companion had a clear, logical brain and he could bear silence; he wasn't full of useless prattle like so many of his contemporaries.

The first person they met was Gilbert Knox, the pathologist. Michael had known him for many years and regarded him as an old and trusted friend.

'A bit far from Barkhampton aren't you? Or is she somebody frightfully important?'

'Don't flatter me, Gilbert! They're up to their eyes in it at Fenshaw and so they've dumped this on my doorstep. I'm filling in for Charles Hastings, he's—'

'Yes, yes, poor old Charlie, I heard about him, they ought to find a permanent replacement.'

'But he'll be back in a couple of weeks — three at the—'

Gilbert shook his head and bit into his bottom lip. 'Don't say you heard it from me, but Charlie won't be going back to work, Mike, not ever. His wife, Sally, and my June are close friends so . . .' his voice trailed away.

Michael sighed, his feelings had done a U-turn and now he hoped that he wouldn't be away for too long. His euphoria at getting away from home had waned. He was feeling mean and selfish. He knew how hard Angie found it to cope when he was away. Besides, Debbie wasn't really going to come across with the goods. It was all a dream, a wonderful, wicked fantasy.

'Can I take a look, Gilbert?'

The pathologist led the way out of the bright sunshine and into the dim interior of Garrick Hall and through to the kitchen. He slipped on a pair of gloves and, as the two policemen looked on, he probed and poked the mortal remains of Isobel Sheldon-Harris. A photographer clicked and flashed, and another technician was busy with a video camera.

Michael's only experience of death was, as now, combined with violence and mystery. As he viewed the contorted body, he thought, surely there must have been another answer? Surely they could have talked about it, worked it out, somehow? His mind flew back to the tramp, murdered for a bottle of meths: surely they could have talked?

'What have you got, Gilbert?' He asked, pulling his thoughts back to the present.

Gilbert stood up and put his hands on his hips. 'Well, strangled of course, with a piece of nylon baler twine, the kind used by farmers all over the country for anything from tying gates to keeping their trousers up. Not a new piece, so forensics will have some fun with that. Find a gate swinging open and you've probably found the origin of our murder weapon.' He didn't smile as he said this and Michael realized that he was quite serious.

He bent down again. 'By the state of her clothing, she put up a fight, but there are no obvious cuts or bruises on the body. There again, it looks like she was surprised from behind.'

He gently pushed her skirt to one side, exposing her genitalia. Michael involuntarily looked away, it seemed like an obscene intrusion. Lady Sheldon-Harris would never have exposed herself in such a way, even to a friend. Maybe to a lover, but even then . . .

'Looks as if she's been sexually assaulted,' Gilbert said, 'this looks very much like semen in the pubic hair here.' He replaced the skirt. 'Time? — Last night sometime. I'll tell you more after the P.M. She's certainly been dead ten hours, more I'd say, but this kitchen's quite warm. That could distort things a bit. I'll get back to you as soon as I know anything more.'

Michael thanked him and he and Barnes made thier way to the front of the house. A young fresh-faced constable stood by the front door; he was extremely thin. He introduced himself to Michael as Constable Johnson; he was, he said, local.

'So? What can you tell me?'

Johnson produced his notebook. His bony hands shook as he turned to the relevant page. His hair had been cut too short and he had shaved a little too close, a small angry cut was visible on his chin. He'll maybe make sergeant, Michael thought, but he'll not get much further than that.

'Right, Sir,' Johnson said, when he found the right page. 'Lady Isabel Sheldon-Harris aged fifty-nine, was found at about eleven-thirty this morning, by her daughter and her daughter's friend. They were expected for lunch, and felt that there was something wrong when Lady Sheldon-Harris didn't appear to be at home. They climbed through an upstairs window and they found Lady Sheldon-Harris in the kitchen. They 'phoned the local doctor, who 'phoned us.'

'And where are they now?'

'In the sitting room, Sir, with the doctor. I hope that's all right, Sir. Only the lady doesn't seem too well. I haven't let anyone else near, Sir, not until the experts arrived.'

Michael crossed his arms in front of his broad chest. 'Is this your first murder, Johnson?'

'Yes, Sir, it is.'

Michael made no comment, but went on to say, 'And you say you're local?'

'Yes, Sir. I live three miles away.'

'Good, now put your notebook away. We'll come

back to your notes in a minute. Did you know Lady Sheldon-Harris?'

'I had met the good lady, Sir.'

'Good Lady?' Queried Michael.

'Sorry, Sir, just a term of speech.'

Michael smiled. 'So was she? Good, I mean, was she a good lady? What was she like?'

'Well, Sir . . . '

For one awful moment Michael thought Johnson was about to say that one shouldn't speak ill of the dead.

'She were a bit of a strange body, if you'll pardon the pun, Sir. She were always calling us out, saying that things had been stolen and asking us to investigate. We'd come out and have a look around, but there was never any sign of a break-in. Then she'd say that maybe her husband was responsible. They don't live together you see.'

'Divorced?'

'No, Sir. I don't think so. Anyway, we'd tell her that we couldn't interfere in a domestic matter. She'd often as not fly into a rage and curse Sir Theo and we'd go off until the next time. Tell you the truth, when the call came from here today, we thought it were her again, you know . .'

'What sort of things did she infer had been stolen?'

'Well, that was just it, I mean look at this place, it's loaded with valuables. But she'd think that someone had stolen her library book, or her address book, although once she said someone had stolen a mattress off one of her beds.

It wasn't really police business. One got the feeling that she was just out to make trouble for Sir Theo. But that wasn't all that was queer about her.' Constable Johnson lowered his voice. 'She were one of those, you know, spiritualist, or clairvoyant or some-such as that. She reckoned that the spirits spoke to her. She were a strange body, she were.'

DI Harper paused for a while to take what in he'd heard, then he said: 'So, tell me, what's the set-up with Sir Theo and her, what do you know about the family?'

'Not a lot, Sir. Except that Garrick Hall is Sir Theo's ancestral home. The Sheldon-Harris's have been here for generations. Lady Isobel is his second wife. He married her before my time, of course, Sir. I don't remember the first lady Sheldon-Harris. This one's been here since I was a youngster. Lady Isobel Sheldon-Harris and Sir Theo didn't have any children, but she's got a daughter by her first marriage, Charlotte, that's who found her. Sir Theo left home about three years ago to live with his shepherd.'

'His shepherd!'

'No, no, Sir. She a woman; not what you're thinking at all. Perhaps I should have said shepherdess. She's a really fit girl as well, a cracker.' Constable Johnson blushed a little. He coughed. 'It caused an almighty stir in the village at the time, but things have cooled down a bit since then. They live at the lodge, Garrick Cottage it's called, it's always been the shepherd's cottage and he moved in with her. Now, I don't know how much truth there is in this, but they do say that Lady Sheldon-Harris refused him a divorce at the time and has continued to refuse. It's a shame because they've got this kid, a little girl.'

'How old?'

'Four or five, not sure exactly.'

'I thought you said they've been together three years?'

'Yes well, rumor has it that she was his fancy bit and she had the kid with him before she moved here, but that's just rumour. She doesn't call him dad, but then that's nothing to go by these days, is it? She's a nice kid, goes to school with my Daniel. She's not all stuck up or anything. You know what I mean, don't you?'

'The woman he lives with, what's her name?'

'Zoë, Zoë Elliot, — only everyone calls her Mrs Sheldon-Harris, although I know for a fact they're not married.'

'And she's a real cracker, is she?' Michael smiled. Johnson blushed. 'Yes, Sir.'

'So do I take it that you know her personally?'

'Not exactly. She does a sort of open day every year at lambing time. School groups and that sort of thing. Me and my wife took the kids last spring, and we met her then, and the wife sees her at the school. She seems like a real nice young lady.'

Michael felt a flash of surprise that Johnson had a

wife let alone children in the plural, he seemed far too young. He stared out across the valley. In the distance, a girl could be seen approaching the house over the meadow. She walked awkwardly as if in pain. She wore tight blue jeans and a long navy sweater. Green Wellington boots protected her feet. In her hand she carried a small aluminum milk can. From a distance she had the look of a very young girl. As she neared the Hall, Michael could see that she was older; perhaps even in her late twenties. She glanced quickly at the police cars, paused for a second as if to register the activity and then she continued on her way.

'That's her,' Johnson said. 'She'll have been to milk the cow.'

Michael raised his eyebrows. 'Mmm,' he said. 'I see.'

'That's all I know about the situation really,' Johnson said. 'Rumour had it that Lady Sheldon-Harris wouldn't be content until she'd ruined him. I believe she made pretty heavy financial demands upon him.'

'Well,' said Michael nodding in the direction of Zoë Elliot. 'Distractions like that have to be paid for.' And Constable Debbie Smith crept unbidden into his mind.

Chapter 53

Zoë tried to walk past the Hall as if she were untroubled and unconcerned. But walking jarred every bone in her body, and she found herself moving with an awkward irregular gait. She was finding it hard to breathe, and she had to keep stopping in order to catch her breath. The normal twenty-minute walk took her almost three-quarters of an hour.

There were a whole lot of police cars clustered on the Hall's front drive, and the place was buzzing with activity. When she reached the cattle grid, she paused. Her ribs were hurting, especially when she took a deep breath, so she grabbed little snatches of air, trying to take the oxygen in without expanding her lungs, an effect that made her giddy and light headed. She knew there was something seriously wrong with her, she knew she should get Dr Armstrong to take a look, but she didn't want to explain how she'd come by her injuries.

She took as deep a breath as she could, and continued on her way. A policeman standing at Garrick Hall's front door lifted his hand and pointed toward her, and the two men with him looked up. She could feel their gaze following her as she turned toward the cottage.

It was four o'clock; Theo would be home with Elizabeth. She had telephoned her mother and begged her not to come. She had then taken an hour nap, and then got up and insisted on going to the farm to give Andy his orders for the next day and milk the cow. Everything must appear normal, the more normal it seemed the better it would be; if she tried really hard she might even believe in the normality herself.

Her mother had objected at first, but Zoë had persuaded her that it was best that she stay away. The last thing Zoë needed was a whole lot of questions. She looked back toward the Hall. Like it or not, questions were going to be asked and answers would have to be found. It was only a matter of time before they — the police — came knocking on her door.

She continued on her way with Bracken slinking at her heels. He, too, was behaving oddly. He was probably affected by her mood or by all the activity around the place, she didn't know which.

She turned the corner of the drive and saw, parked in the turnaround outside the cottage, her parent's car.

'Oh, no,' she said. 'Oh, God, no.'

She entered the cottage and, quietly as she could, crept into the kitchen to put the can of milk into the fridge. There was still plenty of milk left from the morning's milking, and she pulled it to the front and placed the fresh milk toward the back. Then, pasting a smile upon her face she went through to the sitting room.

Elizabeth was sitting on Josh's knee, and her

mother, was nursing a mug of tea. Theo seemed to be pacing up and down.

The conversation came to an abrupt holt. She felt sure that they had been talking about her.

'Hello, everybody,' she said cheerfully. 'Any tea left?'

She had to sit down. If she didn't, she was afraid she might collapse. She slid onto the sofa, and snatched in a gulp of air.

'You know, we seem to drink so little milk these days, it hardly seems worth keeping a house cow,' she said.

All the adult eyes stared at her, a collective look of amazement.

'What?' Zoë said. 'What did I say?'

'Zoë!' Lavinia exclaimed, 'Isobel's been murdered, and all you can think about is the house cow?'

'Seems appropriate,' Zoë said. Isobel, Isobel, Isobel, all anyone ever thought about was Isobel. No one ever thought about Zoë, and what life was like for her. Couldn't they see that her problems far outweighed any of Isobel's? Anyway Isobel's problems had been wiped away now, hadn't they?

'Come on, Ma, you know how she treated Theo and me, and little Betsy. I can't pretend I'm devastated, I didn't want her to die, especially I didn't want her to die in that way, but—'

'Zoë! You should never speak ill of the dead,'

409

Lavinia said.

Josh put his hand up, the child wriggled from his knee. 'Zoë's right,' he said. 'There's no point in pretending that she was some sort of a saint, just because she's dead. Even so, Zoë, I don't think you should let the police hear you talk that way, they might think you had something to do with it.'

Theo looked at Josh as if he'd just sold his soul to the devil. At the same moment Elizabeth charged across the room and threw herself into her mother's arm.

Zoë's ribs got the full force of the child's enthusiasm, and Zoë let out a cry of pain.

'What is it, darling?' Lavinia rushed over to her.

'Nothing, nothing at all,' Zoë gasped. 'I fell, and I hurt myself, that's all.'

Oh, God, she was going to die, the pain was excruciating. She caught her mother and Theo starring at each other. Theo sucked in his bottom lip.

Lavinia tugged at Zoë's sweatshirt; there was little Zoë could do to stop her revealing her upper body. Zoë's ribs had darkened into one huge, deep, angry bruise.

'My God,' Lavinia breathed. 'Theo, you must take her to the doctor. This looks really serious.'

But after one glance at her Theo turned his back, he had his head bent forward as if he were trying to control himself. Zoë was pretty sure she knew what he was thinking, but she was too frightened to ask.

'I think we should go,' Josh suddenly said. 'If that's what Zoë wants?'

Zoë gave him a weak smile. Dear Pa, always avoiding confrontation, always wanting to bury his head in the sand, always living by the rule of what you didn't know couldn't hurt you. Dear, dear Pa, thank God for men like Pa.

'Don't be silly, Josh — we must stay and help. Zoë must have a doctor, look at this bruise, how did you say you did it, darling?'

Zoë plainly saw her mother catch Theo's eye as she explained once again how she'd tripped over the dog.

'I think we should go,' Josh said again.

'Please, Ma — please, we're better on our own. Besides the police are bound to come and see us and—'

'Precisely, that's why I think we should be here. So we can back you up. Give you an alibi or something.'

'Please Mummy — please go.'

Josh got up and gave Elizabeth a hug. 'I expect you've been longing for us to go so that you can eat some of those poor fish's fingers,' he said.

Elizabeth giggled.

'You know what, Betsy,' he went on. 'I've got a really nice pair of alligator shoes at home, but I don't wear them very often, because I don't like to think of the alligator going barefoot.' He paused as if waiting for the house to collapse in laughter.

He was met with three responses. Zoë said, 'Oh

411

Pa.'Lavinia gave him the blackest of black looks, and Elizabeth asked him what a alligator was.

Josh shrugged. 'I thought it was rather a good one,' he said.

'It was, Pa,' Zoë said, wiping away a tear that had been close to the surface.

'Come on, Vinnie,' Josh said. 'We're over-staying our welcome.'

Lavinia turned to Theo. 'Would you like us to stay, Theo? We could get supper and put Betsy to bed.'

'I put a casserole in the oven at lunchtime,' Zoë countered.

'Come on,' Josh said yet again.

'Perhaps it's best,' Theo said.

Lavinia looked a little hurt, but soon rallied round. 'All right, darling, but you will call us if you need us?'

Zoë nodded.

They left.

'The police are bound to come,' Theo said after he'd watched them drive away. 'Zoë? What will you tell them?'

'About what?'

'The bruises.'

'The truth.'

'Which is?'

'That I tripped over Bracken,' she lied.

412

Chapter 54

Michael decided to talk to the doctor next. Unlike Johnson, he was not inclined to offer any information unless specifically asked.

Doctor Armstrong had a pointed, rather hooked nose, his eyes were deep set, almost hooded, and his glasses dangled from a cord around his neck. His hair was receding from his forehead and was left long on his neck as if to compensate. His shirt stretched tightly over his pot belly, but the collar looked too big for him, reminding Michael of a turtle peeping from it's shell.

The sitting room was large and oblong. In the middle of the long wall was an elegant white marble fireplace, to either side of which stood comfortable armchairs. Dr Armstrong sat in one, and Michael took the other. A large brown sofa faced the fire; it didn't match the chairs, yet it was a happy companion to them. That's what good taste is all about, he thought, knowing what will go together and what won't. When Michael had arrived in the room Charlotte and Flora had been curled up on the sofa, their arms intertwined in mutual comfort. They left when he suggested that they take a turn round the garden to get some fresh air, although looking out of the long casement window he saw that they had gone no further than Charlotte's car and were closeted together in the front seats. The sitting room carpet was a rich dark green, a perfect background to several exquisite Persian rugs. The walls were papered in a plain creamy yellow, enhancing the gilt-framed pictures. Thick green velvet curtains swagged the elegant windows.

Michael knew little of antique furniture, but glancing around the room he noted that it sang of harmony, perfection and, most noticeable of all, wealth. He felt uncomfortable, and he began to wish that he'd asked Dr Armstrong to call at the station and give his statement. But the man seemed agitated. He'd already informed Michael that he had house calls and an evening surgery to get to.

'Did you know Lady Sheldon-Harris well?' He inquired. He had a sinking feeling that this was not going to be an easy interview, a fact confirmed by Armstrong's reply.

'Which one?

'You tell me,' Michael volleyed back.

'I knew the first one, very well. I delivered her son right here in this very house. It's hard to imagine, now, considering all that's happened,' he nodded his head — 'Yes, this is where Sir Theo paced the floor, waiting for news of the baby.' He moved his hands in an expansive manner, 'and afterward, when William was born, he sat in that chair there, the one you're sitting in, Inspector, and I sat here where I am now, and we wet the baby's head. Yes, I knew Lady Anne Sheldon-Harris very well.'

Michael wondered if he should show any sort of reverence for the chair. 'And the second Lady Sheldon-

Harris? Lady Isobel Sheldon-Harris, — was she a patient of yours?'

Dr Armstrong's face clouded.

'She was for a very short time, not long,' he said shortly.

'Then you knew her. What can you tell me about her?'

'If you mean her medical history, you know better than that, Inspector. Even if I did know anything I couldn't tell you, not without a court order. Besides, I only attended her for a short time, and that was a very long time ago, just after she moved here. And then, well,' he cleared his throat. 'We had a slight disagreement and she changed over to another surgery. And socially,' his voice rose in volume, 'I didn't know her at all, nor had I any desire to. And that's all I can tell you. Now, if you will excuse me, I do have a medical practice to run, and thanks to your over-keen constable, I'm extremely late for my house calls.' He looked at his watch. 'I'm certain to be late for evening surgery.'

Michael exhaled loudly. 'Dr Armstrong, the woman is dead. Somebody killed her. I need to know everything about her, everything. Do you understand?'

Dr Armstrong looked annoyed. He was obviously not used to being questioned in this way. He was more used to asking the questions, not answering them.

'As I said, Inspector, I know very little about her medical history, and all the badgering in the world won't help to extract facts that I've never known, nor will it help me to remember the few things I did once know.' He waved his hand in the air, dismissing his statement. 'Oh,' he said impatiently. 'It's all too long ago.'

Michael decided to try another line. 'Dr Armstrong, let's begin at the beginning. When and where did you first meet Isobel Sheldon-Harris?'

Dr Armstrong snorted; he rubbed his hands together. 'I'd seen her a few times before I met her, she and her husband, the first one, that is, used to do this, this . . . well, it was a sort of an act, a mind reading thing. It was quite the rage, all our friends used to hire them to perform at parties, they were quite good and very popular. But the first time I really met her was here, in this very room about a week after William was born.'

'William?'

'Anne's baby. I just told you, Theo and Anne had a son, William.'

Dr Armstrong was like a tide that had turned. His face took on a bitter look. 'Issie Bridges, as she was then, was supposed to be a friend of Anne's.' he snorted again. 'Some friend! She came down to look after Anne when William was born. Well, I say she came down to look after her, but they had a nurse of course, and a nanny for the baby. It turned out that Anne hardly knew the woman, she'd only met her a couple of times, and then she turns up saying she's come to look after her. Anne had had a difficult birth. It took

416

her some time to recover and Isobel was supposed to be here to cheer her up, but even in the early days you could see trouble was brewing.' He shook his head. 'Such a powerful woman, Isobel.'

His tone became friendlier, more confiding. Michael sat holding his breath, praying that Dr Armstrong wouldn't be interrupted.

'You know, I can't describe Isobel quite the way she was. She had a charisma, a power. She was entertaining, amusing, daring, and, providing you agreed with her, she was great fun, but cross swords with Isobel Sheldon-Harris and you understood.'

'Understood what?'

'Her power — her danger. She had a way with her, and she couldn't bear not to get her own way.' He crossed his legs as he spoke, and then began to swing the upper leg to and fro in an agitated movement, exposing his extremely white ankle as he did so.

'That's how it happened, you see. She set her sights on Theo and the Hall. She fancied herself playing Lady of the Manor and she couldn't bear not to have her own way. She plotted and enticed Sir Theo to marry her. She was one of the most immoral and determined women I have ever met.'

'And you crossed swords with her?'

'Yes, I'm afraid I did. As I said, she turned up just after William was born and stayed for three months.

417

Everyone could see what was happening — everyone except Theo. She was an attractive woman in those days, the curvaceous sort that used to cause quite a stir in my youth. Theo was bowled over. Anne didn't have much time for anything except the baby. A silly thing, you know, to lavish all your love and care on a baby and forget the existence of the child's father,' he spoke, as if giving Michael a warning.

Michael nodded in agreement. 'So what happened?'

'Well, what do you think happened?' The doctor asked and waited, as if expecting Michael to answer. After a moment or two he continued: 'Isobel ended up accompanying Theo to various social gatherings, and still Theo didn't see the trap he was falling into. The County was scandalized. But Theo insisted there was nothing in it, whilst Isobel of course implied there was everything in it. Anyway, Anne eventually heard the gossip and came to her senses, and Isobel was promptly dispatched to whence she came and everyone thought they had seen the back of her. But then, come the summer she came back.' Michael would not have been surprised if Dr Armstrong had added, 'Ha, ha, I told you so.'

The doctor was in full swing; his eyes had a faraway look.

'I can remember it as if it were yesterday. I was here, you see, the day she came back. We were sitting out there on the east lawn. Anne, Theo, myself of course, and young William the baby. I think the nanny was there as well. It was a wonderful afternoon — warm and balmy. Anne and Theo had seemed so happy together.' He paused as if he were savoring the summer's day all over again. He cleared his throat. 'Anyway, as I was saying, she turned up, large as life. She was driving a very expensive, very flash red sports car. I don't remember the make. Oh, she had a way with her all right. What an entrance! She stopped the car and got out, gave Anne a little peck on the cheek, shook hands with me and then held both hands out to Theo and did the 'Theo darling' bit all over him. It was frankly embarrassing and quite obvious that she had laid claim to him.

'Anne was clearly upset. Isobel stayed on at the Hall despite Anne's unease. Apparently Isobel's marriage was breaking up and she needed somewhere to stay. She knew how to manipulate, you see — she knew how to use people. She flirted outrageously with Theo, dropping hints all over the place about their relationship. Everyone was talking about it.'

Dr Armstrong paused for breath and swallowed. 'Look, Inspector, I really can't tell you what happened. All I can say is that she tricked me into behaving in a very foolish manner, I said something out of turn, something that ruined a good friendship.' He stared ahead of him and bit into his bottom lip. He was tempted to tell all. He remembered it so clearly; his pride had been badly wounded. Isabel had gone to see him. She hadn't been

419

registered with him. He hadn't had her notes or anything. She'd said she thought she was pregnant, and she'd hinted that Theo was the culprit. She'd said she was worried to death, and that she didn't know what to do. She'd told him that she didn't want to upset Anne or break-up Theo's marriage. She hadn't let him examine her; she just wanted his advice. He'd been only too willing to believe that Theo had misbehaved. He hadn't even questioned it. He hadn't been of any help to her medically, she'd said she had moral objections to abortion. But he'd certainly unwittingly helped her to snare Theo. He'd been very upset on Anne's behalf, and he'd behaved very foolishly.

He'd taken it upon himself to speak to Theo; he hadn't said that he'd spoken to Isobel. He couldn't, it was confidential, it wouldn't have been ethical. He'd just told Theo that he'd heard a rumour that she was pregnant and that Theo was responsible. Theo had absolutely denied it. He'd said he'd never touched the woman apart from the odd kiss and cuddle. Dr Armstrong blushed as he remembered the way he'd behaved. Theo and he had ended up by having a blazing row. Anne had broken her heart when she heard the rumour, he hadn't been the one to tell her — she hadn't got it from him. But Isobel had been determined that Anne should know. It had all been part of the plot, and eventually, she'd had her way and a kind friend had spilled the beans. Not long after, Anne had tackled Theo and then left, taking the baby and the nanny with her. She'd refused to say where

420

she was going.

Isobel acted the wounded woman, wrongly accused, her reputation ruined. Theo had gone in search of Anne, and Isobel had stayed on at the Hall. Every time Anne tephoned, Isobel answered and said that Theo didn't want to speak to her.

'You said you crossed swords with her?' Michael's voice jolted him back to ther present

'Yes, well, when Anne and Theo seperated . . . to tell you the truth, I took Anne's side. There were so many rumours, you see, about Theo carrying on with Isobel. I didn't believe old Theo. Well, I mean, would you?'

Michael shrugged his shoulders.

'I told Theo that I didn't think I was the best man to serve him or Isobel as their GP. Theo accepted it without argument. Anne divorced him and he married Isobel.'

Dr Armstrong bit into his lip again; he ran his finger around his collar. He was feeling hot; his face coloured as he relived that embarrising moment at a medical conference some years later. There had been no baby, she'd told some that she'd miscarried whilst Theo was away, and to others she just looked indignant and said that her pregnancy was just an evil rumour. Later he'd found out that Isobel Sheldon-Harris had had a hysterectomy, just after her daughter Charlotte was born. Theo hadn't put her in the family way at all. In fact, Dr Armstrong now believed he'd been telling him the truth all the way along. He'd never

421

been unfaithful to Anne — he'd just been very foolish. Isobel had played the wronged woman, and Theo fell for it. But then Theo had been willing, very willing. Isobel had been a very, very attractive woman.

Dr Armstrong lifted his hands to his temples and rubbed them in a circular movement.

He'd learned all about Issie Bridges about three years later. He'd met an old colleague of his at a medical conference, Hoskins his name, obs and gynae. He teased him about living in a sleepy village where nothing happened. Dr Armstrong had never been a big drinker and that night he'd had one or two too many. He'd related the Sheldon-Harris affair, and Hoskins claimed that he knew the woman, Isobel Bridges. He remembered her from her mind-reading act. The description had been unmistakable. He'd known her daughter's name and everything. There had been no doubt. Then Hoskins told him that he'd given her a hysterectomy. She'd had a bad case of fibroids, — she went to him privately. He remembered the circumstances because she paid him in cash; she'd even asked for a cash discount.' Dr Armstrong shook his head.

Dr Armstrong looked straight into Michael's eyes. 'She was a con woman, Inspector, from beginning to end. I'd took her at her word once. She was a very clever woman, she misled me. A little suspicion here, a hint of scandal there. I suppose I wanted to believe the worst. It's amazing how one can be coaxed into believing a complete fabrication of lies.'

'Yes indeed,' pondered Michael. 'But can't you be more specific?'

'She lied to me, and, because I believed her, someone I cared about was hurt, that's all I can say. She set out to sabotage Theo's marriage and she used me along the way.' His jaw tightened. 'I did confront her. I don't know why I did now — my pride was hurting, I suppose, and as I say I'd been very fond of Anne, more than fond if the truth were known.' He lifted his hand. 'Don't get me wrong, there was nothing like that. I admired from afar, as you might say, she was a lovely woman.

'Anyway, I came down here and confronted her. It was the middle of the afternoon. I didn't want to see Theo. What I had to say was between Isobel and me. She was a strange lady. "Come in," she said, "and have some tea." She acted as if I'd just popped by on a social visit. "Calm down," she said. "It's true that I told a little fib or two, but all's fair in love and war, wouldn't you agree?" She had this look of superiority on her face. As you can imagine, I was flabbergasted. "What about Anne, and little William?" I said.' The doctor shook his head. 'Do you know, — she laughed — laughed until she was bent over, she really did. I could have killed her.'

The doctor didn't seem to see anything amiss in his last remark, and Michael let it go.

'Anyway, she told me to watch my blood pressure.

And she said that Theo had never really loved Anne. She said that Anne was a cold fish behind the bedroom door. I tell you, it's a wonder I kept my temper as well as I did. Anyway, she said that Anne was bound to get married again, and then William would have a new father. I vowed and declared that I would never set foot in the Hall whilst that woman lived here, and I do believe I've stuck to my word.'

'And did Anne marry again?'

'Oh yes, she was right there, nice chap I believe, I never met him. Anne and I drifted apart after she left here, but I do know that William never got on with his stepfather, and Isobel wouldn't have him here, although I doubt if Anne would have let him come. So William lost out both ways.'

'Do you know where Anne Sheldon-Harris and the boy are now?'

'The boy died, drowned in that big ferry disaster just off the French coast. He was on a school trip, his body was never found. As for Anne, she lives in London, I think. Her married name's Hamilton.'

Michael was desperately trying to absorb the facts. 'Doctor Armstrong, is there anything more you can tell me, either about Lady Sheldon-Harris or the family? Anything, no matter how small or how trivial you may think it to be?'

'I don't think so, you know all about her new act I suppose? These clairvoyant meetings she runs, — I don't know any details, but a lot of my patients go to see her and a lot of the poor souls have handed money over to her, money they can ill afford.' He nodded his head. 'Once a con man always a con man. I really can't tell you more than that, except of course, you knew that Theo had left her?'

Michael did know, but he lifted his eyebrows as if it were news to him.

'About three years ago.' A smile played on his lips, revenge looked sweet. 'Not that much to tell really, on the face of things. Theo employed this girl as a shepherd. Then he took an instant and rapid liking to sheep. Always tending the flock as you might say.' He laughed aloud at his weak joke.

'Rumours flew around the village, and then, as predicted, they moved in together. He just picked up his clothes from the Hall and left, and that's how it's been ever since. She has a child, and Theo looks on it as if it was his own. Lavishes all the love he might have lavished on his own son. She's only got to have an earache and he's in my surgery like a shot.'

'You buried your differences then?'

'Oh yes, years ago. It was her, Isobel, I had the argument with. I couldn't stand her. Theo's been a fool but he's a good man.'

Michael looked out of the window, the roof of the lodge was just visible. How, he wondered, could they all live so close together? Why didn't Sir Theo get out?

'I know what you're thinking,' Doctor Armstrong said. 'How do they stick it, living so close together. Well, I

425

think Isobel figured she'd worked hard to earn her place here, and Theo, — he can't afford to buy another house, he's had a few knocks in the last few years and keeping Isobel in this house has cost him a pretty penny. He's cut down on his workers considerably, and Zoë, that's his lady friend, she does as much work as a man.'

'But why doesn't he just sell up and move on?'

'I don't know inspector, except that his family has been here for hundreds of years. You'd better ask him that question.'

Yes, Michael thought, I will.

Dr Armstrong looked at his watch. 'I'm sorry,' he said. 'I must get on.'

'Yes,' the DI said, looking toward the lodge. 'So must I.'

Chapter 55

The body was removed, the little black van driving off slowly and carefully with its grisly load. Michael watched it disappear from sight, and wondered why there was so much respect shown for the dead and so little for the living. Isobel Sheldon-Harris wouldn't care how fast she was driven, unless it was true that the souls of the dead hovered above the bodies they had recently vacated.

Men and women seemed to be all over the place; taking fingerprints, and photographs, and searching, searching everything; drawers were opened, diaries, letters, even notes to the tradesmen, were read, sorted, and filed away. Bedrooms and bathrooms were carefully scrutinized. Fluff and dust disturbed, and made-up beds unmade. Carefully placed cushions were moved and replaced. Room by room, every nook, every cranny, every corner, was examined and recorded.

Flora and Charlotte were asked to go to Fenshaw police station to make statements and Michael made preparations to interview Theo Sheldon-Harris and his lady-love.

But just as he was leaving the Hall, Gilbert Knox caught up with him. 'Michael, a word with you.'

Michael gave him his full attention.

'Look, don't take this as gospel, obviously I'll

427

check it thoroughly when I do the PM. But you know, there's something not quite right. I mean, it doesn't look to me that there's been any sexual activity—'

'But you said there was—'

'Semen? There is, but it's not in the right place, or the wrong place, depending on how you view the matter.'

'Explain, Gilbert, you've lost me.'

'Either chummy got over excited before he got penetration, or he masturbated over the body, or . . . '

'Or?'

'It was planted.'

'Planted — but why would anybody—'

'To lead you lot up the garden path. I'm not absolutely sure, mind you, but it looks that way. In fact, I'd say it was the latter. I'd say it was planted, but don't get too excited, I'll need to check up on a few things.'

'Thanks, Gilbert, you've just increased my possible suspects by fifty percent.'

'There, and I thought you'd be delighted, and pat me on the back, and tell me what a clever boy I am.'

'Oh all that, and more,' Michael said.

'Well,' the pathologist said. 'I could be wrong, I'll let you know as soon as I have anything.'

Michael thanked him and turned toward Garrick Cottage. It was almost dark. His large frame moved slowly and purposefully: a man who knew exactly what he was doing and why he was doing it.

The valley was beautiful, idyllic and so very peaceful in the dusky light. To his left ran a walled garden; a few late roses overhung the chalk and flint perimeter, even though several mild frosts had already left their mark. To his right ran an open pasture, separated from the driveway by a deep ha-ha, and beyond the meadow, a thick wood, the yellow leaves still clinging reluctantly to the skeletal trees.

At the far end of the walled garden stood the lodge. It was built of brick and flint, single storied, and in the shape of an L. The longer side of the L ran parallel to the drive, with only a narrow strip of garden crammed with yellow and bronze chrysanthemums separating the two. The roof of the cottage was so low that Michael could easily have reached up and touched it. Below the eaves ran a line of four small windows.

The first two windows were in darkness. Michael slowed his step as he reached the third. Looking in, he could see a roaring log fire, a sofa and easy chairs, a television set and a large oak coffee table. A Barbie Doll was lying on the top of the table, she was in a state of undress, and in a position not unlike the one they'd found Isobel Sheldon-Harris. The furniture looked old and comfortable, it was certainly not antique and was a far cry from the elegant pieces that graced Garrick Hall. On the windowsill stood a huge vase of flowers, mauve chrysanthemums and sprigs of blackberry with deep purple fruit and burgundy leaves.

Michael paused as he neared the lighted kitchen

429

window. Because of his height and the lowness of the window, he felt he was peering into a doll's house, — a scene where puppets played their parts. It was a large room in relation to the rest of the cottage.

From where he stood, he could see a stone kitchen sink surrounded by a few outdated Formica kitchen units and an electric cooker, but on one wall stood a lovely old pine dresser stacked with cheap, but pretty, willow pattern earthenware. In the center of the room, and reaching almost as far as the window, was a pine table at which sat a family. A family that needed no introduction — Zoë Elliot, Theodore Sheldon-Harris and the little girl, Elizabeth.

Sir Theo wore a tweed jacket and baggy cord trousers. His hair was swept back from his head, he had a broad brow and reminded Michael of someone, but he couldn't think whom. Zoë was wearing old jeans and a shirt untucked at the waist; the sleeves were rolled up to her elbows, exposing some sort of a purple mark on her arm, a bruise? A tattoo? Surely not, it was far too deep and large, a birthmark perhaps? He'd have liked a closer look, but Zoë had spotted him looking in at her and she was already rolling her sleeves down and fixing the button. Her blonde hair was pulled back and held in place with a raggity green scarf. And she was . . . Michael paused in his thoughts, . . . beautiful, her skin was clear and . . . but then she turned and he noticed the bruising just above her left eye, and the scratch marks on her cheek. Her skin was perfect on one side of her face but on the other it showed signs of violence and injury.

They were eating what to Michael looked like a hearty stew, or at least the child was eating. The parents seemed to be moving the food from one side of their plates to the other. God, he was suddenly very hungry.

A border collie growled as Zoë opened the door to his knock. She spoke to it and it flopped down in the corner of the porch.

'Please come in,' she said. 'We've been expecting you.'

She led the way into the kitchen. Elizabeth looked up with lively curiosity, she was very like her mother, except that her straight hair had more of a redish tinge, and her turned up nose was peppered with freckles.

'Do you mind if I put the fireguard up and switch the television on for Betsy, and then we can talk in peace.'

She didn't wait for him to reply, but led Elizabeth into the sitting room. She was having difficulty in walking; he'd noticed that earlier on in the afternoon, her gait then had seemed childlike, now she seemed as if she were in pain. Moments later, dull murmurs could be heard from the television. Theodore Sheldon-Harris sat in complete silence waiting for her to return.

Michael's large frame seemed to fill the tiny cottage. He felt like Gulliver in Lilliput.

'Please sit down,' she said, rapidly clearing plates

431

onto the draining board and wiping the table down. She'd loosed her hair, an attempt, he thought, to hide her damaged face. A large portion of stew remained in a casserole dish and Michael looked at it longingly.

Zoë followed his gaze. 'Oh, have you eaten? There's lots left if you'd like some, it's lamb casserole.'

'I thought I'd go to the village pub . . . but—'

She spoke before he could finish, 'Yes, of course, they do a good range of bar meals up there. Can I offer you a drink then? Or perhaps you're not supposed to drink whilst on duty?' Again she did not wait for him to answer. 'Coffee perhaps? Or tea?'

'Yes please, a cup of tea would be lovely,' he spoke hastily, before all offers of subsistence were withdrawn or overruled.

Ian Barnes's shadow crossed the window. Sir Theodore sighed as if it was all too much.

Michael got up and let him in, and both policemen seated themselves at the kitchen table. There was an awkward silence whilst Zoë made the tea and handed it to them, neither she nor Sir Theo joined them in a cup. Sir Theo sat as if deep in thought, his face was devoid of expression as if he was holding everything inside himself.

'Right,' said Michael. 'Can I have your full names?' Sir Theodore seemed to return from his trance, he got up and pushed the door closed. As he stood, Michael realized that he was both taller and broader than he had at first thought. He took a sip of his tea from the thick earthenware cup. I bet Lady Isobel never had her lips around anything but bone china, he thought. Then wondered why that should matter, he was here to solve a crime, not sit in judgement of other people's lifestyles.

'Theodore Henry Felix Charles Sheldon-Harris.' Theo said slowly, giving Barnes twice as long as was needed to write it down.

'Zoë Louise Sheldon-Harris, well not really Sheldon-Harris, it's Elliot really, but I call myself Sheldon-Harris because . . . ' Her voice trailed away.

Ian Barnes looked up from his notebook and gave her a scathing look.

Michael didn't like him looking at her in that way, it wasn't his place to judge her. She was just a girl. What the hell was she doing with a man of Theo Sheldon-Harris's age anyway? She looked like she was a sweet girl, she was about Debbie Smith's age. Well if she'd hitched up with Sheldon-Harris, Debbie might be prepared to . . .

'How old are you, Sir Theo?'

'Forty-eight. Look, suppose you tell us exactly what has happened.'

'And you? Mrs Sheldon-Harris? How old are you?'

'Twenty-six.'

'Look here Inspector—' Theo started.

'What have you heard?'

'That my ex-wife has met with an accident.' His eyes didn't leave Michael's face.

'An accident?'

'Well, Jeremy Armstrong said she'd been murdered, strangled.' He gave an insincere laugh. 'But that can't be true, can it?'

Zoë put her hand up to her cheek, a gesture not missed by either of the detectives.

'But surely there has to have been a mistake?' Theo added hopefully.

No one spoke for a moment. Zoë was fidgeting in her chair as if she was finding it difficult to get in a comfortable position.

'I mean,' Theo went on. 'Who would want to murder Isobel?' His tone was not very convincing, and Michael thought he probably knew very well who might want to murder her.

'I'm afraid it's true, Sir Theodore. Your ex-wife was murdered some time last night.' He glanced at Ian, afraid that he was going to correct him and remind him that Isobel Sheldon-Harris was not his ex-wife at all.

'So,' Michael went on. 'Perhaps you can tell me all you can about Lady Sheldon-Harris. Her general timetable, the way she ordered her life. You can also tell me all you know about anyone who'd benefit from her death or anyone that had a grudge against her.'

Zoë looked straight into his eyes. 'That's easy,

434

Inspector. Lady Sheldon-Harris had no order to her life, none at all.'

'Zoë!' Theo said warningly. He held up his hand as if to physically ward off what she had said.

'And,' she continued, ignoring her lover's discomfort. 'As for motive, we had the best motive, and more grudges toward that woman than the whole of Norfolk put together.'

Sir Theo had risen to his feet. Once again, Michael was surprised at his size.

'Take no notice of her, Inspector, she's doesn't mean what she's saying, she's not been very well.' Then he changed his tack. 'She's joking, aren't you darling? Zoë, this isn't the time—'

'It's true, Theo, they'll find out sooner or later, there's no point in telling them differently, because *someone* will tell them.'

Theo slumped back in his seat and put his head in his hands.

'Perhaps you'd like to elaborate on that, Ms Sheldon-Harris,' Ian said.

For some absurd reason that he couldn't quite fathom, Michael wanted to tell her to be quiet. To hold her tongue, say no more than was being asked of her.

'Where shall I begin?' She coughed, and there was deep gruff rattle in her chest. The policemen looked at each other.

435

'I'll tell you what sort of woman she was. A few months ago she turned up at Betsy's school. She said she was worried about the child's emotional stability, she explained who she was, and she asked if the headmaster thought Betsy was confused with her mother living in sin with another woman's husband. She even suggested that Betsy might be better off in care.'

Angry tears clouded her blue eyes. 'The headmaster called me in. He laughed at her, he didn't say as much, but it was obvious that he thought she was pretty crazy. He kept saying that hell hath no fury like a woman scorned, but even so. It was horrid.'

Theo reached out and took her hand. 'Sweetheart, why didn't you tell me?'

'And what would you have done? Spoken to her and told her not to do it again? Slapped her wrist perhaps?'

'I'd have killed her,' he said quietly.

The room went quite quiet. Theo's face creased into a smile. 'I didn't mean that,' he said. 'It's just a way of—'

'She did daft, irritating things,' Zoë interrupted, 'like she'd ring up and cancel my milk, or she'd order expensive glossy magazines to be sent with our newspapers. Oh, I know it sounds petty if you look at any one instance, but put them all together, — it was awful.' She drew in a breath, her lungs made a squeaky, wheezy noise.

'I gather you and she didn't get on, ' Michael said

dryly, and, shielding his eyes from Ian Barnes, he winked at her.

He turned to Theo. 'And you, Sir? Did you have any other grudges?'

Theo shook his head. 'No more than I deserved. You don't walk out on your wife of fifteen years and expect everything to be honky-dory, do you?'

Michael thought of Angie. 'No,' he said. 'I don't suppose you do.'

'She made trouble for us in every way she could,' Zoë said. Michael noticed how white her face was, and when she picked the teapot up to pour them some more tea, he saw that her hand was shaking.

'And who would benefit from her death?' Ian asked. Michael shot him a look. It was obvious that the pair sitting before them would benefit.

Theo shrugged and looked blank as if he couldn't understand the question. But Zoë piped up. 'Really, Inspector, isn't it obvious? We would, of course. She wasn't going to rest until she'd cleaned Theo out. He'd have had to have sold the Hall to raise enough money for a settlement, and—'

'That's not necessarily true—' Theo countered.

'Did you have any other means of raising the sort of cash a divorce would cost?' Ian Barnes asked.

'I don't think that's any of your business,' Theo said. He looked irritated. 'Look, Inspector, the situation

437

never arose, there was no way I would sell my family home, and if a divorce meant that, then we'd have stayed married. After all, nobody cares about it nowadays, do they?'

Zoë looked pained. Was that her value? Michael wondered; she was worth a lot, but not enough to sell the family home?

'So what was she asking? And how would you have raised it?'

But Zoë answered, 'He could have sold the tenancy, but without that, we couldn't have afforded to run the big house anyway.'

Theo put his head in his hand and looked despairingly down at the table. He sighed. 'You see, Inspector, I really don't have very much money.'

Ian smiled and nodded, as if to say, ' A likely tale.'

'I got a mauling from Lloyds in the early nineties. I had to do a sale and lease back. I'm a tenant here now.'

'But the deal didn't include the Hall?'

'No.'

'What's it worth?' Ian asked.

Michael once again shot him a look of disapproval.

Theo threw his hands up in the air. 'I don't know, I've never had it valued.'

'She did,' Zoë said.

Everyone looked at her.

'What?' Theo said. 'When?'

'Couple of months ago.'

'How'd you know? Why didn't you tell me.'

'Savills came, or it might have been Strutt and Parker, one of the big boys. Anyway, a really charming man came around and said he wanted to value the cottage. I asked him why, and he told me.'

I'll bet they did, thought Michael. She could get me to tell her almost anything. He smiled at her, but she didn't respond. He felt hurt at that. Couldn't she tell that he was willing to help her?

'And did you let him?'

'There wasn't much point in *not* letting him, was there? Anyway I thought if I got in a good light with him he'd value it low. I told him all about the situation.'

'You shouldn't have done that, Zoë,' Theo said softly.

'Oh, Theo,' she started to say something, but was overcome with a fit of coughing. She excused herself, turned her head, and spat into her handkerchief. Michael could have sworn he saw blood. When she'd recovered, she said, 'He knew she was mad, she'd told him all about Randall, — that's a man that was hanged a couple of hundred years ago. They farmed on my parent's land as a matter of fact. Anyway, Isobel was convinced that Theo was Randall's reincarnation, and I was the mistress and together we murdered Randall's wife.'

Michael ignored the reincarnation theme. He'd heard it before, several times in fact, from Charlotte, the doctor, even the gardener. Instead he picked up on her parent's.

'So your dad's a farmer, is he?'

Zoë gave another strained cough. 'Sort of,' she said.

'Sort of?'

'He's a landowner.'

'Didn't lose *his* land in Lloyds then?' Ian asked.

Michael had the distinct feeling that he was gloating. He's jealous, he thought, he's jealous of the wealth around here.

'No,' Zoë spat, and coughed again. 'He almost lost something far more precious.'

'Oh?'

'His self esteem,' Zoë said simply.

And Theo looked at her and shook his head.

Michael cleared his throat, he wished Ian wouldn't be so hard on her, she was just a girl, a slip of a thing. She hadn't had anything to do with the murder; she was much too — much too what? Outspoken, innocent, what?

'Where'd you get the bruises?' Ian suddenly asked.

'Look, are we under suspicion?' Theo said, rising from his chair then sitting straight back down again.

'Just let the lady answer the question, Sir,' Ian said.

But before Zoë could speak, Theo said, 'She fell in the farmyard, the dog went for a rat and tripped her up. I was there, I saw it happen.'

Zoë looked at him, Michael thought she had a look of utter amazement on her face.

Michael smiled. 'I think that's about all, except of course, I have to ask you where you both were last night?'

'Here,' Theo said. 'We were here all night, we watched TV for a while and then we went to bed, about ten I suppose. We go to bed early because Zoë gets up to milk the cow at the crack of dawn.'

Michael noticed that Zoë's face looked whiter than ever.

'And you were here all night?'

'Of course,' Theo said.

'Mummy wasn't,' A voice from the doorway said. 'I had a bad dream, and I woke up and cried, and Theo came to me.'

Theo reached over and took Zoë's hand in his.

'Mummy was asleep, I told you. We didn't want to wake her, did we?'

Michael wished Ian would wipe that stupid grin off his face.

'No,' said Betsy. 'I woke again, and I came to find Mummy but she wasn't there.'

'I was awake all the time Betsy. I didn't see you.' Theo sounded desperate. 'She's mistaken, Inspector. She woke and I went to her, Zoë was asleep, she was next to me, I swear to God she was, she was with me all night.'His voice was raised and edged with panic.

'No,' Elizabeth insisted. 'You were sitting up in bed, and you were snoring.'

'You must have been dreaming, Betsy. I'd have seen you, I stayed awake on purpose.' His tone was gentler now, but the panic remained.

Zoë burst into another fit of coughing. Michael thought she sounded seriously ill.

'I think that will be all, for now,' Michael said, 'Be in later, will you? We might pop back and see you.'

'But—' Ian objected.

Michael put his hand up. 'The lady's none too well, Ian. We'll pop back later.'

Ian nodded, and followed his superior to the door. But when he got there, he paused and, as if a brilliant idea had just occurred to him, he said. 'Ms Sheldon-Harris? Are those the clothes you were wearing yesterday?'

'Yes,' Theo said eagerly. 'That's right, isn't it, darling?'

Zoë opened her mouth, but Elizabeth spoke first.

'No, Theo, Mummy was wearing her blue sweatshirt, the one with all the fluffy sheep on it. You remember.'

Zoë closed her eyes.

'Could we have the clothes you were wearing yesterday, Miss. For elimination purposes of course.'

Everyone looked at Zoë.

'I, er, I haven't got them.'

442

'Really?' Ian said. He nodded his head triumphantly. 'Now why aren't I surprised?'

Michael shot him yet another look.

'My mother took them, um, for washing . . . my washing machine has broken down, you see.'

'I see, all right,' Ian said, he looked toward the coat pegs. 'This yours, is it?' he took Zoë's Babour jacket down.

Zoë stared blankly ahead of her.

'We'll take this for starters then, shall we?'

He produced a large plastic bag from his pocket and flipped the coat inside.

'Perhaps you could give me your mother's 'phone number? We don't want her washing away your proof of innocence do we?'

Ian Barnes scribbled the number down in his notebook. And they politely said goodbye and left.

Chapter 56

The two policemen retraced their steps toward the Hall, as they neared it they saw that the house was lit from top to bottom. A thin dusting of frost had formed on the roof and touched the tips of the Virginia creeper.

'Looks like a Christmas card,' Michael said. 'All it needs to complete the scene is a coach and four, and perhaps one or two ladies in crinoline dresses, and a suitable greeting, of course.'

'What? Like, A happy Christmas and a peaceful death?'

'You're a right cynic, Ian, aren't you?'

'And you're a fanciful bastard if ever there was one.'

They laughed, then Michael said, 'What's all this good cop, bad cop, lark? I thought that sort of thing only happened in the movies. Besides, you're barking up the wrong tree.' He pointed to the bag containing Zoë's coat. 'She didn't have anything to do with this.'

'I think you're wrong, she's as guilty as sin. She wants the big house,— use your brain, did you see where they were living? Compare that to Garrick Hall. And she wants the title, what woman wouldn't want to be a Lady rather than a single mother? You're not seeing it straight.' He snorted. 'You took a shining to her, didn't you?'

Michael sighed. 'I thought she was a nice girl, but that doesn't make any difference to my opinion. If she were guilty she'd never have spoken about Lady Sheldon-Harris in that way.'

Ian was smiling broadly. 'Ah, that's the point you see, she's been privately educated, and she's clever.'

'How do you know that she was privately educated?'

'I'm a good detective,' he shot back.

'Her accent? It wasn't that plummy.'

'Posh enough though, wasn't it? And daddy's a land owner.'

'Even so, I doubt they have lessons in murder, even at Wycombe Abbey,' Michael said.

'Wycombe Abbey?'

'A posh girls school, down south.'

Ian turned his mouth down at the corners. 'Is that where she went?'

'I don't know, it's the only girls school I know of, and I only know that because I went to a grammar school close by. Scabby Abbies, we used to call them,' Michael smiled. 'Let's just say that the nick-name was totally unfounded.'

'Mmm, well, I think she, or she an an accomplice, did it.'

'Obviously, there's a man involved. Even if the semen is a plant, it had to come from someone.'

'Sir Theodore?' Barnes asked.

'I doubt it. It would be like leaving a calling card wouldn't it?'

'A boyfriend then?'

'Sure, one she's not terribly found of, no doubt.'

'Then who?'

'As I said, Ian, you've got it wrong. You're probably thinking what the killer wants you to think.'

Ian Barnes frowned. 'It's her all right, probably the two of them together.'

'It could be him.' Michael suddenly said. 'But it's a gut feeling that she's not involved.'

'I'll go over to her mother's and pick up her clothes, shall I? I doubt they're there, but we'll give her the benefit for now.'

'Yes, then we'd better get back to them, and get a DNA sample and some prints for elimination.'

'I'll drop this into the lab on my way through.' Barnes held up the coat.

'Yes, let her have it back as soon as possible.'

'Why? Is it the only one the poor little rich girl's got?'

'You really have got it in for her, haven't you?' Michael said.

'No, not at all. I just know she's hiding something, that's all.'

Michael stopped in his tracks. 'You know, Ian, I

think you're right. I just don't think she's hiding a murder.'

When Ian drove off to visit the Elliot's, Michael Harper went to the village pub to eat supper and glean what he could from the locals.

Although Micael had no way of knowing, the bar of the Queen Victoria was very much busier than on most Tuesday evenings. Sonny, the landlord, was reaping unexpected benefits from Lady Isobel Sheldon-Harris's sad demise. The lounge bar was silenced when Michael entered and Sonny's, 'What will you have, Sir,' seemed loud and unnatural.

All eyes were on him as he ordered beer and pie and chips, which turned out to be very good indeed, more so because he had been so hungry. The hum of conversation returned, but in muted tones, and Michael was in little doubt that the murder featured high on the list of topics, although he overheard nothing that could be of use to him. No one spoke directly to him except Vera the landlady, who remarked that there would be a hard frost that night.

Michael was just about to down the rest of his pint, when a small ferret-like man, who had been standing at the bar all evening, sidled over to him. He had sharp black eyes that darted over the room as he spoke. His hairline was well receded; attempts had been made to bring the few remaining strands forward in an unsuccessful illusion of a full head of hair. His skin was sallow, and his forehead scared with needle-like scabs as if he had collided with a thorn bush. His thin bony hands bore similar scratches, and his nails were long and dirty.

'H'evening, Governor,' he said, as he approached the table where Michael sat.

Michael nodded.

'Sparks the name. I'm Sir Theo's gamekeeper, or at least I was. You must be the gent 'as come from Scotland Yard to h'investigate the killing of poor Lady S.' Sparks added and subtracted h's as the fancy took him.

Michael found it hard not to correct his grammar. 'Not quite Scotland Yard,' he said. 'But yes, I'm here to look into the matter. Did you know her?'

'Bless you, Sir, Did I know 'er? She were a wonderful woman, Sir. Very 'umane she were, better be far than most of the so-called gentry round 'ere.'

This was a new Isobel Sheldon-Harris, and Michael became instantly interested. He got to his feet. 'Can I get you another drink, Mr Sparks.'

'No, Sir. No. You see, I wouldn't want 'ole village seeing me take a drink off the coppers, if you h'understand me. No h'offence meant, Sir.' His sharp eyes scanned the room.

Michael understood perfectly. But before he could reseat himself, Sparks changed his mind.

'Well, Sir. As h'I've already been seen talking to you, I don't suppose it would do no 'arm. Why not? A small double whiskey would suit me well.'

Michael smiled and, wondering how a double whisky could be described as either large or small, he went to the bar to fulfill the little man's request.

Sparks leaned very close to Michael as he spoke, Michael found himself leaning backwards, repelled by his foul smelling breath and saliva sprayed speech.

'I were the keeper down at the 'all, until Sir Theo sold the shooting rights, that is. The guns brought in a townie, college trained 'e were and h'all that. Puts far too many birds down, 'e does, the h'estate is far too small to 'old so many birds. Too many guns shooting too many days, as well.'

Michael drew in a deep breath; the last thing he wanted was to listen to a sacked keeper's moans and groans. He ought to be getting back to Garrick Hall. He ought to be ringing Angie; she'd wonder what had happened to him.

'So you were made redundant?' Michael said. 'Where do you work now?'

'I h'aint, Govenor. I can't get a job. I'm one of Mr Blair's h'unemployed. That's me, I'm a casualty of government cutbacks.'

Michael wondered what Mr Blair or the government had to do with anything. But Sparks hadn't finished.

'The country's in a sorry state when a trained man like me can't get h'employment. I knew me job, Sir, and a better keeper you would not find nowhere.' He swigged

449

down two thirds of the whiskey. 'I asked Sir Theo for the shepherds job, when young Andy Culper left, and do you know what 'e says? Says I weren't h'experienced, me not h'experienced! Why, I knows this h'estate like the back of me 'and. And h'I've been dealing with animals all me life. Then lo, and be'old he sets on that slip o' a thing, what could she know about it, at 'er age?'

Michael fidgeted in his seat; he ought to get going. Sparks had nothing to tell him. He ought to ring Angie; she'd be in a foul mood if he left it much longer.

'Well, then when Sir Theo moves in with 'er, I saw what it 'ad all been about. No wonder I didn't get the job, I 'adn't got any frilly little knickers to drop for him had I? Mind you, frilly knickers didn't serve Trev Skinner very well, did they.'

'Trev Skinner?'

'The h'old foreman, he's one o' *them*, you know, *them*. Likes to put on women's clothes, a translucid or something.'

'Transvestite?' Michael asked helpfully.

'Oh, whatever, — something like that. Sir Theo sacked 'im when the Elliot girl came.'

Michael was confused, but he didn't say so, he hoped that things would become clearer as the conversation advanced.

'And what has this to do with Lady Sheldon-Harris?'

'Well, when all this 'appened, when he went like, Lady Sheldon-Harris came to see us, me and my Ruth, said she'd been left high and dry, and she 'andn't got no money, but she still wanted Ruth to clean for her. 'Cause, she couldn't afford to pay 'er much, on acount of 'er not getting much from Sir Theo.'

'Ruth is your wife? And she cleaned for Lady Sheldon-Harris?'

'That's what I said, didn't I?'

'Did your wife go in to clean yesterday?'

'No, not yesterday, she had a bit of a cold you see, and well, as I said Lady S didn't pay much, so I says to Ruth, 'don't go,' I says, 'stay at 'ome and keep warm'. But she went in today, she did. But there was no one 'ome, or so she thought, and to think that that poor woman was lying dead. In a right old flurry my Ruth has been since she 'eard. I didn't really want to come out and leave her tonight.'

Michael nodded as if he understood. Sparks gave him a sideways look and finished his drink. He placed the glass down heavily within inches of Michael's hand. His face looked more ferret-like than ever.

'There's just one other thing Governor. Lady S, well . . . you see . . . '

Michael held his breath, a revelation was about to be made, the case was about to be cracked.

'Well, she 'adn't paid my Ruth for a couple of weeks and she h'owes her, like, over sixty pounds she h'owes her.'

Michael thought Sparks probably expected him to put his hand in his pocket and produce the money.

'I think you'd better see Sir Theo about that,' he said.

Sparks snorted. 'That mean bugger! I don't suppose we'll see that money then.'

'Tell your wife that I'd like to pop in and see her in the morning, ask her to stay at home, would you?' Michael said.

A thought seemed to illuminate Spark's face. 'Course, Ruth didn't earn much, she cleaned more as a favour than for the money, so we'll just leave it, shall we? We'll forget what's due, Governor. It wasn't much, just a few bob.'

'I thought you said, sixty pounds?'

'Oh no, Governor. You must 'ave mis'eard me. It were nothing.' He rose abruptly and made his way back to the bar where he was immediately surrounded by a group of men, who murmured urgent questions at him.

What was that all about? Thought Michael, and, as if in answer, Sonny the landlord, who had obviously been listening to every word, came over to wipe the table.

'Social security,' he whispered. 'He suddenly remembered who he was talking to and everyone knows his missis doesn't declare her wages, — claim all that's going from the state, they do.'

Michael smiled. 'Well, that's none of my business. But tell me, — his forehead, — does he often sport such impressive scratches?'

'Sonny winked. 'Put it this way, a good gamekeeper makes an even better poacher. But even he can't avoid them thorn bushes in the dark. Skinner has the same problem, always prowling about, spying on that young girl.'

'Skinner? That would be the old foreman, right?'

Sonny glanced around the room with obvious discomfort. He rewiped the table bending close to Michael as he did so.

'Look, Inspector,' his voice was barely above a whisper. 'I've got a business to run. If I'm seen talking to you, well — half my customers have got something to hide.' He looked alarmed. 'Nothing strictly illegal. I mean there's no drug trafficking or anything like that, but, you know, a bit of infidelity, the odd fiddles at work, perks really, you know the kind of thing. Folks have a drink and it loosens their tongues. I hear a lot of gossip in this bar, and it's from my customers that I hear it. And my customers are my bread and butter. I'm sure you understand?'

Michael understood, but it made no difference, he had a job to do. Before he could form his thoughts into words, Sonny said, still in little more than a whisper, 'So, if you'd like to leave, Sir. Ordinary like.' He glanced around the room again. 'We'll be closing in three hours. Pop back then, use the side door, I'll leave it open, just go up and make yourself at home. I'll be up as soon as I've closed the pub.' Sonny gave another quick look around and scuttled off to the bar.

Michael felt rather silly as he called a cheery, 'Goodnight and thank you.' And in a rather furtive way he slipped from the bar, got into his car and made his way back to Garrick Hall.

Once through the main gates he pulled over to the side of the drive and rang Angela from his mobile. She wasn't in a bad mood at all; in fact she was as bright and as cheerful as he'd ever know her.

'You're in a good mood,' he said. 'Found yourself a boyfriend, have you?'

'Yes,' she replied. 'As a matter of fact I have. And he's wanting my attention so I'll have to go.'

Michael was stunned, this wasn't the way Angie usually spoke; she hadn't joked that way for years and years.

'And don't ring me too early tomorrow, I'm off to get my hair done in the morning, and in the afternoon I'm going to buy myself a bicycle.'

'What?' She was joking of course; Angie hadn't ridden a bicycle for years. 'Oh?' he quipped back. 'That so you and your boyfriend can go up to the common?'

'That's right,' she giggled

'Right, I won't ring you before seven then.' He

said goodbye and switched off the telephone.

It was good to hear her sounding so buoyant He wondered what had made her so happy. Then a thought struck him, a thought that wasn't very nice. Perhaps, he thought, perhaps she wasn't joking.

Chapter 57

'Mummy? It's Zoë.'

'I haven't been called mummy in a long time, not since—' Lavinia gave a nervous little laugh. 'You called me mummy this afternoon, as well.'

Zoë ignored her mother's remarks and went on, 'I need you to do something for me. The police may 'phone you. I want you to tell them that I gave you some of my clothes to wash, and that you've washed them. It's important, do you understand?'

'Yes, — No, Zoë, I don't understand. Has this got something to do with Isobel's death?'

'No, they're checking up on everyone, Ma, and they want my clothes. The ones I wore yesterday, and I said I was wearing the same ones, but then Betsy told them I was wearing my blue sweatshirt, that one you brought me from Wales, the one with the fluffy sheep on it, and then they asked me for it and I lied, and said my washing machine had broken down, and that you were doing some washing for me, only it hasn't.' The words spluttered out in one long breathy sentence.

'Slow down, darling, take it from the beginning.'

Zoë repeated what she had said. But was hardly more coherent on the second airing.

'But why don't you just give them the clothes,

you've nothing to hide, have you?'

Zoë was quite silent for some seconds.

'Zoë? Oh God. Zoë, what happened? Did she threaten you? What happened?'

'Mummy, it's not what you think, really it isn't.'

'Then just give them the clothes.'

'I can't.'

'Why can't you? It's the only logical thing to do.'

'I haven't got them anymore.' Her voice fell. 'I burned them.'

This time it was Lavinia who was silent.

'Ma, are you still there?'

'Yes, darling, I'm still here. But we'd better not talk on the 'phone.'

'Why not?'

'You never know who might be listening. Don't worry, darling, we'll handle it.'

The receiver went dead.

Zoë carefully replaced it; then, turning, she started as Theo's form came into view. She didn't know how long he'd be standing there, or how much he'd heard.

'We have to talk, Zoë, and I'm not sure how long we've got,— before they come back, that is.'

She nodded her head and allowed him to lead her over to the sofa, but before she'd sat down a thought struck her, 'When do you think they'll bring my Barbour back, Theo?'

457

'I don't know, does it matter? You've got something else to wear, haven't you?'

'But I need it,' she wailed. 'There's something in the pocket I need.' She put her hand up to her aching head. She wasn't thinking straight, how stupid could she get, she'd left the morning-after pill in her coat pocket.

'What? What do you need?'

She should tell him, throw herself on his mercy and hope that he would forgive her, hope that he would understand. But she couldn't, it would spoil everything. She'd had too much heartache in her life to risk the one relationship that really mattered to her.

'Penicillin,' she said. 'For the sheep, I left it in the pocket.'

'Is that all? Well, for goodness sake, I can go to the vets in the morning and pick up some more. Which was it?'

'What?'

'Long acting or short?'

'I don't remember,' she said.

'Zoë, Zoë darling, I love you. I'll always love you no matter what you've done.' He closed his eyes. 'I know you had good reason, my God I do, but you'll have to tell me all about it, otherwise I can't help you.'

She sank down onto the sofa. 'You think I killed her, don't you?'

'No. No, of course not,' he said. But she could see that he was lying.

458

She held his eyes, maybe it was better to confess to a murder than . . . Oh God, she was living in a nightmare, soon she'd wake up.

'I didn't kill her, Theo.'

'You went out last night,' he said. He looked away from her as if he felt guilty for mentioning it. 'Betsy woke, she'd had a nightmare, and I got up to her.'

'Maybe I was in the bathroom,' she said.

He gave a sad half-smile. 'I waited up, only I must have dozed, that's what Betsy says. I saw the Land Rover come back. And then you were showering for ages—'

She held up her hands. 'Okay, it's a fair cop, will you take me in, now?' She laughed but without animation.

But Theo was still looking away from her. 'Then this morning in the farmyard—'

'All right, Theo, I'll tell you.' She took a deep breath, but the pain shot through her, she coughed, and then couldn't stop.

'You have to get that looked at,' he said.

The coughing subsided. 'I'm all right, I bruised my ribs, that's all, when I fell. Look Theo, if you want to know where I was last night, just ask.' She was having to think quickly, very quickly. 'I went down to the farmyard. One of the new Suffolk crosses has an abscess on his back, and it worried me, so I went to take a look at him.'

'In the middle of the night?' he sounded unconvinced. 'Why didn't you tell me this before? Why didn't you tell the police?'

She could tell that he wanted to believe her, and she knew that he couldn't. 'Because when I bought that ram you were horrified at how much he'd cost. I felt I'd probably made a bad choice and that you'd be angry. And as for telling the police, they'd never have believed me.'

He frowned. 'For God's sake, Zoë. Have I ever been angry with you, for anything? Besides, how could you be held responsible for a sick sheep?' His voice was raised. 'Why did you burn your clothes, Zoë? Answer me that?'

'They were, filthy.' She shuddered, they really *were* filthy; she never wanted to set eyes on them again.

'Then why didn't you wash them?'

'Because of what was on them,' she said, tears coursing down her cheeks. That was true enough. The coughing returned.

'What, Zoë? What was on them?'

'All the muck from the abscess, I . . . I . . told you . . . I . . . I lanced it and it went all over me.'

Theo was tight lipped, he didn't believe a word of what she said; she could see that.

'Why are questioning me?'

'Because I don't like this silly game we're playing. Tell me the truth, Zoë.'

'You're worse than the police. I didn't . . . .' but her coughing drowned out everything else she tried to say.

460

Chapter 58

'Bloody hell, you should have seen it, Mike. Loaded they are, there's money dripping out of their finger tips.'

'Plenty of money, but no clothes, hey?'

'Does that surprise you? She must have 'phoned her mum as soon as we'd left. She was a pretty cool customer as well, and did I tell you? She's a Lady as well. Lady Hulver, if you please.'

'But you didn't get the clothes?' Michael said, a smile on his face. Ian Barnes had obviously suffered some sort of culture shock.

'Asked me in, they did, Lord and Lady Hulver. Took me into what they called, 'the drawing room,' — wasn't anything more than a living room, — well, a posh sort of living room. Better than that one they take you round at Sandringham, you know, where the Queen makes her New Year speech.'

'Christmas day.'

'What?'

'Christmas day, she makes her speech on Christmas day.'

'It's pre-recorded, she doesn't disturb her Christmas, does she? Anyway the house — huge it is, they call it a castle but it doesn't look much like one, it hasn't got a moat or anything.'

'And what were the parents like?'

'As you'd expect. La-de-da and a bit above the likes of me.'

'And the clothes?' Michael prompted. They were walking up from Garrick Hall to the cottage for the second interview of the evening.

'Cool, she was, said she'd brought them straight home and washed them. So I asked to see them, and she produces this pair of jeans, — well they might have fitted the Elliot girl about ten years ago, but they'd never fit her now. So I asked about the sweatshirt. You'll love this. Apparently whilst her ladyship was ironing it, she caught the logo with the iron, and guest what? It was ruined. So do you know what she did with it?'

Michael shook his head.

'She threw it on the wood burner! Now there's a surprise. What do you think?'

'I think she's lying,' he replied and looked rather sad.

'That's not all I have to report. Guess what was in the girl's jacket?'

'A signed confession?' Michael said dryly.

'Well, there was a lot of junk, sheep medicine and sheep pills and some funny little orange rings, and a penknife, but guess what else?'

They were nearing the cottage. 'I think you'd better tell me, Ian, we're almost there.'

'Orange string,' he said dramatically. 'Orange string. A bloody great length of it.'

They passed the sitting room window and saw that Theo and Zoë were sitting on the sofa, both seemed to be staring into the fire. The television wasn't on, and neither seemed bent on any occupation.

Theo answered the door, and brought them through to the sitting room. Zoë didn't even lift her head to acknowledge them.

'Little girl in bed?' Michael asked as if he were paying a purely social call.

No one answered.

'I thought we'd just run through the events of last night one more time, if you don't mind, and then tomorrow I'd like you both to come over to Fenshaw. I'd like a sample of your finger prints and a swab for DNA comparison.'

That grabbed their attention.

'Look,' Theo said. 'I don't think that will be necessary, it's obvious we couldn't have had anything to do with it.'

'Funny that,' Ian said, 'that's what they all say, and do you know what I reply?'

Again no one answered.

'I say, that in that case, you won't mind humoring us then, will you?'

Zoë and Theo looked at each other; the stress between them was palpable.

'Your little girl says she woke in the night. What time would that have been?'

'I don't know,' Theo said. 'I didn't look at the time. It was the middle of the night, I mean it wasn't morning, it wasn't getting light or anything. As for Betsy coming in our room and not seeing her mother, well I can explain that.'

Ian Barnes gave him a look that was almost a sneer, as if to say, 'go on then, explain it.'

'It's a bit embarrassing,' Theo said. 'You see, we'd just made love, and Zoë didn't have any clothes on, well of course she wouldn't have, not in bed, would she? I mean, she didn't have her nightdress on. And so when Betsy came in Zoë snuggled under the duvet, and I pretended I was asleep.' He gave a false laugh. 'Didn't want her going off to school and saying something she shouldn't'

Zoë flopped forward and put her head in her hands.

Barnes tapped his pencil on his notebook, he hadn't written anything down.

'Let me get this straight,' he said. 'Betsy woke up because she was having a nightmare, and you, Sir, went to comfort her. I seem to remember that you reminded Betsy, when we were here earlier, that you'd not wanted to wake her mother up, right?'

Theo, looking very uncomfortable, nodded.

'So then you went back to your room and you woke her up, and you made love?'

'No, no, she was awake when I got back.'

'But you didn't go into the child, Mrs Sheldon-Harris?' Michael asked gently.

'Yes,' Theo answered for her. 'She did, but Betsy had fallen asleep again.'

'So then you made love?' Ian asked.

'Yes, and then a little later Betsy came through, and Zoë hid and I pretended I was asleep.'

Ian Barnes had a broad smile on his face. 'Right,' he said, nodding his head. 'That all sounds highly believable.'

'Did either of you hear any strange noises last night? Anything unusual?' Michael looked toward the door where the collie lay. 'Did the dog bark for instance?'

Sir Theodore spoke again. 'We can't actually see the Hall from here, our windows all face either onto the drive or away from the house. The few windows we have on the back, face into the walled garden. The lodge was built that way to give maximum privacy to the big house. Anyone visiting my ex-wife, needn't have come past here, they could just as easily use the back drive. We really didn't know what went on down there, either last night or any other night.'

Zoë spoke then. 'We weren't interested in what she did. She seemed interested in our every movement, but we just wanted her to leave us alone. We just wanted to get on with our lives. We saw nothing last night, and we heard nothing.' She glanced at Theo for confirmation. 'The first time we realized something was amiss was when we saw all the police cars this morning.'

Zoë picked up her head and stared straight at Michael. 'We can't pretend, you know,' she burst out, 'it would be hypocritical of us to pretend.'

Theo patted her hand; he gave her a warning look. But then he himself added.

'What Zoë means, is that we would be lying if we said that life without Issie won't be a lot easier and a lot pleasanter for us both. We only wish a less violent solution had come about.'

'You mean a natural death?' Ian said, and sniggered.

'Good Lord, no, Inspector!' Theo retorted. 'Divorce, if only she'd have agreed to a divorce and a reasonable settlement. We never wished her dead, never. Now if you're finished with us?' he put his arm around Zoë, 'I'd like to get my wife to bed, you can see she's not well.'

'Your wife?' Ian said.

'For Christ sake,' Theo snapped 'A figure of speech, we're an item — as you people would say. Zoë may not be my wife in law, but she's certainly my wife in every other way. Now, if you don't mind?'

He stood up and helped Zoë to her feet, and Michael was once again struck by his size, he was a very big man indeed. Zoë, who was a girl of average size, barely reached his shoulder.

'Ralph Fiennes,' Barnes said. 'That's who you remind me of.'

'Good bye, 'Theo said, and he held out his hand.

Michael took it and shook it. It seemed a strange action considering he was about to ruin the man's whole life.

Chapter 59

Ian set off to Fenshaw to collate the information they had gained so far and to liaise with the experts from the scene of crime. It was late, but both agreed that time was of the essence. Michael took himself off to the Queen Victoria. As invited, he let himself in by the side door, ascended a steep flight of stairs and entered Sonny and Vera's private sitting room.

The room made him shudder. Everything, from brightly painted artex walls to highly patterned garish carpet offended him. He seated himself on a brown vinyl sofa and stared in dismay at the beige tiled mantelpiece, which displayed a collection of china and glass animals; dogs, cats, horses and elephants competed for attention. To the right of the fireplace stood a glass display cabinet, full to bursting with more of the same.

He must have been staring intently at the hideous display as he didn't hear Vera Crisp enter, and was not aware of her presence until she said in a rather breathless voice, 'Oh, hello, Inspector, I see you're admiring my little collection then?' She nodded her head as she spoke and she had a look of pride on her face.

Michael jumped. 'Oh, um, yes, lovely,' he said, 'lovely.'

She went over to the mantelpiece and removed a

pink glass giraffe. 'This one's called Oswald,' she said, her head tilting back and forth and a fixed smile on her lips. 'They've all got names,' she nodded. 'But I can't always remember them. Well, I've got so many now.' Her eyes opened and closed in time to the movement of her head.

Michael found the action quite hypnotic; he wondered if he too were nodding back and forth. His mind displayed a vivid picture of Vera's false teeth nodding up and down in time with, but detached from, her head, and he wanted to laugh. He must be getting tired, or perhaps he was just getting old and senile.

Vera Crisp was a plump, rounded woman, in her late fifties. Her grey hair was once dyed auburn, but had lightened into a pale orange. Her tired skin was plastered in a thick layer of tan makeup, her cheeks highlighted with a rosy blusher, her eyelids were spread with pale blue eyeshadow and her lips outlined in a vivid red. She wore a high necked dress of some sort of stretchy fabric that cruelly clung to her ample figure. Michael thought that a low-necked dress would have been more the order of the day. She could have achieved a cleavage that would have qualified her for barmaid of the year, although which year he wasn't quite sure. She moved slowly and, in contrast, talked very fast. She continued to show Michael her favorite ornaments until Sonny Crisp finally arrived.

Sonny, as rotund as his wife, was completely bald and sported an impressive double chin; his hands were soft and podgy. Michael guessed him to be about sixty. He had the sleeves of his off-white shirt rolled up, exposing his short, fat, rather hairy, arms. Maroon braces supported his baggy grey trousers, his shoes needed a clean and he didn't look as if he had shaved that day. He gave Vera a sharp look and she immediately ceased the verbal tour of her precious glass animals.

'Sonny doesn't like my little collection,' she said apologetically.

Sonny shot her another damning look.

Michael smiled at her, then he said, 'Tell me what you know about the Sheldon-Harris family.' He addressed his question to no one in particular.

Vera wriggled excitedly. 'Well, you'll never guess.' She then went on to relate the tale of Theo going off with Zoë, followed by Isobel's connections with the world of spirits. Michael didn't bother to explain that he had already heard several versions of both stories, or that he'd probably hear a few more before the case was over. He patiently listened, noting any small differences in this new edition.

'Of course,' Sonny said, 'we don't know what goes on down at the Hall. None of that lot ever comes in here. We get the guns from the shooting syndicate, of course, but that's as close as we come.'

'Who are they — the guns?' Michael asked.

Sonny raised his eye to the ceiling. 'Well there's

that chap Banks, owns the BMW garage on the Fenshaw bypass. And there's Chad Stephens — he's a builder from Stalham. There's Tony somebody or other, — he's a loud mouth, him, don't know what he does though. Sonny continued in this vein, reciting a list of names, half names and occupations. Michael made notes, another good job for Ian Barnes; it was all good training for him.

'But,' said Sonny. 'If you want to know about the shooting side of the estate, you were talking to the right chap tonight.'

Michael raised his eyebrows.

'The weasel, you know, Will Sparks. If anyone saw anything down in the park last night, Will Sparks would be your man. He spends more time about Sir Theo's business now, than ever he did when he worked for him.'

'You mean he's a poacher.'

Sonny pulled a face. 'That I couldn't say.'

'Or won't say?' Michael asked.

'I do have a business to run,' Sonny said with a smile on his plain round face.

Vera looked uncomfortable. 'Ask the guns, they'll tell you about the weasel. A lot of birds go missing, Inspector. They haven't caught him though.'

'Yet,' said Sonny. 'He'd be better named the fox, he's that sly,'

'He would and all,' Vera said, her breathy voice held a tone of complete dislike.

'He pays for his beer, same as everyone else, Vera,' Sonny said, giving her a warning glance.

'There's another one knows more about Sir Theo's business than he ought,' Vera said.

Sonny shook his head. 'She's talking about Blossom Skinner,' he said.

'Blossom Skinner?'

'Trev, Trev Skinner. They call him that, behind his back mind, not to his face. He has a liking for ladies garments, but he's harmless.'

'He watches that girl,' Vera said. She looked straight into Michael's eyes. 'He gives me the willies he does. Wears hairslides and wigs, and like Sonny says, women's clothes. Why his misses puts up with it, I don't know.'

'She maybe has no choice,' Sonny said. 'He's harmless enough, Inspector. All talk and lacy knickers, he is.'

Vera put her hand over her mouth and laughed.

'Tell me about the syndicate. Who's the keeper now that Mr Sparks has left?' Michael wasn't sure if he was going in the right direction, but he had a hunch he was.

'A chap called Peter Evans. He lodges with Mrs Coe at the post office. He comes in here on a shoot day and takes a pint off the guns, but doesn't ordinarily come in here. The guns are a load of get-rich-quick, wide boys, and that about sums them up. They run the sweep for twenty or

472

thirty pounds a head, — it's as if money's lost its value when they're around.'

'Have you any idea how Sir Theo and Lady Sheldon-Harris got on with them?'

Sonny scratched his bald plate. 'Now, thereby hangs a tale!' He looked at Vera. 'Shall I tell him?' he said winking at her.

He didn't wait for Vera's reply but went on. 'I assume Sir Theo gets on all right with them, otherwise he wouldn't rent the shoot to them. I've not heard that he doesn't get on, anyway. As for her, Lady Sheldon-Harris,' he chucked. 'I'd say she and they didn't see eye to eye. In fact it all came to a bit of a head last Thursday. She 'phoned your lot, and said that half the guns didn't have shot-gun certificates. Of course, the police had to check, well, they would, wouldn't they?' Contempt had crept into his voice. 'Well, I mean, most people don't carry their licenses around with them, do they? Young Johnson, he's our local copper, was a bit enthusiastic. He wouldn't let them take them into the station the next day or anything, he wanted to see them then and there. I suppose he'd got a bit carried away with all these school shootings in America. Well, none of the guns are exactly local, they couldn't just pop home and get them, so the day was abandoned and they'd only done a couple of drives. You can imagine what they had to say about Lady Sheldon-Harris in here last Thursday night. The language was something special, I can tell you. I wouldn't have liked to have been in her shoes.' He chuckled again. 'I'm not surprised that she was murdered. I'm just surprised she wasn't shot with a twelve bore.'

'So the syndicate drink here after the shoot?' Michael asked.

'Oh yes. They've got the sense to support local business. It's an improvement since Sir Theo ran the shoot himself. When that lot shot, they sipped their G and T's in a much grander style.' Sonny chuckled again.

'I'd have liked to have been a fly on the wall when Arthur Banks went to see Sir Theo last Thursday night. Old Arthur was two parts drunk, and I know he was going to ask for some money back. I bet Sir Theo could have killed his missus.' Sonny Crisp fell suddenly silent. He looked over to where his wife sat in one of the brown vinyl armchairs. His face had lost much of its colour.

'Oh,' he said, 'Oh, my God.'

It was well past midnight when Michael reached Fenshaw police station. Barnes was waiting for him.

'I just had a call from Gilbert Knox,' Barnes said. 'He says he was right about the stuff being planted, or to use Knox's expression, "The semen was not deposited as the result of normal intercourse." He says the old girl hadn't had a poke for years, says it had practically healed over.'

'What?'

'Well no, he didn't say that, but I bet she hadn't.

It's right about the plant though. He also said that she was probably strangled by someone smaller than her, something about the direction of the rope. Got it right, haven't I? It's the Elliot girl, it has to be. If we find her clothes we've got her, those clothes are somewhere in that cottage, but they won't be for much longer, they'll be getting rid of them. In fact, they're probably off somewhere now, dumping them, we should have brought her in tonight.'

Michael bit into his bottom lip. 'She won't get rid of them tonight. I've put a man on surveillance.'

'So you *do* think it's her?'

'No, but in the light of all the evidence, it wants following through.'

'Pick her up first thing then, shall we?'

'What about him?' Michael said.

'He couldn't have done it, he's too tall, for a start.'

'That's Gilbert's speculation, he can't be sure. I don't know about bringing her in. We ought to do a bit more groundwork, find out who her accomplice is.'

'She'll crack, — once she's here. She may be clever when she's on her own ground, but it'll be different when she's on our turf.'

'I don't know.'

'Leave it any longer and the evidence will have gone.'

Michael sucked air in between his teeth. 'Okay, organize it for the morning, not too early, let her get her kid off to school first.'

Ian gave him a broad smile. 'Oh, by the way, Debbie dropped this in,' he said handing him a green holdall. 'There's a note for you on the top.'

Michael took the bag, removed a small white envelope and split it open. The note said that tomorrow,— Wednesday — was her day off and that she'd be in Fenshaw, and she was happy to help him in any way he saw fit. He crammed the note in his pocket and, whistling, he made his way to the Kings Head.

Chapter 60

Debbie Smith came out of the bathroom; she was completely naked. He stared at her in amazement; her body was more beautiful than he had ever imagined, and here she was offering herself to him. He held out his hands and she smiled at him. He was dying from the need of her. He could feel his erection pressing against his stomach, he thought he might explode before he'd got close to her.

She pulled back the bedclothes and slipped in beside him, her legs seemed extraordinarily long, her toenails were painted a very pale pink. Her skin had a dark olive hue as if she was of Mediterranean extraction and her bush was very thick and dark like the hair on her head. She had a stud pieced into her belly button. Her breasts were small and neat, her nipples were large and dark and the areola extensive.

She leaned over him, supporting herself on one elbow, and looked down on him, he stretched himself out and parted his legs a little. She smiled, her lips were a dusky pink and her eyes were very brown and very clear and she mesmerized him.

She put a hand up to the back of her head and slipped the comb out of her hair, the thick dark mane tumbled over her shoulders and down over his chest. She rested one leg over the top of him. His erection was huge, he could feel it pressing against her thigh, he'd have to be inside her quickly, otherwise he'd come. The proximity of her was too exciting, he couldn't hold himself in check much longer.

Her fingers crept over his belly and down, down, until she held his penis in her hand, she looked at him and she seemed pleased. Then she slid on top of him. He raised his hips, so that he could slip inside her; he could feel her moist labia welcoming him, he caught his breath, she was going to ride the tiger. He moistened his lips; he'd been waiting so long for this. He almost had the tip inside her, she was moving above him in a circular movement, he couldn't get it in; she was always just beyond his reach. He raised his hips a little more. She took him in her hands again and drew his foreskin back as far as it would go, she squatted above him; he was about the enter her and . . . too late, with a cry, he ejaculated.

He gave a hoarse cry as his body gave a last convulsion. He turned his head away from her, and when he turned back he saw that the hair that cascaded over him was not dark at all, but a soft, silky, blonde waterfall, and the eyes that stared into his were not brown, but a startling blue.

He murmured his confusion, and tossed his head from side to side, she slipped from the bed and started to walk backwards away from him.

'Zoë, Zoë, don't go. Stay, stay here,' he called as she faded away from him.

478

His eyes snapped open and he sat bolt upright, his heart was hammering in his chest, and he was drenched with sweat, he looked at his alarm clock, it was one-thirty, he'd only been in bed for half an hour. His left hand was still clutching his penis, which was delightfully sticky.

'Christ,' he said aloud. He began to laugh. A wet dream, at his age! He couldn't remember the last time that had happened. There again, he couldn't remember the last time he'd made love, and he hadn't masturbated for years.

He flopped back on the pillow. Sex was something he'd put on one side; he'd sort of hoped that it would find him when the time was ripe. Well maybe the time had come, and maybe he had to seek it out himself. Maybe it wouldn't come to him unless he looked for it, and perhaps he should start looking now, before it was too late.

His hand moved in a long forgotten rhythm, and his erection returned with renewed vigor. How could he have forgotten how good it felt? How could he have put such an exquisite pleasure to one side?

Debbie had delivered an invitation with his bag. He had her home telephone number, she'd offered to give him a hand. Well, she could give him a hand with this if she wanted. His hand was flying up and down now — yes indeed, she could well assist him in this particular venture.

Chapter 61

Zoë slammed a chicken in the oven, and straightened her back. She'd thought she might go and see Dr Armstrong on her way home from taking Elizabeth to school. She could maybe get some more pills; maybe it wasn't too late. But something deep inside, told her it was. She was sure she was pregnant, she felt almost hysterical about it, talk about bad timing. She ought to go and see the doctor about her chest anyway, but today she was breathing easier. After the murder, she really didn't want to face Theo's old friend. She didn't want to explain what had happened to the first lot of pills. She looked out of the window, her face a mask of misery; she had stopped believing that everything was going to be all right.

She watched transfixed as Harper and Barnes drew up to the cottage door. Oh no, not again. There was a white van and a police car behind them, but she took no notice, she assumed they were going on to the Hall.

And that's all she remembered, except for those dreadful, dreadful words *murder, murder, murder.* Those two men, intruders in her home, were bringing it down around her ears. Thieves, robbing her of all she loved, all she held dear. Men, upright citizens in positions of power, entering into her life and breaking her heart. *Murder, murder,* they were accusing her, how could that be?

Someone, the young one, Barnes, had his hand on her wrist. She thought they were going to handcuff her. They didn't, but she wouldn't have cared. They had stripped her of all her dignity, choked the life out of her with that one foul word, m*urder*. The van had reversed up to the cottage, its back doors gaped open, inside was like a dark threatening cave, a place where once entered you would never return as the same person, a kind of death. *Murder, murder,* why wouldn't her brain work? It was as if she were floating, very, very, slowly, taking everything in, yet not able to collate anything, everything was in the wrong order. Her thoughts were jumbled and messy.

There was a man on either side of her. Barnes the young one, had a tight hold on her wrist, his face was twisted into a sort of a sneer. He looked as if he was enjoying himself. Harper, the Inspector on the other side of her, cupped her elbow with his hand. He had a sad but steady look, as if to tell her not to worry, that everything would be all right. She wanted to laugh at him; she knew that nothing would ever be all right ever again. Stupid old fool, with his macho looks and his pea sized brain. *Murder, murder,* if he was half a detective, he'd know what had happened the night before last. Was that all it was? Two nights ago? How could a life be destroyed in such a very short time, and not just one life, not just Isobel's, but her life, and Theo's, and Betsy's, and her parents.

'In you go, Miss,' One of them said, but she didn't

know which one, her senses were confused, her orientation was out of line. *Murder, murder.* The steps at the back of the van seemed very steep, they weren't; they just seemed that way, as if she was trying to climb an insurmountable obstacle. She felt as if she were hauling herself up, and as if the policemen were pushing her from the rear. The operation seemed to take a very long time.

She slid herself onto one of the two wooden benches that ran along the side of the van, there were slats in the wood, and she pushed her finger down between them. She was losing her grip on reality, she had to hold onto something that was real.

She could hear Theo's voice, snatches of words clustered together, 'not necessary . . . could have driven her . . . common criminal.' He was getting so het up, didn't he understand that it didn't matter anymore. She'd never see him again anyway, and Betsy — oh God, she'd never see either of them again.

Theo's face appeared at the door, Barnes pulled him away, and said something. She heard Theo very clearly then, he was shouting. 'Suspect, don't be such a bloody fool, Zoë didn't kill her, I did. I did it, not Zoë.' *Murder, murder, murder.*

She leaned her head against the back of the van, and closed her eyes, but opened them again with a jolt when the van moved away. There were two men in the front, both of them in uniform, she looked around her, she was in a sort

482

of a cage, hemmed in like an animal, a dangerous animal. *Murder, murder.* Between her and the men in front was a thick dirty Perspex screen. What did they think she was going to do? Creep up behind them and strangle them? *Murder, murder.*

She shrank back into the corner of the van, drew her legs up to her aching chest and wrapped her hands around her knees. She'd known all along that they would come for her, ever since Monday night she'd known, it was her destiny. She couldn't tell anyone the truth, because they'd tell Theo, and she'd rather Theo thought of her as a murderer than a betrayer.

She'd never in her life been to Fenshaw police station, why should she? She'd never been on the wrong side of the law; she'd never even got a parking ticket.

The van was driven into a large yard and backed up to a red brick building. One of the policemen got out and banged on what looked like a shining steel door. Some moments later it was opened, and she was uncaged and taken into a small windowless waiting room. The walls were painted a battleship grey and were bare apart from three notices reminding offices of the correct procedure for prisoners in the secure waiting area. *Prisoner?* Is that was she was, a prisoner? How could that be? *Murder, murder, murder.*

She sat on a painted wooden bench. There seemed

to be a lot of activity, uniforms were going in and out of another door. No one met her eyes.

'Won't be long now,' the van driver said. 'They're just processing someone before you.'

Why was he smiling at her? What was there to smile about? Was she supposed to join him in his mirth? Didn't he know why she was there? Didn't he know that her life had come to an end? Or did he know, and it was just that he didn't care?

A camera swung round the room, she looked up at it, it stared blankly back at her. She wondered who was watching her from beyond the stout door. She wondered if they were nodding their heads saying that they recognized the mark of Cain. But Isobel had been her rival, not her brother. Her thoughts led her to the twins, what would they say if they knew? She sniffed, she tried to control her bottom lip, but it shook and trembled on its own accord. She wiped her tears away with the back of her hand. But as soon as one lot was away another flood came. What did her tears matter anyway, what pretence did she have to keep up? What did anything matter now? She stopped wiping her cheeks, bent her head and let the tears fall.

Michael put his head around the door.

'Do you want to bring her in,' he said.

The van driver stood up, and, putting his hand on her arm, he guided her toward the door. She tried to shake his hand away, but he held onto her. She didn't want any man to touch her, ever again.

She was taken into a room with a counter, a computer and a constable, at least Zoë thought of him as a constable; she liked the sound of all those C's together. What was she thinking about? Had she finally lost it? Had she finally gone mad? Harper and Barnes stood either side of her and the van driver disappeared somewhere; she didn't see him go.

She was asked her name, her address, her date of birth, and her age. She'd told Inspector Harper all that yesterday, she couldn't see why she had to recite it all again. She was asked where she'd been born and if she'd ever been in custody before. Then she was placed against the wall and measured.

'Five, five,' the policeman said.

She thought about arguing, she was sure she was almost five-six, but what did it matter anyway?

'This old man he played five, he played . . . ' A raucous drunk brushed against her, his breath smelled foul, and his clothing was torn and extremely dirty; Zoë felt suddenly very alone and frightened.

'Come on, Tinker, this way,' the drunk was hustled away from her.

'Time of arrest?' The duty officer asked.

Harper looked at his watch. 'Eleven-fifteen.

'And the offence is?'

'Suspicion of murder,' Barnes said, his face

immobile.

Murder, murder, murder, when would she get used to it, when would the word leave her head.

'Any comment made at the time of the arrest?'

Barnes shook his head. The custody officer tapped the computer keys on the keyboard.

'Listen,' the man on the desk said to her. 'The Detective Inspector will now explain why you're at the police station.'

Barnes cleared his throat. 'Inquiries have been made that have led us to believe that Ms Elliot is the . . . '

Zoë stopped listening, she looked up above the desk, a monitor showed the room where she'd just been held, three policemen and two youths now occupied the bench where she had been sitting. They all looked extremely bored.

Barnes had finished speaking and the man at the desk finished tapping.

'Right, Ms Elliot.' The custody officer said. 'So you understand that you are here to be questioned?' He gave her a piece of printed foolscap. 'These are your rights, please read me a section so that I can be sure you're able to understand them.'

She picked out a sentence and read it.

'It's Zoë, isn't it? Your first name?'

She looked at him then, a big man of about fifty, with a full head of grey hair, cheeks covered in old acne

486

scars and small brown eyes. He'd used her first name and the sound of it on an official's lips made her want to cry again.

'You have the right to speak to an independent solicitor free of charge. You have the right to have someone told that you have been arrested. You have the right to consult the codes of practice covering police powers and procedures.'

Zoë frowned. She had the right to? No, she had no rights; they had been taken away from her when the heavy steel door of the station had closed behind her. If she really had rights, then she could just walk out of there.

'You may do any of these things now, but if you do not, you may still do so at any other time whilst detained at the police station. Do you understand, Zoë?'

She nodded. But no, she didn't understand, she didn't understand how she'd got there, or why she was accused of this heinous crime. Couldn't they tell by looking at her that she shouldn't be there?

The policeman was droning on, how was she expected to take it all in? Her back ached, she'd like to sit down, but she didn't want to ask. She wanted no favours from them, they were her enemies now.

'If you are asked questions about a suspected offence . . .'

Her mind wandered away. She had a clear picture of Hulver and the pony she rode as a child.

' . . . something you later rely on in court . . . '

Her mother was laughing, and Fen the Labrador was just a little black puppy.

' . . . may be given in evidence.'

'Do you understand, Zoë?' Harper asked.

She gave no indication either way.

The Custody Officer handed her the form she had put down. 'This is for you to read and keep,' he said. She took it from him, folded it into four and put it in her pocket.

'You should read that,' Barnes said, not unkindly.

'Would you like to see a solicitor?' the man on the desk asked.

'Her partner's sending for one.' Harper said.

She looked from one to the other, she was dazed, it was as if she wasn't really there, but looking from the outside in.

'Are you fit and well?'

She nodded, but it was a lie, she was far from well.

'Are you on any medication?' She thought about the pill left in her coat pocket. Maybe it wasn't too late, maybe she could get some more.

'I was,' she said. 'Only they took it away, it was in my coat pocket.'

'That was for sheep,' Barnes said.

Zoë looked at the floor.

'Where's the coat now?' the Custody Officer asked.

'Norwich.'

'What were they for?' Barnes asked.

Zoë looked right through him. It was none of his business.

'We'll get you to see the doctor, and he can prescribe whatever medication you need,' the Custody Officer said

She continued to look at the floor.

'Have you ever tried any self harm?'

Does trying to abort a baby count? She wondered. She suddenly felt very tired. She picked her head up and rolled her neck around and around. She probably wasn't pregnant at all; she was being dramatic and fanciful. She shook her head.

'Right, nearly done now, turn out your pockets.'

She dipped into the pockets of her jeans. She pulled out a dirty tissue, two ten piece coins, a short piece of orange string, and the folded form she'd just been given. The two detectives looked first at the string and then at each other. Barnes had an 'I told you so,' look on his face.

The man on the desk handed the form back to her and slipped the rest of the pathetic little trophies in a property bag, and sealed it. She wasn't quite sure why they kept the tissue, maybe they thought she might choke on it, or maybe they weren't thinking at all.

'One last thing, then you can have a break. Just sign here to say that I've explained your rights and entitlements to you.'

Zoë signed.

They led her down a long corridor, the walls were painted the same battleship grey, and the floor was hard painted concrete. They turned a corner and she gasped in horror as they directed her toward a cell.

'Right, let's have your shoes off.'

'What?'

'The shoes.'

She was wearing a pair of navy leather deck shoes. She slipped them off and handed them to him.

'And the belt.'

'But . . . ' she slipped it from it's carriers and handed it to him.

'In you go then,' the policeman said.

'But . . . ' she gave the very feeblest of protests, then, turning away from him, she entered the small cold room.

'It'll warm up in a minute. I'll get you a cup of tea, shall I?'

She didn't answer, but scurried over the tiny room and perched herself on the low bunk, which was little more than a raised platform. The sad little cell was perfectly clean, but smelled strongly of stale sweat and urine.

'Milk and sugar?'

Somewhere in the bowels of the cells the drunk was still singing his song.

'Just milk,' she said. Then she plucked up her courage and asked, 'How long will they keep me here?'

'In don't know, love. Your husband's sent for a solicitor. When he comes they'll no doubt question you, and then they'll take it from there.'

She smiled weakly.

'That cut on your lip, do you want a doctor to look at it?'

She shook her head, an action that flicked the hair away from her forehead and exposed the bruise, which was looking more impressive by the hour.

He closed the door with a hollow bang, and she heard the key turn in the lock. Why where they locking her up, surely they knew she wasn't going to run away? Surely they knew she was harmless? In any case, she had nowhere to go.

The cell was freezing cold, there was a very thin vinyl covered mattress on the hard bunk, atop of which was a blue blanket. There was no pillow, behind the door was a lavatory made entirely of stainless steel, its cistern was hidden somehow in the wall. The window, which filtered in the dull October light, was constructed of solid glass bricks so that she couldn't see out into the world. She realized that she wanted to pee, but she couldn't quite bring herself to use the facility.

A few moments later, the hatch on the door flopped down, and she was handed a polystyrene cup of strong tea.

Then the hatch was slammed shut, and she was left alone, with only her fear for company.

Chapter 62

Tiggy, lying on her stomach, stretched out to her full length and held onto the top edge of the mattress. Alex lifted her hips; she gave a low guttural growl as he entered her.

She pushed back onto him. 'I love you,' she said.

'I love you too,' he replied, running his hands over her back. She really did remind him of her mother. The woman he still loved, and feared he always would.

The telephone rang.

'Let it ring,' she said.

He quickened his pace. She gasped as he bore deeper into her.

He ran his hands down her back again, swept under her and grasped her breasts.

The telephone continued to ring.

'It's probably important,' he said. 'Maybe the hearing's been cancelled and we can go and have an indulgent lunch together.'

'No chance,' she said drawing herself up on her knees and pressing backwards. 'I have a client at two. This was meant to be instead of lunch, not as well as, remember?'

The insistent ring continued.

'Leave it, Alex, they'll get tired in a minute.'

The ringing stopped.

She pulled away from him, turned around, and lifted her hips to him.

'No,' he said. 'The other way, sweetheart, please?'

'Why? Can't you bear to look at me?' She was laughing. 'Because I like to look at you, all of you.' She brought her head up and took him in her mouth. 'I like the taste of you as well.'

The telephone rang again, and continued to ring.

'The other way,' he said. 'Please.'

She smiled and turned back onto all fours.

It wasn't that he didn't like to look at her, she was beautiful, she was lithe, and sexy, and clever, and lovely. She was everything a man could want. But she wasn't Lavinia, and from her back view he could just about pretend she was. Her body was so like that of her mother, slimmer — much slimmer, younger, unravaged by childbirth, but nevertheless very like it. He pushed himself inside her. What was he to do, he would never love anyone else, Lavinia was his drug, his heroine. Tiggy was his substitute, his methadone, the only way he could survive. He knew it wasn't fair on Tiggy, and for that he felt dismay. Tiggy loved him, and as far as he was capable, he loved her. But not enough, it would never be enough.

The telephone bell echoed on through the room.

'I can't stand this,' he said. 'It's bound to be important.' Without missing a beat, he reached over to the side of the bed.

'You can't take a 'phone call whilst you're fucking,' she said, and giggled.

'I can, that's why I'm so good at my job. I'm great at mixing business with pleasure.' He gave an extra hard thrust and snatched up the receiver.

Tiggy wriggled and made little mewing noises.

He rubbed her buttocks and slowed his pace.

'Yes? . . . Lavinia!'

He felt Tiggy's body stiffen, she'd grown away from her mother over the past months. He knew that he was the obstacle that stood between them, and he enjoyed the fact that he'd taken something precious away from Lavinia. It was his payback, after all she had denied him. She had taken her love away from him and now he was taking something she loved away from her.

Now he was in a position of power, with Tiggy's body sheathing him and Lavinia on the other end of the telephone. He was suddenly tongue-tied. She'd want to speak to Tiggy, of course. What should he say to her? 'Sorry, Vinnie, Tiggy can't come to the 'phone right now. You see we're making love and I'm about to shoot my load, right into her sweet, Elliot pussy'. Or 'I'm sorry, she can't speak at the moment, I've got her on her stomach, and I'm entering her from behind, you know how much I always liked that position, you must remember, it enabled me to worship your perfect, beautiful back.' The thoughts were amusing, but fleeting. It was he she wanted to speak to, not her daughter.

'What?' he pulled out of Tiggy and sat back on his knees. 'Why? . . . Well what did they say?'

Tiggy rolled over and mouthed, 'What is it?' She looked as alarmed as he felt.

Alex put his hand up and gesticulated for her to be quiet.

He'd half lost his erection; he wasn't even looking at Tiggy but putting his full concentration into the telephone call.

Tiggy sat up; she was now looking extremely irritated. 'What is it,' she said quite loudly.

He waved his hand again. 'Quiet, I can't hear what she's saying.'

Tiggy went down on her knees and took him in her mouth, she sucked and played and teased, and although he wasn't exactly flaccid, he wasn't responding either.

'Don't panic, Vinnie,' he said. 'I'll be there as soon as I can. And I'll bring Tiggy, she ought to have a solicitor.'

He replaced the receiver, and Tiggy lifted her head.

'What?' said Tiggy. 'What is it?'

'Theo's wife's been murdered, and Zoë's been arrested.'

Tiggy began to laugh. 'Your sending me up.' Then she looked at him closer. 'You're for real, aren't you?'

He nodded his head. 'I said I'd go down there, and I said you'd go with me.'

496

'But, but . . . I'm a corporate lawyer, I know nothing about criminal law.'

'Then I'll teach you. I know all there is to know about it.'

'I thought you were due in court this afternoon?'

'It's an interim, my junior can deal with it, you'd better cancel your client. Now get dressed, we must get going — no telling what Zoë will have told them. I don't suppose she'll have the sense to stay quiet.'

He felt weak. Lavinia had been in such a state. But it was he whom she'd turned to, she knew he was there for her. A warm glow settled in the pit of his stomach. She needed him, she trusted him. He wouldn't let her down.

Tiggy pushed herself back into the pillow and watching his face carefully, she said, 'Alex, thank you for doing this for Zoë.'

'I'm not doing it for Zoë,' he said quickly. His words hung in the air for just a little too long. They held each other's eyes. He smiled then and patted her hand, 'I'm doing it for you, of course,' he lied.

He struggled from the bed and started to throw some things into a bag, whilst Tiggy went into the bathroom, a few moments later the telephone rang again.

'Vinnie? . . . I told you, I'll be there . . . Yes, we're leaving right away . . . You know that, Vinnie. I've always been here for you, and I always will be.'

He replaced the receiver, and it was then that he

lifted his eyes and saw Tiggy listening in the doorway.

'Half a loaf is better than none,' she said. She shrugged her shoulders and smiled; but she looked immeasurable sad.

'It's not the way I want it to be, Tiggy. It's just the way it is.'

She nodded. 'I know,' she said. 'I've always known.' And he saw that there were tears in her eyes.

Chapter 63

'So you see, you must let Zoë go, she didn't do it — I did it'

'Right, I see. Willing to sign a confession, are you, Sir'

Theo blanched, 'If that's what it takes for you to let Zoë out of here, yes.'

Michael sighed. 'Okay, let's run through it one more time, shall we?' He shuffled some papers about on his desk. You went down to Garrick Hall,— what time did you say it was?'

Theo's eyes shifted about the room. 'About midnight?' he asked.

'I don't know,— you tell me.'

'Yes. Yes, that would be about the time.'

'And you and Lady Sheldon-Harris had a few words.'

'That's right, she wouldn't agree to the divorce.'

'So you got into a fight and you strangled her?'

'Yes, yes, I didn't mean to do it. I just lost my temper.'

Michael doubted whether Theo Sheldon-Harris had ever lost his temper in his life.

'And you strangled her, with?'

'With?' Theo looked uncomfortable.

'Her dressing gown cord? Or your bare hands?'

Theo tapped his fingers on the desk.

Come on, thought Michael, I've given you a fifty-fifty choice, now get to and make a guess.

'The...cord?'

Michael shook his head.

'My bare hands.' Theo said triumphantly.

Michael shook his head again. 'Actually, it was Colonel Mustard, in the library with the candle stick. Not very good at this, are you, Sir?'

Theo's Adams apple jerked in his throat. And Michael watched in alarm as tears filled his eyes and then cascaded over his cheeks.

'It's a serious offence to waste police time, you should remember that before you make up stories.'

'But don't you see, she can't have done it.' Theo sobbed. 'If you knew her, if you knew what kind of person she is, you'd know that it can't be her, it just can't be.' Theo took a handkerchief out of his pocket and wiped his eyes.

'She must be something special, Sir, for you to be willing to take a murder wrap for her. But . . . ' He didn't finish his sentence, Theo Sheldon-Harris was distressed enough as it was. There were all sorts of things that he'd have liked to have said, most of all he'd liked to have said, that deep down, he didn't believe she was capable of it either. But he had no reason to say that, except a gut feeling, and gut feelings never had held their own in a court of law.

He'd have also liked to tell Theo how much he envied him; he couldn't imagine loving anyone the way Theo loved Zoë. He hoped he might feel that way one day, before it was too late.

A tap came on the door. Ian put his head in. 'Zoë's solicitor's here,' he said.

'Zoë? It's all very friendly, isn't it?' Theo said.

'Less intimidating,' Michael replied.

'Can I—' Theo began. The appearance of Ian Barnes had dried up his tears.

'No, that won't be possible.'

'I haven't even asked yet.'

'You can't see her, Sir. You're a possible witness.'

Theo nodded and dragged himself up from his chair, he seemed suddenly old. 'Will they have finished? The men at the cottage? Only Betsy—'

'They were back half on hour ago.'

Theo nodded and left the room.

'Did they find anything at the cottage, Ian?' Michael asked once they were alone.

'A large quantity of nothing, I would say. Bags and bags of it, it'll take a while to go through it all, but there's nothing obvious.'

Michael scraped up a bundle of papers. 'Right, let's see what little Miss Elliot has to say for herself.'

'You still don't believe it can possibly be her, do you?'

'Rule number one in police work, Ian. Anything and everything's possible.' He paused at the door. 'However, I'm not going to stop looking at other possibilities.'

'She'll crack, Mike. She'll tell us who her boyfriend is.'

Michael pushed the bundle of papers under his arm. 'Ian,— it's not a boyfriend. The semen was planted for the soul purpose of misleading us. We were meant to find it. Probably so that some innocent bugger would be accused, and have irrefutable evidence against him, or so that we'd spend our time looking for a man and not a woman. Whatever, one thing's for certain, this person, the one who's calling card we found, is not a friend of the murderer. So it might be as well to ask Zoë, who her enemies are, not her friends.'

Rodney Burton was good-looking in a boyish sort of a way. His hair was a little too long to be called smart, but it might have been described as trendy. He had a rounded, babyish face, which made it difficult to assess his age. He had soft green eyes, blonde, gingerish hair, and a podgy turned-up nose. He'd consulted with his client for all of ten minutes, during which time she had said absolutely nothing either to confirm or deny the charge. He and Zoë were already ensconced in the interview room when Michael and Ian got there.

Michael needed no introduction to Rodney; he'd

had dealings with him many times before. Rodney was perhaps, one of, if not *the* worst lawyer he had ever come across. He'd have liked to have told Theo to get her someone better, given him a few suggestions even, but that wasn't within his power.

The four of them settled themselves in the tiny room. The walls were clad in royal blue hessian, the floor carpeted in blue and the chairs also upholstered in blue; it was a change from the usual battleship grey.

Zoë looked ill, her face was a terrible pasty white, and dark shadows lurked beneath her eyes. She was nursing a cup of water, and he noticed that both her hands were shaking. They had taken away her clothes and she was dressed in a thin white overall that was several sizes too big for her. She sat opposite the two inspectors with her lawyer on her right. She didn't meet his eyes but stared straight ahead of her, fixing her eyes somewhere in the middle of his tie.

Ian Barnes flicked on the tape. 'This interview is being recorded and may be given in evidence if your case is brought to trial. We are in an interview room at Fenshaw Police Station.'

Michael kept his eyes on Zoë as Ian recited all the necessary information. She didn't blink, but sat as if paralyzed.

Ian recorded the time and identified those present, then he said, 'You do not have to say anything. But it may harm your defense if you do not mention when questioned—'

'I don't want to say anything,' Zoë said. 'Can I go back to my cell now?'

She's ill, Michael thought. She's lost the plot; she doesn't know what she saying or what she's doing.

Rodney Burton, put out his hand to her. 'Wait for him to finish,' he said.

Only when Ian *had* finished, she seemed to have forgotten what she had said, and once again she sat motionless staring at Michael's tie.

Ian started the questioning. In fact, Michael had very little input, Rodney Burton less, and Zoë nothing at all.

Ian was saying, 'I must warn you that if, from now on, you fail, or refuse, to account for anything, a court may draw its own conclusions on why you have not done so.'

Zoë looked over at him as if she'd only just noticed that he was speaking, then she turned back to Michael. She'd placed the cup on the table in front of her some time ago and had spent most of the time rubbing her hands and worrying her fingers with a tissue. Afterwards Ian would compare her actions to that of Lady Macbeth.

'I can't get rid of it,' she said. 'I can't get it off.'

Michael saw that the black dye from the fingerprint ink was embedded in her nails. 'I'll get you a special wipe,' he said.

He leaned toward the tape. 'Inspector Harper and

504

Inspector Barnes are leaving the room.' He flicked the tape off. 'We'll take a break shall we?'

He ushered Ian out of the room.

'What'd stop it for? I was getting somewhere, she was about to break.' Ian was irate.

'Oh yes, and pigs can fly I suppose. Look, Ian, I don't like it, she doesn't look well.'

'She refused to see the doctor.'

'Yes, well, I think she should. All those bruises want cataloging. All we need is for her to say she got them in police custody.'

Ian's bleeper, bleeped. He went over to the desk and picked up the telephone.

'Ian? There's a couple here, say that they've come to see Zoë Elliot, they say they're her lawyers.'

'She's already got a lawyer.'

'Well it looks like she's got two more.'

'I'll come through.'

Ian sighed. 'Rich bitch's found herself a couple of high powered lawyers. Does that sound like the action of an innocent woman?'

Michael watched him as he scurried through to the front desk. He put his hands on his waist and stretched. He couldn't have explained to anyone why he felt so relieved.

Chapter 64

She closed her eyes, waiting, waiting. Her whole life seemed to have been spent in waiting. Waiting for Steve to love her, waiting for Isobel to divorce Theo, waiting, waiting. But today had been the longest wait yet. Today had lasted a hundred isolated years. Now here she was, flat on her back on a hard couch waiting for the doctor to come and examine her. How long did he think it took to wriggle out of a plastic overall and a pair of socks? He'd been gone ages. Would he know by looking at her? Could he tell what had happened by the marks on her body?

It was all Tiggy's fault, it was she that had bowled in and asked,— no demanded, that they stop their interviewing immediately and get her to see the doctor, or police surgeon as they grandly called him. The young one, Barnes, had looked irritated, but the other one, the older one, had looked relieved, what was he hoping for? That the doctor would find evidence that would trap her?

Tiggy had amazed her; she couldn't get over how she'd taken charge, nor how she'd bossed the police around, quoting this act and that act at them. Not that they'd objected. At least the older one hadn't, he'd seemed only too please to get the doctor in, She'd spent the whole day telling them she didn't want to see a quack. But there'd been no arguing with Tiggy, even as a child she'd always got the upper hand. She was well suited to the role of lawyer.

Somewhere, a long way off, she could hear the drunken man singing, and someone else shouting, and telling him to shut his mouth. She pulled the sheet up to her chin, she wondered what the time was, she had no idea; she seemed to have lost all sense of time. It could be ten o'clock in the morning, or three in the afternoon. No, it was later than that, because the doctor's room had a window, high up it was, and covered with bars, but she could see the sky and she could see that the sky was darkening towards evening. It must be quite late, because a lot of things had happened. Fingerprints and photographs and swabs for DNA. Where was the doctor? She wished he'd come and get it over with.

The room was, like most of the rest of the station, painted grey. It was spartan, containing a cupboard, a computer, — wherever you looked these days there was a computer, — the couch she was lying on, and a chair. Unlike the cell in which she'd spent a good part of the day, the room was stiflingly hot.

The doctor seemed nice enough, — for one of *them*. He was a small, thin, elderly man, with bony hands and hollow cheeks. He wore a well-worn tweed suit, gold rimmed glasses and a perfectly laundered shirt and he had a confident no-nonsense manner about him.

He'd introduced himself as Dr Thomas and he called her Miss Elliot. For the first time since entering the police station that morning she felt she was regarded as a person of worth. But then again, she thought, she might be wrong.

There was a tap on the door, and it swung open. 'All right to come in?' Dr Thomas asked, entering.

He smiled at her, 'Now young lady. I hear you've got a bit of a cough.'

'I'm all right,' she said. She sighed with relief, he'd listen to her chest, give her some cough medicine and that would be that. She hardly needed to have stripped off for that, need she?

He started to pull the sheet down. 'Let's have a listen to your chest, shall we?'

He had his stethoscope in his ears, but as he lowered the sheet, he pulled it away from them and let it spring around his neck. 'However did you do this?' He gently lifted her breast and examined the huge purple bruise.

'I fell,' was all she said.

'Wherever from? The Eiffel Tower?' he smiled. 'Roll over onto your side, this is pretty major stuff, tell me if I'm hurting you, won't you?'

She rolled over onto her side and faced the battleship grey wall. How could she begin to tell him what hurt? Everything hurt; every bone and every muscle. But most of all she hurt inside, she was full of secrets and deceptions, and that was the greatest hurt of all.

'Let's have you sitting up.'

508

He helped her to a sitting position and, replacing the stethoscope, he listened to her back and to her chest.

'How did you say you did this?'

She didn't answer him, but for one brief moment their eyes met.

He seemed almost embarrassed. 'Right,' he said briskly, 'let's have a look at the rest of you.'

She lay down again and Dr Thomas examined her lip and her injured forehead. Then he folded the sheet up from the bottom exposing her bruised legs.

'When was your last period?'

She didn't answer.

'I said—'

'I finished just over three weeks ago.'

Bend your knees up will you?'

'No I—'

'I'm not going to hurt you, I just want to see these bruises on the inside of your legs.'

Zoë bent her knees and let her legs fall a little apart. She could feel Dr Thomas's warm gloved hands gently touching her skin.

'How did this happen?' he said. His voice was very soft and very reassuring.

Tears choked her and she couldn't speak.

'Okay, lie back now.' He pulled the sheet up around her, stripped off the rubber gloves and stuck them in a bin. 'I'll be back in a minute.' Then, just as he got the door, he turned; his face was a mask of concern.

'Don't worry. It'll be all right,' he said. He held her eyes, this time without embarrassment. Then he turned toward the door. Dr Thomas shut the door very gently as if Zoë was asleep and he didn't want to wake her.

Once outside he strutted to the desk. 'Get an ambulance organized, and get me St Mary's on the 'phone. I want to speak to the casualty officer.'

Michael came over to him.

Dr Thomas held out his hand. 'Mike! I didn't know you were here.'

'I didn't know you were the duty surgeon.'

'I've been on the rota for years, punishment for my sins!'

'So how's . . . ' Michael nodded towards the door of the examination room.

Dr Thomas pulled a face. 'Sorry sight, whoever did that to her, wants hanging.'

'Right,' said Michael, he gave Ian a look of triumph. 'That's why I'm glad she agreed to see you. I didn't want her claiming she'd been beaten up in police custody.'

'Beaten up. Mike? Beaten up? Zoë Elliot's been the victim of rape, a pretty nasty, violent rape, it was too. She's got at least one broken rib, if not two, and I wouldn't be at all surprised if her lung isn't punctured.'

Michael and Ian looked at each other.

510

'Christ,' Michael said. 'Her lawyer's will have our guts for garters. I said she wasn't well, I said she should see a doctor. But she wouldn't.'

'What are you smiling at?' Dr Thomas asked Ian.

Ian smiled even broader. 'I think,' he said, 'you've just solved a puzzle for us Doctor. I think we now know where a certain little bit of planted evidence came from.'

Chapter 65

Angie Harper put the little dog down on the bed beside her. It snuggled up to her and laid its head on her stomach; it licked her fingers and then her face.

'Don't do that Butch,' she said pushing him away from her. 'I don't like to have my face licked.'

The dog sighed and settled down with his head once again on her stomach. She flicked on the television set. She was about to take a sip of the hot chocolate drink she'd made for herself, when the dog heard a noise and, pricking his ears and pulling up his head he knocked her elbow, and some of the chocolate spilled over her chest and arm.

'Oh, Butch,' she said, brushing down the front of her nightdress. 'It's a good job that wasn't hot, it would have burned me.'

The dog cowered and licked her arm where the chocolate had been spilled. It felt quite nice to have his rough little tongue on her skin; she just didn't like it licking her face. She sighed; Michael certainly wouldn't approve of the dog being on their bed. She wasn't even sure he'd approve of the dog being in the house at all.

Years ago, when they were undergoing barrages of infertility tests, their GP had suggested that Angie get herself a pet, a dog perhaps. He'd referred to it as if it was some sort of hobby, suggesting in a patronizing way that her childlessness was her own fault, that if she'd only relax Mother Nature would take her natural course. Michael had been keen enough; it was she that had refused, feeling that the idea of a dog was being suggested to placate her, and that the dog would be a permanent replacement for the longed-for child. In her heart she was certain that pregnancy would follow a successful coupling and blamed Michael for the lack of that success. She'd been ever hopeful, mapping out her life in menstrual cycles, demanding and refusing sex as the calendar demanded. She couldn't remember the day she'd actually given up hope. Perhaps it was only very recently, the day she'd got the dog. Always before she'd painted herself a vision, all too often she'd seen harassed mothers with baby strollers and canine friend tugging at a lead. When Angie had a child it would take center stage, not share space with a dog. So adopting a dog was paramount to admitting defeat.

She sighed again and caressed the top of the puppies head. She hated the name Butch and wondered if she could subtly change it. Hutch? Touch? She giggled. Sam had suggested Crutch. He was quite a lad was Sam, he had a great sense of humour. Michael seemed so dull in comparison.

She'd only met Sam two nights ago, at puppy training class, although Everton, Sam's Labrador cross German Shepherd, didn't seem to need much training, Sam had him well under control. Sam was such good fun, the comic of the group, always saying that it was the owners that needed training, not the puppies. Everybody seemed to like him, even Sheila the class leader. Well who wouldn't like him, — he had a joke or a quip for everything; he really lightened the mood.

She'd arranged to meet him up at the common the following day to exercise the dogs and run over one or two of the things Sheila had taught them. A tingle went down Angie's spine, thoughts of Sam did that to her. It wasn't that Sam was a particularly attractive man, he wasn't nearly as attractive as Michael. He was rather plain in fact, with a bit of a stomach on him. That's why he'd got Everton, he told her, to exercise his figure back into shape. His face was rather round and he was balding. He was younger than Angie, probably in his early thirties. Angie wasn't sure of his exact age, and she hadn't had the courage to ask him. But the best thing about him was that he was unemployed. She smiled to herself; it seemed an odd qualification. Michael wouldn't approve, but it meant that Sam was free, free as a bird, free as Angie. In the two days since she'd met him, they'd made all sorts of plans. They'd talked about everything, she'd asked him about being on benefits and he hadn't made any fancy excuses like he was over qualified or that decent jobs weren't available. He'd just told her that he was a man of simple tastes, and if her Majesty's Government were kind enough to pay his rent and give him enough to feed himself and the dog, then there was no point in tying himself down to a nine to five job. If he needed any extra, he managed by doing a bit of this and a bit of that; he'd always scraped by. He'd managed to convince her that his unemployment was a sort of virtue, — he was harming no one, now was he?

Mind you, she hadn't been that easily convinced. They'd been standing outside the Bakers Oven, drinking tea from polystyrene cups, unable to go inside because of the dogs. Sam was telling her that in France they'd have been able to take the dogs inside, the French weren't as neurotic as the English when it came to pets. She'd bought the tea of course; it wouldn't have been right to expect Sam to pay out of his measly little allowance. She'd also bought him a jam doughnut, — he'd said he was starving. His Giro wasn't due until the next day and he hadn't eked his benefit payment out very well that fortnight. Everton had lost his collar and he'd had to buy him a new one. It was at that point that she'd suggested, very casually, that if he'd had a job he'd be so much better off.

'Of course I would,' he replied, there'd been no resentment in his voice; he hadn't minded her saying it. 'But think about it, there's only a certain number of jobs to go round, and if I took one of them, it would be one less for some other poor bugger.' He swore a lot did Sam, but it didn't offend her. Michael would have hated it, he wouldn't have understood that it was just a form of speech, that Sam used swear words like other people used adjectives. There was no harm or offence meant in it. Sam had gone on to say that this imaginary person probably wouldn't be able to live on the unemployment pittance the way he did. For instance, due to the fact that he'd had to buy Everton a new collar, he'd not had enough money to buy himself an electricity card. How many people did she know that'd be able to cope without heat and light until the Giro came?

She'd had to admit that she didn't know anybody that would be prepared to freeze and starve. She'd given him some money of course; just enough to buy a meter card and get himself a few groceries. She'd had to handle it carefully, mind you; he'd already told her that he never borrowed money and that he was dead opposed to taking charity. She'd had a job convincing him that the money was neither. In the end she'd had to be quite firm and she'd told him that Everton needed light and heat, even if he didn't. And Everton needed more than one meal a day; after all he was a growing puppy. Sam had reluctantly taken it for the sake of the dog. She'd been very clever turning it around like that, in the end she'd convinced him that he was doing her a favour. Michael gave her far too much housekeeping; she often didn't know what to do with it all. Like Sam, she was a woman of simple needs; she just didn't need all that money, especially now that Michael was temporarily away from home. She hadn't told Sam exactly what Michael did for a living, she'd said that he was a civil servant. Sam had wrinkled his nose and said that it sounded extremely boring and she'd agreed and said he was right, it was too boring for words and therefore she wasn't going to talk about it. She instinctively knew that he wouldn't approve of Michael's profession.

He was an odd one was Sam, he'd obviously come from a good background, she could tell that by the way he spoke, despite his free and easy use of swear words; and he was knowledgeable too, he'd read all sorts of things. Freud, Jung, as well as a lot of the classics, although at present, he told her, he was into Science fiction, Stephen King and the like. He talked a lot about the books he was reading.

Angie finished up the remainder of her hot chocolate. It seemed strange to be excited about such a simple thing as a walk up on the common. It felt almost as if she was going on a date. That was ridiculous of course, but that's what it felt like. Sam was so attentive, they got on really well; it was as if she'd known him all her life.

Sam would have to leave town ages before she did to get up the common, because she had her new bike, complete with little basket on the front to carry Butch. Sam would have to walk up there or take a bus. Maybe she should get Sam a bike, Everton would love running beside him. Sam said he really believed in using bicycles, he said they were 'ecologically a very sound mode of transport'. He sometimes said things like that, using all the right words. If she'd have repeated that to Michael he'd have laughed and said something like it would take him some time to answer a nine-nine-nine on a push-bike. That was the difference between Sam and Michael. Michael was always putting her down, whereas Sam listened to every word. But there was no point in comparing them, Michael was miles away and thoroughly disinterested in her life, and Sam was here and as different as he possibly could be.

Chapter 66

'So,' said Michael, 'let me get this right.'

They were sitting in the bar of the Kings Head, both nursing half-pints of beer. 'You're saying that Zoë Elliot crept out in the night, got herself raped, and incidentally, half beaten to death. Then, on her way home, she pops into Garrick Hall and murders Lady Sheldon-Harris, plants a bit of semen, scraped no doubt from the inside of her thigh, which wouldn't be that easy to do without leaving a bit of her own DNA behind. Then she dashes home and hops into bed with her old man?'

Ian Barnes sighed and took a long draught of his beer.

'It's full of holes, Ian, and you know it. For one thing you don't know that she was out of the house on Monday night, we only have what the child said, and how old is she? Four, five? Not old enough to be thought of as a reliable witness.'

'No, no, you don't follow me, I'm not saying it's the way you just said, we may never know exactly how it was. But first of all, you don't know that she didn't leave her DNA behind, do you? The results aren't back yet.'

Michael raised his brows as if to concede defeat.

Ian went on. 'What I'm saying is, that she has to have had an accomplice, and she arranges with him to get knocked about a bit, so it looks like she's been raped, and I might remind you that there's no evidence that she has—'

Michael looked incredulous, 'No evidence! That's not what the rape crisis center at the hospital says!'

'I don't mean the injuries, I mean, that there's no sign of, you know . . . '

'Semen? Suddenly too delicate a word for you, is it, Ian?'

'Look, there's no sign of anything, no clothes, nothing on her body—'

'Apart from the odd broken rib and about a hundred bruises you mean? Anything else she'd washed away.'

'Yes, why doesn't that surprise me?' He tutted. 'That's exactly what I'm talking about, why isn't there any evidence on her clothes? Why'd she make sure everything was washed or destroyed?'

'Because she couldn't bear looking at them?'

'It doesn't add up that way to me.'

'Why are you so sure it's her, Ian?'

Ian Barnes pulled in his lips. 'You're thinking exactly the way she wants you to think. Don't you see, the rape is her alibi.'

'Then why didn't she come straight out with it, *"It couldn't have been me, your honour, because I was being raped at the same time as Lady Sheldon-Harris was being . . ."* Why didn't she say that?'

'I told you, because she's clever, very clever, she wants us to wheedle it out of her.'

'Well, Ian, whether we wheedle it out of her or she tells us, the fact remains that she couldn't have been violated and murdering at the same time. And if you think that her friend, accomplice, or whatever you want to call him, helped her plant his own DNA, then you're crazy. No one would be fool enough to do that.'

'Supposing, it's Sir Theo's semen she's planted?'

'What on earth for?'

'Well, what sort of will has he made? Maybe she gets the lot when he—'

'Ian, you're off your head, you're so certain it's her, you can't get your logic straight. We don't have the death penalty any more, remember? What use would his will be to her?'

Barnes supped the rest of his pint thoughtfully. 'Well, I *know* she did it, I just know.'

'Here's a thought,' Michael said. 'Supposing the man that raped Zoë, is the same man that killed Lady Sheldon-Harris?'

'But it wasn't a man.'

'No, no Gilbert didn't say that, he said apart from the DNA evidence, which suggests a man's involved, it could have been a woman. That's only because the perp was shorter than Lady Sheldon-Harris was, and she wasn't a small woman, was she? There's a lot of men five-seven and under.'

'But why would he, — you know, leave his DNA behind? Everyone knows about DNA in semen, everyone.'

'Everyone? Not in a sleepy little village like that one. Maybe Gilbert was right the first time. Maybe chummy masturbated over her. It's just as likely, in fact it's a darn sight more likely. Maybe he's a real woman hater, he rapes Zoë and then he does for Lady Sheldon-Harris and just to show his contempt for her . . . ' Michael's eyes scanned the room as he spoke.

'You expecting someone?' Ian said.

'No, it's just that I ought to ring Angie, my wife.'

Ian sighed. 'I ought to be getting home, my misses will have my grub on the table.' He stood up to leave. 'Well, we'll know more when the doctors let us talk to the girl again.'

'That might be sometime. Her lawyer,— it's her sister by the way,— is guarding her like the crown jewels, and the doctors agree with her, they won't let us near her. So meanwhile it's back to good old fashioned police work I'm afraid. But I'll tell you one thing for sure. There's two crimes here, not one. We're investigating a rape as well as a murder. And personally, I don't think that the two are in the least bit connected.'

'Come on, Mike. Zoë Elliot went out that night to meet someone—'

'We don't know that for sure.'

522

'But you're saying she went out and got raped.'

'We don't know *when* she got raped, it could have been in broad daylight. Anyway, if she did go out that night we don't know that she was meeting someone. She might have gone out to tend to a sick sheep, or maybe she just couldn't sleep, and took the dog for a walk.'

'In the middle of the night? Do me a favour.'

'I told you before, Ian, all things are possible.'

'Possible, but not probable.' Ian seemed struck by a thought. 'Okay, humour me. Let's say she was raped that night. Well, don't you see? What a wonderful way to get back at whoever did it. Murder the woman you most hate, and plant the rapist's calling card on the deceased. He's picked up for a murder he didn't commit. He can hardly use the rape as an alibi. Zoë Elliot gets away with murder, she doesn't have the trauma of going to court on the rape charge, and she's got her man into the bargain.' He grinned. 'I knew we'd crack it,' he said. 'I knew it. All we have to do now is find the man. Poor bugger, she was going to make him pay dear for his sins, wasn't she?'

Michael was shaking his head, and laughing. 'I don't think so,' he said. 'She's not that clever, public school education or not, she's not that good.'

'Hi, I'm sorry I'm late,' Debbie said as she joined them.

Michael smiled at her, he looked as if any moment he might burst into laughter. 'Debbie, I'd like you to meet

523

my colleague, — Ian Barnes — Debbie Smith.'

They shook hands and Michael offered her a drink. She opted for white wine and Michael and Ian had another half-pint of Adnams. Then Michael excused himself, saying he had to make one quick 'phone call and then he'd be free for the rest of the evening. He went out into the cold night air with his mobile in his hand.

Angie was in excellent form; she told him that she'd bought a bicycle and been up on the common; she'd had a wonderful day. He told her that he didn't know when he'd be home. That was all right, she replied cheerfully, it didn't matter, she was perfectly all right at Barkhampton without him.

Michael flicked the telephone off, and returned to the bar, whistling. Ian had had to go as his wife was about to bin his supper. He'd left a message saying he'd see his colleague at the station first thing in the morning. Michael took a sip of his beer. It was cold and nutty.

He put the glass down on the bar and rested his arm lightly on Debbie's shoulder. 'I'm going to be quite honest with you, Debbie,' he said. 'I could wine you and dine you,— and I will take you out and give you a good meal, — that's not the issue. After dinner, I could try a little subtle seduction. But which ever way round, it won't change the fact that I aim to get you into bed. And it won't change the fact that I'm a married man. So if you find that idea totally repulsive, maybe you'd better get home to your mum right away?'

Twenty-eight-year-old Debbie smiled at him. 'I'd like another glass of white wine Michael, if I may?' she said. Her eyes were shinning very brightly, she looked as if Michael had just offered her the pick of a fleet of Ferraris

Michael smiled. 'Tell you what, Debbie, why don't we go up to my room now and order a bottle of wine from room service. It's quieter there. I can tell you all about the case, — you might have some thoughts on it.'

He could hardly believe his luck when she slid from the barstool and said, 'That's a good idea,' and, taking his hand, she led him toward the lifts.

Chapter 67

'You might feel better if you talked about it.'

Zoë turned her head and looked into Pat Specter's eyes. She was a short thin woman, with a lined face and dancing blue eyes. Talk about it? How could she? What good would it do? If she told, then Theo would have to know; know that she'd betrayed him, and their love.

Dr Specter stroked her forehead. 'I know how difficult this is for you, you may not even remember all that happened . . . ' On and on she went in her lilting Irish brogue.

Remember? Remember? Of course she remembered. Every word, every detail, she even remembered her every thought. That night would live with her for the rest of her life. It would run and rerun through her head just as it was now, and she'd think, just as she did now, of all the things she ought to have done differently.

'Because I don't want to,' Zoë had hissed down the telephone on that fateful night.

'Come on, Zoë, for old times sake.'

'Old times were pretty miserable,' she'd spat back.

'You're mad for me, you always were,' he'd said.

'I am not.'

'Prove it,' he'd said. 'Prove it by coming. You daren't come, because you know you can't resist me.

Midnight, up by the release pen in Garrick wood.'

'I'm not going to the woods in the middle of the night.'

'You'll be there,' he'd said.

She hadn't intended to go, but it was something Theo had said. How could she turn the whole thing around and blame Theo? He'd said that Steve was staying at Hulver, her father had invited him to shoot, and he'd said he wouldn't mind if . . . And she'd snapped at him and asked what he wouldn't mind,— wouldn't mind if she slept with him perhaps? And then Theo had said, something about laying a ghost . . . Oh God, if only she hadn't gone. She hadn't told Theo that it was Steve on the 'phone, she'd said it was Tiggy, but she could tell that he didn't believe her. Why couldn't Theo have left it at that? Why didn't Theo believe that she loved him? Why had she for one moment questioned her feelings for the man she hoped to marry? Why had she got so confused? Why had she decided to prove to herself that she really didn't give a damn about Steve? She'd decided that she'd meet him face to face and finish it, once and for all. She'd tell Steve Jarvis exactly what she thought of him, and she'd explain that Theo was her world now, and that Steve was in the past, and that's where he would forever remain.

Theo always fell asleep as soon as his head touched the pillow. She'd crept from the bed, and pulled on her working clothes. Then she'd driven through the village,

527

down through the farmyard and up the causeway. There she'd parked the Land Rover and continued on foot up to Garrick Wood, arriving there five minutes before midnight.

Steve was already there; he'd opened up the keeper's hut and switched on the battery lamps.

'Knew you'd come,' he'd said smugly.

His confidence made her angry.

'I only came to tell you to get lost, and leave me alone,' she'd replied. She was holding the keys to the Land Rover in her hand. She felt both angry and euphoric, Steve Jarvis meant nothing to her, she was right; she was over him. She'd met him face to face and the chemistry was gone. She could go now. Go home to Theo, and when she got there she would tell him what she'd done. She had lain her ghost, and she was finally free to love him. She was free to have his child, to live and love him and to grow old with him. Her heart was lighter and she actually smiled. She could remember that triumphant smile so well, so very well.

'Goodbye, Steve,' she'd said.

He reached out and caught her wrist, the Land Rover keys dropped to the ground, she bent and tried to retrieve them, but Steve held her fast.

'Let go, Steve,' she'd said. 'It's over.' She still wasn't in the least bit frightened, she was more annoyed than anything.

'Then why'd you come?' He laughed, and she could smell that he'd been drinking.

Why had she gone? She already knew that she was over him, every time she lay in Theo's arms she knew that. So why had she come?

Steve made a grab for her waist and pulled her down onto the damp leaves. He hadn't just been drinking; he was very drunk, yet the alcohol didn't seem to have affected his strength.

It had all happened so quickly, and she'd seemed powerless to stop it. She'd fought, fought as if her life depended on it, and there were vivid moments when she'd thought it had. But she should have fought harder, screamed louder; someone might have heard her. But he was stronger and bigger than she was.

'Come on, Zoë, you know you're gagging for it. You always were, never got enough of it in the old days.'

Her sweatshirt was pushed up under her arms, the night was cold and damp, and yet she was hot and perspiring. It seemed that Steve had twice as much of everything she had. Double the number of arms and hands, double the strength, and double the energy. Her thighs were bruised as he snatched at her clothing, her jeans were down below her knees, her panties torn and roughly pushed to one side, then, with a searing pain, he was inside her. But instead of that long forgotten pleasure, she felt only pain; and still she fought. He pushed her hands back and pinned them above her head and pounded into her.

'Steve, this is rape,' she spat, twisting and turning

and trying to get out from under him.

'You're loving it,' he said. 'I like this new wildcat approach, Zoë. You always were a bit of a Miss Mouse, always were a bit too much of a pushover. Is that the problem then, Zoë? Theo not given you a good enough seeing to these days?'

Damp leaves clung to her hair, and stuck to her bare skin.

'Stop, Steve, stop now. I won't say anything if you stop now.'

'Oh, God,' Steve cried out, and Zoë felt him pulsating inside her. 'Oh, God. Oh, God. Oh, Zoë, you always did do it for me.'

He collapsed on top of her, releasing her hands. For a moment she couldn't move, he was a dead weight. Then he propped himself up on his elbow.

'I don't know how it was for you,' he said. 'But that was one of the best for me.'

Her hands now free, she hit out at him and brought her short strong nails down the side of his cheek.

'I hate you,' she spat. 'I hate you. Now get off me.'

He laughed. 'Whatever the lady wants,' he said rolling off her and tucking his arms above his head.

'Christ, Zoë, you certainly know how to please a man.' His trousers, a rather smart pair, and his underpants were pulled down to his knees, and he lay with his legs slightly apart, his belly and his now flaccid penis, exposed to the night air. His perspiration glowed in the light from the hut.

Zoë struggled to her feet. She was filthy; a mixture of dead leaves and mud adhered to her clothes, her body, and her hair. She pulled her jeans up around her waist, her panties were in shreds, she was wet between her legs, very wet, and she knew that Steve had broken his own rules and not worn a condom.

She fumbled in the dead leaves and found the Land Rover keys.

'Not going already, are you, darling?' Steve smirked. 'You always used to like an encore.'

She went over to him and looked down on him. He had a stupid supercilious smile on his face. She brought her foot back, aimed it at his groan and pushed it forward with all her might.

Steve may have been drunk, but his reactions were as fast as they ever were, and before her foot had reached him, his hand shot out and caught hold of her ankle and she staggered and fell heavily.

He rolled over on top off her. 'Don't even consider it,' he said.

She felt a spray of saliva on her face as he spoke.

'You're mine, Zoë, all mine, and I shall have you whenever and wherever I please.'

She brought her knee up sharp and thrust it into his groin; he rolled off her and doubled up in pain. In a flash she was on her feet and headed away from him, staggering through the wood, ignoring the brambles and twigs that scratched her face and hands.

She was more angry than frightened. 'Don't mess with me, Steve, or you'll find yourself in a lot of trouble,' she'd screamed as she got away from him.

She stumbled blindly on, glancing back every so often, but he didn't seem to be following her, she slowed her pace and tried to recognize her surroundings. She was quite lost, and she was sure she was going in the wrong direction for the Land Rover. She stopped dead still for a moment and listened, she heard a starter motor; Steve must be leaving. She waited another few minutes and then backtracked the way she had come. She reached the clearing by the keeper's hut, all seemed quiet. The lights were off and the door was shut. She let out a breath and relaxed. Then she heard him, he was very close, a slight crackle of leaves underfoot, and something else,— she could hear his shallow breath. He had returned, or perhaps she'd been mistaken in hearing his engine start up, either way, he was standing close by, she could hear him breathing. The cold hand of fear stroked her spine. ' Steve, don't mess about,' she said. She nearly added that he was frightening her. But her pride wouldn't let her do that. Steve would never actually hurt her, would he? He was drunk and pushy, but she was sure he wouldn't do any actual harm to her. Without the lights from the hut, the wood was pitch black. She moved forward, her heart thumping in her chest, all the time telling herself not to panic, but her body refused to obey her and she trembled. 'I know you're there, Steve. You're not frightening me, if that's what you think,' she said boldly, trying at the same time to control her shaking limbs. *Don't run, don't run, don't panic,* she told herself, but her legs took no notice, and she broke into a run, bumping into the trees and tripping over fallen branches. She could hear the crackle of leaves as he followed her, and she knew she had to get away, she knew that her life depended on it.

Then came the moment of her undoing, she looked back over her shoulder, tripped, and pelted headlong into a tree. She lay on the ground trying to orientate herself. She'd hit her head and her lip was cut. Then she froze, he was standing immediately above her, the toecap of his boot touching her arm, it moved back away from her, then crashed forward with a mighty force into her chest. She cried out in pain as the air wheezed out of her lungs, she put her arm out to protect herself, but the boot crashed down again, and there was something else, he was laughing; a mad manic laugh that didn't sound like Steve at all. He must have gone mad, completely mad. She curled up into a foetal position, tucking her head into her chest as another and another angry blow hit her. After some moments he stopped and she suddenly felt a warm liquid at the back of her neck, and knew that he was urinating on her. Oh God, he would kill her, she was going to die out there in the woods, and no one would know where she was. The cascade of moisture stopped, and she sensed that he was looking down on her again. She heard a snort and then the rustle of leaves as the he walked away.

She waited curled up in a ball for a very long time, then cautiously, she unraveled herself and, getting to her feet, she made her slow painful way back to the Land Rover. But all the time she sensed that he was watching, and could easily attack her again, and she shook with fear.

Once in the vehicle she didn't look back, but drove at speed, down through the valley, up through the farmyard and on through the village of Garrick-in-the-Willows, she saw not a soul. She imagined herself reporting what had happened to the police, Theo would insist on it, she knew he would. Only then she'd have to explain what she was doing out in the woods with Steve at midnight. The police wouldn't believe her, she doubted if Theo would. It sounded feeble enough, even to her own ears.

She'd slipped into Garrick Cottage, and then in the privacy of the bathroom she'd scrubbed herself clean, only there was no way she could get the taste of it all out of her mouth or the shame of it off her skin. Her clothes had all but dried out by the time she'd got home, but she wanted nothing to remind her of that night, she'd bundled them up into a black rubbish bag; she would take them to the farm in the morning, and burn them.

She'd tiptoed into the bedroom. Theo was fast

asleep he didn't even stir when she got into bed beside him.

Now here was Dr Specter suggesting that she might not remember all of it. Did she remember? Oh yes, Dr Specter, she remembered all right, every word spoken, every angry action, every insult inflicted on her body, she remembered, she would never, ever, forget.

She put her hands down between her legs, she still felt bruised and violated; no amount of scrubbing would rid her of the wretchedness and shame that she felt. Her hand traveled up to her belly, what if? Oh, God, no, not Steve's. Please, God, don't let that happen.

'Dr Specter?'

'Pat, call me Pat.'

'I . . . I . . . '

'Yes?'

'I didn't kill Theo's wife.'

Chapter 68

Debbie Smith disappeared through the bathroom door. Michael stared after her, boy, what a night; the sort of night he'd only ever dreamed about. He shook his head and smiled broadly, he was dreaming; he had to be; he'd wake up in a minute.

But no, Debbie's knickers were lying on the bottom of the bed; he reached forward and grabbed them. They were the strangest of garments, they looked normal enough from the front, but the back of them was little more than a string of material. A G-string, he supposed they were called. He had no idea that girls actually wore such things, it cut up between her buttocks, exposing that wonderful rounded sexy arse. They ought to be banned. He'd never be able to look at Debbie's bum again without seeing those gorgeous cheeks poking out and asking to be stroked. And that wouldn't be very convenient in Barkhampton station, would it?

She came out of the bathroom. 'Sorry it's so early,' she said. 'Only I'll have to pop home and change, and then it's a good hour's drive to work.'

'What'll your mum say? You not going home last night.'

Debbie flopped down on the bed, her long olive body crossing his. She stretched, like, thought Michael, some exotic feline.

'I'll tell her I couldn't make it, because . . . ' She curled her body around, and ran her tongue from his navel to the end of his penis. 'Something came up.'

'It'll be coming up again, if you carry on like that,' his excitement was visible.

She took her knickers out of his hand. 'I'll have to go,' she pulled them on, and slipped into her bra.

Michael didn't think he had ever seen a more beautiful woman, firm fleshed and nicely rounded. Nice breasts with huge dark nipples, deep-set navel with the merest hint of hair running down to her mound of Venus. A very well named part of Debbie's anatomy.

'Do you wear those kind of knickers for work?' he asked.

'Thongs?'

'Is that what you call them.'

'Yes, and yes,' she said.

'And how do you expect a frustrated old bastard like me to keep his hands off you? I'll be done for sexual harassment, I will.'

'You still frustrated?'

'Not now, not this very minute, but I have been for about ten years, and I'll probably . . . ' he looked at his watch — it was five-thirty, 'be frustrated again by seven-thirty.'

She leaned over him and kissed him. Oh, that kiss,

those lips, that tongue.

'Ditto,' she said, and kissed him again. 'I hope you won't keep your hands off me,' she giggled. She pulled his hands around her waist and rested them on her buttocks. 'Hold out 'til tonight can you?'

'Tonight?' He couldn't believe his luck, she was offering to come back.

'Yes. I'll come over after work, and then I'm on lates tomorrow, so I won't have to get up early in the morning.'

She got off the bed and finished dressing.

He too dressed. 'I'll walk down to the car with you. I'll get reception to cut you another key, then if I'm not back you can let yourself in.'

'Thanks,'

The girl on the reception desk gave him another plastic keycard without question and Michael handed it to Debbie.

He walked her to her car. It was almost six o'clock and the morning was cold and frosty.

'I'll see you tonight then?' he said.

'Yes,— and Michael — thank you.'

'No,' he said. 'Thank you.'

They smiled and kissed, and parted.

Michael hummed as he went back up in the lift. He studied himself in the reflective wall surface, pulling his stomach in and turning from side to side. He'd watch his

538

diet from now on; he didn't want her to go off him.

The police station at Fenshaw stood just off the Market Square and was just around the corner to The Kings Head Hotel. Michael decided that he might just as well have breakfast and go into work, there was no point in sitting in his room thinking of the delectable Debbie.

True to his resolution, he had a breakfast of mueslie, yogurt and orange juice, and although his mouth watered at the sight of the piles of eggs and bacon, it watered a deal more at the thought of Debbie Smith's buttocks.

Michael's temporary office was small and painted a light cream colour. It already seemed filled to capacity with files and reports. Tomorrow, more men and women were due to be drafted in. Telephones would start ringing; Barnes would produce piles of reports from house to house inquiries. Statements would be read and re-read. Key lines underlined and matched up to other statements. The search had started; a mistake, if made, would be found — and they always made mistakes — didn't they?

Ian didn't arrive until gone ten; he'd collected the PM report and some bits and pieces from Garrick Hall that could have some relevance.

Michael was starving, his frugal breakfast had not satisfied him for long, and now he was famished.

'Come on, Ian, let's grab some breakfast at The Kings Head, bring those reports with you.'

Before Ian could protest, Michael had left his office and was striding back toward the hotel. Ian Barnes was far too much in awe of Michael to protest that his wife Gabbie had already fed him more than adequately.

The Kings Head was an imposing eighteenth century building overlooking the Market Square. The rooms were high and grand, remnants of a bygone age. The service was good and personal. As they entered, the attentive receptionist informed them that breakfast had finished, but that morning coffee was being served in the lounge.

Michael ordered large coffees and a Danish pastry for them both. After all, he'd been on the go all night, he must have burned off a few calories, — more than a few in fact.

Ian groaned as a young blonde girl placed the large cinnamon Danish in front of him. She was wearing a bright badge that said that her name was Vivian and that she was happy to help.

Ian pursed his lips. 'She can help me anytime, Mike. What say you?'

Michael smiled; an image of Debbie's rounded buttocks slipped into his head. 'I'm well satisfied with what I've got, thanks, Ian.'

They ate and drank whilst scanning the PM report, it was concise and to the point.

'Lady Isobel Sheldon-Harris, aged fifty-nine, five-seven inches tall, nine stone two pounds. Time of death,

between ten pm and one am. Cause of death, strangulation.'
A lurid account of her stomach contents followed, along
with other details such as the size and weight of various
internal organs.

A hand written note was added on a postit, which
said that Gilbert Knox would like to meet Michael at
Garrick Hall, if at all possible.

'What's that all about?' asked Ian.

'That means that Gilbert has a theory. A PM
reports facts, and there,' he said making a sweeping gesture
toward the wad of paper, 'are the facts. But Gilbert's a great
guy for figuring out the how and the whys, things he
wouldn't really want to write down.'

Michael bundled the papers together. 'We'll drop
these in at the station, then we're off to see Mrs Sparks.'

Chapter 69

Ruth Sparks showed no surprise when she opened the door to two policemen. Her hair was neatly curled. She wore a pink hand-knitted jumper and a plaid skirt. A string of artificial pearls of poor quality peeped from the neck of the jumper. Michael suspected that both the hair and the pearls were for his benefit. She invited them into the tiny cottage, which stood on the very outskirts of the village.

They were then led into a very small sitting-room-cum-kitchen, in the center of which stood a table covered with a checked oilcloth, and with three painted wooden chairs pushed under it. On the far wall stood a black iron range, the like of which Michael had not seen since his childhood, and which Ian had probably never seen at all. The fire in the range burned with a cheery glow. To each side of the range stood comfortable armchairs, with a rag rug between them.

The cottage looked like a folk museum exhibit of the 1930's, but Michael felt a bewildering sense of wellbeing.

'My Granny and Grandad lived in a cottage just like this one,' he said — a strong sense of approval in his tone.

Ruth Sparks smiled at him and patted the permed curls. The smile revealed an even set of very white dentures, so false, that they gave her face a comic look. Her eyes were dark and deep set.

'Would you gentlemen take a seat,' she gestured toward the table and chairs.

It was then that Michael turned and saw the television set — its bulk oppressive in the small room. Michael experienced a deep feeling of disappointment. You've spoiled it, he thought aggressively. He took the seat facing the television and throughout the interview he was constantly aware of its presence. It was almost as if a forth person sat in the room betraying his fantasies.

Ruth followed his gaze and said with pride, 'Twenty-eight inch screen, Inspector.'

'Very nice,' said Michael.

'Of course, it's only rented,' she said wistfully.

They accepted the coffee she offered. She rose and went into the next room; a cold blast of air circulated the tiny kitchen. Michael didn't need to enter the sitting room to know what it contained. It would be the best room, the one saved for high days and holidays. There'd be a plump three piece suit, probably of a beige moquette material, a small coffee table, probably Formica, on which would stand a handmade crochet mat and perhaps an ashtray, although no one would ever consider smoking in Ruth Spark's best room. In the corner would be a glass fronted china cabinet, in which was stored the best tea service.

Ruth appeared carrying three china cups, two of

which had ugly black cracks in their side; the third had, at one time, had its handle reglued, a blob of yellow glue bulged out from the injured limb.

She produced a bottle of liquid coffee and carefully measured a spoonful in each cup. More and more, Michael was reminded of his grandparents, and the sweet milky coffee Mrs Sparks produced lulled him into thoughts of his childhood.

'Here you are,' she said. 'A proper cup of coffee, not like all the stuff you get from these percolators and things these days.'

'No indeed,' Michael said looking dismally into the pale beige liquid.

Mrs Sparks sipped contently for a moment. 'Now, Sir, what's old Sparks been telling you?'

Michael was a little taken aback. He'd like to explain to her, without causing offence, that it was she, not he, who was there to answer the questions.

'I was expecting you yesterday, that's what Sparks said, but he gets muddled these days. Is it right that you've arrested the fancy bit?'

Michael ignored her and said, 'Mrs Sparks, let's get down to it, shall we? Your full name?'

He ran through the usual routine questions and then continued, 'And when did you last see Lady Sheldon-Harris alive?'

'Well, Sir. She were always alive when I saw her.'

He studied her face. No, she wasn't being funny or obstructive.

'Of course,' he said. 'So when did you last see her?'

'Last Friday, Sir. I left at about one o'clock — perhaps a bit later, as I gave the kitchen a good do that day.'

'And was there anything unusual? Anything you think we should know about?'

She thought; no, there had been nothing, everything had been the same. Lady Sheldon-Harris had been looking forward to Charlotte's visit. She'd been close to her daughter lately.

'You see, she'd forgiven her for being . . . well not quite as you'd like your daughter to be.'

'I'm sorry,' Michael said. 'You've lost me.'

'Well she was one of them, you know, a lesbian. But when her Dad got ill, it brought Lady Sheldon-Harris and Lottie, that's what they called her, Lottie, together.'

Michael wrote a note in his book, he didn't dare look at Ian he was afraid he might giggle. He thought of Debbie's cheeky cheeks and then he didn't dare have eye contact with either Mrs Sparks or Ian.

'She got me to make some scones for when Lottie came to tea on Monday. I told her they'd be stale, I told her I'd make them on Monday morning when I went in, but she didn't want that. Good job I didn't, seeing as I were sick and all. Anyway, I made the scones and she said she'd put them in the fridge. She didn't have much idea about things like that.'

'So you normally work on . . . ?'

'Monday, Tuesday, and Friday, but sometimes she asks me to do a bit extra, if she's got one of them there clients coming for a consultation. To tell you the truth, I'm glad of the extra money, what with Sparks being unemployed.' She rolled her eyes to the ceiling, as if her sympathy for her husband's lack of employment had long since disappeared, but loyalty forbade voicing her thoughts.

'Only I had a bit of a cold on Monday, so I didn't go in.'

'Was Lady Sheldon-Harris a good employer?' Ian asked, his voice was eager and he looked as if he was concentrating. Michael suspected that he was doing anything to avoid drinking the pale beige liquid masquerading as coffee.

Ruth stuck her bottom lip out. 'Good enough, Sir. She was always moaning of course, but them sort always does. She'd never got enough money,— a joke aint it? Did you see her standard of living? And she was minting it with all that spirit stuff. She were good mind, I'll say that for her; she deserved to get a bit put by.'

'Did Lady Sheldon-Harris entertain much?'

'Visitors? In the summer, quite a few, mainly those that came for a reading or whatever she called it, you know, to get in touch with them that had gone. Then there was that solicitor woman, dead snotty she were. Sometimes Charlotte would visit, but always on her own. Lady Sheldon-Harris didn't take to the girlfriend, you see.'

Ruth explained how she'd gone to the Hall on Tuesday morning, only to find the doors locked and the place deserted. She had spoken to Tom Farrow and passed the time of day with him. She had got back home at about ten o'clock.

'Of course I thought it funny. She'd never done that before, gone out I mean, and not let me know, not left a key or anything, — but I didn't think anything bad had happened. Of course I saw the car there, that's why I hung about for a few minutes. I mean Lady Sheldon-Harris wasn't one to go anywhere on foot. Then I thought that perhaps she'd gone off for a couple of days with Charlotte, in *her* car. I supposed she had just forgotten I was coming in that day, being as I didn't go in on Monday.'

She went on to say a little of how Lady Sheldon-Harris ran her life, but she was unable to tell them anything of great importance.

'One last question,' said Michael. 'Where were you last Monday night?'

She looked startled. 'Here, of course,' she looked proudly at the television set. 'Watching tele'.'

'And Mr Sparks?'

'He was here with me. Why? Has anyone else said otherwise?'

Michael thought she seemed defensive. He smiled and got up to leave.

'Inspector,' she said. 'Neither of you has drunk your coffee, you've let it get cold. Shall I make you a drop of fresh?'

'Oh, no, no, no thank you,' they both said a little too eagerly.

They made their way back to the car, with Mrs Sparks watching them from her open door.

'What a dump,' said Ian. 'The only thing worth having was the television set.'

Chapter 70

'But don't you see Vinnie? By sending for Tiggy and Alex, you've made her look guilty.'

Josh and Lavinia were on their way over to Garrick to see Theo and pick Elizabeth up; the news of Zoë's arrest had shattered them both.

'Oh? And how'd you work that out?'

'Well, they're going to say that an innocent woman doesn't need three lawyers. Theo has already got her a local chap.'

'Yes, Rodney Burton. You know him, don't you? A terrible lawyer — he'd have found Jesus guilty.'

'Better men than him, did,' Josh retorted.

'Oh, Josh, you know what I mean. Stop being unreasonable.'

'I'm not. I'm only saying that the police will think it's odd that we've called in a barrister.'

'Alex isn't just a barrister, he's family.'

'Is he?' Josh said, a tinge of sarcasm in his voice.

'You know what I mean. Stop trying to make this harder than it really is. Why are you going this way?'

Josh had cut in by the Schoolhouse and was making his way across a rough track toward Garrick Cottage.

'Theo says that there's a load of reporters round the

main gate. The last thing we want is for them to get wind of who Zoë is.'

Lavinia nodded. 'They already know, a reporter 'phoned the Castle this morning.'

'What did you say?'

'Nothing — I switched over to the answerphone.'

They passed Garrick Hall on their left, and bumped over the cattle grid.

'It's a nightmare, isn't it, Josh?'

'Yes, but the comforting thing about nightmares is that you always wake up.' He patted her hand.

Lavinia shifted uncomfortably in her seat. 'I think there's something I should tell you, Josh.'

Josh looked panic stricken. 'Don't, unless you're sure I'll want to know it,' he said.

They bumped onto the main drive and turned a slight bend.

'Damn, look,' Josh said, 'they're all over the place.'

Two reporters were standing in the trees not far from the cottage; one of them was smoking a cigarette. Several more men and women were gathered around the main gate, and a television van was pulled onto the verge just outside.

'When I stop the car, Vinnie, get out and run like hell into the cottage.'

'I certainly will not — I shall hold my head high

and proceed with dignity.' And that's exactly what she did.

'But, she's in hospital and they won't let me see her, ' Theo's voice greeted them as they opened the door.

'Why not?' Sebastian, the younger of Zoe's twin brothers replied.

'Oh,' Lavinia said. 'Thank God, the twins are here.'

'Because they say I'm a possible witness,— to what, I'd like to know?' Theo turned and greeted Zoë's parents, kissing Lavinia on both cheeks and shaking hands with Josh.

'Did I hear you say she was in hospital? Why? What's wrong with her?'

'Her fall, you know, the one in the farmyard. She's cracked her rib and they thought she'd punctured her lung, but she hasn't, thank God.'

'You know that's not true, don't you, Theo?' Lavinia said.

'What, about her rib?' Sebastian looked surprised.

'No, no, about her fall. She couldn't have got those bruises just by falling.'

The room went very quiet.

'Are you saying that she fought with Issie?' Theo said quietly. It was a question that had popped in and out of his head a dozen times, and one he hadn't dared voice until that moment.

Tears sprang to Lavinia's eyes. 'I don't know,

Theo,— I just don't know. Had Isobel been in a fight? I mean did she have bruises?'

'I don't know, the police haven't told me. Lottie identified her, I didn't see her, after . . . well you know . . . after she was dead.'

'No doubt one of her spirit friends will pop down and tell us what happened,' Josh said.

Everyone turned their heads and looked at him, but nobody laughed.

'Let's get practical, Theo, they won't let you see her, but they'll probably let me, I'm her mother. But I'll need to know what to say to her.'

'Ask her what happened of course,' Josh said.

'And do you think she'll tell me? Just like that?'

No one replied.

'Precisely,' Lavinia said. 'Look, Theo. Put some of her things together, nightdress, toiletries and the like, and I'll take them into her. Surely they can't mind *me* doing that. Tiggy and Alex will be here soon, we'll ask them what to do.'

'There's something you should know before they come,' Theo said. 'Zoë went out on Monday night.' He felt sick even saying it, but he had to tell someone what was troubling him. 'Betsy told the police that she wasn't here.'

'But she's a child,' Quentin said. 'No one will believe her,'

'But don't you see, she *was* out. She crept out in

the middle of the night, and was gone for two hours.'

'Is that what the charade about her clothes was all about?' Josh asked.

Theo nodded; did he tell them the whole story? Or leave it at that. These were people that loved Zoë; they'd help her if they could.

'She destroyed the clothes that she was wearing. She burned them in the incinerator at the farm.'

The room was very quiet; nobody met anyone else's eyes.

'She was with me,' Quentin suddenly burst out.

'What?'

'There's an owls nest in Two-penny Hollow. I took her there to see it.'

'This isn't helping, Quen,' Lavinia said.

'But?'

'But nothing, you see I *know* where she was on Tuesday night.'

She had center stage now. Josh put his head in his hands. She looked directly at Theo, 'I'm sorry, Theo, but she met Steve Jarvis and . . . you see Steve's always been willing to do practically anything for money, dishonest things I mean, and it seems, — he'd do the same for love, he's always been very, very, fond of Zoë.'

'What are you saying?' Quentin said.

'I'm saying that your sister and Steve . . . '

'Murdered Issie?' Theo said. 'No. No, never in a

thousand years, Lavinia.'

'I know it seems astounding, Theo. But I saw him that night, the night of the shoot. He went off at eleven-thirty and came back in the early hours.'

'How do you—'

'How do I know?' She was extremely agitated. 'I saw him go — I was in the kitchen finishing things off and I saw him come down the back stairs and drive away. Then I didn't sleep very well, and I heard Fable barking, — real din she was making. I looked out of the window and I saw him return. Then the next day—'

'Those scratches on his cheek!' Josh exclaimed.

Lavinia nodded.

Again there was a long silence. Finally Josh said, 'Steve may not be your usual honest Joe, but murder, I don't see him stooping that low. Besides what was in it for him?'

'A final act of love,' Lavinia said. 'He treated Zoë pretty badly in the past, maybe this was his way of recompensing. Or maybe Zoë just persuaded him to help her.'

'Ma! You can't believe that Zoë would do that, you just can't,' Sebastian said.

Her hand was clamped over her mouth and tears streamed down her cheeks. 'I don't know what to believe anymore,' she wept, 'I've looked at it every which way, and I can no longer think straight.'

It was Theo, not Josh that put his arm around her.

'Lavinia, I don't know where Zoë went that night, but I do know that she didn't go anywhere near the Hall, and she didn't have anything to do with Issie's death.'

Lavinia sniffed. 'How can you be sure, unless . . .'

'Unless?'

'Unless you did it yourself.'

Theo took his arm away from her, the situation was getting worse; it was reaching nightmare proportions.

'Look here folks, whatever Zoë was doing and wherever she was, we have to keep this to ourselves.' Sebastian said. 'Steve's gone back to Scotland now, and there's no need for anyone to know about him going out in the night. Neither is there any need for anyone else to know that Zoë went out. If she wants us to know anything then she'll tell us. Theo's right, Zoë couldn't have anything to do with murder. We all know that, but there's no sense in giving the police a nice little motive and a nice little opportunity now is there?'

Everyone nodded their heads.

'I suggest we don't even tell Tiggy and Alex.' Quentin added.

'Why not?' Asked Lavinia.

'We don't trust Alex, Ma,' he looked at his brother to include him in the statement.

'I don't understand?' Josh said.

'We don't like the way he looks at Ma, he's shifty somehow,' he laughed. 'It's almost as if he fancies her.'

'We'll keep it to ourselves then,' Lavinia said quickly.

Everyone nodded their agreement

Chapter 71

Michael entered Garrick Hall grounds via the main gates and drove very slowly past the lodge. A couple of reporters were hanging about outside the cottage, they were looking very bored.

'Poor sods,' he said. 'No peace while she lived, none now she's dead.'

'You still think she's innocent, don't you?' Ian scoffed.

'And you still think she did it?' Michael batted back.

Ian pulled a face. 'I think she was involved,— yes, I do.'

Michael stopped the car just outside the lodge. He lowered the window. 'Can I help you, gentleman?'

'I'm from the Mercury. Just waiting to get an interview with Sir Theodore. Is it correct that his mistress has been charged with murdering his wife?'

At that moment Elizabeth's small freckled face appeared at the kitchen window, her nose pressed close, deforming her features. The other man, who hadn't yet spoken, lifted his camera and snapped wildly at the child. Click-click, click-click. Michael was not a man to show his anger and, even now, although his fury mounted, he appeared calm.

'You know you can't use those, don't you? At least I hope you know that.'

The man lowered his camera.

'I'm Detective Inspector Harper from Barkhampton. There'll be a press conference at ten o'clock tomorrow morning. I'll try and answer any relevant questions then. Meanwhile, just to clarify matters, no one so far has been charged with this murder—'

'But we heard she'd been arrested,'

'Someone is helping us with our inquiries. But no one's been charged. As I said, I'll try and answer your questions tomorrow, meanwhile perhaps I should remind you that taking photo's of a four-year-old child, is not, in my opinion, nor I suspect in the press complaint board's opinion, relevant to the case, nor is it worthy news coverage.'

He began to shut his window then he lowered it again.

'By the way, Gentleman, from here to the road is private property, and Sir Theo has every right to throw you out. I would advise you to join your colleagues at the gates before that happens.

The two men gave tight-lipped smiles and, with only the slightest of backward glances they set off in the direction of the main gates.

Gilbert Knox hadn't arrived, so Michael and Ian settled themselves in Michael's Golf to wait for him.

'Right, Ian, what have we got so far?'

Ian began flicking through his notebook. He pushed his dark hair back from his forehead, and ran his index finger up and down the cleft in his chin. Michael studied him and realized that Ian Barnes had only narrowly missed being very handsome.

'Well, Lady Sheldon-Harris was certainly not popular. It seems that she made a career out of giving her husband and his new love a bad time. If you think about it you can hardly blame Zoë Elliot for— '

'Let's just stick to the facts, shall we?'

Ian smiled and shrugged his shoulders.

'It either was, or was made to look like rape, right? So what does that tell us?'

'That Lady Sheldon-Harris was a darned sight more attractive when she was alive than when she was dead? Or that it must have been very dark that night?'

'Very funny, Ian. Now let's be serious.' Michael had to turn his head, afraid that Ian would see him smile.

'To be honest, Mike. I *was* being serious. But I know what you're getting at; this wasn't an opportunist, a one off, someone that just happened to be passing through. This was someone who wanted her dead. This wasn't a thief, — the whole place is packed with goodies. Nothing in the house is disturbed, so if something was taken, then whoever it was, knew where to look.'

'Someone who wanted her dead,' Michael said,

thoughtfully.

'And someone, who wanted to shift the blame onto a man,' Ian added.

'Or another man, it doesn't have to be a woman.'

'Okay, a small man who wanted to shift the blame onto another man.'

'Or a man who hated her so much that he didn't care that he left his genetic fingerprint behind.'

'But everybody knows about DNA and body fluids.'

'You've said that before, but not everyone does know, Ian,' Michael shook his head, round and round they were going; he was missing something. It was staring him in the face and yet he couldn't see it. 'You know the statistics as well as me, Ian. Most murderers know their victims, and in a case like this, — the eternal triangle as it were . . .'

'Is Sir Theo clever enough to admit to it, — like he did, — get the facts all wrong, so that we send him packing and—'

'It's hard to believe. But he admits himself, that he had motive, and I dare say if we probe a bit deeper we'll find that he had the opportunity.' Michael was quiet for a moment. 'But then the semen, why the semen?'

'To confuse us even more. It's not going to be his, is it?'

'I can't believe he's capable of that. You should

have seen him with the little girl, he doesn't seem capable of hurting anyone. At least, not the type to strangle. He'd use poison or fiddle with the brakes of her car.'

'But then it wouldn't fit in with her reincarnation theory, would it? She had to be strangled, like that old farmers wife in the seventeen hundreds.'

'You're not suggesting that we can pin this on the spirits are you, Ian?'

Ian grinned. 'That might be what the murderer's hoping. But you know, strangulation is usually a spur-of-the-moment thing. A lot off people are capable of it, if provoked enough.'

Michael had a sudden vivid recollection of a fight he'd once had with Angie. He'd got as far as putting his hands around her neck before he'd come to his senses and walked away, — but that was just it, he had walked away.

Gilbert Knox tapped on his window and he jumped. Both detectives got out of the car and shook hands.

'Brought this for you,' Gilbert said handing him a plain manila file. 'Fingerprint report.'

Gilbert was a gentle eager-faced man, with iron-grey hair, who talked with his small sensitive hands. He touched everything with care, no matter what it was, as if each object was precious and fragile. He had rather a hooked nose and a small mouth, which made it appear difficult to smile. His clothes never varied; a dark pinstriped suit and an old school tie, although Michael did not know which school. As always, Gilbert appeared excited and enthusiastic. He was a man dedicated to his work; he enjoyed piecing together the jigsaw puzzle of murder. So much could be learned from the silent dead, so many secrets heard from cold blue lips.

They proceeded into the kitchen of Garrick Hall, — a room the forensic team had finished with. There was nothing there to speak of a violent death apart from the forensic teams residue and a chalk outline indicating where Lady Sheldon-Harris's body had lain.

The kitchen overlooked the path where Zoë walked every morning and evening. It was by no means a modern room, although it was littered with every modern kitchen appliance, dishwasher, microwave, food-mixer, and even a small television set. The AGA was of a yellowed cream colour, which told Michael that it must have been installed some years ago. It gave off a welcoming warmth. The room was large, about twenty feet or so long and almost square. A large scrubbed pine table stood in the center, with eight matching pine chairs around it, and a continuous pine worktop ran around three of the walls. Beneath these were fitted a wealth of appliances interspersed with solid pine cupboards. The room, once clean and tidy, was now marked with fingerprint dust and patches of purple die, giving the impression that nothing had ever been cooked in it. Michael wondered if it had been installed by Lady Sheldon-Harris, or Theo's first wife, a thought which brought with it another question; did a Lady lose her title on divorce? Could there be more than one Lady Sheldon-Harris? After all, if he had his way, there'd be more than one Mrs Michael Harper.

They settled themselves at the long kitchen table. Michael thought that the three men looked out of place in such a female domain, but he'd never dream of voicing such a sexist remark.

'Right,' Michael said. 'Tell me all.'

'You did get my report?'

'Oh yes, we did.' He turned to Ian. 'I read most of it, but Ian here, has read it all, haven't you, Ian?'

Ian cleared his throat. 'Most of it,' he said.

'Hmm,' Gilbert coughed. 'Well, what do you make of the lubrication?'

'Lubrication?' Ian and Michael said in unison.

'You read *most* of most report, did you?' He nodded. 'I see,' he said scathingly.

Michael thought that Gilbert looked more hurt than annoyed. 'You know how much paper work we have to wade through in cases like this, Gilbert,' he said defensively.

Gilbert smiled and shook his head. 'Maybe I should just tell you the facts and what I surmise from them. But why I should do your detective work for you I don't know, you'll get the glory when this chap is caught.'

Michael pretended to rub his eyes. 'Come on, Gilbert, you'll have us all in tears soon. Spill the beans.

What's this about lubrication.'

Gilbert Knox held up his hand. 'Patience,' he said. 'I'll start at the beginning. As you know she was strangled with a piece of baler twine. Not a new piece, it had traces of hay and mud on it, the sort of stuff every farmer worth his salt carries about in his work-coat pocket.'

Ian shot Michael a look of triumph.

'It wasn't a very long piece of twine,' Gilbert went on. She was strangled from the rear and the murderer used a downward pressure. He was also quite strong and Lady Sheldon-Harris didn't have much of a chance. Although, there again, she wasn't a particularly strong woman, her bone density was poor; she'd lived on a very poor diet for many years. Her clothes were torn, but very halfheartedly. There were minute traces of blood under the nails of her left hand, group O, rhesus positive, the commonest group there is, but we've got a good DNA fix on it. And as you know, there was semen found on the top of her thigh and in her pubic hair. And guess what? In with the semen were traces of lubrication, not spermicide, please note, but lubrication, the sort used on all the best known brands of contraception, except that they're not used these days very often. Most people like to kill two birds with one stone, — you know, guard against disease and pregnancy, and lubricate, all in one go. But occasionally the woman, or even the man's, allergic to spermicide, so one can buy these.' He produced a packet of condoms from his pocket. 'Look, spermicide free, but does contain a water based lubrication.'

Michael took the packet from him.

'Do you have to ask for these specially, from behind the counter, or are they on general sale?'

'Sorry, — you just go in the chemist and pick them off the shelf.' Gilbert replied. 'But it does narrow the field a bit. There's three in a packet, and he'd only have used one. But it kind of proves my theory. The semen was planted, and what's more it came from a man with an above average sperm count, so it's probably a younger, rather than an older man. The big boys are always banging on about men losing their sperm count; well, this chap could father a nation if he put his mind to it.'

'His mind?' Ian asked innocently. And both Michael and the doctor laughed.

'But the really surprising thing is—'

A young officer coughed as he entered the room. 'Excuse me, Sir. We've finished with the sitting room,' he said pleasantly. 'The little study is going to be the hardest, there's documents and diaries going back years and years.'

Michael rubbed his chin. 'Get a WPC to go through the diaries, women have a keener sense than men. Set her up with a photocopier and get her to xerox anything she feels might be relevant.'

'Careful, Mike,' Ian said, as the constable left the kitchen, 'that sounded like sexism to me.'

'Too darned right it is, Ian. If Lady Sheldon-

Harris's diary says she saw Zoë looking terrible, it probably means she looked ravishing. Now, another woman would know that, but that young man wouldn't. But back to the drawing board.'

'Yes, as I was saying, two surprising things, the blood under the nails and the semen don't belong to the same person.'

Ian's mouth twitched into a smile, 'So there were two of them?'

'Looks like it.'

'And the other surprising thing?' Michael asked.

'Her wedding ring was missing, she could of course have taken it off herself, but she was definitely used to wearing one, and she was wearing it either when she died, or up to a few hours before she died. That's it, really. They're the facts. Make of them what you will.'

Michael smiled. 'So that's it? Simple as that? You've called me all this way, and you're not going to give me your theory?'

Gilbert closed his file. 'You know, Mike, murder is often a lot less complicated that it first seems, the obvious is often the only possible truth.'

But nothing seemed very obvious to Michael. 'Spell it out to me,' he said.

'Well, see where she was found? There was no real struggle, yet someone wanted us to think that there was a struggle, she was walking away from the back door. If you ask me, she let that person in, and it was someone she trusted.'

'That lets Zoë off the hook,' Michael said.

'She let them in, and then she turned her back on them, and they grabbed her from behind and strangled her. They took her wedding ring, for robbery? Her purse was in her handbag on the side there. No, I'd say that it was a symbolic gesture.'

'She trusted Sir Theo,' Ian said. 'Zoë Elliot says she was always calling him down here. She might have let Sir Theo in, he might have been in front of her, and Zoë could have crept in behind and—'

'Let's leave Zoë Elliot out of this for a minute. Has Sir Theo's mouth swab come back yet? Do we know what his profile is?'

'Not yet. Later this afternoon, I hope. I've asked them to rush it through.'

'And Zoë's?'

'It's not her blood under the fingernails.'

Michael felt a terrific surge of relief. He was being ridiculous, as long as he got his murderer, what did it matter who it was. Yet somehow he'd confused Zoë and Theo's situation with his own. If they got out of their difficulties there was every chance he might get out of his.

Michael got up to leave.

'Aren't you going to look at that report?' Gilbert asked. 'Only I took a peek. Theodore Sheldon-Harris's fingerprints were found all over this kitchen.'

Chapter 72

The inquiry continued. Countless people were spoken to; their comments recorded and statements taken. Whilst the detectives toiled, Zoë lived in a sedated haze, and Theo experienced the full range of emotions from anger and aggression to sorrow and loneliness, and still they would not allow him to visit her. Lavinia and Josh took Elizabeth home to Hulver. On visitation rights, Lavinia had faired no better than Theo in delivering her effects to the hospital. She was told that Zoë was heavily sedated and the doctors advised no visitors.

The farm manager George Vickers was questioned. 'She was a good enough worker,' he said of Zoë Elliot. 'But the whole situation is impossible for me.' He was a good-looking man of about forty-five, who did not speak without thinking carefully about what he was going to say. Michael felt irritated by the man's slow analysis of every question. He had dark auburn hair, dark eyes, and a small, mean looking mouth. Michael noted that the man never actually smiled. He wore a smart checkered sports jacket and grey flannels, more like a gentleman farmer, than a farm manager, Michael thought. It was obvious from the onset that the man had one or two axes to grind.

'Of course, Sir Theo's put himself in an impossible position. The farm wouldn't have survived if Isobel had lived, we'd certainly have gone bankrupt. Sir Theo tends not to think too far ahead, and he never troubled to think of others. I'm speaking in confidence, of course, Inspector,' he added meaningfully. 'He never thought of me, for instance. If the farm had gone bust, what would have happened to me? I live in a tied house, Inspector. I'd have lost both my job and my home.' He paused as if to give Michael time to appreciate the gravity of the situation. 'You see, Sir Theo was keeping two women, two homes, two cars, and now he's even landed himself with a child to support.' He spoke as if Elizabeth had appeared that very morning. 'Zoë is a tremendous drain on his resources, and his resources come from this farm, and I'm the one that does the work. I'm the one that's been trying to keep the whole show solvent.'

'What was the relationship like between Miss Elliot and Lady Sheldon-Harris.'

Vickers weighed his answer. 'Not good, of course.' He thought for another moment. 'It's hard for me to comment. By the way, she called herself Mrs Sheldon-Harris, not Miss Elliot. That must have rankled a bit, mustn't it?' He paused and gave it more thought. 'I spent all my time trying to please them all. I'm afraid Sir Theo made a great mistake when he brought Zoë Elliot home, she's not even a good shepherd,' he added bitterly.

'I thought you said she was a good worker,' Michael said.

'Oh, she is, but that doesn't mean that she knows

what she's talking about. You know who she is, don't you? She's Lord Hulver's daughter. Now you tell me, how can a girl brought up like that, possibly know anything about sheep? Besides, shepherding's a man's job, not a woman's.'

Michael smiled, the depths of Norfolk obviously hadn't heard about equal opportunities, or if they had, they were doing their best to fight it.

'So, how did *you* get on with Lady Sheldon-Harris?'

Once again Vickers waited some moments before he answered, his small mouth drew together as he thought.

'Well, you may think it's just sour grapes, but I can assure you it isn't.' he paused yet again. 'We used to get on quite well. She often used to ask me to make up the numbers for a dinner party, then I started taking Charlotte out a bit, this was four or five years ago, before Sir Theo left. Then Charlotte decided that—' He paused, this time quite abruptly, and closed his eyes. 'You see, this is difficult for me. Lady Sheldon-Harris came to see me and ordered, actually ordered me not to repeat what I knew. A lot of things were said, the gist of which was, that I did as I was told, — if I wanted to keep my job, that is.'

'And so you kept quiet?'

This time Vickers didn't stop to think. 'Of course I did.'

'But,' Ian said. 'Surely, Sir Theo would be the one to sack you, not Lady Sheldon-Harris.'

'You didn't know her. She'd have found a way. Sir Theo was putty in her hands. She could get him to do anything she wanted. Until he met Zoë Elliot, — then things changed around here.'

'I assume this was about Charlotte's sexual orientation?'

'You know about that then?'

Michael thought of the two girls, Charlotte and Flora, comforting each other in the car outside the Hall on the day that the body was discovered. He should have known then, but he hadn't, he hadn't seen anything unusual in it. Perhaps he *was* getting old and stale.

'The last few years I've spent my time avoiding all of them, Sir Theo, Isobel, and especially Zoë. I only look after the arable side, I don't have anything to do with the stock. You might say that it's Sir Theo's little enterprise. You'll gather however that things around here have been more than a little tense.'

Michael and Ian made their way back through the village. Michael looked at his watch.

'We'll pay a visit to Sir Theo, and then we'll go and see if the quacks will let us interview Zoë.'

'Fat chance of that,' Ian said.

Sir Theo answered the door, and showed them into the kitchen. The sink was piled with dirty dishes and there were more dirty mugs on the table. Sir Theo followed Michael's eyes and made an ineffectual attempt to clear it away.

'I'm sorry, without Zoë I can't seem to get it together. When will you let me see her? I don't mind one of your lot being there — I mean, I do mind of course, but it's better than not seeing her at all.'

Michael felt a surge of irritation, and when he analyzed it, he knew it sprang from a deep-seated jealousy. Sir Theo had found someone to love and he'd had the guts to throw caution to the wind and do something about it. He'd upset everyone, but he'd had the courage to do it. Michael envied that courage and wondered if he'd have it in him to do the same.

'Don't you have someone to clean for you, Sir Theo?'

'Lord no, Inspector. These women expect to be paid the earth, — besides, it's a small enough place, and Zoë manages quite well.' He seated himself heavily at the table and sighed. 'I'm sorry,' he said. 'I'm not feeling myself today. I suppose it must be the shock. And the worry, about Zoë, that is. Have you seen her today? How is she, do you know?

'If it's any comfort to you, you're not alone. The doctors have banned us for the time being, Sir Theo.'

Theo sighed. 'Isabel burnt up so much of my energy, now she's gone, it's left a sort of void. The thought of not having her around, was like crying for the moon. I never seriously thought I'd ever get it, now I have, and Zoë and I should be . . . she has nothing to do with this, Inspector. I know her, and I know that she's simply not capable of such a thing.'

Michael didn't comment, but he nodded in understanding. Ian, however, looked totally perplexed.

Sir Theo showed surprise when asked about Lady Sheldon-Harris's missing wedding ring.

'But she always wore it. In fact she lay great store by it. She swore she'd never take it off, and, as far as I know, she never did. You see, Inspector, I was Issie's prized possession, — not much of a prize, I know. But that's the way she saw it. She said that she would never let me go, and she said that she would never take the ring off whilst she was . . . alive . . I . . um . . . ' Theo's words trailed away. He bit into his bottom lip.

Michael knew he'd thought of something. 'What is it?'

Sir Theo shook his head. 'Nothing, it's nonsense, but . . . Well, my wife was always talking about a chap named Randall. He and his mistress were hanged for his wife's murder, years ago in the seventeen hundreds.' He paused and shook his head. 'It's nonsense, of course it is, only . . . well she believed it, she really did . . . and . . . '

'And?' Ian sounded irritated.

'That's what convicted them, the murderers. The mistress was wearing the wife's wedding ring.'

'Not suggesting the spirits are responsible, are you,

Sir?' Michael asked.

Theo shook his head. 'No, no of course not, but . .'

Michael opened the fingerprint report that he'd placed before him on the table. Prints belonging to Lady Sheldon-Harris, Charlotte, and Flora had been found all over the house. Likewise Ruth Sparks, the cleaner. The gardener, Tom Farrow's, prints were found on the outside of both the front and the back door. But the biggest surprise had been Sir Theo's prints, which were found in the kitchen, the workshop and the drawing room.

Ian took the lead; he sounded very aggressive. 'You're prints were found at the Hall, and yet you tell us you rarely went there.'

'I don't, not if I can help it, but on the day before all this happened she telephoned me and said that a fuse had blown, and would I go and fix it, otherwise she'd have to get an electrician in to do it. Have you any idea how much that would have cost?'

'Miss Elliot said it was a light bulb. She said that Lady Sheldon-Harris 'phoned for you to change a light bulb.'

'That was earlier in the day, in the morning.'

'So you went to the Hall twice on Monday?'

'Yes.'

'And you didn't think to tell us this before?'

'I didn't think it was important, Inspector,' he paused, reminding Michael of the farm manager Vickers.

'You see, I didn't tell Zoë I was going, — it would only have caused another row. She really couldn't bear me having anything to do with Isabel. You've no idea how hard it was, Inspector, trying to appease both women, trying to keep them both happy.'

'Did you and Zoë have many rows, Sir?' Michael asked.

At the same moment, a perplexed looking Ian asked, 'Why did you need to keep both of them happy?'

Sir Theo turned to Ian first. 'You're young,' his tone was accusing. 'You can't begin to understand. I love Zoë, I feel so much for her, more than I've ever felt for anyone in my whole life.' Sir Theo's eyes looked watery. 'And as for little Betsy, she's given my life a whole new purpose. But the more I loved my new family, the guiltier I felt about Isabel, or rather, the guiltier she made me feel. How can I explain? Because I had love and she had none, she made me compensate.' He stared intently into Michael's face. 'Am I making any sense, Inspector?'

Michael thought of Debbie Smith and of Angie, and knew that if it came to the crunch, he'd be offering Angela a more than generous settlement. Yes, he understood Sir Theo perfectly.

Ian Barnes's face still held a look of puzzlement. 'But surely to be loyal to one woman meant you just couldn't be loyal to the other?'

Sir Theo looked toward Michael who came to the

rescue.

'I think I know what Sir Theo means,' he said.

'I'm sorry, inspector, I can't remember what you asked me now?' Theo said.

Michael noticed that his hands were shaking.

'You said that you didn't want to have another row with Zoë, and I asked you if you had many rows?'

'My first instinct, Inspector, is to tell you that it's none of your damned business, but I suppose if I say that, you'll class me as a hostile witness?'

'Put it this way, that attitude won't help you, and it certainly won't help Zoë and it might just hinder us. Our sole aim is to get this business over with as soon as possible, so that we can all carry on living our lives.'

Theo nodded his tired head. 'All right. No, we don't argue often, and when we do, it's always about money. Not just money,— the money I give to Isobel. I never was able to explain it to Zoë.' He opened his hands and looked up toward the ceiling. 'I agreed to give Isobel money, in recompense for the love I'd never given her, even before I met Zoë. Zoë couldn't understand that.'

Theo brought his hands up to his chin. 'You see Issie had made it big, she didn't need my cash. She was a rich woman, she made a fortune from her, what shall I call them, — meetings? Yes, meetings. She'd deny it of course, but we all knew what sort of money she was taking. So you see, it wasn't the money she wanted, she wanted me to be short of it. Suffer a little for my happiness. And frankly, I thought it a fair exchange for Zoë and Betsy.'

Theo got up and began to pace around the room. 'You know, when I left her, Issie that is, I really, really didn't think she'd mind. Our marriage was over. Once she got all that supernatural stuff in her head, — that was it. It's not my thing, you see — all this past life stuff. Overnight she became a vegetarian, booze was banned,' he smiled. 'I used to hide a bottle of scotch in my dressing room. She moved into a separate room, — and all sorts of things like that. She became convinced that I was this Randall chap reincarnated. Then when I picked up with Zoë, she was even more convinced. She was sure I was going to murder her again in this life. Ironic isn't it?'

He sat down again, opposite Michael.

'She wasn't a bad woman, not really, she was just a little crazy. Funnily enough, in the last few weeks she'd almost mellowed. In fact, that last night, when I went down to fix her fuse, I cut myself, — she wouldn't actually touch me, of course, she had a thing about touching anything of mine, especially any of my bodily fluids.'

Michael looked confused.

'You see, she believed that I was, well — evil, not *me* exactly, but the person I used to be, in the last life. She thought that if she came into contact with me, it would somehow contaminate her. When we were together she'd even use her own crockery — wouldn't even wash it up

578

with mine.' He shrugged. 'It's what she believed,' he said. 'Anyway I bathed my hand and she found me a bandage, and she was perfectly reasonable. She even said that it was time we sat down and worked things out.'

He smiled. 'You'd have to know what she was like three years ago to appreciate how far she'd come. I can't describe how mad she was then, she used to do the craziest things. Do you know? Once she sold the flock! Andy 'phoned in a hell of a state. She'd actually advertised my sheep and sold them way below the market value. The first thing that Andy knew about it, was when the buyer came to collect them! Andy did his homework, and found that most of the farm equipment was in the small ads in the Farmer's Weekly. It all took a bit of sorting, I can tell you.'

'But you should have—' Ian began.

'What? Had her thrown into jail? Humiliated her in front of her friends? I thought of it, but you know, I think I'd already humiliated her enough, don't you?'

Michael returned to the subject of Sir Theo's last visit at the Hall on the day that Lady Sheldon-Harris died. 'So you went to the Hall at about?'

'The second time? About six in the evening, I suppose.'

'Fixed her fuse, cut yourself, and? Anything else that's slipped your mind? What did you talk about?'

Theo pulled a face. 'I had a drink of herbal tea, terrible stuff. We talked about Charlotte, and she asked me if I could let her have some money.'

'Who, her or Charlotte?'

'Her of course. You don't understand, Issie always asked me for money.'

'And you refused?'

'I had to, I don't have any.'

'What's happened to Lady Sheldon-Harris's first husband?'

'He's terribly ill, near death's door. Issie was very upset about it. I believe it's going to be a slow and painful illness.' Theo looked down at the floor.

'And your first wife? Do you have an address for her?'

Theo looked miserable. He took a large red address book from the side of the dresser and handed it to Michael. 'You'll find everything in there. Please let me have it back when you've finished with it.' He held his head up straight. 'You can count Anne out, Inspector. She wouldn't enter the Hall. She wouldn't enter the same room as Issie, not even to kill her. I know that for a fact.'

'A bit like Dr Armstrong?'

'Ah, you know about that business then. Stupid man, he always loved Anne, right from the first, but the old fool spent years hating Issie, rather than making himself and Anne happy.'

Theo looked out of the window.

'Take some advice, Inspector. Grab at happiness

whilst it's there, be greedy for it. Unlike sorrow, it doesn't last for long.'

Michael swallowed as the image of Debbie Smith standing by the bathroom door slid into his mind.

'I believe that there was a problem with the shoot last week?'

'Problem? No I don't believe so.' Theo's face looked blank.

'Oh I thought that Lady Sheldon-Harris—'

'I'm sorry, Inspector,' Sir Theo interrupted. 'You mean the business with the gun licenses, and all that? Of course, you'd have a report on it. I must say, I thought it a bit much, your chaps coming on heavy like that. They could have left it until the end of the day, or at least asked the guns to drop the certificates into the station later in the week. There was no need to break up the day.'

'I believe the syndicate came to see you?'

'Hardly the syndicate, Inspector, just one of them. We sorted it out, no problem. I agreed to put in another strip of cover in exchange for his loss. It ended quite amicably, and in future they'll all carry their certificates with them.'

'Did you talk to Lady Sheldon-Harris about it?'

'Now what would have been the point of that? Let her know I was rattled? Give her some ammunition? Besides, in a way, she was right. You hear dreadful things these days. One ought to be certain that everyone has been approved of by the authorities.' He smiled. 'Her timing was a bit out, that's all.'

'You seem very forgiving,' said Ian.

Theo smiled a little more. 'She's dead, Inspector, it's easy to forgive anything when you're sure it can't be repeated. I feel surprisingly kindly toward Issie right now.'

Michael was about to tell Sir Theo that providing the doctors approved, he saw no reason why he shouldn't visit Zoë the following afternoon, so long as a WPC was present and the case wasn't discussed. But then he had a change of heart; he was letting his own situation influence him. Sir Theo could wait, another day would make no difference.

Predictably, once they had left Sir Theo, Ian analyzed every word he'd said. 'Funny how Sir Theo felt loyalty to both women, isn't it?'

Michael winced. 'To tell you the truth, Ian. I understood everything he said, but anyone who hasn't gone through a bit of a rocky time would just think he was talking gobbledegoop.'

Ian shrugged. 'I understood what he said all right. I just didn't see what he was trying to tell us.'

Michael smiled at the distinction.

Chapter 73

Tiggy pushed her food about on her plate, making it into little piles, trying to mash it down in order to make it look less appetizing.

'Eat up, darling,' Lavinia said. 'You can't help Zoë if you're weak with hunger.'

Tiggy swallowed the smallest morsel. No one seemed to understand that food was her enemy, only by controlling her appetite could she feel in charge of her life. She couldn't pinpoint the exact day that the realization had dawned, — when she had known for sure that she was actually fighting an enemy, she only knew that over the years the war had got more intense. More bloody.

'Eat up, darling,' her mother said again. 'You're getting so thin — you'll waste away.' Lavinia smiled but she looked extremely unhappy.

'I'm not very hungry,' Tiggy said. It was a lie, she was starving. All the problems with Zoë served as an excuse, but now she fell back on her loss of appetite. She should have told the truth; told her mother, that if she gave in and indulged herself, then her enemy would win the battle. Every battle lost plunged Tiggy into a deep and terrifying depression. She must always be on her guard, if she gave in and ate, even a little, then she'd immediately be filled with regret and self loathing, a loathing that only making herself vomit would alleviate. Why didn't anyone understand that, why couldn't they see how fat, how out of control, she was getting?

She pushed the food around some more; the roast potatoes glistened in the light, — laughing at her and tempting her. The broccoli was perfectly cooked and looked green and sweet, her mother had tossed it in butter and pine kernels; it was one of her favorite vegetables. The chicken looked plump and succulent.

She put some of the chicken on her fork, then pushed it off again. If she were to eat just one small piece she might be tempted to finish the plate. Even if she could manage to eat just a small piece it would ruin everything. She had to stay trim, trimmer than her mother, she had to make Alex love her best. But she was so hungry. She'd eaten a quarter of an apple for breakfast and sipped a cup of black coffee, and then she'd run around the park for an hour and a half. All that activity should have burned off the calories a bit; maybe she could afford to eat just a little.

How she wished Alex was there, he'd had to go back to London for the day. The twins were over in Kings Lynn picking up some errands and even Betsy was having a nap. Her mother, as usual, had cooked enough food to feed an army, saying that she expected the twins home any minute, but they hadn't as yet arrived, so it meant that all of Lavinia's maternal instincts were lavished on her younger daughter.

She cleared her throat. 'Do you have any salad, Ma?'

'But—' her mother began to protest.

'To tell you the truth, I'm a bit off roast food.'

Lavinia raised her eyebrows.

'Don't look like that,' she said. 'I'm not getting strange fancies, I'm not pregnant or anything.'

Lavinia seemed to wince as if she'd been slapped across the face.

Tiggy looked down at her plate. A baby would solve a lot of things; it was the one thing Lavinia couldn't give Alex. It would tie her to him irrevocably. She'd abandoned precautions months and months ago, but her periods had ceased long before that. The gynecologist said it was because she'd got so thin, how little he knew. He hadn't seen her standing naked in front of a mirror, he'd only seen her lying flat on her back — she must look thinner when she was lying down, because head-on and naked, she looked enormous.

'There's salad in the fridge,' Lavinia said. 'Help yourself.'

Tiggy took her plate through to the kitchen and scraped the meal into the waste bin. She sighed; it felt good to be rid of it.

Her mother had followed her through. 'Hey, that should have gone in the chicken bucket.'

'Ma, you can't feed chicken *on* chicken.'

Her mother sighed. 'Well, Fable would have eaten the meat, it's a waste to bin it.'

Tiggy opened the fridge door, she pulled out two lettuce leaves and a tomato, then she placed the tomato on a board, halved it, threw half in the bin and put the other half on her plate.

Her mother watched her every move.

'Tiggy, there's not enough there to keep a sparrow alive.' She put her arm around her shoulder. 'Darling, I'm worried about you.' Lavinia's smile seemed awkward. 'You haven't got one of those illnesses — Anorexia, or whatever they call it?

'Don't be ridiculous, Ma. I'm just not hungry, that's all. I can't stop worrying about Zoë.' She patted her mother's hand. 'I usually eat like a horse. Anyway, I can't be anorexic, look at the size of me, I'm as big as a house!'

Her mother guided her over to a chair. 'Darling, you're not huge, in fact you're terrifyingly thin. You have a distorted body image. Surely Alex—'

'Alex likes me the way I am,' she snapped getting up from the chair. 'He's not into fat middle-aged women.' Her mother certainly wasn't fat; Tiggy knew that, but she wanted to find some words that would wound.

Lavinia sighed and walked toward the dining-room. At the door she turned and smiled. 'Bring your food through darling, there's some mayonnaise or some French dressing in the fridge, but I don't suppose your appetite will stretch to such high calorie accompaniments.' Her words were loaded with sarcasm.

Tiggy flounced over to the fridge and snatched the bottle of mayonnaise from the shelf; she placed a large spoonful on the side of her plate and followed her mother into the dining room.

'Good heavens,' said Josh as if he'd just woken from a deep sleep. 'You on a diet, Tiggy?'

'No, I am not,' she replied dipping the lettuce leaf into the mayonnaise as if to prove her point.

She stuffed the leaf into her mouth and followed that with the tomato. It was the biggest meal she'd eaten for a week and she felt bloated and guilty. Her conscience immediately began to punish her. If only she'd stuck to the salad and not added the mayonnaise; all salad dressings were terribly fattening, everyone knew that. It was her mother's fault. If she hadn't been so scathing about Tiggy's meal she'd never have been tempted.

'There's treacle tart, with cream, or custard sauce, for pudding.' Lavinia announced, placing the dessert on the table.

Tiggy hadn't even noticed her clearing the table; she'd been too seeped in the misery of her failed diet.

Lavinia cut slices of the tart and placed it on plates. Tiggy leaned over and took the largest piece and topped it with a huge dollop of thick cream.

'Well done, darling,' Lavinia said. 'You have no

idea how happy it makes me to see you eat.

Tiggy looked at her mother through lowered lids. I'll bet it does, she thought, you'd like me to get fat so that Alex stopped fancying me, wouldn't you?

Tiggy ate the first slice of tart in record time and asked for seconds. Her mother looked very pleased, as if she had personally solved all Tiggy's problems. Tiggy ate the second piece of tart, again, very quickly.

She sat back in her chair. She felt disgusted with herself, how could she? How could she have stuffed herself in such a way, it was stupid — ridiculous — what was she thinking of? She must get rid of it; she must, before it turned itself into fat, before it did her any harm.

She excused herself and made her way to the cloakroom, where, with practiced ease she rid herself of her great enemy, her sinful meal.

When she returned to the dining room, her parents were talking about Zoë. Josh smiled at her. 'I was just saying to your mother,' he said. 'Thank God we don't have to worry about you, Tiggy. Thank God you're settled and happy with your lot.'

Chapter 74

Michael spent another steamy night with Debbie, and, as she was to be off work on Saturday and Sunday, he was promised a weekend he would always remember. But the thrill and excitement of Debbie had incubated problems for him. Guilt, and fear of discovery, rested heavily on his shoulders. He'd spoken to Angela on the telephone, but briefly, and for the first time ever, she seemed contented with her own company.

'I'll try and get home for a few hours this weekend,' he'd said.

'No, it's all right, love, I've made some plans.' She'd told him then, all about her little dog. He'd had the strangest reaction; he'd felt almost jealous of the little beast. He couldn't work his feeling out at all. He should be pleased, he should be delighted, so why wasn't he?

'I'm going to take him up to the common,' Angie said.

'Great, I'll come with you.'

'No, that's all right, Mike. I know you're up to your eyes in it.'

'No, I'll come, Barnes can take over here.'

'I've arranged to meet a friend, Mike.'

'Oh,' he said and didn't know why he felt so rejected.

It was perfect, Angela was happy, and that left the field clear for he and Debbie. So why didn't he feel elated? He tried to put his feeling in order. It wasn't jealousy at all, it was more a kind of envy. Angela seemed to have found contentment, whilst his world was reeling in turmoil.

He admonished himself. He didn't have the time nor the energy to brood on his or Angie's feelings, he had a case to work. He'd leave his personal life to one side, — things would probably work themselves out; they usually did.

On Friday Michael made his way to Norwich, the search team having turned up the name of Lady Sheldon-Harris's lawyer. Ian was left at Fenshaw Police Station to compile reports.

The offices of Crouch, Crouch and Thrumbrell, were just off Elm Hill and Michael had to park the car what felt like miles away and make his way on foot. On arriving at the office, he was asked to wait for what seemed to him an intolerable length of time. He was reminded of his own tactic of keeping a suspect waiting; hoping nerves might snap.

The office he was eventually shown into was tiny, no bigger, he later told Ian, than his own bathroom at home. Although the office had impressive wood paneling, its lack of size inspired no confidence in Michael, and he wondered if clients felt the same as he. The desk was perfectly clear except for a blotter pad with a clean sheet of blotting paper in it and an inkstand with a pen next to it. A bookcase stood against one wall; on the lower shelf were several scrolls of paper displaying impressive red seals. On the shelf above stood a handful of law books, no more than a dozen in total. Michael looked around him and thought back to his little office in Fenshaw, with its muddle of papers and files.

Julie Saunders was a woman in her late forties. Her hair was cut in a short, rather severe style. She wore a crisp white blouse and a full black skirt. Despite her gilt earrings, hint of mascara and delicately applied lipstick, she had a masculine air about her.

Aggressive, Michael thought, — a theory confirmed when she spoke in her deep, slow drawl. I bet she hates blokes like me, he surmised.

She shook hands with him, seated herself and indicated that he should do the same. 'Now Inspector, tell me, how can I help you?'

'I believe you represented the late Lady Sheldon-Harris of Garrick Hall?'

Her eyes widened, and, for a split second, her mouth literally fell open. 'Do you mean to say that dear Issie's dead?' Her voice was filled with disbelief. Michael wasn't sure if her shock was genuine or not. The murder had been featured in both national and local newspapers; could it be that she hadn't seen any of them?

'I'm afraid so, sometime on Monday night,— or the early hours of Tuesday,' Michael said, rather coolly. The affection she showed toward Isobel Sheldon-Harris, didn't sit well with him, it didn't quite fit. He was about to say more, but the solicitor interrupted.

'But why wasn't I informed? Why were we not told? And how exactly did she die? I only spoke to her on Monday.'

Michael drew in a deep breath. 'To answer your first question, I'm informing you now, and I'm afraid she was murdered. I'm surprised you haven't heard, it's been all over the media.'

She waved her hand, as if to say she never bothered with such things. Then she leaned back in her chair and brought her hand up to her face and shaded her eyes in a dramatic, and Michael guessed, an uncharacteristic gesture.

'Murdered? Are you sure, Inspector? Are you sure?'

'Yes, very sure.'

'But how? Are you sure it wasn't suicide — she was a very tormented woman.'

Michael felt deeply irritated; he hadn't had enough sleep. Debbie had taken it out of him, he'd really have liked to have been curled up in bed, preferable with Debbie by his side.

'Unless she was a contortionist, and managed to strangle herself from behind. I think we can assume it was murder.'

Julie Saunders put her hand up to her neck. 'Strangled,' she said. 'You do know about the local farmer that was hung for—'

'Oh yes, but I think the murderer lives in this life, not one that's gone before,— nor the one to come.'

'I really don't like your attitude, Inspector. There's no need to mock, you know. Stranger things have happened, and Issie fervently believed that she'd die of strangulation.'

'You believe in all that, do you?'

Julie Saunders shifted her eyes about the room. 'She was very good you know, she told me things that she couldn't possible have known.'

'Oh yes?' Michael said and smiled.

'I've never quite understood why policemen don't receive some sort of training, to help cope with breaking the news of a bereavement.' She looked at him with small hard eyes.

Michael was unperturbed. 'We do receive training, Madam, but we usually reserve our skills for the victims relatives, or very close friends. Correct me if I'm wrong, but I understood you to be neither.'

Her face visibly hardened, but she did not speak.

'However, I'm sorry, madam, if I've upset you.' His tone of voice betrayed the fact that he was very far from sorry. 'Now, can we get down to business?'

Julie Saunders had made a quick recovery, and spoke in her low slow drawl. 'What is it you what to know?'

'Everything, of course. Every little detail.'

They had an immediate dislike for each other. Michael hated this sort of woman and she apparently hated his sort of man. She smiled and raised her eyebrows.

'Everything? Well that might take some time. You're sure you want everything?' Her smile was insincere.

'Please?' he said.

'Very well. I'll ask Cassandra to locate Lady Sheldon-Harris's file.' She spoke into the telephone and moments later, Cassandra, a drab woman who did not aspire to her name, appeared carrying four large navy-blue files stuffed with papers. She placed them on the desk and left, returning a few moments later with four more files of a similar size and again two minutes later with two more. It was Michael's turn for an open-mouthed stare.

'You asked for everything,' Julie Saunders said smugly.

'Hell! How long have you been looking after Lady Sheldon-Harris's affairs?'

'Almost four years, since her husband walked out on her.'

'Perhaps, Miss Saunders, you'd like to save me some time and trouble and tell me what's in these files?'

Her face showed him that she'd like to do neither. But she did briefly describe the background of Sir Theo's defection. It was interesting hearing it from Lady Sheldon-Harris's point of view. Michael couldn't help thinking of

Angie.

'Why didn't she just divorce him?'

'She would have done, but only in her good time, and on her terms. Let the swine wait, that was our tactic.' A smile played on her lips.

'I suppose after five years he could have divorced her?'

'Yes, you're right, but only up to a point. You have a layman's simplified understanding of the law.' She spoke as if Michael himself was simple minded. 'You see, Sir Theo filed for a divorce when he and Lady Sheldon-Harris had been apart for two years. Of course we advised Lady Sheldon-Harris to refuse, and we told him that he would have to wait for a further three years. Then this year, we told him that Lady Sheldon-Harris would agree to divorce him as long as she could bring forth her own petition on the grounds of his adultery. It was rather sweet really, he was so relieved, and he withdrew his petition so that Lady Sheldon-Harris could submit hers. There can only be one petition in the courts at a time.'

'And?'

Julie Saunders smiled. 'I'm afraid she changed her mind again. So poor Sir Theo had to start, all over again. Clever, wasn't it? You see, Sir Theo had to be persuaded that he must make adequate financial provision for her, and he simply wasn't willing to do that.'

'And how long did you say that this has been going

on?'

She smiled. 'It could have gone on much longer. I got the feeling that Sir Theo was not keen on a big court case. He was afraid, you see. He wanted to have his cake and to eat it.'

'What was he afraid of?'

'Losing his money, of course. He thought he'd been very clever, he got rid of all his assets. He did a sale and leaseback on the estate. But he still owned the Hall outright, so we felt it only fair that he keep the tenancy and we had the Hall. He would have agreed in the end, you know. A husband can't just throw his wife on the scrap heap when he finds a younger more palatable replacement. No, Inspector, Sir Theo was about to pay dearly for his pleasures.'

Michael swallowed. Was that what he was doing, throwing Angie on the scrap heap?

'But didn't he do the sale and leaseback in the early nineties? He had a big debt to pay, didn't he?'

'Lloyds? Huh, yes, well, that was his excuse, but Lady Sheldon-Harris was pretty sure that he'd salted that money away, probably in a Swiss bank account or an off-shore company. No, no, he'd been planning to leave her as far back as the early nineties, Inspector. He'll deny it of course, but that's what that was about. And if it had come to court we'd have convinced the judge as much, and he knew it.'

'But surely, this state of play couldn't have gone on forever.'

'As I said, Inspector. He'd have given in eventually. It really was only a question of wearing him down. We are in the process of negotiating with his lawyer. But of course, it isn't particularly easy. Property values have risen, and the Hall will have to be revalued again. Sir Theo was told he had to pay for the new valuation and so he was tending to drag his feet. These things take time, Inspector.'

'Lady Sheldon-Harris has run out of time,' he said, but his thoughts wondered to Miss Saunders fat fees.

'Did he do it?'

'Who?'

'Sir Theo,— did he kill her?'

'I don't know, Madam. Do you?'

She smiled indulgently at him.

'How much was she worth?' Michael said.

'Without the settlement?'

'Well she didn't get a settlement, did she?'

'I don't know, she certainly wasn't very well off.' Julie Saunders shifted in her chair.

'I thought she made a lot of money from her Spiritualism?'

'I've no idea, we never really discussed her personal finances.'

'But surely, if she was worth a packet. And Sir Theo wasn't worth as much, she could have ended up paying him!'

Julie Saunders spoke cautiously and with deliberation. 'I think she put her little bits and pieces off shore. It was her money Inspector, money she'd earned through her own talent. He had no right to that money.'

'Legally?'

'Morally,' she said.

'I thought you lot dealt in the law, not morals.'

She gave him a long hard look.

'Who benefits? Do you have her will?'

'It's in the vaults. I'll get Cassandra to fetch it.'

Whilst they were waiting, she said, 'It's the tiniest bit embarrassing, Inspector, but I know I'm one of the beneficiaries.'

'Yes?'

'She's left me some of her jewelry, you see, in a past life, Issie was my sister, well, that's what she believed, and what with Charlotte . . . this is just a tad delicate, Inspector. But Charlotte probably won't get married . . . '

Michael was enjoying her discomfort.

'You see, she's chosen a different way of life, and when the will was made, Issie wasn't very pleased about it. In fact she was quite shocked. She's come round to it now, and I expect she would have changed her will but—'

Cassandra entered with another file, this time a thin brown one.

Miss Saunders took it, and dismissed her.

'Here we are, apart from a few small bequests, the jewelry to me, and something to her cleaner and gardener, she left all her personal wealth to her ex-husband Gerald Bridges. I believe they made identical wills.'

'Nothing to her daughter? Nothing at all?'

'I suppose the daughter would have got it when the ex-husband died. I know Issie hoped by then . . . Charlotte would . . . well you know, be more normal.'

Michael watched carefully, Julie Saunders's façade was beginning to crumble.

'She was always here you know . . . Charlotte, always on at me to persuade her mother to settle. She didn't see that the whole point was to make Sir Theo suffer. Men like him ought to suffer. They can't just walk out on their wives,— discard them as if they were empty crisp packets. It's not fair and it's not right.'

Her face had become rather red. Michael would have liked to ask how long it had been since Julie Saunders's husband had left her. But he didn't.

Michael turned a page in his notebook. 'Do you have an address for Mr Bridges?'

'You can't possibly think it was him? The man's terminally ill. I remember Issie telling me about him some time ago, she was terribly worried about him.' She frowned. 'She may even have spoken about him when I spoke to her on Monday.'

'You spoke to Lady Sheldon-Harris on Monday?

How can you be sure it was Monday?'

'Because it was the only day, apart from today, that I've been in the office.'

'And could you tell me the nature of that call?'

'Oh, the usual sort of things. She wanted an injunction, to stop Zoë Elliot from using the footpath near the house, and she wanted some redecoration done, she wanted me to write to Sir Theo's lawyers, and . . . '

'And what?'

'Well, she was getting softer on him. Not the girl — never the girl. But I felt as far as Sir Theo was concerned . . . well, I felt she was weakening her resolve. I had to remind her . . . '

'To make him suffer?'

She looked at her watch. 'Is there anything else?'

'I don't know, is there?'

She drew her lips together. Her nostrils seemed to grow visibly larger. 'I'm a very busy woman Inspector.'

'I'll have all these files collected, if that's all right?' And because he could see that she was about to protest, he added curtly. 'You'll get a receipt.'

He turned at the door. 'I'll let you know when the funeral is. No doubt you'll want to go?'

'Go? I don't think so, Inspector. I don't usually attend client's funerals.'

Michael was left wondering what to make of her. The interview had begun with poor dear Issie, and ended with, only a client.

He said a brief prayer that, should it come to divorce, Angie would not find her way to the doors of Crouch, Crouch and Thrumbrell.

Chapter 75

Saturday, four days after Lady Isobel Sheldon-Harris was found dead, dawned clear and bright, with a sharp hoar frost to remind everyone that autumn was rapidly making way for winter.

The inquest had been set for the following Monday, and Michael knew he'd have to work hard in order to assemble all the facts ready for presentation.

Debbie was going off to buy Christmas presents. 'Bit early, isn't it?' he'd said. 'It's not even November.'

'I like to be organized,' she replied. 'Perhaps you could help me by telling me what you've put on Santa's list?'

He laughed. 'Nothing,' he said, 'except you,' and he kissed her. 'Christmas came early for me this year. I've got all I want now.' He kissed her again. 'Now be a good girl, and don't spend too much money.'

How had this happened? They were like an old married couple, no, not that, more like teenage lovers, but not that either, there was no anxiety in their relationship. All the anxiety and fear was outside, beyond their world. Ian knew what was going on, he could hardly help but know. But Michael didn't care. He was fifty miles away from home, fifty miles away from the nagging clinging Angie. And he didn't give a damn. He would grasp life whilst it was on offer and if he had to pay later, then so be it.

Ian was pacing up and down when he got to the office.

'All sorted is it, Ian? Know exactly how it happened, do you?'

Ian Barnes pulled a face. 'We should know, we've got all the facts, there may be one or two pieces missing, but—'

'But you're as foxed as me, right?'

'I still think it's got something to do with Zoë Elliot.'

'Well of course it has, but only indirectly.'

'Will they let us see her today?'

'We're to 'phone at eleven. But I did think we'd let Sir Theo visit her, we'll have a WPC in the room, of course, and—'

Ian was giving him a very funny look.

'What, what is it?'

'It's his blood.'

'What?'

'Under Lady Sheldon-Harris's nails. It's his.'

Michael sat down heavily. 'Good God, and the semen?'

'Not his. He probably planted it, but it's definitely not his. The blood is though, there's no doubt, she must have scratched him, and in doing so she picked up the real killers DNA.'

'Good God,' Michael said again.

'Still think you ought to let him and Zoë get together?'

'I want forensics back at that cottage. I want every item of his clothing brought in, including the stuff he's wearing.'

'But we know he was in the Hall. Didn't he say he changed a bulb in the morning and fixed a fuse in the evening?'

Michael sighed. 'Of course, and he cut himself, and Lady Sheldon-Harris bandaged it for him, that's how the blood got under her nails.'

'The last time he spoke he said that she wouldn't touch him, she believed that he was evil and that she'd be contaminated or something. Is he now saying she bandaged it for him?'

'No, but it's what he will say, isn't it? We have to have more to go on than that.'

'Well, what have we got?'

'Front door locked, back door locked. Key to the back door on the floor. So Chummy was either let in, or he had his own key, and he pushed her key out when he put his key in. Then he either locked himself out or he pushed the key back through the letterbox. Take your pick, there's only her prints on the key.'

'Who *had* keys?'

'According to Charlotte and Ruth Sparks, no one.

Lady Sheldon-Harris was funny about giving out her door keys.'

'Motive? Well, only two really — Sir Theo and Zoë Elliot. Unless you think a bitter twisted solicitor capable of murder in order to get her hands on a few bits of jewelry. The daughter had nothing to gain, — everything's gone to the ex-husband. Who, incidentally, we should find and pay a visit.

Go and see Charlotte Bridges, she's staying at The Knight's Gate, it's in Haymarket Lane. I've told them it will be at least a week before they can have access to the Hall and sort out dear Mama's things. Get her dad's address.' Michael paused, his forehead creased. 'And, Ian, ask her where she was on Monday night.'

Charlotte Bridges and Flora Gouch were in the hotel lounge when Ian Barnes arrived. There was, it seemed, some sort of discussion going on.

'It's all right for you to be so bloody calm, you're not involved are you? I tell you, Flora, I nearly had a bloody fit when I saw his will.' Charlotte lamented. She was pacing up and down. 'And to think of that woman wearing mother's diamond and emerald ring, it's too awful to think about.'

Flora seemed perfectly calm. 'It's all right now though, isn't it? I mean, okay, so you didn't get the jewelry or The Hall, but—'

'Shut up and listen,' Charlotte snapped. 'I'm just

trying to explain,'

'Can I just say one thing?' Flora asked.

'Do shut up.'

'But, Lottie—'

'What?' Charlotte sounded very irritated.

'There's a policeman eavesdropping on our conversation.'

Charlotte looked both horrified and angry.

'How dare you?' She spat. 'How dare you spy on bereaved people.'

'I thought it would be tactless to intrude directly on your grief,' Ian said moving forward with his notebook in his hand.

He undid his topcoat and sat down. 'Just a few questions, the usual things,— only you were a bit upset on Tuesday, Miss Bridges.'

'I had just found my mother murdered.'

'I appreciate that, Miss. That's why I've come back today, to clear a few things up.'

'Go ahead,' Flora said. 'I'm sure this won't take long, will it?'

Ian smiled at the round-faced girl. 'Not long at all, Miss. I just need to know where you both were on Monday night.'

The girls looked at each other. Then Charlotte put her hand out and rested it on Flora's shoulder. 'We were at home, together, we had an early night, didn't we, darling?'

Flora blushed, and, as a consequence, Ian Barnes blushed too. 'Yes. Yes,' she said. 'That's right, we went to bed early.'

'And home is?'

'You've got our address, it's a two and a half hour drive away,' Charlotte snapped.

'Fine — just one more thing, I wonder if you could give me your father's address, Miss Bridges?'

Ian thought he saw Charlotte blanch, but it could have been a trick of the light. Her dad was very ill; poor girl, one parent murdered and the other near death's door.

'What on earth for?'

'He's the beneficiary of your mother's will.'

'So? You can't believe he had anything to do with it. He's a sick man, he couldn't possibly—'

'Just the address, please, Miss.'

She sighed, took his notebook from his hand and wrote out an address for a house on the South Coast and handed it to him. 'He's not there at the moment, he's in hospital having chemotherapy.'

'And the address of the hospital?'

'You're not going to bother him there, are you? He'll be home soon.'

Ian bit into his bottom lip. 'No, no of course not.' He shut and opened his notebook. 'Finally, have either of you thought of anything that might help to find your mother's killer?'

'She wasn't *my* mother,' Flora said. 'My mother lives in Acton, and she hasn't got an enemy in the world. She plays bingo every Thursday and that's as near as she's ever come to a fortune.' She was eyeing Charlotte as she spoke.

'Stop it, Flora,' Charlotte said. 'Mr Barnes will think we're always fighting.'

Ian snapped his notebook shut. 'Just a lovers tiff I expect. Me and my missus are always spatting,' he said seriously but barely supressed a smirk.

He thanked them for their help, and reserved the right to go back and question them again should the need arise.

He'd got in his car, and started the engine when his mobile rang. It was the desk sergeant. They were looking for Inspector Harper, the hospital had just telephoned. Zoë Elliot was insisting on discharging herself, and they wanted to know what they were to do with her.

Chapter 76

It wasn't how Zoë had planned it; it was just the way it happened. Inspector Harper had arrived at the hospital and offered her a lift home. And for some stupid reason that she couldn't quite fathom, she felt grateful to him. Grateful that he was taking her home and not taking her back to the police station. But then, when she'd asked if she was no longer under arrest; if he was letting her go, he'd looked sad and said, 'for the time being' in a non-committed sort of way. She hated him again then, and wondered if she should have taken Tiggy's advice and stayed in hospital where, Tiggy assured her, no one could touch her. But she was desperate to see Theo again, and they were fending him off, she knew that. Even her mother hadn't been allowed to see her. Tiggy was the only one, she'd brought her clothes and toiletries in.

The bruising had turned to a livid rosy purple, but the cut on her lip was healing, and her ribs felt a lot better now that they were strapped up. But every time she coughed, her chest still vibrated and produced a searing pain. It was, the doctor said, because she had a touch of pneumonia in her lower lobes, whatever that meant; it wasn't uncommon in injuries such as hers he reassured her and the antibiotics she'd been given would soon kick in and sort it out; it was just a matter of time. And that was the one thing she had, plenty of time.

The doctors and nurses had been wonderful, so kind and understanding, but all the kindness and understanding in the world couldn't alter the facts. She'd been raped and beaten by a man she had once loved. And she was accused of murdering the wife of the man she now loved, and it was all very well for counsellors and doctors to say they understood. The fact was, no one would ever understand the injustice of it all, it was wasn't their fault, it was just a cruel, mean, fact.

With Tiggy's advice, 'don't say a word unless I'm with you,' ringing in her ears, she slid into the car beside Inspector Harper, and fastened her seat belt.

Michael smiled. 'How'd you feel?'

She tried to shrug her shoulders, but the action hurt her chest. 'Fine,' she was going to say. But tears pricked her eyes, and she came out with. 'Totally depressed and exhausted.'

'The sooner we get you home, the better then,' he said, and he looked at her with anxiety.

'Does Sir Theo know you're coming?'

She shook her head, but even that seemed to hurt her chest.

'He'll get a nice surprise then. Is Betsy with your mum?'

She smiled; she'd never heard anyone call Lavinia, mum. Ma or mother, or mummy. Never mum. 'Yes, I'll 'phone her later, I need to talk to Theo first.'

Michael nodded.

The rest of the journey was conducted in silence, and it wasn't until they neared the entrance of Garrick Hall that Michael spoke again.

'You must tell us who did this to you. You know that, don't you?'

'Supposing I don't know who did it?'

'Then you must tell us what you do know, and we'll do our utmost to find him.'

She nodded, she could understand the rape, well almost. Steve had been drunk and he'd always regarded her as a very willing partner. Indeed, sometimes they'd played hard-to-get games, and why did she agree to meet him in the woods if she had no intention of . . . Yes, she could understand the sex bit. The part that puzzled her, was how nasty he'd turned, kicking her and hurting her. She'd have never have believed that of Steve, never.

They entered through the main gates and Michael drew up outside Garrick Cottage. The door of the lodge flew open, but it was Lavinia, not Theo, that rushed forward and opened the car door.

'Ma,— what are you doing here?'

'Tiggy rang me, and, — oh, my darling, my poor child, she told me what happened to you. Why didn't you tell us? Why didn't you confide in us?'

Zoë allowed her mother to help her to her feet. Michael got her bag from the car, and walked with it to the door.

'Does Theo know?' Zoë asked.

Lavinia shook her head. I thought you'd want to tell him yourself. She'd ignored Michael, she hadn't even nodded her head to him, but now she spoke. 'You'll get him, Inspector, won't you? He went back home first thing on Tuesday morning. He won't be able to deny it, I saw him leave and return.'

'No, Mummy, I don't want any charges brought I—'

'Who are we talking about?' Michael asked.

'Steve,' Lavinia said as Theo appeared around the corner with Bracken at his heels.

'What about him?' Theo said. Then he set eyes on Zoë. 'Oh God, you're home. Oh, darling, thank God.'

She winced as he put his arm around her.

'He raped her, Theo, all this nonsense about her falling in the farm yard. That's where Steve was that night, hurting Zoë.' Lavinia's eyes were sparkling and her face was red and animated.

Theo's face had turned into a stricken mask.

Lavinia put her hand up to her forehead. 'Oh, God, I'm sorry, I wasn't going to say anything. I was going to let Zoë tell you . . . I just feel so bloody angry . . . I'm sorry.' She turned to Zoë. 'I'm sorry, darling.'

Zoë could bear it no longer, the spell in hospital seemed to have made her weaker, not stronger, and she staggered.

Theo caught hold of her, and the policeman and Lavinia followed them into the cottage, where, settled on the sofa with all three of them fussing over her, Zoë explained what had happened on the night that Isabel was murdered.

She was tearful, and every other sentence was interspersed with, 'Theo, I'm so sorry,' but eventually most of the story came out, finishing with, 'And so you see, I thought I heard his car start up, so I went back the way I had come. But I couldn't have heard it, because he was still there, and I tripped and fell and— Theo, he kicked me, just as if I was a piece of dirt, he kicked me, and . . . '

'Yes darling? Then what?'

'He just went away. I waited for a while, I thought he might come back, but he didn't, then I got up and I made my way back here.'

'Which way did you come, did you pass the Hall? What time was it?' Michael asked.

'I was in the Land Rover, I came through the village. I don't know what time it was, the middle of the night.'

Michael had his notebook out. 'Where can I find this man?'

Lavinia was about to speak. But Zoë spoke first.

'No, I don't want it taken any further, let it be.'

'You'd better let the police have him, Zoë, because

if I get to him first I'll—' Theo began.

'Excuse me,' Michael interrupted. 'But this isn't actually up to you, this is a police matter, and like it or not, I'm still investigating Lady Sheldon-Harris's murder.'

'He had nothing to do with that,' Zoë said. 'I've just told you where he was, I've just told you what happened.'

'You're still protecting him after what he did to you?' Theo said.

'It's not a question of protection, it's a question of the truth,' she replied.

'The truth is, he raped you, he could have killed you, and he should be made to pay.'

'And his family, Ailsa and the children, should they pay too?'

Michael coughed. 'This is getting us nowhere. The thing is, Zoë, like it or not, Steve, — what's his last name?'

'Jarvis,' Lavinia volunteered.

'Steve Jarvis was out and about, on this estate, at the time of Lady Sheldon-Harris's death. And so it seems, were you.'

'She's told you what happened, for God's sake.'

'Then she won't mind if I verify it, will she?' he sighed. 'I'm sorry, Zoë, but I do have a job to do.'

Zoë couldn't speak; she hadn't intended telling Theo in front of anyone else, let alone her mother and this stupid dumb policeman. And she hadn't intended dropping

Steve in it, in fact she'd been very careful not to use his name. She never wanted to see Steve Jarvis ever again, she wanted the whole thing put to one side, where it would rot and be forgotten. She put her hand down and rested it on her stomach. But would she be allowed to forget? She hadn't told Theo that bit, and she hadn't told him about going to Dr Armstrong for the morning-after pill either.

Chapter 77

Tiggy adjusted the sleeve of her smart navy suit; the woman in front of her was rabbiting on. It was typical, how come she'd ended up with this particular client? She didn't deal in criminal law, or at least she wasn't supposed to. But there'd been a lot of snide remarks about her dealing in it when it suited her, they were referring to her sister Zoë's case of course; and there'd been no one available to see Mrs Smith as Janet had gone down sick, so Tiggy had drawn the short straw.

'So you see, I went and bailed him out and then—'

Tiggy was jolted into speech. 'What do you mean you bailed him out? He beats you up and then you go and—'

'Yeah, well, it's like I said, I'm stupid, aint I?'

'If a man hit me I'd leave him in goal to rot.'

'Oh, would you?' The woman said mimicking Tiggy's upper class accent. 'That just shows 'ow much you know about love, don't it?'

Tiggy moistened her lips; she shouldn't have commented. It was her job to listen and advise, not condemn. But her sentiments were not the same as Mrs Smith's, not the same at all. Steve Jarvis should be thrown in goal and the key should be thrown away, there was no two ways about it.

'There's worse things than getting beat up. Men can treat you worse than that, you know. As long as they loves yer, then you can forgive 'em anything.'

Tiggy had the uncomfortable feeling that the woman was reading her mind. She was unhappy referring to Mrs Smith as a gypsy. It seemed not quite politically correct, nevertheless that's what she was, a true Romany at that, her deeply lined skin was a deep mahogany colour, her long black hair was streaked with grey, and she wore copious amounts of heavy gold jewelry

Tiggy dug her fingers into the roots of her hair; she ought to be at Hulver. Her mother had 'phoned to say that Zoë had discharged herself from the hospital. She ought to be there, making sure that Tiggy didn't say something she shouldn't.

'So 'ow much is this going to cost me?' The woman asked, her eyes narrowing into two black slits.

Tiggy was about to suggest that she ask the clerk on the way out when the woman cut in.

'You got problems, aint you, Dearie? Give's yer 'and, let me 'ave a look.'

Tiggy swallowed. Problems — her? Well if you disregarded the fact that the man she lived with was in love with her mother, and her beloved sister was being accused of murder, and she had an uncontrollable eating disorder, then of course she didn't have problems.

'Come 'ere, lets 'ave a look.'

Tiggy wanted to say that she wouldn't dream of having her palm read, but all the same, she thrust her hand across the desk.

The gypsy studied it, and with a worried expression, she looked up at Tiggy.

'You've got trouble ahead, Dearie. You're crossed in love. Look — see,' she pointed to Tiggy's palm. 'Someone's not being quite straight with you, Dearie.'

Tiggy wanted to say that Alex was being perfectly straight with her. He'd never pretended that he'd stopped loving her mother, maybe it was her mother that wasn't being straight. Maybe her mother still loved Alex?'

Tiggy snatched her hand away, she didn't believe in all that nonsense.

'I think we should get on, Mrs—'

'Madam Maureen — that's what they all calls me, it's my professional name so to speak. Look,' she made a grab for Tiggy's hand. 'Why don't we just swap our expertise? You do the legal stuff and I'll tell yer fortune, exchange is no robbery, now is it?'

Tiggy smiled. 'Unfortunately, I can't do that, I only work here and—'

'Who's to know though, Dearie? Who's to know?'

'Me, I'd know.'

The gypsy woman rolled her eyes.

'Shall we continue?' Tiggy asked.

Mrs Smith sighed. 'Well, all right, so as I was

saying, I bailed him out and I takes him back to the caravan. Only whilst I were gone, I'd shut the dogs up in the van and my friend comes to see me and the stupid cow lets them out.'

'And that's when they savaged the farmer's sheep?'

'Yeah, well, so yer see, it weren't my fault, can't 'ave been, can it? Can't 'ave been Rose's fault neither.'

'Rose-a-Lee?' Tiggy asked incredulously.

'Yeah, she tells fortunes an' all, but she's no good at it. She just tells 'em what they want to 'ear. She's not a true Romany you see, her family come from Poland during the war. She's not one of us.'

Tiggy nodded as if she understood.

'Yeah, well, as I said it were either Rose's fault for letting them out, or it were 'im — Bill — 'cause if he 'adn't 'ave needed me to bail 'im out, I wouldn't 'ave left the dogs, would I?'

'I see your logic,' Tiggy said, 'but I'm afraid the court won't see it that way.'

'Then they bloody ought.'

Tigyy smiled. 'Yes, well — I think the best thing you can do is plead guilty, but we'll tell them the circumstances and hope they'll go lightly on you.'

'And then what?'

'They'll probably fine you, and . . . ' Tiggy paused. 'They may easily decide that the dogs should be put down.'

'What? Caesar and Samson? They can't make me do that, can they?'

'The dogs did attack a flock of ewes with lambs at foot.' Tiggy referred to a sheet of paper. 'Eight lambs were killed and another three had to be destroyed, along with four ewes.'

'That weren't the dogs fault. They panicked, stupid animals. If they 'adn't 'ave run all over the place, then Caesar and Samson wouldn't have chased them. Rose saw it, she'll tell yer.'

Tiggy moistened her lips; the woman was behaving in a very stupid way. How was she supposed to cope with ignorance on this scale?

'I'm afraid the court won't see it that way, Mrs Smith.' She looked at her watch. 'I'm afraid our time's up. My advice would be to plead guilty with mitigating circumstances, and ask the court to show leniency toward the dogs, and make sure you keep them under control.'

Madam Maureen rose to her feet, and grabbing Tiggy's hand in both of hers' she solemnly shook it. 'Oh, dear, oh, dear, always such trouble.' Her black eyes darted first down at Tiggy's palm and then up at her face. 'But I'll tell you what, I'd rather double my troubles, than 'ave 'alf of yours, Dearie.'

Tiggy gave an involuntary shudder as she opened the door and wished her client goodbye.

Chapter 78

'No, Ian, the local lads can't question him. I want him brought down here and I want him today. Send someone to fetch him.' Michael was irritated, it should have been obvious that he'd want to interview Steve Jarvis himself.

'It's Saturday, and it's a hell of a drive,' Ian said.

'It's a hell of a crime, murder and rape, Ian. Someone will want the overtime.'

Ian compressed his lips. 'What charge?'

'Stick with the murder, we'll see if he uses the same alibi as Zoë Elliot.'

'He's hardly likely to do that, is he?'

'He may decide it's the lesser of the two evils.'

It was almost one o'clock. Michael had arranged to meet Debbie in the bar of the Kings Head. He looked at his watch, he was running late; he rushed up to his room, splashed his face with water, ran a brush through his hair and presented himself in the bar.

Debbie was deep in conversation with the barman when Michael joined her; she was already sipping a glass of orange juice. Michael got himself half a pint of beer and nodded toward one of the little tables on the edge of the room.

'See-yer Debs,' the barman said.

'Yes,' she replied, 'See-you Jason.'

'Friend of yours?' Michael asked.

'You forget, I was born and brought up in Fenshaw.'

They seated themselves at the table.

Debbie took a sip of her drink and said, 'There's things you should tell me, and there's things I should tell you.'

'I know you're twenty-eight,' he said.

'I don't know how old you are, but—'

'Too old for you, that's for sure, but I guess you're referring to the fact that I'm married?'

'Seems to be a bigger stumbling block than your age.'

'How about you? You're not going to tell me you're married, because I know you're not, unless it happened in the last twenty-four hours, but is there someone? Someone special?' He clenched his teeth, he didn't really want to know, but she was sort of forcing the issue.

'Yes, there's someone very special. That's why we need to talk.'

He slumped back in his chair, so that was it, it had just been a one-night stand, well, a three night stand, three wonderful nights. But it wasn't just the sex; it was the way she was, the way people warmed to her. She wasn't showy or snobby, and she listened to what people said, and she sympathized without being overpowering.

'Shall we cut the talk till later? Let's go to bed, shall we?'

'Mike, this is serious.'

He closed his eyes, if he didn't say it, he'd spend the rest of his life regretting it. 'I've fallen for you, Debbie, that's pretty serious too.'

'I know, Mike, but there's something I should tell you.'

'About this someone special? I'd rather not know about him, if it's all the same to you.'

Disappointment was gnawing away inside him. If she didn't go on about it, he could just about laugh it off, pretend that it didn't matter that much, pretend that his great big policeman's heart wasn't breaking. What a fool he was, thinking that a girl like Debbie could be serious about a man like him.

'Mike,— you fool, you know all about the someone special, you look him in the eyes every time you shave.'

Say it again, he wanted to say, just so as I know I've got the meaning right. But she was still talking.

'The thing is, Mike, my family's not that well up in the world. My dad's a carpenter and my mum's a cleaner. Although she's grandly called a chambermaid, she's really little more than a cleaner.'

He smiled, he realized that he was sweating, he was literally hot under his collar with relief. 'Where do you think I come from then? Buck House? Is that the best you can do for a confession?' he took a gulp of his beer. 'I can do much better than that. I've got a wife that I don't love. A marriage that died years ago and a lover I'd kill for.'

'Oh, Mike, you don't mind?'

'About what? Being married to someone else? Of course I mind. But that's the state of play.'

'No, you fool, about my mum being a cleaner?'

'Do you mind?'

'No, she's my mum, she's done a lot for me and my brother, but I thought *you* might mind. She's asked you for Sunday lunch, you see, and I really want you to come. But you better be prepared, — we don't live in a posh house. And for my parents it's called Sunday dinner, not lunch.'

He was smiling at her, shaking his head, loving her with all his heart.

'It's a nice house, — my dad's done all sorts of fancy things in it. But at the end of the day it's still a council house, least it was before they bought it.'

He put his hand on hers; it looked tiny in comparison to his. 'I think they'll mind far more when they discover that I'm married than I'll mind about them, Debbie.'

'I already told them, you've already met my mum, you see.'

'What?'

'She works here, she does your room.'

Michael nodded. 'I see, then I'll have to be a lot more tidy in future, won't I? I wouldn't like your mum to think I wasn't housetrained.'

She laughed, but then went serious again. 'And your wife, what will you do about your wife?'

'What would you like me to do?'

'Divorce her, of course,' Debbie looked down at her shoes and added in a very soft voice. 'Divorce her, and marry me.' She looked up into his eyes. 'I know it's not that easy, but you did ask.'

He put his arm around her. 'You're right, it's not that easy, and there's our jobs to think of. It would go down like a lead balloon at Barkhampton. Give me some time, Debbie, just give me time.'

He took another sip of his beer. 'What did you tell your parents, anyway?'

'I told them you were separated,— well you are this week, aren't you?'

'That'll be news to Angie.'

She nodded sadly.

'Look, Debbie. I could bore you to tears telling you all about me and Angie, but I won't. I could go on about her; say she doesn't understand me, all the usual crap. The fact is — I think she probably understands me very well. I never understood her, which is where the trouble lay. I've not been a brilliant husband to her, and I probably wouldn't be a much better one to you. I could walk out on her tomorrow, send her a note, — tell her I'm not coming home. But it's not my way. I'll have to go back, and I hope I'll be able to make the break, but I can't promise you that. I don't know if I've got the guts to do it, she's not a happy woman, and she relies on me a lot. She hasn't got much of a life. Do you understand?'

'She's got the dog.'

'How'd you know about the dog?'

'I met him, when I went to pick your clothes up.'

'Yes, that's right, why didn't you tell me she'd got herself a dog?'

'I didn't know you didn't know, did I?'

He lifted his shoulders and laughed. 'God, I'm not so good at the deception game am I? I'd forgotten you'd met Angie. She already seems fonder of the dog than she does of me. Nice animal, is it?'

Debbie nodded. 'It's really cute, but if I were Angie, I'd choose you every time.'

He kissed her on the cheek. Then he asked thoughtfully, 'Do all the staff here know?'

'Know what?'

'That you're — what's your mum's name?'

'Ida.'

'Ida's daughter?'

'Of course, that's how I know that she does your room. Kate behind reception told mum that I stayed with you.'

'And you don't mind that they know?'

'No, the more people that accept us as an item, the better.'

'Why's that?'

'You'll find it harder to go.'

He pulled her close to him and kissed the top of her head.

'It couldn't be any harder than it is already,' he said.

Chapter 79

Monday, November first, turned out to be another clear bright day, with a low, bright, pale-yellow sun surrounded by an azure blue sky. The inquest, set for eleven o'clock, was held in the local Coroner's Court. There were no surprises; the inquest was, as expected, adjourned pending further inquiries. It was with visible relief that the party exited into the bright autumn sunshine, made even brighter by the flash of press cameras.

A great number of people had attended, but they were drawn mainly from the media. Charlotte was there leaning on Theo's arm and exposing her sorrow to the mass of photographers whilst her friend Flora faded unobtrusively into the background. Ruth Sparks and Tom Farrow the gardener both turned out in their Sunday best. Zoë had wisely stayed away, distancing herself from Isabel Sheldon-Harris in death as she had in life.

Steve Jarvis was also absent. There was no reason, apart from curiosity, for him to attend, although he was staying with his mother in Hulver, due to the fact that the police had asked that he stay locally until the matter was cleared. Although in truth neither Michael nor Ian thought they had a good enough case to hold him.

He'd arrived very late on Saturday night, and, as Ian said, he was full of swank and indignation. He'd denied everything, he'd even said that Lavinia was mistaken. It was true he'd been out for a cigarette after dinner, he didn't think it quite polite to smoke in the castle. But he certainly hadn't been out in the car, nor had he met with Zoë Elliot.

Michael and Ian had done their best, but Steve Jarvis was not to be intimidated nor tricked. He'd gladly give a mouth swab, if they'd tell him why they wanted it. So they told him that semen had been found on Lady Sheldon-Harris. His next remark would have been music to Zoë Elliot's ears, but no one knew that at the time.

'Blanks were they?' he'd asked. ''Cause that's all I fire these days.'

'What exactly do you mean?' Michael asked.

'I had a vasectomy when my youngest was born. My wife can't have any more and . . . ' He'd caught Ian and Michael looking at each other. 'They weren't blanks were they? I'm in the clear then, aren't I?'

'Not quite, there may be a rape charge to face,' Michael said.

'Rape? I never raped anybody and if Zoë say's I did, then she's lying. Or has she handed in her dirty knickers covered in blanks?'

Ian said later that he was either a mind reader or he was innocent.

'Or he was sure that Zoë wouldn't let him down,' Michael said.

'He's crazy. After the way she was beaten, even a

saint would turn him in.'

Michael shook his head. 'I don't think it was him, Ian.'

'But the girl said—'

'The girl implied, it was the mother that said.'

'But then she admitted it was him—'

'That raped her yes, but she didn't say it was him that beat her, did she? She didn't say that she'd seen his face. Besides, she clearly said that he was wearing boots, and by the look of the damage he did to her, it fits. Steve Jarvis had been at a dinner party at Hulver Castle, I don't suppose boots are the dress code under Lady Hulver's table, do you?'

'You think she's shielding someone else?'

'I don't know. *Oh, what tangled webs we weave, when once we practice to deceive.*'

'You thinking of Zoë Elliot?'

'I was thinking of me actually, Ian. I had lunch with Debbie's parents yesterday, which reminds me, — her little brother. I said I'd arrange for him to have a ride in a police car.' He wrinkled his nose. 'Can you get someone to arrange it for me?' he looked at Ian. 'Sorry, does that piss you off?'

Ian smiled. 'No, Mike, I'll get someone on to it.'

'Thanks.' He thought for a moment. 'They're really nice people.'

'Does that surprise you? Debbie's really nice.'

'No, I didn't mean it that way. I just don't like deceiving them, that's all. They think I'm separated.'

'Well? I thought you were, as well.'

Michael looked miserable. 'I am, it's just that I haven't got around to telling my wife.'

'Ah, I see, won't she like it?'

'Not a lot.'

'Right,'

'Tell you what, Ian. Pop over to Barkhampton and have a wild sexual affair with her, would you. Allow me to catch you in *flagranti delicto*, then I can get into a rage and walk out.'

'Sooner arrange the ride in the police car, if it's all the same to you. I hate the sight of blood.'

'Wise man, so do I.'

Chapter 80

Zoë came out of the bathroom. She had ignored it long enough. All the signs and symptoms had been there for weeks. Now a little blue strip had confirmed what she already knew.

She slid onto the bottom of the bed, and shivered. It was seven o'clock in the morning. Andy would be there soon delivering the milk. Almost a month had passed since the murder, but she was still considered, by Theo, not fit enough to do the early morning milking and Andy had taken over the chore. She wondered if her life would ever get back to normal, she could no longer rememeber what the word normal meant.

Theo was propped up in bed, he'd made tea and he handed her a mug.

'How you feeling?' he said.

'Fine.' She took the mug from him and sipped at it. Although she didn't look up at him, she knew that his eyes were fixed on her. 'I'm pregnant, Theo.'

'Yes,' he said, 'I know.'

She closed her eyes, he knew everything, he must do; otherwise he'd have been jubilant, ecstatic even.

'You're afraid that it might be his, aren't you?'

She nodded. 'After it happened, I went to see Dr Armstrong and I got the morning-after pill, only they made me sick, and in any case, I couldn't take them all because they went away with my waxed jacket.'

'It's mine,' he said and took another gulp of his tea. 'But if you don't want to run the risk, then I'll understand, and we'll start again.'

'How do you know it's yours?' she said.

'How do you know it's yours?' he replied.

She smiled then. 'Theo, you clown, it's inside me.'

'That's right, that's how I know too.'

'Oh, Theo, why do you make it all sound so easy?'

'Because the rest of life is hard, Zoë. Our love has never been a very complicated thing. We've never hidden it or denied it. It's the one part of my life that's always been up front.'

'But what if—'

'Would you love it the less. You don't love Betsy any the less because she's not mine, and neither do I?'

She sniffed. 'I don't suppose so, but it's your child I want, not his.'

'Then you must do what you think is best. But would you do just one thing for me first?'

'What?'

'Marry me?'

'But we can't?' She frowned. 'Can we?'

'There you go again, it's very straightforward, and you're making it sound extremely complicated.'

'We can't get married, just like that, can we?'

'Well, Westminster Abbey might raise a few eyebrows, but I think a simple little ceremony at a registry office would surface?'

'It's not the way I planned . . . '

He rubbed her tummy. 'Things often aren't, but it doesn't mean they're not worth doing.'

Theo and Zoë were married three weeks before Christmas at the little registry office at Fenshaw. Quentin and Sebastian acted as witnesses; Lavinia, Josh, Tiggy, Alex and Betsy were the only guests.

Afterwards they all went off to McDonalds — Betsy's choice, and they all laughed a lot, but avoided each other's eyes lest the act of legalizing the relationship be deemed to be important, when each had spent so many years assuring others that it was not.

It wasn't until Elizabeth was tucked up in bed, and the Hulver guests had left, that Theo and Zoë finally took stock and talked about the past, the present, and their hopes for the future, it was then that they both became silent and morose.

'We'll sell up,' Theo said. 'Sell up, and move on.'

'That would be silly after all we've been through to stay here. You love Garrick, it's your life.'

'No, Zoë, I thought it was. But my life's with you and Betsy and the new baby. Garrick hasn't been the same since I had to sell out. Farming's hitting an all time low, and this government seems bent on destroying the country way of life. Maybe it's time to call it a day. The land I owned is rented back to me now, it's not the same as owning it. In fact, at the rate we're going, it'll be difficult to run a big house like Garrick Hall on my income.'

Zoë propped herself up in bed. 'That's such defeatist talk. We'll have to diversify. My mother did, and very successful she was too. Besides, we have to be better off now that . . .'

'Now that Issie's dead?'

Zoë nodded.

'Funny, isn't it? Her death has cleared the path for so many things, how can someone's death make so many people happy. It doesn't seem quite right, does it?'

'It's made some people sad too,' Zoë said defensively.

'Who? Name one single person.'

'Lottie.'

'Apart from Lottie.'

'Ruth Sparks.'

'She didn't really like her. I'll grant you she liked her wages, but that was about it. Besides we'll need a cleaner ourselves if we move up to the big house, won't we? Ruth's as good as anyone so she won't lose out.'

'Farrow?'

Theo shook his head slowly.

'Okay, not Farrow. Well there must be someone — there must be. I know. That woman she used to see, the

635

medium, Mrs Hapgood, she'll be sad. And all those customers who got her to talk to the spirits.'

'They should be pleased for her, shouldn't they? Glad she's joined the spirit world.'he winked at her.

'Theo, Let's not talk about her anymore. She's still ruling our lives. We talk about her all the time. It's like she's more alive, since she died.'

'Yes,' he said. 'I know. Unsatisfactory isn't it? I'll tell you what, if there is a spirit world, she's up there having a real good laugh at our expense.'

'It's not her doing it, Theo, it's us. We're doing it to ourselves. We're eating ourselves up with it.'

He kissed her on the forehead. 'That's the way it'll be until they catch whoever's responsible.'

'Only if we let it,' she said reasonably.

He kissed her again, and settled down in the bed. It was their wedding night, and the first time for a very long time that they hadn't made love. It was as if Issie had at long last had her way and forced herself between them.

Chapter 81

Michael Harper was courting, that was how Ian Barnes described it. It was a stupid description. Michael was still married to Angie; separation, let alone divorce hadn't been mentioned, certainly it had never been fully discussed. Mind you, there hadn't been much time for conversation, he'd only been home a couple of times. To be precise, he'd actually been home four times since he'd started working at Fenshaw, but he'd only met up with Angie on two of those occasions. Then she'd been in a rush to get somewhere, puppy club or was it puppy playgroup? Michael thought he'd never heard anything so daft. But it kept her busy; it kept her out of his hair. She hadn't even asked him when he'd be home next. He'd given up his nightly telephoning, although it hadn't been planned that way. She was always out, taking the dog for a walk or to the aforementioned activities. And if he did catch her in, she had as little to say to him as he had to her. So he just paid the bills and put money into the housekeeping account and at night he lay with Debbie Smith, and the arrangement suited him very well. It was as if both he and Angie had found themselves someone to love. And in Angie's case, thought Michael, the someone couldn't answer back.

November had turned into a month of cold and wet drizzle. Damp fog descended upon the land and hung across the countryside like a depressing impenetrable blanket. The crisp morning frosts and sunny afternoons of October faded from memory, as did the murder of Isobel Sheldon-Harris. By the time December arrived, bringing with it early snow and treacherous roads, even Michael had to admit that the trail had gone completely cold. No one would admit to giving up, of course, but other crimes demanded attention and the Sheldon-Harris murder was no longer a number-one priority. Charles Hastings, the DI that Michael was standing in for, died, and that in turn raised questions of possible long-term solutions. It was suggested that Michael, not Ian Barnes, apply for the job and that in turn caused animosity on the part of the younger man.

Ten days before Christmas, with only the slightest of hints, Ida Smith, Debbie's mother, invited Michael home for the weekend. 'Much nicer than staying in that hotel week in and week out,' she'd said. With that simple invitation, the Smith's acknowledged Michael's importance in their daughter's life, and Michael knew he must soon face up to what had happened to him and more importantly, what had happened to his marriage.

The spare room was prepared, a new bedside lamp was purchased, and a brand new bale of blue towels. And although Debbie could be heard to murmur, 'Oh, Mum, stop fussing,' her delight was plain for all to see.

He arrived on Friday night, only minutes before Debbie, bearing a bottle of scotch for Fred Smith and a bunch of flowers for Ida. Knowing that the family was far form wealthy, he brought a large joint of sirloin to supplement the family's larder, saying that it was a gift to him from a farming friend.

The beef, eaten on Sunday, was delicious. After lunch Debbie went upstairs to change in preparation for an afternoon walk.

Whilst she was upstairs, Michael endured an awkward silence. Of course he knew they wouldn't ask him about his wife, but all the same he had an uncomfortable feeling that they just might. It was a relief therefore, when Ida brought the conversation back to the piece of beef.

'It was really nice, Mike, the best bit of beef I've had in ages. You've got some generous friends.'

'Yes,' he agreed.

'Wasn't Sir Theodore Sheldon-Harris was it? You know, that case you've been working on. Wasn't him that gave it to you, was it?'

'No, no, it wouldn't be right to take gifts like that, not with the case still open.'

'No, of course not. I mean, if it had been him, I'd have thought it was some sort of bribery and corruption. I mean, everyone knows that that Zoë Elliot's no better than she ought to be, despite she's the daughter of a Lord.'

Michael sucked in his breath, someone else set against Zoë; maybe there was no smoke without fire.

'Married aren't they? His wife not cold in her

grave, and they go and get married. Not sort of decent, was it? Not to go ahead and do it so soon. Someone told me she was pregnant, is that right?'

'I believe she is.' He daren't, — he mustn't, defend Zoë: there was no need.

'She was all over him at the inquest, I saw her picture in the paper, two-faced little so-and-so. You should have seen the way she behaved herself in the hotel that night.'

Earlier Michael's eyes were becoming heavy; an afternoon sleep had seemed preferable to a country walk. But now he sat bolt upright.

'You're saying that Zoë Elliot stayed at the Kings Head?'

'Oh yes, that's the funny thing, she stayed in the room you've got, her and a friend of her's, I didn't see the friend, but then I think he went home, because she picked someone else up. I saw it with my own eyes.'

Michael was on the edge of his chair. 'Wait a minute, when was this?'

'Didn't I say?'

Michael shook his head.

'The night before the murder. I checked with the hotel register. Then the next night — you had the room.' Ida turned her nose up. 'You could see what she'd been up to as well. Poor old Sir Theodore, I expect she was looking for someone younger.'

Debbie came into the room. 'Who, me? Should I be looking for someone younger?'

'Right on,' Michael said. 'But your mum's just been telling me that Zoë Elliot stayed at the Kings Head with a friend, but—'

'But then she picked someone else up.' Ida interrupted 'Of course the friend could have been Sir Theodore Sheldon-Harris, I don't know, I didn't see him. And I don't know that he went home, he might have been there as well, sort of a three—'

Fred Smith gave her a warning look.

'Well you do hear of those sorts of things going on, you'd be surprised what I see in my job. All I know is that she picked up another bloke, and took him back to her room.'

'Mum! How do you know all this?'

'It was that night, you know, when half the staff had gone down with the flue. Mrs Crosland, — that's my supervisor—' she added, for the benefit of Michael, '— asked me to go in and help with this reception they were having, it was some sort of convention, although if you ask me, it was just an excuse for a load of men to get away from their wives and get stoned out of their minds.'

'Mum, just tell it how it was.'

'Well, she was there, in the bar, she was sort of flirting with all the blokes, I mean she's a nice looking girl, then this particular chap brought her dinner, they went in the restaurant together, and they were all lovey dovey.'

'Perhaps it was a friend of her's?' Debbie said.

'Yes,' agreed Michael, thinking of Steve. 'Perhaps it was.'

'Very good friend, by the look of it. They went up to bed together.'

'How do you know that?'

'I know because I saw them in the corridor. They went to his room — I saw them. I had to take room service to the room next door. Then later they must have gone to her room, I know because,' she lowered her voice, 'they left things there. I tell you Mike we were so short staffed, — I was waitress one minute, chamber maid the next, and hall porter the next.'

'And you actually saw them disappear into the room together?'

'Fall into the room, more like. Their hands were all over each other, it were like a scene from an X movie. Not that I've ever seen one, of course.' She added rather prudishly. Debbie shook her head. 'And then next day, well, I had to clean the room. You could see what they'd been up to.' She looked at Debbie a little embarrassed, 'Well I mean, you'd think they'd flush them down the toilet, wouldn't you.'

Michael squeezed his chin between his thumb and his forefinger. 'Did you see her in the morning? Did she have any bruises, or cuts or anything?'

'I didn't see her, that's another funny thing. I start at seven, and she'd left before I got in, she didn't even stay for breakfast, she left the money for her room on the dresser.'

'In cash?'

Ida nodded. 'That's right, good job I'm honest, isn't it? I could have easily pocketed it and made out it wasn't there. '

Michael was looking at her.

'I wouldn't do anything like that, of course.' She sounded quite put out.

643

Chapter 82

'Bloody mobile,' Michael cursed as he stood in the porch of Debbie's house, the signal had been weak the evening before, now it was non-existent. He shook the little oblong of black plastic as if hoping to shake some life into it.

He snapped the flap shut and went back into the house and asked Ida if he could use their telephone. He conscientiously put fifty pence in the box that lived by the side of the Smith's telephone and dialed Ian Barnes's number.

A child answered, and, with an air of disappointment, brought his father to the 'phone.

Michael hated doing this; he hated that Ian had been proved right, but he hated more, that Zoë, sweet, innocent looking Zoë, had proved to be the villain of the peace.

But Michael was a big man, big enough to admit that he was wrong when all the evidence was staring him in the face.

'Ian? You were right, we've got her.'

'No? How? When?'

'Meet me at the station, I'll tell you all about it.'

Debbie, who, coming down the stairs, had overheard what was said, frowned, and Michael had a feeling of *deja vue*.

'Can't it wait until tomorrow? Mum's made a trifle for tea.'

Why was it he thought of Angie and Angie's mum, and a far-off time when he was a lowly constable?

'I'll be back by teatime.' He pecked her cheek. 'I just need to check a few things out. Thanks to your mum, we've had our first big break.'

Debbie put her hand up to her cheek as if she'd just been stung.

Ian was waiting at the station when he arrived. 'We'll bring her in again, she's fit enough now, this time we'll lean on her a bit.'

'She's pregnant,' Michael said.

'Huh, she's only about two minutes gone—'

'I know, but we must be sure this time. We have to find the man she was with. Ida wasn't too specific, but I gather the place was littered with condoms, and a used syringe, no needle just a plastic syringe, like the one's Zoë Elliot uses for injecting sheep, an ideal thing for planting semen exactly where you want it. It all fits, brilliant isn't it? What a plot, con some chap into literally giving out. Make sure he lives one or two hundred miles away, and you've got an untraceable suspect. It's brilliant and it's fool proof.'

'Almost,' Ian said. 'If you'd not been screwing the chambermaid's daughter we'd not have got onto it.'

'Yes,' Michael said. 'The things I'm prepared to do in the name of justice.'

They both laughed.

'So, who was it she booked in with?' Barnes asked.

'No one seems to know. She booked under her own name,— Zoë Elliot, double room for one night only.'

'We could show Debbie's mum a picture of Steven Jarvis.'

'I'd rather not do that, in case I want her to look at an identity parade.'

'What do you suggest then? Get every employee of, what's the firm called?'

'Oakley's Greetings Cards.'

'Oakley's Cards, lined up and get Ida to sift through them?'

'No, just the males of medium built, dark, mid to late twenty's.' Michael laughed. 'So the field should be narrowed down to about fifty!'

The drive to Garrick cottage seemed to take forever. Both knew from experience that there was little point in planning what was to be said, things rarely worked out as planned.

'Here's how I see it,' Ian Barnes said as they sped through the village of Garrick-in-the-Willows. 'She books a room with her boyfriend, it might or might not be Steven Jarvis, it might even have been Sir Theo.'

'That'd be a bit daft, when they have a perfectly good home twelve miles away, wouldn't it?'

'Yes, well, she books in with someone, her lover

then, and they have a bit of a tiff—'

'Or he had to be somewhere, like having dinner at Hulver with her parents?'

'Right, and then, whilst he's away socializing, our Miss Zoë gets bored and picks up some entertainment. And then she has this brilliant idea to get rid of Lady Sheldon-Harris and throw the trail right away from her,' Ian said.

'She'd have to have come prepared.'

'Maybe he was the one that came prepared.'

'Okay, but then what?'

'Well, as soon as the chap she's picked up has gone back to his own bed, she goes to Garrick Hall and does for Lady Sheldon-Harris.'

'Okay, but what about her injuries?' Said Michael.

'Obvious isn't it? Lover-boy comes back from his evening at Hulver and finds out what she's been up to, and he beats the shit out of her. Or maybe when she got home that morning Sir Theo beat the shit out of her. Yes, that might be it, she gets home at some ungodly hour and he's none too pleased with her and—'

'She was raped, Ian. There's no two ways about it.'

'Okay, then the bloke she picked up beat her up.'

'Why?'

'Because he's like that, that's the way he gets off. Or maybe she changed her mind and he was all psyched up for it.'

'Mmm, we have to get the owner of the semen.

First thing tomorrow, find out how many employers Oakleys have, and find out exactly who was at that convention, everyone mind.'

'And Zoë Elliot?'

'Lady Sheldon-Harris now, Ian.'

They drew up outside the cottage.

'We won't take her in today, unless of course she realizes we've on to her and throws in the towel. We'll just see what she has to say about staying at the hotel. We won't give too much away.'

Theo answered the door with Elizabeth close on his heels. He didn't immediately ask them in, he looked drawn and weary. 'Yes? What now?' He said.

'May we come in?' Ian said. Michael could see that his partner could barely contain his excitement, he, on the other hand felt exceedingly depressed.

'It's Sunday afternoon,' Theo replied.

Neither policeman acknowledged the day of the week.

'Oh, all right then,' he said, and then as if he'd relented a little, 'I'm just making a cup of tea.'

He led them through to the kitchen

'It's Lady Sheldon-Harris, we really wanted to talk to.'

For a moment Theo looked confused. He sat down on a kitchen chair and shook his head. 'You know, it's funny, when you say Lady Sheldon-Harris, my first thought is to tell you that my mother's been dead for many years, then I think of Issie, and . . . well, you know. I can't quite think of Zoë as Lady Sheldon-Harris, perhaps it's because she can't think of herself as that either.'

Ian Barnes looked irritated. 'Is she in?'

Theo got up and went over to the kitchen sink. 'She having a lie down,' he said.

'We'd like to speak to her, if possible?' Michael said gently.

Elizabeth stood in the corner of the room, her eyes casting a rebellious stare in their direction. Michael smiled at her, but was met with an unflinching fixed gaze.

'And supposing I say no, it's not possible, supposing I tell you it's not convenient just now?'

'Then we'll quietly wait here until it is convenient,' Ian said.

Theo indicated that they should sit down, and the men sat, both on one side of the kitchen table.

'I'll take her some tea and wake her,' he said.

Theo poured some hot water from the kettle into the teapot, swished it around, tipped it away, added tea, and filled the pot up with water. Then he placed the pot on the table and covered it with a tea cozy. Michael thought about his own usual way of making tea with a teabag and a mug, and he smiled.

Theo took cups and saucers from the dresser, and poured four cups of tea. He placed a jug of milk on the table and a sugar basin. He then poured a glass of milk out for Elizabeth and handed it to her. The whole operation was carried out in complete silence.

He carried one of the cups of tea out of the room, and Michael and Ian could hear him gently waking Zoë and telling her that they were there to see her. The child still watched their every move, making Michael feel somehow ashamed of what he was about to do.

Michael stood up as she came into the room. Barnes remained seated. Neither of them had touched their tea.

'Sorry to trouble you on a Sunday afternoon, Lady Sheldon-Harris,' he said.

'Zoë's fine,' she said.

'Just one or two questions, if that's okay, Lady Sheldon-Harris,' Ian Barnes added, he was enjoying Zoë's discomfort. Michael shot him a look.

Zoë caught Theo's eye and rapidly looked away. She slid into a kitchen chair and Elizabeth wriggled onto her lap still clutching the glass of milk.

'Yes?'

'I'm sorry to go over this again, only we've had a witness come forward, and we thought perhaps you'd like to change your statement?'

Zoë looked at Theo again, and Michael thought that they both looked very frightened.

'Where were you on the night of Monday the

Twenty-fifth of October?' Barnes asked.

She looked extremely sad. 'I told you, I was here and then I went to Garrick Wood.'

'With Steven Jarvis?' Michael asked.

She glanced at Theo. 'I don't want to press any charges.'

'Why not,' Ian interjected. 'You got beaten within an inch of your life, and yet you're happy for him to get away with it?'

Michael could see that she had tears in her eyes.

'There's been enough trouble already,' she whispered.

Theo leaned over and took her hand. Elizabeth wriggled and looked sulkily at Michael and Ian.

'Perhaps you can explain, how a witness saw you at the Kings Head Hotel on the night of the twenty-fifth, the night Lady Sheldon-Harris was murdered. Perhaps you'd like to explain how your name appears in the register for that night.'

Michael felt almost guilty as he watched a mask of confusion sweep over her face. He wasn't enjoying watching her being caught out.

'But that's ridiculous.'

'Where's the Kings Head?' Asked Theo.

Michael had an urge to lighten the mood, it had to be a mistake, this couple weren't capable of murder; they were muddled and open, not devious villains. He wanted to laugh and say that the Kings Head was on the Kings shoulders and that he was sorry to trouble them, they'd be going now.

'Darling, it's that big hotel in the Market Square at Fenshaw,' Zoë said.

Never been there in my life,' Theo said.

'And you, Lady Sheldon-Harris?' Ian Barnes asked.

'I do wish you'd stop calling me that,' she snapped. 'I prefer to be called Zoë.'

'Just answer the question, Zoë, please.'

'What question? I wasn't at that hotel. I swear I wasn't.'

'Have you ever been there?'

Zoë ran her fingers through her hair. 'I sometimes pop in there to use the loo, — if Betsy gets taken short when we're in town, but it's not a place I frequent. It's always full of commercial travellers.'

'How would you know that, if you never go in there?' Ian shot back.

'It's that sort of place,' Zoë said. There was desperation in her voice.

'And if we were to tell you that a witness, a very reliable witness, saw you there on that night, what would you say to that?'

'I'd say that your witness is lying through his teeth, because I was nowhere near the place. I think I should

652

'phone my sister.'

'Zoë was here Inspector, with me, apart from the time she was . . . well, you know, and then she'd only gone for about two hours.'

'You'd be willing to come to the station and take part in an identity parade would you, Zoë?' Michael asked.

'Of course, so long as your witness is straight. Because it wasn't me, it really and truly wasn't me.'

Michael pushed his chair back from the table, and Ian followed suit. Their cups of tea were untouched, as was Theo's.

'We may ask you to come to the station in the morning and make a statement,' Ian said.

'But I've already made a statement, you know where I was.'

'We know where you say you were,' Ian replied vindictively.

Zoë trembled, tears filled her eyes, and she placed her hands across her chest, as if trying to comfort herself. Would the nightmare never end?

Chapter 82

Pulling off his trainers, Sam Jeffrey's stretched himself out in the chair, and sighed. He was onto a bloody good thing he was, and no mistake. He whistled softly and Everton wandered over to him and put his head on his knee. He caressed the dog's smooth head. Oh yes, this time he'd really fallen on his feet.

Angie came through to the sitting room with a cup of tea in one hand and a ham and cheese sandwich in the other. Poor bloody cow, she thought he didn't know who her old man was. Civil bloody servant! As soon as he'd heard the bloody name he'd known. He hadn't been positive, not when she'd first said, not until she'd asked him back to her place for supper, then he'd seen the 'photos and there'd been no doubt. But of course he had known, deep down, the minute he and Angie were introduced he knew. Harper's not an unusual name, but it just had to be him. You never forgot the first time you had sex, and you didn't forget the first copper that collared you either. No, Inspector — he was just a detective sergeant then — Harper, had been the first of many to slap a pair of handcuffs on him.

What poetry it was, here he was living the life of Riley, courtesy of his old rival's dosh! What a laugh, what a sell! Here was Harper's little wife making him feel at home, feeding him and his dog, doing his washing, and even giving him a bit of spending money.

Angela smiled at him and went back into the kitchen. He could hear her tidying up, she was pleased as punch to have him there; it gave the stupid lonely cow something to do. He got up and, taking the television controller from the shelf beside the fireplace, he flicked the sports programme on. On his way back to his chair he picked up a little silver snuffbox from off the mantle and slipped it in his pocket. He immediately thought better of it and replaced it, she might discover that it was missing, and he had bigger fish to fry, far bigger fish. He didn't want to spoil things; everything in good time. He nodded, yes, everything in good time.

Angie wasn't a bad sort — she was all right, her heart was in the right place, or at least her purse was. She was as plain as a pikestaff mind you, and as gullible as anyone he'd ever met, but she was okay. A bit of a mumsy sort of woman, but what could you expect, being married to the Harper fossil?

He got up and went into the kitchen. 'What you up to Angie-baby? Here, why don't you sit down and let me do the clearing up?'

She shook her head. 'No, Sam, I won't hear of it. You're a guest and I'm going to treat you like one.'

He put his arm around her waist, he felt her shudder and saw colour flush her cheeks. God, this was so easy. He wasn't sure how he felt about bedding her, but he guessed that it would be all right; after all, you didn't need to look at the mantleshelf whilst you poked the fire, did you? And his sex life couldn't exactly be described as active at the moment, now could it? He smiled and breathed heavily into her neck. Any port in a storm, as his old mates from the Scrubs used to say. This time it was his turn to give an involuntary shiver. He didn't want to go back there, no — no way — so he'd have to be careful, very careful. Of course he hadn't got her into bed yet. It all took time; he'd done well to get this far. Oh, it was such poetry! There was Inspector Harper off working all hours God sent, trying to net the criminals, when all the time his wife was entertaining one of the biggest, — well maybe not the biggest, but one of the best, — well okay, not the best. But he was bloody good at what he did, and he'd not been caught, — well not too often.

If he pulled this one off, he'd have really gone to the top of the league. The laugh of it was, Harper would be far too embarrassed to do anything about it, what could he do anyway? Everything that he'd got from her so far had been a gift and taking gifts wasn't a crime, now was it? And if he could pull the rest of the plan off — well, he'd consider himself made.

She'd told him all about her childlessness, everything, right down to the smallest, most intimate details. Some of the things she'd told him had been a little near the mark; who'd she think she was talking to, her mother? He knew more about Harper's sex life than his own bloody GP. 'I bet I can get you up the spout,' he'd said to her that afternoon. God, she'd blushed to the roots of her hair, then she'd stuttered and told him that she was a married woman and that he was a very naughty boy. But he could tell she was thinking about it. Even a dimwit could tell that she wanted it. God, that would be such bloody poetry, wouldn't it? Take old Harper's money *and* leave a cuckoo in his nest. Leave him with an unsatisfied wife to boot. Once a woman like Angie had tasted the sort of fruit he had to offer, she'd never be interested in bedding a pathetic copper ever again, now would she?

He gave her a peck on the back of the neck and returned to the sitting room. On the way he caught his own reflection in the hall mirror, he stopped and studied himself. He wrinkled one eyebrow and then the other, and experimented with a lopsided smile. Then he blew himself a kiss and resumed his interest in the athletics.

Fifteen minutes later Angie joined him, settling herself in the corner of the sofa.

'Do you mind the sports channel Angie-baby? Shall I have a look what else is on?'

'No, no, you enjoy it. I quite like seeing the running.'

He moved over and joined her on the sofa. He picked up her hand.

'You know Angie-baby, you're a good sort. Your

old man's mad leaving you on your own. He wants to look out, else some chap's going to steal you from right under his nose.'

She was squirming now, she tried to ease her hand away from him, but he held it fast, enjoying her embarrassment, knowing it would leave her vulnerable.

'Tell you what, Angie-baby. If my Giro comes tomorrow, I'll treat you to fish and chips, how'd you like that?'

She relaxed a little. 'Oh, Sam, that would be lovely. That'd be a real treat for me. But I can't let you pay, — you fetch them and I'll pay. You can't go spending the little money you have on me.'

'Well, if you're sure? I do need every penny at the moment. I told you about my old mum, didn't I? Well things have got really bad now. I'll either have to go back to Manchester to look after her, or somehow find the money for the nursing home.' He paused, she was a bit slow was Angie.

'You see, Mum's problem is that she owns the house, so they expect her to pay her own fees. Of course once the house is sold it won't be a problem, it's knowing what to do in between times.' He paused again.

'You could rent the house out,' she suggested.

Wrong answer Angie, she wasn't quite as slow as he thought.

'Yes, that would be one solution. I suppose the best

plan would be for me to go back there to live and look after Mum myself though, wouldn't it? I mean, I'm not being mercenary or anything, but that house is my inheritance. Of course, I'd go up there like a shot, if it wasn't for you.'

'Me?'

'Yeah, you. I'd miss you and Butch more than I can say. I do so love our walks on the common, and our little meals together here.'

She was blushing again. Blushing's fine on a teenager but it looks a bit over the top on a middle-aged woman, he thought.

'How much do you need to find?'

Well done Angie, I do believe you're cottoning on at last, he thought.

'A lot, Angie-baby. A hell of a lot. And before you offer, the answer's no. I couldn't possibly—'

'But, I wasn't going to—'

'You're too good hearted, Angie, it's a good job it's me, and not some unscrupulous bugger that'd take advantage of your generosity.'

'But, Sam I—'

'No, no, let me finish.' He held both her hands and looked deep into her eyes. 'You see, I've never met a woman like you before, Angie. You're all heart, — it's as if you know the sort of life my mum's had. Did I tell you about the fire? No, I didn't, did I? It's hard for me talk about it of course, both my little sisters, and my dad, gone in the

659

space of a few hours.' He covered his face with his hand. A dramatic gesture designed to cover his mouth that threatened to break into a smile. Her eyes were watering already.

'I was only little, not quite five, but I can still remember seeing my mum dash into my bedroom and rescue me. She tried to go back in for my sisters, but the firemen held her back. Can you imagine what it must have been like for her?'

A tear was making slow but steady progress down Angie's cheek.

'Anyway, Mum always said that I should hold onto that house, no matter what. All her memories are there, you see.'

Angela's brow furrowed. 'I thought you said it burned down?'

God, she was quicker than he thought.

'Yeah, it did, insurance paid for it to be rebuilt though. That was typical of my parents. They hadn't thought to insure Dad's life, but they'd made sure they insured the house. They always wanted me to have a roof over my head, you see.'

Angela nodded.

'But you know my principles. I never borrow money and I never accept charity.'

Oh dear, she was looking relieved.

He stroked the back of her hand. 'You've got

beautiful hands Angie-baby, did anyone ever tell you that?'

She was blushing again.

'Anyway, as I was saying. You know my principles, but you know, I don't think I have any right to make my mum suffer because I'm too proud to take help when it's offered. Especially when the offer comes from someone like you. Someone who I have an understanding with. So thanks, Angie, if you really mean it, and I know you wouldn't have said it, if you didn't. You're not the kind of woman to lead a chap on. I shall pay you back mind, it's just a loan. Once I sort Mum's affairs out you are going to have it all back, every penny of it.'

'How much . . . '

'Twelve hundred pounds a month. I have to pay up front, — it's a bugger isn't it? Still, when you think about what that woman did for me, it's no more than she deserves.'

Angie wasn't blushing now; in fact she looked quite white and pasty.

'It's a lot, Sam. I could give you a cheque, but then I'd have to go to the building society in the morning to put it back in the account. Michael wouldn't under—'

'Forget the cheque, Angie. I don't want to cause a problem between you and your old man. Tell you what, I'll stay here tonight, and then we can go to the building society in the morning and draw it out together. It's better if I have cash anyway, — I don't want them social security creeps stopping my giro, do I?

Chapter 83

The last thing Michael and Ian arranged before parting on Sunday evening was a trip to Manchester the following morning.

'Phone through to the local boys and let them know what we're up to. We'll ask for the man to come forward. If he doesn't, we'll ask for volunteers to give us a DNA sample, then we'll see whom we're left with. Set it up with Manchester CID will you?

It had been almost six when Michael got back to Debbie's house. 'Not too late for tea am I, Ida? My mouths been watering all afternoon thinking about that trifle.'

Ida Smith instantly forgave him and assured him that he wasn't late at all, they never had tea very early on a Sunday. Debbie was not quite so quick to forgive. In fact she went on and on about it. Flouncing and sulking and slamming doors; even so, it didn't stop her accompanying Michael to the Kings Head for a night of passion. Once again Michael was reminded of his youth spent with Angie. What was it about women? They gave you their bodies, but only in exchange for your soul.

Debbie was due on duty at Barkhampton at eight the next morning, so Michael got up with her at five-thirty and joined her for a continental breakfast in the hotel dining room. After he'd seen her on her way, he went to his office to gather all he would need for his trip across country.

Ian arrived at seven-thirty, and they were about to leave, when the desk sergeant put his head around the door.

'Your Christmas present just arrived early,' he said. 'There's a woman out here, a Miss Skinner, says she knows where Zoë Elliot was on the night of the murder, says she knows someone who saw her.'

Another witness? God, this was their lucky day. He'd been convinced of Zoë's innocence, he'd have staked his life on it, but another witness! How wrong could he be?

'Where is she?'

'I put her in the interview room. I gave her a cup of tea and said you wouldn't be long.'

Michael hesitated. This was important, really important.

'You'll have to go to Manchester on your own, Ian. You know how we agreed to handle it. I'll stay here and do what I can. With any luck we'll have this tied up by the end of the day.'

Ian, pulled a face. 'One small request, Mike? Let me come with you when you bring her in? I want to see the look on her face when she finds out we've outsmarted her.'

Michael nodded sadly. He almost felt that Zoë had let him down, that it was a personal thing. He'd based his passion for Debbie on Zoë Elliot, and, like Debbie, she'd turned out to be not quite who he thought she was. Ian was watching him carefully, he's gloating, Michael thought, he's bloody gloating.

By ten o'clock that morning Ian Barnes was seated opposite Tim Oakley, Managing Director of Oakley's Greeting Cards. He was a jolly, red faced, man of about sixty, he had grey short cropped hair, very square shoulders and a square chin. He had a large bulbous nose on the end of which was perched a pair of modern, heavy framed, red glasses, which he constantly adjusted, pushing them up his nose and easing them off his ears as if he couldn't quite get them in a comfortable position. His smile revealed large yellow teeth.

The premises of Oakley's Greeting Cards were situated on a modern industrial estate. The factory itself was a monument of glass and steel as was the adjoining office block where Barnes now sat.

Tim Oakley's office was large and airy. It had a thick pile carpet in an insipid shade of green. The walls were painted a similar shade. The curtains and the modern desk were of a darker shade of green, and even the filing cabinets, banked across one of the walls, were painted green.

Ian Barnes felt happy, very happy. He liked Mike Harper, but the fact was, Mike was stale. Ian had known all along whom the murderer was, and Mike simply wouldn't listen. Admittedly he hadn't known how she'd managed it, but now that he did know, he felt very smug. Let's face it, he thought, poor old Mike's past it, well past his sell-by date. Mike had let sex blind him to the truth. He'd really fancied Zoë Elliot, right little toff she was, as well, and poor old Mike had let a pretty face and a posh voice go to his head. Well, the report would show that Ian was right all along; and that wouldn't do his job prospects any harm.

'It's about a conference you held at the Kings Head in Fenshaw on Monday twenty-fifth October of this year.'

Tim Oakley frowned. 'Sunday twenty-fourth and Monday twenty-fifth, yes that's right, it was a sales convention. We had no trouble, Inspector. Everything went off very smoothly, everyone behaved themselves very well.'

'So I believe, Sir. Unfortunately on that night, Monday twenty-fifth, or in the early hours of Tuesday morning, a woman in a small village about twelve miles away was murdered.'

Tim Oakley blanched. 'Goodness, and you think one of us had something to do with it?' he pushed his glasses further up his nose.

'Bear with me, Sir. I'm not really at liberty to tell you the whole story. But do remember that this is a murder inquiry, and we do have good reason to believe that one of your employees may, and I use the word *may,* have been involved.'

Tim Oakley was becoming paler by the minute; he removed his glasses and rubbed his eyes.

'Oh, dear, oh, dear, I do hope the press don't get hold of this. You see we have such a good reputation. We are

— and I hope you don't think that I'm being immodest,— but we are well known to be excellent employers,' he replaced his glasses. 'We employ the best, Inspector, the very best, and we look after our staff. To think that one of them might be a murderer! Well it doesn't bear thinking about.'

Ian held up his hand. 'First of all, there's no reason why the press should be involved, and secondly, if we have your cooperation there's no reason why this shouldn't be cleared up in a matter of a few hours.'

Tim Oakley swallowed. 'How can I help, Inspector, you have my full cooperation, of course you do.'

'I'd like a list of everyone who was at that conference. How many do you employ by the way?'

'About five hundred, but this was just for the sales staff, about sixty people in all.'

'All men?'

'Gracious no, most of my sales staff are women, they're much better than men when it comes to persuading buyers.' He seemed to think better of his last remark and said, 'Not that much persuasion's needed, the product sells itself.'

'So how many men were there at Fenshaw that night?'

'I don't know off hand. Mrs Gunn, my secretary, could tell you exactly. I think it was about thirty.' He spoke into the intercom.

'And these thirty or so men? Are they all here today?'

'Most would be, it being a Monday, but not all of them, some are out on the road.'

'Those that are here. Can you gather them in one place for me, I'd like to talk to them all together.'

An hour later, twenty-five men were gathered in the staff canteen with coffee being served to them. A high pitched buzz of conversation permeated the air, until that is, Ian Barnes got up to speak. Then the room was suddenly thick with silence.

Ian knew which one it was. As soon as he'd explained that on the night of October twenty-fifth, someone in the room had shared a bed with a young lady in the Kings Head at Fenshaw, he'd known. He'd never seen a man lose his self-control so visibly. He watched, almost in fascination, as the man's face paled and beads of sweat formed on his forehead. He'd have liked to have flung his hands in the air and shouted 'yes, jackpot,' as he watched the man's hands shake, and the cup of coffee he was holding spill and saturate his blue and white striped shirt. Perhaps he'd been just a tad unkind when he'd suggested that whoever had spent the night with Zoë Elliot might well be in need of urgent medical attention.

Ian said his piece and then suggested that if that man were present he might like to come and join him for a chat in Tim Oakley's office.

'Who was the man who spilled his coffee?' Ian asked once he and Oakley had left the canteen.

'You think it's him, don't you? Well you couldn't be more wrong. He's one of our best sales reps. He's been with us for a very long time, over five years I should say off hand.' Once more the glasses began their perilous journey, sliding on and off Tim Oakley's nose.

'Is he married?'

Tim Oakley got up and walked over to one of the green filing cabinets. From a drawer marked Reps, he withdrew a slim green file and handed it to Ian. The name Anthony Bird was written in the top left hand corner. A sheet of foolscap told Ian that Anthony Bird was five feet eleven inches tall. He had brown hair and brown eyes, he was twenty-nine years old and was married with two children, both boys. He lived on the outskirts of Manchester.

It was a full half-hour before the knock came on the door. He's been shut in the gents — shitting himself, thought Ian.

The brown hair talked of in the file was exaggerated, most of it had probably been lost since the file was started, but all the other particulars proved correct and up to date.

Tim Oakley was dismissed and Ian asked Anthony Bird to sit.

'I expect you know what this is about, don't you?'

'Hepatitis, or Aids,' he said, and swallowed. 'I've

669

been thinking. Hepatitis, that's curable, right? But Aids! Oh Christ, suppose I've given it my wife? Do I get to take a test? I should be all right, we used protection you see,— she insisted.' Beads of sweat once again appeared on his forehead.

I'll bet she did, thought Ian.

'I'd never done anything like that before, she came on so strong. I was flattered I suppose, and I was a bit drunk, and she was very pretty and . . . Oh Christ, my wife will kill me.' His face was ashen.

Bloody suffer, thought Ian Barnes, unkindly.

'Suppose you tell me all about it, from start to finish.'

Anthony Bird frowned. 'Why are the police involved?'

'I'll ask the questions.' Ian felt great; this was the reason he'd joined the police force, to catch out people like this silly little man who couldn't keep his woody in his pants. He was at his mercy now.

'What happened? She came on to me, that's all. We had dinner. Christ she even paid for it. Then we went back to my room and, Christ, I don't need to give you a blow by blow account, do I?'

'How many times?'

'What? How many times did we do it? Christ, what's it matter? What do the police want to know that for? Law against doing it more than once in Fenshaw, is there?'

Ian put the tips of his fingers together and waited.

'Two, I think, or it may have been three, I just don't remember. No,— it was two.'

'And then what?'

'She gets off me,' he blushed. 'She went on top you see, and she cleans me up. Then off she goes, back to her own room. She wouldn't stay the night.'

'I tried to see Zoë, that was her name, Zoë, in the morning, but she'd already left. That was it'

'So you were in your room, not hers?'

'That's right, she insisted, — all prepared she was as well. But what difference does it make? She's not claiming sexual harassment is she? Because if she is—'

'I'll need a mouth swab from you, and I'll need a statement. There's a squad car outside. They'll take you down town and arrange it. Thank you Mr Bird, you've been very helpful.'

'But what about the Aids test? Will my wife need one?' he frowned. 'Why are the police involved?'

Ian swung back in his chair. 'You're an accessory to murder, Mr Bird. You'd better cooperate with us — try and convince us that you're an *unwilling* accomplice.'

Chapter 84

Three days later, a metalic blue Golf could be seen weaving its way through Garrick-in-the-Willows, followed by a white and blue police car and behind that a windowless white van.

In the driving seat of the Golf sat Ian Barnes with Mike Harper by his side. Michael was holding a thin, buff coloured file. Two uniformed policemen were in the car behind and two more in the van.

'Slow down, Ian, there's no need to hurry, not now.' The cars made an abrupt right turn into the gates of Garrick Hall and crawled slowly past the lodge. Zoë was standing at the kitchen sink washing up. She lifted her head as the car approached and put her hand up to her mouth.

Ian stopped the car and Michael got out and strolled over to the cottage, he was still holding the buff coloured folder. The ever faithful Bracken gave a cursory bark as Michael tapped on the door.

'Quiet, Bracken,' Zoë whispered. 'Please, please be quiet.'

She went to the door and unlatched it; the police car and the van had drawn to a halt behind the Golf. Zoë put her fingers through her hair.

'Yes?' her voice was little more than a whisper.

'I won't keep you now Lady Sheldon-Harris, but if

it's all right with you, I'd like to come and have a brief chat with you later, say in half an hour?'

She was drying her hands on a tea-towel and she continued to do so, long after all the moisture was absorbed.

She nodded. 'Fine,' she whispered. 'Theo will be home by then.'

Elizabeth came through from the sitting room and clung warily to her mother's legs. Michael gave her a broad smile. Which Elizabeth returned with a scowl.

Michael nodded and got back into the car, the little convoy proceeded toward the Hall, where it parked, blocking in a white Porsche. Michael signaled to the uniformed police to wait in their vehicles.

Ruth Sparks opened the door.

'Inspector,' she seemed pleased to see him. 'I'm just giving Miss Charlotte a hand with sorting through her mum's things. Sir Theo wants them sorted and gone before Christmas. That little madam up there can't wait to get her foot in the door.' She nodded her head toward Garrick Cottage. 'I'll give Miss Charlotte a call.'

Charlotte appeared followed by Flora. Michael had the feeling that they'd been fighting.

'Just the person,' Flora said. Perhaps you can help us sort out a little problem?'

'I'll try,' he said, a little bemused.

'Well, I say that if we're not sure about who owns a certain item then we should either ask Theo, or, failing that, give Theo the benefit of the doubt and leave it here for him.'

Charlotte's face looked like thunder.

'Oh, shut up, Flora. Inspector Harper doesn't want to know about our petty little squabbles,' she snorted.

'It's not petty at all. You see Inspector, Lottie believes that everything belonged to Lady Issie and therefore, now belongs to her. That doesn't sound right to me, what do you think?'

'Flora, just shut up.'

'Why are you here Inspector?' Charlotte asked. If she'd have looked beyond him at the little group of vehicles on the drive she might have known, but her eyes didn't stray that far.

'I'm here because I believe we've caught our murderer.'

Charlotte took a step backward. 'Really? Who is he?'

Michael shook his head. 'Not he, she. Why do you think it's a man?'

'Nothing, I just thought it seemed more like a man's crime. I found my mother's body, remember? Her clothes were all torn and,— well, she looked as if she'd been raped.'

'Yes. Well, she hadn't.'

'Zoë Elliot? You've come for Zoë Elliot? She's not here — they haven't moved in yet, although you can see that she's dying to.'

'No. It was a woman all right, but not the new Lady Sheldon-Harris, she has a cast-iron alibi.'

'Theo? Well you can't believe what he says, he's under her spell.'

'Might we come in Miss Bridges, it's cold standing on the doorstep.'

Charlotte and Flora moved to one side.

'Go in here, shall we?' He indicated the sitting room and everyone with the exception of Ruth Sparks, who said she'd go and make a cup of tea, filed in front of him.

They all sat down on the welcoming sofas and Michael opened his file. Your mother was found with certain clues on her, Miss Bridges, it seems that a strangers genetic makeup was left on her body, probably immediately after her death.'

'What sort of genetic makeup? Do you mean to say she *was* raped? Only when Lottie just asked you, you said that you thought not,' Flora said.

'She wasn't, it was made to look like rape, it was clever too, there was even a splattering of semen.'

'Then it has to have been a man,' Flora said.

'Not necessarily. As I said, this was extremely ingenious. The murderer obtained and planted this vital clue, didn't he, or she, Miss Bridges? Very clever — get a man to make love to you, — use a condom, carefully draw his semen up into a syringe perhaps, and—'

Flora put her hands down on her stomach, 'Oh, no, oh, no. Lottie, tell me you didn't, you haven't, tell me?'

Charlotte was silent; her eyes were fixed straight ahead, her lips pressed closely together.

'Charlotte Isobel Bridges I am arresting you on suspicion of . . . '

'No,' Flora screamed. 'I don't want this child, I don't want it.'

Michael and Ian looked at each other.

'I woke up. We were staying at the Kings Head. Lottie's was supposed to have seen her mother that day, but they'd had a row on the telephone — they'd fought about her father's will. So we stayed at the hotel overnight because Lottie decided she'd go over the next day. Anyway, then *we* had a row, and Lottie went down and had dinner on her own. I went to bed, I wasn't hungry, and as I said, I woke, and she was . . . ' Flora looked around the room. 'She was injecting me with this stuff'

'Injecting?'

'Yes. . . Oh, not drugs, not in my arm, not with a needle . . . She said it was a joke, an experiment she said, — to see if it could be done. Oh, God, I've missed twice. I didn't dream it could be that. I'd forgotten about it, what with the murder and all that. Lottie, how could you do that?'

Charlotte was staring at the ceiling. 'Why don't you just shut up, Flora,' she said.

'We had another row, and she went off into the

night, she came back about four o'clock in the morning and said she wanted to go home, only then, as soon as we got back to London, she changed her mind and decided to drive back again. We'd made up by then, you see, and then when we found her mother dead, we thought it best not to mention the night before.'

'You checked into the hotel under the name of Zoë Elliot?'

'Lottie did, she thought it was a lark, she was going to let Theo know so that he'd think she was having a bit on the side. It wasn't my idea, Lottie's sort of got it in for Theo, and she can't stand Zoë.'

Flora turned to Charlotte. 'Why Charlotte? Why did you do it? Your mother was a pain in the arse, but why kill her?'

Michael smiled. He knew; he knew very well why Charlotte had killed her mother.

'Do shut up, Flora.' Charlotte snarled. 'It's bad for you to get upset in your condition.'

'My condition! Oh, I don't believe this. You trick me and then you . . . Lottie . . . your own mother?'

'She was never a mother to me, she walked out on me, remember? I was only a child, Dad brought me up, not her, then he was stupid enough to . . . '

Michael repeated the caution. When he'd finished, Charlotte said, 'She went ballistic because I brought the car back, it was just rotting. She was terrified that Theo would

677

find out.'

Michael nodded; it was the final piece of the jigsaw.

'Take her away,' he said. But then just as she'd got to the door, he asked, 'But why pin the blame on Sir Theo and Zoë? They'd done nothing to harm you.'

'I didn't want Theo to get the blame. I've always been very fond of Theo.'

Then why plant his blood under your mother's finger nail?'

'I didn't know it was Theo's blood, there were all these dressings in the waste bin, I thought one of the trades people had cut themselves. I thought it might . . . '

'Mislead us? It did, but why didn't you just assume that it was your mother's blood?'

'She wouldn't have put it in the waste. She was terrified that Theo might get hold of some of her bodily fluids. She thought he might harm her with it.'

'But why did you use Zoë's name?'

Charlotte's eyes narrowed, 'Obvious, isn't it? I really did intend to make Theo think that Zoë had been playing games behind his back. Then when I thought of my plan, it seemed better still. I've have rejoiced if she'd got the blame. If it wasn't for her, Theo would have given Flora our child, I wouldn't have had to resort to a stranger in a bar. Theo's so handsome, he and Flora would have made a beautiful child, our child . . . I'd have looked after it

Inspector, I'd have made a good parent for it.'

Flora was sitting on the sofa rocking backwards and forwards.

Charlotte was led away, and moments later the doors of the white van slammed shut.

'You really think you're pregnant?' Michael asked Flora.

She nodded, 'I've never missed before.'

'You'll be able to get some help.'

'I don't know if I want help, I'll have to decide what to do. When she first suggested a baby, I was quite keen, and then I felt I couldn't bear the idea. Now, I'm not so sure again.'

'You've time, you'll have to get some counseling.'

'She used to take the money to Jersey, — her mother's money, from the meetings. They were afraid that Theo might get his hands on it.'

'Yes I know, her father looked after it for her, didn't he?'

Flora nodded. 'There was a lot of money, she often took anything from fifty to a hundred thousand over in one go.'

'Yes, yes, we know.'

'But then her father died.'

'Yes, the weekend before she—'

'Murdered her mother. I had no idea, Inspector, if I had I'd . . . '

'Have told us?'

Michael only half believed her.

'We'll need a statement. If you'd like to go with Inspector Barnes, there's a car outside.'

She went with Ian to the door and was helped into the back of the police car.

'I'll be back in an hour or so.' Michael said to his partner. 'I think I owe Sir Theo and Zoë an explanation.'

'You don't owe them anything,' Ian said sulkily. 'It's a murder investigation, people get in the way, toes get trodden on.'

Michael scratched his neck. 'Yes, but these toes didn't deserve to be trodden on, not quite so heavily anyway.'

Chapter 85

First the white van then the police car passed by the widows of Garrick Cottage.

'I'll never see a police car ever again, without feeling sick,' Zoë said.

Theo put his arm around her.

'Flora was in the back of the car,' he said.

'Perhaps Harper has found a new scape goat,' Zoë said bitterly.

A few moments later the blue Golf turned into the graveled area in front of the cottage.

'I'll make some coffee,' Theo said.

'Why? Why do you feel you have to entertain them every time they come here?'

Theo shrugged. 'Just being polite, I suppose.'

Zoë felt close to tears, when would it end? She felt lonely and persecuted. Her life seemed to be on hold, as if she was in a constant state of flux, waiting for a catalyst that would make her world set, and, at last, be stable.

Michael tapped on the door. This time Bracken lifted his head but didn't bother to bark.

'Even the dog's given up,' Zoë muttered as she went to open the door. She didn't invite him in, but just stood to one side so that he could pass. Then followed him into the kitchen.

'Just making some coffee,' Theo said. 'Would you like some?'

Theo filled the coffee filter and switched it on.

'I just came to tell you the state of play,' Michael said.

Zoë and Theo looked at each other but neither spoke.

'We've just arrested Charlotte Bridges for the murder of her mother.'

'What?' said Theo. 'Surely not.'

'I saw Flora being driven away,' Zoë said.

'You've got to be wrong about Lottie, Inspector. In the last few years she was devoted to her mother. She was always here. Issie didn't get on with Flora, but that's not a reason to murder your mother, now is it?'

'Money,' Michael said. 'That's the motive, and it's the oldest one in the book.'

'Money? But Isobel and I hadn't reached a settlement. Issie had no money, apart from what she made with her meetings, and Lottie was part of that.'

'What do you know about Isobel's late husband Gerald Bridges?'

'Gerry? He's a good sort,' Theo said. 'He did very well for himself, owns a string of nights clubs, two in London, one in Paris, and I believe one or two more as well. But you said late, husband. Is Gerry dead then?'

Michael didn't reply to the question but opened the

thin buff file. 'He also had clubs in Brussels, Lyon, two in Amsterdam, and it's three in London,' he said reading from a large sheet of paper. 'He even had one or two in the Caribbean.'

'Oh?'

'He had a house on the south coast and a house in Jersey, and yes, let me see, a property in Montecarlo, one in the south of Spain, he owned a company in Gibraltar, and we haven't finished checking yet.'

'I said he'd done well,' Theo said. 'Issie would have done better to have stuck with him, wouldn't she?'

'Issie did, stick by him, that is, or at least they had a good relationship in the later years of his life.'

Theo lifted his eyebrows.

'He died,' Michael said. 'Saturday, twenty-second October, three days before your late wife.'

Theo sat down on his chair and sighed. 'I'm sorry. Poor Lottie, she never said. She must have been distraught, she loved him very much.'

'She never said, because she didn't want anyone to know. You see Gerald Bridges left everything to his ex-wife, Isobel.'

'Good Lord, not to Lottie? She must have been upset about that.'

'She killed her mother, so that she could get her hands on her father's money?' Zoë said, her face creased into a frown. 'But why? She only had to wait, it would have

683

been hers one day.'

Michael smiled. 'Funnily enough, it wouldn't have been hers, although I don't think Charlotte understood that. Gerald and Isobel made identical wills about a year ago. They'd decided they were soul mates, apparently. They left each other everything they owned. Charlotte didn't get a mention. I expect the surviving parent would have included her at a later date.'

'But if Gerry was dead, surely it would all have gone to Issie and then when Issie died, the money would go to her next of kin?'

'That's right.'

'Well then, Lottie gets it.'

Michael shook is head. 'No, her next of kin is her husband.'

'I see,' Theo said. Although it was as plain as anything that he didn't.

'You, Theo,' Zoë said. 'You'll get all of Isobel's money.'

'Yes,' Michael said, and we're not just talking about Gerald Bridges's business enterprises, but the chaps that crunch the numbers back at HQ think that Charlotte ferried at least two and a half million to Jersey over the last few years.'

'Good God,' Theo said.

'The ironic thing is, that if all this had been known to your lawyer, then Lady Sheldon-Harris would have had to pay you a big divorce settlement. The other thing is, if Charlotte had waited until after your divorce, then either Lady Sheldon-Harris would have been advised to make a new will or if she hadn't, once you were out of the picture, Charlotte really would have been the next of kin.'

'Then why........?' Zoë asked.

'She misinterpreted the will, and she assumed that if Lady Sheldon-Harris was dead, then she was sure to inherit. She rather jumped the gun, she was probably afraid her mother would do something stupid with the money.'

'We're moving to the big house,' Elizabeth interrupted.

Michael smiled at her, she didn't exactly smile back, but this time she didn't scowl.

'That's lovely.' Michael said.

'How did you know that she'd done it?' Zoë asked.

'I can't go into precise details, but I can tell you that she was clever, very clever. She obtained some DNA, I don't suppose it hurts to tell you that it was semen, and she planted it on Lady Sheldon-Harris's body. To tell you the truth, at one point we thought it belonged to the man that raped you, Steven Jarvis. But he'd had a vasectomy after his last child was born and—'

Zoë gave a cry and put her hand out to Theo, 'Oh,' she said. 'Oh.' She staggered and Theo helped her down into a chair.

'Are you all right, would you like a glass of

water?' Michael asked.

She shook her head. 'I'm fine, just fine.'

Theo slipped his arm around her shoulder. He kissed the top of her head. 'I told you it would be all right,' he whispered.

It was all too much for her. She wiped her eyes with the back of her hand and tried to swallow the lump that had formed in her throat.

'By the way, it wasn't Jarvis that beat up on you?' Michael said. 'You do realize that?'

Zoë moved her head in an action that was neither a yes nor a no. 'I . . . I . . . ' But the words wouldn't form themselves.

'Gail Skinner, the daughter of Sir Theo's old foreman? Do you know her?'

Zoë again gave a gesture that was neither a yes nor a no.

'Anyway, she came to see us. Her dad was full of it, — he followed you that night. Apparently he'd been stalking you for months, he had it in his head that it was your fault that he lost his job. He saw you meet with Mr Jarvis and he saw what happened, apparently he couldn't resist, quite literally, putting the boot in. And he couldn't resist boasting about it. Mind you, I'm not sure if Gail would have come forward, had she not taken her new boyfriend home and found her father dressed to the nines, ginger wig and all.

'We've got him in the station, he's admitted to it. In fact he's rather proud of himself. And we've also managed to obtain the jeans you were wearing that night.'

Zoë moved her lips as if to ask how, but no speech was heard.

'They never got burned that day. Andy stuck them in his car, — must have thought they'd make good engine rags I suppose. Anyway, there's enough DNA on them to convict both Skinner *and* Jarvis.'

Zoë put her head in her hands. Theo stroked her back.

'There's a piano in the big house. I'm going to learn to play it,' Elizabeth suddenly said.

'That's nice,' Michael said.

'I can't believe all you've told us. How did you find out,— about Lottie, I mean?' Theo asked.

'I'd like to say it was brilliant detective work,' he smiled. 'Some of it was, but the break came when the mother of a friend of mine recognized, Zoë's picture in the paper, after the inquest.'

'But I wasn't at the inquest,' Zoë said lifting her head and exposing tear wet cheeks.

'I know, but this lady was sure it was you, because a woman named Zoë Elliot had booked into the hotel in Fenshaw.'

'That's what that was all about?' she said.

'Wait a minute, Inspector. Are you telling us that

Lottie tried to frame Zoë?'

'It looks that way.'

Theo sighed. 'But why? Zoë has never hurt Charlotte.'

'Jealousy. Zoë's got it all, hasn't she?'

Zoë was puzzled, whatever was this big stupid, well, perhaps not quite as stupid as she at first thought, policeman, on about now.

'I don't understand,' Theo said.

'We're moving to the big house, and Theo's not Theo anymore, he's my Daddy, and Mummy's going to have a baby, and it'll be my little brother or sister. And Mummy will get really fat, but she'll still be just as pretty. And we're going to have proper milk in proper bottles like Granny does, because we're getting rid of the cow, because Daddy doesn't want Mummy out all on her own, and besides she'll have the new baby to look after.' Elizabeth slid onto a kitchen chair and folded her arms in front of her; she now had all the grownup's attention.

Michael smiled. 'You may not understand, Sir,' he said. 'But Betsy certainly does.'

688

Coming soon:

The 3rd volume of the Hulver novels

The Fall of the House of Hulver

Josh Elliot is dead. His heir, Quentin, has become
hopelessly entangled with an uneducated waitress and gold
digger, and his younger daughter, Tiggy, is trapped in a
loveless marriage to Alex Kirby, Lavina's onetime lover.
Lavinia doesn't know where to turn. She knows that it will
take all her strength and cunning to salvage the situation
and deliver the Hulver estates intact to future generations
of Elliots. Once again, desperate times may lead to
desperate measures.

For details of this and other Susannah Campbell novels
please contact
Desiderata Press
PO Box 112
Cambridge PDO CB4 3SU